D1742810

THE FIRST ELEMENT

THE FIRST ELEMENT

Mark Regan

iUniverse, Inc.
New York Lincoln Shanghai

The First Element

Copyright © 2005 by Mark James Regan

All rights reserved. No part of this book may be used or reproduced by any means, graphic, electronic, or mechanical, including photocopying, recording, taping or by any information storage retrieval system without the written permission of the publisher except in the case of brief quotations embodied in critical articles and reviews.

iUniverse books may be ordered through booksellers or by contacting:

iUniverse
2021 Pine Lake Road, Suite 100
Lincoln, NE 68512
www.iuniverse.com
1-800-Authors (1-800-288-4677)

This is a work of fiction. Characters, companies, organizations and agencies in this novel are either the product of the author's imagination or, if real, used fictitiously without any intent to describe their actual conduct.

ISBN-13: 978-0-595-36975-1 (pbk)
ISBN-13: 978-0-595-81381-0 (ebk)
ISBN-10: 0-595-36975-8 (pbk)
ISBN-10: 0-595-81381-X (ebk)

Printed in the United States of America

For Rick Miller

Yours will always be bigger

CHAPTER 1

▼

"Beautiful...isn't it?"

He wasn't asking rhetorically. When Bob Hobbs asked a question of his young apprentice, he expected an answer.

The renowned engineer was standing several feet away from his creation with his hands stuffed in his pockets, admiring the vehicle's powerplant with all the pride of a first-time father viewing his newborn son.

"Yeah, Bob. It's great," his young assistant replied with considerably less enthusiasm. A moment later he glanced irritably at his watch and asked with some urgency, "Can we go home now? Julie's pissed off enough at me as it is. If I'm late tonight, she'll cut my ba—"

"Terrance, Terrance, Terrance," Hobbs bellowed theatrically, shaking his head. "Look at you! One of the few young engineers here at GFCT given the *honor* of working on the future of transportation and all you can think about is...is, *pussy!*"

Terrance McChaffee grimaced. He thought about retorting with a wiseass remark but quickly decided against it. Despite the old man's irritating work ethic, McChaffee truly liked and admired him, and was beginning to see him more as a father figure than boss.

And he was fortunate too. Not many engineers recently out of college had the honor of assisting Bob Hobbs, Global Fuel Cell Technologies'—if not the world's—foremost fuel cell engineer. He was never quite sure why, but Hobbs picked him over twelve other equally qualified junior engineers to assist him on this, the company's flagship program. He had taught McChaffee more about the technology in the relatively short period of time they'd worked together than he could have ever hoped to learn remaining a common cog in GFCT's engineering wheel. Fuel Cells were the future, and with the help of this prominent engineer, McChaffee was on his way to becoming one of the most knowledgeable fuel cell engineers in the business. Working with Dr. Bob Hobbs really added to a resume. He had a bright future ahead of him.

But on the other hand, he didn't want to blow it with Julie Newman either. She was the first woman to take an interest in him after his bitter divorce. Adding to her physical attractiveness was her seeming indifference to the financial situation he found himself in after the one-sided settlement.

Because he idolized Bob Hobbs, he never told him about this aspect of his life. Mainly because he was embarrassed about his short-lived marriage and didn't want the celebrated engineer to think him a failure. As far as Hobbs knew, his young assistant was still a care-free bachelor on the prowl.

"Perhaps we were wrong, Terrance," the wizened old man chuckled playfully, turning to look at his youthful charge, "listing hydrogen as the first element in the periodic table of elements. Perhaps hormones would have been a better choice!" He laughed at his own witticism as he watched the younger man give him a sour look.

Ya, young love, he thought to himself, watching McChaffee's anxiety grow. He wasn't so far removed from youth that he'd forgotten how powerful the pull of young love could be—particularly on a Friday afternoon. "Alright Terrance," he said acquiescently while giving the young man a fatherly clap on the shoulder. "I want tomorrow's demonstration to upper management to go without a hitch." He walked up to the prototype vehicle. "Just help me calibrate the AC converter and you can be on your way, Romeo." Bending over the fender and reaching inside the vehicle's fuel cell compartment, he saw McChaffee glance at his watch and smile.

The young engineer cheerfully went to the lab's tool cabinet to grab a voltage meter. Digging through the cabinet he was about to thank his boss for his consideration when he heard an ear-splitting scream followed by the unmistakable, sickening sizzle of electrocuting flesh.

McChaffee spun around and gasped in horror at the sight. His mentor was leaning against the small SUV's fender with one arm buried inside the fuel cell compartment. His feet were several inches off the ground and his entire body was shaking with the distinctive quiver of a man being zapped by 10 kilovolts of raw electrical power. Hobbs' other hand was reaching up into the air like a drowning man desperately reaching for the extended limb of a would-be rescuer. His entire body was beginning to smoke.

"**BOB!**" McChaffee screamed in horror, dropping the voltage meter and running up to the convulsing man. Without thinking he reached out for Hobbs, but before he'd actually touched him the old man somehow managed a facial expression warning him off and reminding him of his emergency procedures. He'd saved McChaffee's life while he himself was dying an excruciating death.

Quickly, almost as if being magnetically repelled, McChaffee jerked his arms away from the burning man. He dashed to the vehicle's cab, staying mindful not to touch it. Frantically, he reached inside and pulled the emergency shut-off switch, and there was a dull thud as Hobbs' smoldering body fell flaccidly across the vehicle's fender.

Terrance McChaffee instantly knew it was too late. Dr. Bob Hobbs, holder of no less than twenty patents for the automotive fuel cell powertrain, lay dead and smoldering on the fender of the retrofitted Nissan Pathfinder.

The investigation lasted a pitifully short period of time and Hobb's death was quickly ruled an accident. McChaffee didn't buy it and said so, vehemently, but no one cared to listen. The world's leading fuel cell engineer killed by a mistake a first-year engineer would make. There had to be more to this!

Even more disturbing to McChaffee was the callous attitude of Global Fuel Cell Technologies' upper management. They treated the tragedy with a cold indifference he found appalling. But perhaps the icing on the cake was how they treated him. When Hobbs' replacement was named, so was his—to McChaffee's utter astonishment. It made absolutely no sense to replace the assistant, unless of course they wanted to get rid of him. Retribution perhaps for all the trouble he caused during the investigation into Hobb's death. He'd never know for sure— no explanation was ever offered. The cold shoulder he'd received from management, which naturally filtered down to infect the lower level employees, infuriated him.

Terrance McChaffee swore vengeance.

"Gentlemen…the threat is real and can no longer be ignored," Laurence Haggerty declared in his darkest, most ominous voice. Standing with his hands clasped behind his back and dressed in a fifteen hundred dollar suit he could ill afford, Haggerty stared solemnly at the projection screen to allow time for his words to make the desired impact on his tiny, but extremely powerful audience.

Haggerty's company, Noble Consultants, LLC, a little-known and highly specialized firm, had been hired by this group known only as "The Committee" nine months ago. Since being retained this was his third, and by far most important presentation to The Committee—a group of men whose decisions impacted the economies of every nation on earth.

This presentation was being held at the same location as the previous two, PETROCOMP's boardroom, located on the 87th floor of the World Trade Center's north tower. The corporation leased floors 83 through 87 for its worldwide executive headquarters, and was the most convenient location for The Committee to meet when necessary.

When they signed the multi-million dollar contract with Noble Consultants, it had been the intention of the three men comprising The Committee to meet with Laurence Haggerty once every six months—at most. However, due to the rapidly growing potential of the threat, that plan had fallen by the wayside.

The Committee never, under any circumstance, communicated in any manner other than face-to-face; and when they did, every security precaution was taken. This included sweeping the boardroom for electronic listening devices. Despite the fact that their meetings took place in the heart of PETROCOMP's executive suites which had twenty-four hour armed security, they took no chances and searched the room for bugs fifteen minutes prior to their meetings. This became standard practice; there was far too much at stake.

Haggerty slowly turned from the screen filled with threatening statistics and looked at his trusted assistant. Seeing his somber nod, Sandra Beach clicked the mouse and brought up the next screen of the PowerPoint presentation.

"As the graph you are now viewing clearly points out," Haggerty continued grimly, "several companies, particularly Global Fuel Cell Technologies and Unlimited Energy Systems, have made substantial progress in the last year. They have reduced component cost by more than four hundred percent, cut the assembly time of the PEM cell—that's Proton Exchange Membrane—by over seventy-five percent, and, to make matters worse, succeeded in extending the life of the cell by more than sixty percent." Haggerty paused for a moment, grimaced then added morosely, "UES has even managed to reduce the cost per kilowatt hour by over fifty percent. This, gentlemen, is a major accomplishment."

There was a long, low whistle. Not surprisingly, Haggerty thought, it came from the Texan. He pretended to ignore the boisterous man's outburst and continued. "I should point out that PEM fuel cells are not the only kind of fuel cells being developed for commercialization. There are Alkaline, Solid Oxide, Phosphoric Acid, etcetera. However, the PEM fuel cell is by far the most versatile and reliable. Which brings me to my next point.

"Perhaps most worrisome is…ah, next screen please, Sandra." Sandra Beach brought up a new, brightly colored graph. "…is that these companies have been remarkably successful in achieving their primary aim—that of unit reliability." Haggerty brought a fist to his mouth and cleared his throat. He then stepped closer to the screen and, using a laser pointer, focused The Committee's attention on the graph of a timeline. "Over the last two years these two companies, UES and GFCT, have achieved ninety-one percent reliability at just under eight thousand hours. And this, gentlemen, was achieved in real world environmental conditions—not a laboratory. Should their progress continue at this rate, they'll achieve ninety-five percent reliability over eight thousand seven hundred sixty hours—or one year—within the next six to nine months."

The owner of Noble Consultants turned from the screen and scanned the faces of his clients. The eyes of all three men were fixed on the screen, their faces showing the desired concern. But not the panic he was hoping for. *Well, they'll panic soon enough,* Haggerty thought as he raised his eyebrows to Beach. She clicked to the next screen.

"These two companies will be in a position to produce and market their products by 2003. They could probably go to market sooner, but their vendor base—fortunately—isn't keeping pace."

"And why not, Laurence?" Haggerty didn't need to turn around to know who posed the question. The English accent told him it came from Kenneth Saxton, CEO of World Energy.

Haggerty shrugged. "In a nutshell, Mr. Saxton…skepticism. Many of these companies are unsure of the viability of fuel cell technology. Consequently, they're reluctant to invest the necessary capital to support the various development programs of these fuel cell companies, not to mention tooling and staffing for production to handle capacity when demand hits. As a matter of fact, some of the more short-sighted companies have pulled out of this industry altogether because they haven't received an immediate ROI—return on investment."

"Fools!" Theodore Kennelly, CEO of PETROCOMP, scoffed.

"Yes," Haggerty agreed. "Surprisingly, the majority of the companies that have pulled out are privately owned, with no board of directors to pacify. Some who have stayed in have increased their components' prices—obviously jittery over the potential of receiving no ROI. This, of course, has complicated matters for our friends. But despite this, as I pointed out earlier, they have still managed to make tremendous progress. Had these few vendors maintained their initial pricing, more than likely UES and GFCT would have reached their published cost targets by now."

As Haggerty paused to take a sip of water, he glanced at his assistant. Knowing her boss as well as she did, Sandra Beach could tell he was still incredibly nervous. She gave him an encouraging smile.

The head of Noble Consultants put the glass down and again faced his clients. "Predictably, had these costs been achieved, Wall Street would have reacted accordingly and UES and GFCT's share price would have surged, probably ending up significantly higher than they already are."

"Amazing, isn't it?" Kennelly said, shaking his head. "How people who are so short-sighted can reach the executive level." All three CEOs chuckled at the derogatory remark clearly aimed in jest at themselves and their brethren in the corporate world. At the last meeting, during a rare period of light-hearted banter, Theodore Kennelly shared with Wendell Finley and Kenneth Saxton, the other two members of The Committee, his monumental folly. Many years ago, while a senior marketing manager for 3M, Minnesota Mining and Manufacturing, Kennelly had adamantly opposed the introduction of the Post-it-Note. He argued that going to market with such a product would make the company look like a "low-end" manufacturer of cheap paper products, rather than the image they were trying to project—a company on the cutting edge of technology. Fortunately for 3M, the vice-president of marketing overruled Kennelly and the Post-it-Note was a colossal success. As is all too common in corporate America, Kennelly was promoted for his efforts despite the fact that he had tenaciously fought to deny 3M what turned out to be one of their most successful products and a generator of tremendous revenue.

Haggerty dutifully smiled at Kennelly's remark and patiently waited for the CEOs to finish their laugh, then continued. "In addition to the technical advances and just as important, the lobbyists for the fuel cell industry are starting to make substantial headway in Washington. They have a sizable number of influential congressmen and senators either in their back pocket or sympathetic to their interests. On the federal level, Congressman Hanson from Vermont is in the process of drafting a bill in the spirit of California's zero emissions law."

"What's their strategy, Haggerty?" Wendell Finley, CEO of ENDICORP asked. "Have you made any progress in penetrating one of the groups?"

Haggerty winced; it was an area in which he hadn't made adequate progress. "I've made some headway with the automotive lobby backed by Global Fuel Cell Technologies, HydroTech and Etran. From what I've been able to ascertain up to this point, their main strategy is to support Hanson's zero emissions bill while pushing for a similar law in several key states—in the event Hanson's bill fails."

"I'm not terribly familiar with this zero emissions bill, Laurence. What does it entail?" the CEO of World Energy asked.

"In a nutshell, Mr. Saxton, the legislation mandates that by 2008, ten percent of the vehicles sold in the United States—or sold in a state with the law—must be zero emission. An amendment was recently added to Hanson's bill requiring that the automotive fleets of all federal agencies be zero emission by that time also."

Saxton nodded thoughtfully then said, "In the greater scheme of things, that's not a lot of bloody automobiles."

"No, it's not," Haggerty agreed. "But it's not an arbitrary figure. It just so happens to represent the minimum number of vehicles the fuel cell industry feels it needs to produce in order to make their business more attractive to the larger, more technically savvy vendors. This, in turn, would allow them to obtain competitive bids and further drive down component cost. At the same time they could tap into these vendors' technical resources, improving the efficiency of their own manufacturing process."

Haggerty took a deep breath; it was time to go in for the kill. "The bottom line here, gentlemen, is that if something isn't done—and soon—fuel cells will begin to nibble away at your markets by 2004. By 2008 they will cut into them dramatically." Haggerty paused a moment for effect and then added dourly, "Once market share is lost to this technology, and the public sees its benefits, there's going to be a domino effect. In fifteen years, twenty at most, about the only thing oil is going to be needed for is aviation fuel, a small number of special lubricants and plastic resins—about five percent of your current combined sales."

Haggerty breathed a little sigh of relief; he could see his message was starting to sink in. The looks on the faces of the CEOs was now deadly serious. Haggerty decided to drive the message home. "In all likelihood, gentlemen, within your lifetime, World Energy, PETROCOMP and ENDICORP will either cease to exist or be nothing more than a shell of their former glory."

The room was silent. As he had on previous occasions, Wendell Finley, CEO of ENDICORP, ignored the no-smoking policy and lit up a thick Havana. All three CEOs were lost in thought. Haggerty nodded at Sandra Beach, signaling her to shut down the PowerPoint presentation. After turning off the projector's lamp, she stood and walked over to the boardroom's door to turn on the overhead lights. Finley, cigar clenched between his teeth, salaciously followed the young woman's movement with his eyes.

Laurence Haggerty was pleased; the presentation had gone well. Looking at the troubled faces of the CEOs, he was sure his contract would be extended—adding badly needed millions into the coffers of Noble Consultants.

It wasn't his intention to tell them—to show just how far he was capable of infiltrating the industry—unless he had to. In the event they should waver, question the need to extend his contact, then he'd open his mouth. But he saw no need to admit to murder—not yet anyway. Even if it was unintentional.

Haggerty cursed himself. He was foolish to take Swenson's advice and hire that bumbling amateur Grossmann. He knew of a better man; a much better man. But like all things in life, quality costs. He wasn't in a position yet to shell out the big bucks for the professionals. But the time might come when he'd have to.

Forced into a career change, Laurence Haggerty started Noble Consultants four years ago in 1995. Up until then, he had spent twenty-five years as a successful attorney specializing in intellectual property rights. An extremely intelligent man, Laurence Haggerty could, when necessary, be very cunning and devious—essential character traits for a successful lawyer. He prided himself on his ability to hold his temper and remain calm under pressure. However, after twenty-five years of seeing the law twisted and the wrong people getting screwed, the system was beginning to wear on him.

Developing a conscience, he knew he would soon lose his edge in the profession. It was time for a change. But the change was forced on him, coming sooner than he'd expected and not under his terms.

Representing a small software company, Haggerty had been infuriated by the judge's decision to grant a continuance allowing the defense more time to "prepare." The delay would have a devastating effect on his client. Each day, Omega Systems was losing thousands in royalties. The defense's strategy to litigate the plaintiff into Chapter Eleven was so blatantly obvious, Haggerty had to bite his lip to stop himself from calling the young judge an idiot when she granted the continuance.

It was a high profile case and the judge issued a gag order. Haggerty, livid over the delay, shot his mouth off to the press, complaining about the judge's handling of the trial and even insinuating that she was in the pocket of the defense's client, one of the largest software firms in the world. The judge, furious, held Haggerty in contempt, declared a mistrial and began proceedings to disbar Haggerty.

Embarrassed by the affair and the negative publicity that ensued, Powers, Hancock, Strom & Haggerty suggested that their newest partner leave the firm—and take his name with him. Disheartened by what the legal system had become, the proceedings against him and the abandonment by his fellow partners, Haggerty didn't fight to retain his license. Six months later he could no longer legally practice law in the State of Virginia.

But his years within the Washington Beltway were not without benefit; he'd learned how to work the system and made several politically well-connected friends. One of these friends was Pat Wheeler, a senior senator from Maryland and fellow Virginia Military Institute alumni. In the sauna of the congressional health club, Wheeler suggested his friend start a firm that would fill a particular "niche." This niche, the senator knew, if handled properly, could provide the right firm with annual revenue in the eight-digit range. The former lawyer found the idea intriguing.

Shortly after his talk with Senator Wheeler, Haggerty started Noble Consultants, LLC. Given the nature of his new firm's specialty, he considered use of the word "noble" rather ironic. After all, there is nothing noble about industrial espionage.

His friend the senator was right; Noble Consultants' services were in high demand. Working on the fringe of the law—many times in violation of it—it wasn't long before his firm had more clients than it could comfortably handle with the necessary discretion. Due to the nature of the business and the risks involved, hiring key people with the kind of discretion essential for this line of work was one of his more challenging tasks.

Soon, however, he had developed an organization with several key operatives fully cognizant of the firm's true purpose, and a support staff that believed what was written in the firm's literature: that Noble Consultants was a company dedicated to assisting its customers with their business development efforts.

Companies from a wide variety of industries—electronics, telecommunications, software and defense, both foreign and domestic—were seeking out Haggerty's services. Noble Consultants made millions while saving its clients billions in research and development costs and slashing their time to market. Finding people inside a company willing to sell trade secrets and desired information was surprisingly easy. Employee loyalty had become a thing of the past; major corporations ensured this by treating their employees like chattel. Payoffs for information were the standard procedure; bribes paid were astonishingly small.

For those less cooperative people, Haggerty and his closest associates found ways of inspiring them if the usual incentives of money and/or sex didn't work. Thankfully, he'd rarely had to resort to those tactics.

Finding ways around patents, or in the case of his pharmaceutical clients, finding creative ways to extend them, was almost becoming routine. Laurence Haggerty was particularly fond of the drug companies—they paid top dollar.

Having spent years practicing intellectual property rights law, Haggerty couldn't understand why the idea of starting this type of firm had never occurred to him before—the concept was so simple. Putting up a token protest, Senator Pat Wheeler accepted Haggerty's gift of a sixty-foot yacht for the idea.

Until recently, Haggerty and Noble Consultants were wallowing in money. But with rumors starting to fly about a burst in the Dot-Com bubble, new business had all but dried up. To make matters worse, one of his close associates, someone he trusted and thought was his friend, quit the firm and demanded ten million dollars to keep his mouth shut. With only twelve million in reserve, the ultimatum couldn't have come at a worse time. A leak to the press concerning the true nature of his firm was the last thing Haggerty wanted; an investigation would bring unwanted publicity and scare away customers. Remaining inconspicuous was essential to the survival of Noble Consultants and crucial to obtaining and retaining clients. Grudgingly, he paid Michael Cochran his hush money and moved on.

After Sandra Beach sat back down from turning on the overhead lights, Haggerty noticed Kenneth Saxton's eyes nervously darting between his two peers—it was time for the close.

"Now, gentlemen, you have—"

"Laurence…" Saxton cut him off. "Would you and Ms. Beach be so kind as to excuse us for a moment? I would like to discuss something in private with my two colleagues."

Haggerty tried not to show his annoyance at being cut short. He had rehearsed the pitch endlessly and was counting on a dramatic delivery to drive home the main theme of his presentation, ensuring an extension of his contract.

"Of course, Mr. Saxton," Haggerty replied evenly with a slight nod of his head. His eyes shifted to Beach and the two of them headed for the polished mahogany door.

"Have Martha fix you and Ms. Beach a drink," Theodore Kennelly added. "We'll call for you when we're through with our discussion." Walking out of the boardroom, Haggerty glanced at his watch. Two thirty-six, a tad early for a drink but what the hell; he could use one. Besides, Martha—Theodore Kennelly's executive assistant—knew how to pour a scotch and water.

Haggerty quietly closed the door behind him and turned to stare at Sandra. She knew by his expression that he wanted her thoughts; but at the moment she had none to give. Unsure of how the presentation was received by The Committee, she only grimaced and shrugged her shoulders. The young woman knew how important this meeting was to her employer; she didn't want to run the risk of offering the man false hopes.

Haggerty let out a tired sigh. "What the hell, Sandra, let's take Kennelly up on his offer." Beach produced a small smile and the two of them walked down the hall to Martha's office. As the two walked past the open door of Kennelly's office they were hailed from within. "Mr. Haggerty, Ms. Beach, in here please." Either Martha Putnam could read minds or Kennelly called her as they departed the boardroom and asked her to fix them a drink. Haggerty—secretly admiring Kennelly's executive secretary—chose to believe the former.

A handsome woman about his age, she had been the first lady to catch his eye since he'd divorced his wife over five years ago. Haggerty was secretly frustrated that his conversations with Martha had yet to get beyond standard pleasantries. But during the short periods he was with her, he couldn't think of anything to say; making him feel like he was back in Junior High.

Martha was clearly an intelligent woman. She had to be to attain the position of executive secretary to the man who ran the world's second largest oil company. And intelligence was a quality Haggerty found very attractive in a woman.

At fifty-six, young, beautiful women no longer made much of an impression on him. He'd recently come to discover that he was lonely and now yearned for someone in his life who could provide him with the kind of companionship he desired. Seeing no ring on her finger, he often wondered if Martha Putnam could someday be that woman. He knew that if he ever wanted to find out the answer to that question, he'd have to work up the nerve to ask her out.

Stepping into Kennelly's massive office Haggerty heard Sandra catch her breath. He could certainly understand her reaction; the place was beyond breathtaking. He recalled he had a similar reaction the first time he set foot into the room.

The lavish décor—eighteenth century French—was offset by marble walls trimmed in dark teak. Plush, sand-colored carpeting covered what Haggerty estimated to be close to a thousand square feet of prime real-estate. Kennelly's massive, ornate desk was set in the corner in front of huge floor-to-ceiling windows that provided a spectacular view of Manhattan.

Behind a bar that was larger than he'd seen in most taverns, Martha was pulling a bottle of Johnny Walker Blue Label from a sparkling glass shelf that held numerous bottles of equally fine liquor. Breaking into a small smile, Haggerty gave her a grateful nod, pleased she'd remembered his fondness for this particular brand of scotch.

"How about you Ms. Beach. Would you like a drink?" Martha asked, dropping several ice cubes into a glass.

Sandra Beach inadvertently looked at her watch and immediately regretted it, thinking she may have embarrassed her boss by implying it was too early to drink. What she really wanted was a Diet Coke, but to prevent any further possible embarrassment to Laurence she told Martha a gin and tonic would be nice.

"Tanqueray okay?" Martha asked lifting the bottle. Sandra broke into a genuine smile; she loved Tanqueray. "Oh, yes. That would be great."

Beach had only been working for Noble Consultants a little over four months and was still very concerned about making a favorable impression. So far she believed she had. She was astonished at how quickly—and deeply—Haggerty had taken her into his confidence. He held back little about the true nature of his firm.

Sandra Beach couldn't be more pleased; her career was starting out on overdrive. She was barely out of law school and passed the bar exam only last month. Prior to graduation she faced a hiring process with Noble Consultants the likes of which she never would have imagined. Personally conducting the search himself, Haggerty inquired whether Florida State's Law School had any exceptionally gifted student. The name Sandra Beach was immediately forwarded to him.

The interviews were grueling, and Beach believed the background check he'd conducted on her was more thorough than what a candidate for the CIA would receive. But she endured the process and it all paid off.

Through the arduous hiring process a rapport began building between the older man and the younger woman. By the fifth interview she was calm and relaxed—it almost seemed to her like she was having a casual chat with her father. It was during this last discussion that she discovered Haggerty himself had been a gifted attorney. Perhaps that explained why the connection and trust between the two developed so quickly.

Initially, she couldn't help but be suspicious. Considering him just another man, she assumed his interest in her was purely sexual. After all, he was divorced and she was a single woman. The fact that he was thirty-two years her senior might—in his eyes—mitigate the fact that she wasn't terribly attractive.

Sandra Beach didn't consider herself ugly, but becoming a Victoria's Secret model wasn't in her future. She did the best she could to look as attractive as possible without adding so much makeup she took on the appearance of a slut. But for her, the fine line between attractive and slutty was difficult—difficult to the point of being a challenge.

At five-foot-seven, one-hundred-sixty pounds, keeping additional weight off was a constant battle; a battle she was determined not to lose. Her shoulder-length strawberry blonde hair was lifeless, forcing her to spend considerable time in front of the mirror each morning trying to put a little curl into it.

Her one true physical asset were her breasts. When men took notice of her, inevitably their eyes would wander to that part of her anatomy—as did Finley's more than once during this, and the earlier presentations. Consequently, she took to wearing low cut blouses to expose as much cleavage as professional decorum would allow.

To her relief, she never once saw Laurence Haggerty's eyes wander to her breasts, and he rarely commented on the way she dressed. If he did, he always said she looked nice, or comments to that effect—he never said anything derogatory. This had a very positive effect on their developing professional relationship.

"There you go," Martha said warmly as she handed the drinks to Beach and Haggerty. He noticed her perfume; its subtle fragrance seemed appropriate for her. "If you need anything while you're waiting, please let me know. I'll call for you as soon as Mr. Kennelly and the others say they're ready."

"Thank you, Martha," Haggerty said as sweetly as he could. His eyes followed her as she walked out of the office. Sandra Beach stepped behind Kennelly's desk, admiring the view of Manhattan. Haggerty joined her. After a minute of silence and several sips of their drinks, he asked, "So Sandra…was I convincing?"

Beach looked at her boss with concern. She scanned the room with her eyes and then mouthed the word: *"Bugs?"* Haggerty shook his head and gave a dismissive wave of his hand, indicating he wasn't worried about that.

She let out a small sigh; she would have preferred not to answer the question. Since there was no way around it, she decided to be positive. "Yes. I thought you were very convincing. Honestly Laurence, they'd be *fools* not to renew your contract." It wasn't a complete lie.

Haggerty turned from her and looked out the window again; his face seemed to tighten a bit. "Well…I'm a little upset Saxton cut me off. My closing statement would have clinched the deal—I'm sure of it." He took a long sip of his drink and continued. "Not having said it, not having reiterated those facts and allowed to reinforce the highlights of the presentation, I feel…oh, I don't know. I guess I feel only ninety-eight percent complete, somehow." He shrugged. "If that makes any sense." He turned back to the young woman and stared at her blankly, frowned, then returned his gaze to the city's skyline and sipped his drink.

After Haggerty and Beach departed the boardroom the three members of The Committee sat silently for several moments, each lost in thought. Haggerty's presentation was powerful and much to their dismay, it justified their concerns.

"It's a lot to absorb, gentlemen," Saxton said quietly.

"Yes, it is," Kennelly agreed soberly. "He brought up some valid points. Clearly, something needs to be done."

"But what?" Finley chimed in while crushing out his cigar. "Plain and simple, it's technological progress…sooner or later it's going to happen." He leaned back in his chair and folded his hands over his ample belly. "Just like a girl turns into a woman," he shrugged, "it's natural progression."

Kennelly looked sharply at Finley and said acidly, "Oh, so you're just going to roll over and play dead. Is that it, Wendell? Let these goddamned fuel cell companies destroy us? Unlike you, Ken and I have shareholders to consider, not just a family dynasty."

The CEO of ENDICORP didn't appreciate Kennelly's tone or his accusation; the look Finley shot him made that clear. Though Finley knew both Saxton and Kennelly held him in contempt, he was surprised that Kennelly would overtly admit to it by speaking to him in such a scornful manner—and so early in their affiliation.

Finley leaned forward slightly in his chair and replied firmly, "Don't put words in my mouth, Ted. That's not what I said! You think that because ENDICORP is family-owned I don't have people to answer to? You think I'm not going to put up a fight? I can't believe you—"

"Wendell, Ted, please…this isn't getting us anywhere," Saxton broke in. Quickly he asked, "When does our contract with Haggerty's firm expire?"

Kennelly stared angrily at Finley a moment longer, then dropped his eyes down to the stack of papers in front of him. He sifted through several documents until he found the one he was looking for. "April thirtieth, 2000."

Saxton slowly nodded as he looked off into the distance and stroked his chin. "Okay, good. That gives us a little time." He focused his eyes on the other two men. "We need to discuss this situation in much more detail, gentlemen. Decide between ourselves what we want to do…how we want to do it."

Finley looked at his watch. "I'm sorry, Ken, I just don't have that kind of time today. I've got a meeting with Brazil's Interior Minister tomorrow and I haven't even started to prepare."

Saxton shook his head. "No, I wasn't suggesting we discuss it today. I don't believe any of us have that kind of time." Kennelly nodded in agreement. "But I think that whatever we decide to do, Noble Consultants will be part of it, and we'll need to renew their contract.

"I suggest we all study the information Haggerty gave us, and give some thought as to what the best course of action should be. Shall we plan on meeting again sometime in November to come to consensus as to what should be done?"

The other two men silently nodded their agreement. "Good. Let's inform Mr. Haggerty of our plan and call it a day."

Kennelly pushed the button on the intercom. "Martha, would you ask Ms. Beach and Mr. Haggerty to join us again?"

"Of course, Mr. Kennelly." Martha entered Kennelly's office to find both Sandra Beach and Laurence Haggerty staring silently out the window. They didn't hear her enter the cavernous office and Sandra Beach started when Martha announced that their presence was requested in the boardroom.

Sandra Beach gave Martha her nearly full glass of Tanqueray and tonic. Haggerty had a couple of swallows of his drink left and quickly finished it off; he considered it a sin to waste exceptionally good scotch. The glass he handed Martha had only half-melted ice cubes remaining. He again thanked her for the drink. The two left Kennelly's office and headed for the boardroom.

Haggerty knocked on the door and they entered. His stomach plunged when he saw the facial expressions of the three men—they appeared to be unconvinced. The three members of The Committee locked Haggerty with an icy stare until Sandra Beach entered the room, then Finley's eyes shifted to her and immediately softened.

"Ah…Laurence, Sandra, please be seated," Saxton gestured to their seats. He sounded far more cordial than Haggerty expected. They walked around the long conference table and took their seats across from the three men. As he sat down, Haggerty regretted drinking the scotch. He'd eaten nothing all day—he couldn't; he was too nervous about the presentation. The drink hit him with an unexpectedly stiff kick. He'd have to concentrate to keep his faculties.

"Laurence, I speak for all of us when I say your presentation…" Saxton paused, looking briefly into the air as his mind searched for the right words, "…gave us cause to think. It's quite evident you've done your homework and fulfilled your contractual obligation. Along with Ted and Wendell, I thank you for a job well done."

Haggerty's face fell; the presentation clearly hadn't gone as well has he'd hoped. He'd failed to convince them of the threat and as a result they weren't going to renew his contract. Worse than that, he was responsible for a man's death—a death that now seemed in vain. He cursed under his breath; the revenue was not only badly needed, it was easy money. Spying on the fuel cell companies wasn't terribly difficult—despite their security measures.

In an instant he thought about all the people he'd have to lay off and how it would be necessary to dramatically cut back on expenses. If only Saxton hadn't cut him off before his finish! Maybe he should try to do it now? He opened his mouth but immediately closed it; his light-headedness made him think better of it.

Saxton continued. "You've given us a lot of data, Laurence; actually too much to absorb in one day." He placed his hand on the thick handout Haggerty had given each member of The Committee prior to starting his presentation. "We'd like some time to study the data further."

Sandra Beach noticed Finley staring at her and she shifted nervously in her seat. What was it about him that made her uncomfortable? It certainly wasn't a bad thing to have an incredibly rich and powerful man notice her. Quickly, she decided to take advantage of the attention and nonchalantly arched her back, forcing her breasts to push tightly against her blouse. It worked. Finley's eyes immediately dropped to her chest. She had his interest.

"Ted, Wendell and I will get together sometime in the next few months to decide what it is we're going to do…if anything. After that meeting we'll contact you and let you know if the services of your agency are still required."

Haggerty let out a silent sigh of relief—he was still in the ball game. Perhaps he'd send them a follow-up report prior to their meeting outlining the final points he didn't get a chance to present. He deliberately kept those facts out of the handout because presenting them verbally would have much more impact. Haggerty wasn't thrilled with the idea of presenting this critical information in written from, but there was nothing else he could do. Regardless, he had every confidence that data would convince The Committee of the need to extend his contract.

"When do you…" Haggerty suddenly stopped and abruptly burped. "Excuse me," he said, his face flushing. He quickly composed himself. "When do you plan on having that meeting? I've got some follow-up material I'd like to send you. I'm certain it will help elucidate the situation facing the oil industry."

"Right now it appears we won't be able to get together until sometime in November." Kennelly glanced at Saxton and Finley. "Is that an accurate statement, gentlemen?" The two men thumbed through their planners and nodded. Kennelly then said drearily, "We're cognizant of the fact that your contract with us expires at the end of April next year." Haggerty pursed his lips and nodded, trying hard not to show the anxiety he was feeling.

"Well, there you have it," Saxton said as he stood up and extended his hand to Haggerty. While shaking his hand the CEO of World Energy added, "You can expect to hear from us by early December. Until then, please keep us informed of any new developments—particularly at UES and GFCT."

"Of course," Haggerty replied. "I'll look forward to hearing from you. And please don't hesitate to contact me if you have any questions prior to December." Haggerty and Beach shook hands all around and left the boardroom. After passing Martha's office Haggerty stopped. He seriously considered asking her out to dinner. If she was both willing and available tonight, he could postpone his flight back to D.C. until tomorrow.

Sandra continued on for a few steps then stopped, noticing her boss no longer at her side. She looked back at him curiously. "Something wrong, Laurence?"

He hesitated a moment before answering. Shaking his head he replied, "No, nothing's wrong. Let's go."

He was disappointed with himself. He couldn't work up the nerve to ask her out. *I'll definitely do it next time*, he thought to himself. *For Christ's sake Laurence, you're acting like a teenager!*

His assistant looked at him suspiciously. Haggerty stepped up beside her and they entered the elevator, leaving the executive suites of PETROCOMP behind them. On the long ride down to the north tower's main lobby, Sandra noticed her boss remained uncharacteristically silent and appeared almost remorseful.

CHAPTER 2

▼

Rick pulled into a visitor's parking space and threw the rented Ford Taurus into Park. Switching off the ignition, he sat back and let out a little sigh. It was a beautiful morning, and the new building he was parked in front of gleamed in the soft golden light of the rising sun.

He had come a long way since May of 1997 when he'd first called Robert Jones of Unlimited Energy Systems to reply to his inquire about a "gasketing challenge." Rick was still thankful Jones took the time to fill out his company's little marketing flyer. The marketing department of Rick's company, Flexible Sealing Solutions, was experimenting with these flyers which were really nothing more than questionnaires, hoping they would generate sales leads. Rick had little use for marketing and considered the department a waste of money and resources. But in the case of UES he had to grudgingly give them credit—they really struck gold.

When he first met Robert Jones, Rick had only been working for Flexible Sealing Solutions—FSS—for six months, and was desperate to find a company with potential to become a significant account. Up to this point everything Rick had worked on had gone sour. He credited his lack of success to the fact that he was working for an incredibly arrogant company. Engineering, staffed by the same people for over twenty years, refused to consider alternative tooling options and processes that would bring FSS into the 90's. Consequently, the company was destine to remain uncompetitive.

As Rick watched the gleaming glass building before him grow brighter with the rising sun, he thought—with a depressing lack of amusement—about his first week with FSS. He was meeting his new co-workers and was introduced to the company's estimator—the person responsible for costing new parts and generating quotes. This man took pride in the fact that he had never, in his twenty-five year career, worked for another rubber company. During their brief conversation he boasted that, "No one can mold silicone as well as us—no one!" Rick was astonished by the comment. He had worked for two other rubber companies in the past that could not only mold silicone as well as FSS, but other rubber compounds as well. FSS refused to even consider molding anything other than silicone—and this would turn out to be the company's Achilles Heel. Rick sometimes wondered just what the hell motivated him to take the job with Flexible Sealing Solutions in the first place.

But this one material mentality would change—it would have to. Rick was doing his best to make management see the light, but it was an uphill battle.

Perpetuating this delusion of superiority was his new boss, David Greene. FSS had recently been purchased by Flexible Tubing Technologies, a manufacturer of specialty silicone hoses. David Greene, who had been working for FTT for three years and was the vice president of sales and marketing, was tasked, much to his dismay, with becoming the general manager of FSS shortly after the acquisition.

On a personal level, Rick liked David. He truly did. His boss was witty and had a good sense of humor. From a business standpoint however, they were beginning to butt heads. And Rick's interest in Unlimited Energy Systems was bringing their differences in business philosophies to a head.

Greene came to FTT from one of the world's largest manufacturer of base silicone. He had been a high level executive who was forced out of the company after being politically out-maneuvered. He never shared with Rick, or anybody else for that matter, exactly why he left his previous employer. But he came to FTT with tremendous knowledge of the silicone industry and, as Rick found particularly irritating, wasn't shy about pointing this out. Thinking himself a brilliant businessman, he was responsible for talking the owner of Flexible Tubing Technologies into buying Rick's company.

Thanks to Reaganomics the previous decade, the economy in the 90's was enjoying record growth. The unprecedented economic expansion fostered an erroneous belief in the boardrooms across Corporate America that if a company didn't expand, didn't grow, it would perish—be gobbled up by aggressive competitors not afraid of taking risks. This mentality launched a corporate feeding frenzy of hostile takeovers, mergers, joint ventures and buyouts—an insatiable hunger that seemed never to be satisfied.

Falling under the spell of this fallacious principle, David Greene persuaded the perpetually apprehensive owner of FTT, Donald Kampnel, to buy Minnawaka

Products. Shortly after the purchase Minnawaka Products was renamed Flexible Sealing Solutions.

Since joining FTT, Greene had been quietly maneuvering behind the backs of the company's other five executives to establish himself as Donald Kampnel's confidant. Persuading him to purchase Minnawaka Products—over the objections of the other vice presidents—was proof that Greene now had the influence he wanted over the owner.

Of course, not all the other executives were oblivious to what Greene was up to. Recognizing him as a thinker rather than a doer, the other managers decided that if they allowed the sneaky little shit enough rope, he'd eventually hang himself. Their strategy worked.

Shortly after the acquisition, Scott Pederson, VP of Manufacturing, suggested David Greene become the general manager of FSS. Greene was terrified at the prospect for the simple reason that he'd actually have to produce tangible results. He discretely tried to pass on the opportunity but Kampnel would have none of it; he like the idea. Amused, Pederson and the other executives sat back and watched from the wings.

David Greene realized he had painted himself into a corner. Along with having to constantly reassure Kampnel that the decision to buy Minnawaka Products had been a good one, he had to turn around its dwindling profitability—and quickly. To do this, he'd have to depend on Rick Miller.

Rick gave David Greene credit for knowing the raw polymer silicone industry; the man could spout off almost every company that bought the product worldwide. But he was clueless as to how these molding companies conducted business. It was a fact he'd never admit. Rick, an industry veteran, tried in vain to explain to Greene how custom-molded rubber products were sold. It was a process that didn't happen overnight. The sales cycle for these goods was typically two years or longer. Greene refused to accept this—*couldn't* accept it because of the situation he'd placed himself in. Consequently, he and Rick began to cross swords.

Because of the pressure he was under, Greene wanted Rick to find and sell components that were ready to go into production—immediately. Of course, these parts would have to have a high profit margin. This fantasy was no doubt the wish of every general manager in the business, but unlike Greene, everybody else knew the reality.

Deliberately ignoring his boss' directive, Rick focused on companies with sealing problems. He, like every successful salesperson in the business, knew that winning the production order for new parts was accomplished by solving the customer's problem. This was a tedious and time-consuming process. The problem had to be understood, solutions proposed, and prototypes tested before the customer would have confidence in the proposed solution. Only then would the business be awarded. And this process took time—usually a lot of time.

Unlimited Energy Systems had the potential of being the biggest sale of Rick's career. A new and rapidly expanding company, UES was developing stationary fuel cell systems that could provide electrical power to individual residences. But developing a gasket that would seal between the anode and cathode plates was a daunting challenge due to the limited space available on the plates to place a seal. In addition, the gasket was expected to seal in hydrogen, the smallest of atoms.

But the reward at the end of the rainbow was almost incomprehensible. One hundred and fifty-seven gaskets were needed for each fuel cell stack. Even if UES sold their product only to new construction homes, the volume of gaskets the fuel cell manufacturer would need was astronomical. If Rick was successful in solving UES' sealing problem, overnight the size of FSS would expand ten-fold.

Initially, David Greene supported Rick's efforts at Unlimited Energy Systems. However, as the pressure began to mount on Greene to turn the company around, he decided that UES was taking up too much of Rick's time and FSS' resources. On top of that, production of the gasket was a minimum of two years away—way too far off. He needed new business now and he wanted Rick to find it. Greene would never admit it, but he was desperately counting on Rick to bail him out.

In an effort to immediately increase the profitability of FSS, Greene decided to raise prices across the board for all parts currently in production. Rick pleaded with him not to do this—they would lose customers. Instead, he argued, make FSS' processes more efficient—God knows they were antiquated. "On the cutting edge of 60's technology," Rick grumbled. But there was no need to increase manufacturing's efficiency, his boss countered; after all, no one could mold silicone as well as they could. Just ask the estimator!

Rick seethed over Greene's inability to see the potential UES had to offer, and his unrealistic demand for quick, profitable business. Being the good soldier he was, however, he did his best to comply. The price increase Greene foolishly imposed hampered Rick's efforts because it forced him to spend a considerable amount of time trying to retain fleeing customers. But through it all, he still devoted the majority of his time to UES. The potential of this company was mesmerizing.

Rick looked at his watch again and decided it was close enough to 9:00 A.M. He'd need a couple of minutes to chat with Mary Lou, UES' gregarious receptionist. As every sales professional knows, it's crucial to immediately get and stay on good terms with a company's receptionist—those that still had them. They were the modern-day gatekeepers; the person who could provide useful and priceless information that wasn't supposed to be known outside the company. They could also track down people who forgot about an appointment. Generally, they made the salesperson's job so much easier.

This morning however, Rick couldn't steer Mary Lou away from talking about her daughter. For the last two years, the receptionist explained, her daughter had been engaged to be married. But something always popped up at the last minute to prevent the ceremony from actually taking place. This month it was the fault of her future son-in-law's mother; she didn't approve of the wedding cake's design. Rick genuinely liked Mary Lou and tried his best not to look uninterested.

Mercifully, her phone finally rang, cutting her off mid-sentence and allowing Rick an excuse to pull out his cell phone and fake a call. As he pretended to talk, he strolled over to the lobby's chairs and took a seat. He immediately noticed a new display. It was a miniature mock-up of a US1 residential fuel cell system.

Blinking blue lights showed the hydrogen atoms path through the machine while red lights simulated electrical generation. Rick shook his head slowly as he gazed at the display; the concept was so simple even he understood it.

Never in his long sales career had Rick been as excited about working with a company as he was by UES. The prospects of this account went far beyond the mere saie of rubber gaskets and hoses. This company, and companies like it, would literally change the world—and refreshingly, for the better.

Although Rick would never be so naïve as to think for one moment that UES was building fuel cells for any reason other than profit, he couldn't help hoping that perhaps in some very small way, there was an altruistic reason for the company's formation.

In Rick's opinion, what Unlimited Energy Systems was doing was on a higher level than simply the manufacture of a product for profit. What UES and other fuel cell manufacturers were doing would have a dramatic impact on how energy was produced first here in the United States, and eventually the rest of the world.

The benefit of fuel cell technology to both mankind and the environment was beyond question—an endless supply of pollution-free energy. Working with a company whose product would change and benefit the world was intoxicating to Rick, and he felt privileged and proud to be part of it. The fact that this account would eventually generate millions of dollars of sales for his company was of secondary importance to him.

It was worth the aggravation—every minute of it—just trying to get his foot in the door here back in May 1997. After calling Robert Jones in response to UES' "gasketing challenge," it took six months and countless phone calls reminding the engineer before he finally got around to honoring his pledge to send Rick his company's non-disclosure agreement.

What a sales call that initial visit was! Robert was kind enough to take the time to explain, in layman's terms, how the device worked:

Fuel, natural gas or any other substance containing high amounts of hydrogen such as kerosene, propane, unleaded gasoline, whatever, enters the reformer—a fuel processor—where it is converted into a hydrogen-rich gas called reformate. The reformate goes into the fuel cell stack where the hydrogen molecules are separated from each other in the presence of a catalyst on the anode side of an electrochemical cell. The protons pass through an impermeable non-conducting membrane to the cathode side of the cell. This membrane is called the proton exchange membrane (PEM), or polymer electrolyte membrane. The electrons pass around the membrane through the electrical load to the cathode side. Around the cathode catalyst the hydrogen protons combine with the electrons and oxygen molecules from the air and produce water. DC power is generated within the fuel cell and is sent to a power-conditioning device where it is converted into reliable, regulated DC or AC power.

The engineer also explained some of the possible uses for fuel cells: units that could power individual houses, whole subdivisions, or factories. They could also act as emergency generators, referred to in the industry as UPS units—uninterrupted power supply. The potential even existed for small fuel cells that could power laptop computers or small appliances.

And of course, automobiles.

Rick considered himself a closet environmentalist and immediately saw that the benefits of this technology went far beyond just clean air. Once widely in use, how many fish and birds would be saved by the drastically reduced chance of an oil tanker running aground or breaking apart at sea, creating another Prince William Sound? Global warming could be slowed or possibly even eliminated. Reducing the amount of fossil fuel burnt would reduce the volume of greenhouse gas produced. This would be an immeasurable benefit to the overall environment.

Then there were the other considerations as well: the eradication of electrical outages due to overhead power lines going down—they would no longer be needed. (Not to mention the aesthetic benefit of not having to view huge metal structures scarring the landscape). The widespread use of fuel cells would ensure the security of the U.S. economy. No longer would we be at the mercy of OPEC and other oil-producing countries. And, perhaps most importantly, how many young service men and women would live to see children and grandchildren as a result of not being called upon to confront every crisis that threatens the flow of crude oil to this country. In Vietnam Rick had come to the conclusion that nineteen years old was awfully young to die.

When he sat back and really thought about it, the use of fuel cells would revolutionize the world for the better. Hydrogen is extremely abundant and can be extracted from any number of sources. Rick couldn't imagine how anybody with half a brain, or any sense of international or environmental responsibility, could not grasp the benefits of this technology.

But there were problems, Robert explained, with bringing fuel cell technology to market. The main problem, not surprisingly, was cost. At the conception of mass-producing fuel cells, generating electrical power by the devices was five times the cost of generation by traditional methods. In time that gap would close, Robert assured him—in fact it already had. Since Rick's first visit in the spring of 1997, electricity produced by fuel cells had come within reach of overall cost parity to power supplied by nuclear or fossil fuel-fired plants.

The other problem was the cost of the fuel cell itself. Because they were not in mass production yet, component cost—all the different parts required to produce one of UES' residential units—was extremely high. In time, and with increased production, those costs would come down, too.

Robert explained that many of their vendors had pledged to absorb as much cost as possible to help UES get to market as quickly as possible. Of course, these same suppliers would expect preferential treatment from UES once in production, and his company intended to provide that.

Research and development would be ongoing at Unlimited Energy Systems. The company would continue to work on new designs to reduce the number of components needed to produce a fuel cell, and develop ways of assembling the units faster and more efficiently. This was a technology that would continuously evolve.

On the flight home after that initial visit, Rick pledged to himself that he would do everything possible to ensure both FTT and FSS fully supported UES. After he advised Donald Kampnel, David Greene and all the business unit managers of the incredible potential for both seals and hoses at this prospective account, he didn't expect cooperation would be a problem. Of course, at that time he didn't know that his own boss—the person who should be foremost in support of his efforts—would be so incredibly short-sighted.

The engineers of Flexible Sealing Solutions and Unlimited Energy Systems were currently on the fifth revision of the stack gasket. This critical seal was sandwiched between the Anode and Cathode plates and ensured the refromate and oxygen only flowed where they were supposed to. Currently, 157 plates were needed to comprise one fuel cell stack.

It had taken a little less than two years for the engineers at both companies to perfect this gasket, fondly referred to as the "bat gasket"—so nicknamed because the cross-sectional design of the seal looked very much like the bat in the spotlight of the preamble to the old 1960's *Batman* television show.

Two years was a long time, Rick would concede to himself, but far from excessive for this type of program. For David Greene, however, two years was an eternity. And as FSS' sales continued to plummet he had no qualms about letting Rick know his feelings. But every time his boss got on the soapbox, Rick took pleasure in pointing out that sales wouldn't be declining had his advice to forego the price increase been taken. He knew, however, that this argument's shelf-life was coming to an end—his boss would only put up with it for so long.

Unfortunately, David Greene's attitude toward the time and resources Rick was devoting to UES was beginning to rub off on other influential people at FTT. Mark Kampnel, the owner's son and heir apparent to the throne, was one of them. Rick was disheartened when he'd heard junior comment in a recent meeting that the only reason he allowed FTT and FSS to continue to work with UES was because he saw fuel cell technology as a threat to their core business— hoses for internal combustion engines. In the unlikely event fuel cells ever replaced the internal combustion engine, he wanted his two companies entrenched with one of the major players in the business.

Working with a company only because you're hedging future bets was hardly the way to foster a healthy, long-term relationship between two companies. But Rick didn't care what the reasoning was so long as he could continue to work with and support Unlimited Energy Systems.

As Kathy Socolowski, UES' buyer, appeared in the lobby to collect him for their appointment, Rick began to dread the coming battle between him and his boss over UES.

CHAPTER 3

▼

Theodore Kennelly sat motionless in his plush leather chair watching the rain splatter against the huge windows of his office. The rain, and its accompanying thick gray haze, reflected his mood. Tomorrow was Thanksgiving, his favorite holiday—at least it used to be. But since Carol was gone he didn't much care for Thanksgiving, or any other holiday for that matter.

He really couldn't blame James Landue and the rest of PETROCOMP's board of directors; after all, he had agreed to come back. He should have resigned. He only had himself to blame for staying on during those last precious months of his wife's life.

Unlike most retired people with wealth, he and Carol didn't plan on spending their remaining years in hot, humid, overcrowded Florida. It took little convincing to get his wife, a Michigan native, to agree to purchase a retirement home in the state's Upper Peninsula. He loved the snow, and he and Carol enjoyed nothing more than becoming snowbound in their well-provisioned, modern cabin.

Calling it a "cabin" was probably a stretch. Sitting on twenty acres of land with three-hundred feet of lakeshore, the five-thousand-eight-hundred square foot dwelling was really more of an estate. But what the hell, calling it a cabin made it seem cozier and it made Carol happy.

Thanksgivings were always spent at the cabin with their two daughters, their husbands and the three grandchildren. By that time there was usually plenty of snow on the ground and while he and Carol cooked, the kids and grandkids had a great time sledding, snowmobiling or building snow forts. Afterward, they'd have a great Thanksgiving dinner—*God*, those were good times!

Then the call came.

Kennelly had spent the majority of his life in executive positions, first in manufacturing at Honeywell and 3M; then, reading the writing on the wall, made the switch to the oil industry by becoming general manager of TEXCOM's Corpus Christi refinery in 1983. He prided himself on the fact that he was probably one of the first executives in the country to recognize that manufacturing was doomed in the United States.

With sadness, he realized that outsourcing would eventually lead to a dramatic drop in the country's standard of living. It was already happening. Manufacturing jobs had been disappearing for a number of years. But now, in 1999, there were few professions that couldn't be sacrificed at the altar of profit. Work such as customer service, engineering and computer programming were going to places like China, India and Bangladesh.

It was a bitter irony few seemed to understand. If everyone in the goddamn country has a minimum wage service job, who's going to have the money to purchase the consumer goods being produced in other countries?

No, the United States was slitting its own throat and would soon have the standard of living of a third world country. The distribution of wealth between rich and poor would grow wider than ever.

As Kennelly watched the rain stream down the windows he grunted, acknowledging to himself that *he* was part of the problem. It was high-level executives like him that would eventually cause the country's economy to implode. Thank God he wouldn't live to see the results of his handiwork.

But his children and grandchildren would.

All one can do in life is play the game. And play to win. Why not? There was no God—no higher authority to answer to. He could, and would crush anybody who got in his way; and do it with impunity. Fuel cell technology would soon be more than just a threat. He had the power to destroy it—and he would.

It was a cold, hard fact—his grandchildren's generation will not have the same standard of living he now enjoyed. Therefore, he was going to bequeath to his grandchildren as much wealth as he could. Carol would have wanted that.

They knew his weakness and exploited it, calling him two years ago with an offer he couldn't resist. He never could say no to a challenge.

Theodore Kennelly retired from PETROCOMP in 1992 as vice president of finance. Typically, he played the political game pretty well, but tired of it toward the end of his career. Consequently, he had not been offered the position of CEO in '92 when William Kramer was fired. With the prospect of heading up the corporation gone and feeling financially secure, he decided to pack it up.

PETROCOMP had gone though three CEOs since his retirement and the company was hemorrhaging cash. They needed a numbers man. When Marcus Corrigan was "broomed" by the board, the board's chairman, James Landue, gave Ted Kennelly a call. Carol claimed not to care that he was being pulled out of retirement, but she did, and it showed; he just refused to see it.

In just two short years as CEO, Kennelly had turned the company around financially—a fact he was proud of. He was the man of the hour; winning the respect and admiration of the board.

But the success came at a price. Nine months into the job Carol became sick. Diagnosed with pancreatic cancer, she was dead three months later. He should have resigned the moment he'd learned of her illness—spent the last few months at her side. But he didn't. He was too goddamned driven to succeed.

He'd never forgive himself, but he swore he would make it up to her by leaving her children and grandchildren a sizeable inheritance.

But this vow was now threatened.

Fuel Cell technology was placing the millions of shares of PETROCOMP stock he owned in jeopardy. The small amount of preliminary research he had done into the burgeoning industry scared the hell out of him.

Something had to be done.

Kennelly knew World Energy and ENDICORP had as much to lose as his corporation did. PETROCOMP was powerful, but not powerful enough. A strong alliance was needed. When he approached Wendell Finley and Kenneth Saxton to suggest the formation of this extraordinary alliance, he was pleasantly surprised—neither CEO hesitated.

But Saxton and Finley wanted to go slow. Conduct extensive research into the industry to determine if action really was required. They had insisted on hiring a consultant. Consultants—Kennelly detested them. They made their money by perpetuating the problem, not solving it. Kennelly particularly hated Laurence Haggerty. Why, he didn't know. The man just rubbed him the wrong way.

He turned from the window and pressed the intercom button on his phone. "Martha, the weather's awful. Would you please check to see if Mr. Finley and Mr. Saxton's flights are on time?"

"Of course, Mr. Kennelly."

He looked at his watch, 8:50 A.M; they were scheduled to meet at 10:00 A.M. A majority of the day was set aside for this meeting. He hoped it wouldn't take them that long to come to agreement on what to do.

He had spent considerable time poring over all the data and information Haggerty had presented them back in August and for the life of him didn't know what to do. The few ideas the consultant did have not only lacked ethics, but were downright illegal. Though the lack of ethics didn't bother Kennelly, at sixty-seven the last thing he wanted to do was spend what remaining years he had left in prison—even if it was "Club Fed." A good attorney would ensure he ended up there rather than a real prison.

No, it would be preferable to eliminate the fuel cell threat by means that were not illegal. But that may not be possible.

"Mr. Saxton just called," Kennelly flinched, Martha's voice snapping him out of his deep thought. "His jet just landed at LaGuardia. He's taking a shuttle helicopter and expects to be here in about forty minutes. I'm still checking on Mr. Finley."

Hopefully, his jet will crash. "Thank you, Martha." Kennelly leaned back in his chair and stared at the ornate ceiling of his office.

The one thing he and Saxton had in common was an intense dislike of Wendell Finley. Although they never discussed it openly, Kennelly didn't trust the ostentatious son-of-a-bitch and could sense Saxton didn't either. For his part, Finley probably thought the same of him and Saxton. But so what? Despite the feelings all around they were able to come together and trust each other enough to confront this common threat. Once they had addressed this issue they could go back to business-as-usual. Back to battling amongst themselves and the lesser oil companies for a larger piece of the world's oil market.

"Mr. Kennelly?"

Kennelly leaned forward in his chair and reached to press the intercom button. "Yes, Martha. Go ahead."

"I spoke with Mr. Finley's secretary. Mr. Finley's jet took off a little late, but should have landed at Kennedy fifteen minutes ago. She expects him to be here in the next twenty minutes or so."

"Good. Please escort them to the boardroom when they arrive. Also, tell Joey I want him to sweep the boardroom now."

"Right away, sir."

Ten minutes later, Joey D'Aleo, head of security for PETROCOMP, stuck his head into Kennelly's office and gave him a thumbs up, signaling the boardroom was free of any electronic listening devices. Kennelly hardly expected Joey to find anything, but his two associates would chastise him if they ever discovered he hadn't followed procedure. Several moments later, Martha informed him his guests had arrived.

Martha placed doughnuts and coffee on the boardroom's long, highly polished table. After she left the room, Saxton, as usual, took command of the meeting. It irked Kennelly that the CEO of World Energy appointed himself leader of The Committee. But at the same time he was glad the Englishman took the initiative—Kennelly didn't want any more responsibility than necessary.

"Well...for my part, gentlemen," Saxton started off, "having thoroughly studied Haggerty's data, I am convinced that if we don't act, and act quickly, we're...as you Americans are so fond of saying...*fucked!*" He grinned at his colleagues, expecting a chuckle but only got a solemn nod of agreement. Slightly crestfallen, he continued. "It's apparent that the Saudi's strategy is no longer effective." He was referring to the Kingdom's efforts to stave off alternative energy development.

As long as oil remained cheap, there would be no incentive for nations to undertake efforts to find alternative energy sources. OPEC had been formed for just that reason and Saudi Arabia, being the largest oil producer, had tremendous influence to force other oil-producing nations to follow suit.

"I have an idea of what to do," Saxton continued. "But I'd like to hear your thoughts on the matter first."

There was a long, uncomfortable pause. Suddenly, Finley barked out, "Drop our prices. Drop them so low that there will be no hope of fuel cell cars competing with the internal combustion engine—from an economic standpoint—for years to come, if ever."

"And how long will we need to subsidize the consumer, Wendell?" Kennelly asked with no attempt to hide his aversion to the suggestion. "How long before the fuel cell companies throw up their hands and give up?"

Finley shrugged, "I'm not sure. But I wouldn't think more than a year."

"*A year!*" Kennelly exclaimed, turning to face him. "Do you realize how much money we'd lose in a year? Christ...we'd come close to insolvency."

Finley reddened. Scornfully he asked, "Do you have a better idea, Ted?"

"Yes," Kennelly snapped, turning to look at Saxton. "Begin research immediately on ways of extracting hydrogen from unleaded gasoline. This has several advantages for us. For one thing, it would make us appear environmentally friendly—green, if you will—to the average consumer. Additionally, our corporate image would be enhanced because we'd be working *with* the fuel cell companies—not against them. But, in actuality, all we'd really be doing is perpetuating the world's dependency on our product." Producing an arrogant smirk, Kennelly folded his arms across his chest and leaned back in his chair—clearly pleased with himself.

Saxton stroked his chin thoughtfully for several moments then said, "Actually, I like Wendell's idea better." Kennelly, shocked, raised his eyebrows and did a double take at Saxton. He then turned to Finley who shot him a smug look. "I believe participation with fuel cell technology would not only lend it credibility, but would open us up to competition with other hydrogen-rich substances for production of, ah…what did Haggerty call it?"

"Refromate," Finley offered.

"Yes, thank you. Refromate." Saxton got up from his chair, clasped his hands behind his back and began to pace. "But, I think Wendell's idea is extreme. To survive we'd have to involve the Saudis, and I doubt they'd embrace the idea—pricing can't go much lower. And I'd be hesitant to approach the other producers. It would be dangerous to have so many players involved. The risk of a leak would be too great.

"No," he stopped pacing. "We'll keep Wendell's idea in reserve; use it as a last resort." He turned to Kennelly. "However, I think your idea has merit, Ted. We should begin preliminary research into hydrogen extraction. Covertly, of course. Perhaps at a later date, form 'front' companies to hide our true intent. Would you like to handle that?" Kennelly pursed his lips and nodded. "Good." The CEO of World Energy strolled over to the window and gazed out at the New York skyline.

After several moments of silence Kennelly asked, "Okay, Ken, what is it *you* have in mind?"

Saxton abruptly spun to face Kennelly, his eyes wild. Crisply, and with startling enthusiasm he spit out, "Discredit it! Discredit the technology. Prove it to be unreliable, dangerous—a farce." The CEO of World Energy offered his suggestion with such conviction he almost seemed possessed.

"And how the hell we gonna do that, Ken?" Finley asked, biting off the end of a cigar to light it. Saxton said nothing. The CEO of ENDICORP lit the cigar, took a few puffs, then, waving it around said, "As we've all learned from our homework, the technology has been around for over a century—and used successfully. It's been on every goddamned spaceship we've sent up."

Saxton walked from the window and stood behind his chair. Placing his hands on it he solemnly admitted, "I don't know how we'd do it." He pulled the chair out and sat down. "That's where I believe Noble Consultants comes in. We commission Haggerty to develop a plan to discredit the technology, or otherwise trash it. He presents his plan to us and if we like it, we renew his contract to implement the plan through to completion." He took a sip of coffee then added, "If, of course, we truly believe it's necessary." Saxton folded his hands on top of the table; his eyes darted expectantly between his two associates. "What do you think?"

Finley shrugged. "Sounds good to me. Hell, better idea than anything I've been able to conjure up." He turned to look at Kennelly. "Ted?"

Kennelly was still steamed that Saxton thought Finley had a better idea than his. But Saxton's idea seemed the most logical of all and Kennelly took solace in that. Nodding his head he said, "Yes. It makes sense to me. Overall, it does seem to provide a...a better long-term solution. Besides, if we don't like Haggerty's plan we can always have him come up with another." Then grumbling to himself added, "Or preferably we hire another consulting agency."

"Capital!" Saxton exclaimed with genuine enthusiasm as he reached for a doughnut. After taking a bite and a sip of coffee he said, "Then, gentlemen, the task before us is to determine how much we compensate Mr. Haggerty, and the amount each of us contributes, in the event we extend his contract."

Finley blew out a thick cloud of blue smoke. "As for who pays what..." he began to thoughtfully examine his stogie, rolling it between his fingers. "I think it should be proportional—three ways—based on percentage of market share."

"Of course you would," Kennelly quipped, making no effort to mask his ire. "ENDICORP will have the smallest share." Finley didn't reply. He only smiled and shrugged indifferently.

"Well, World Energy will certainly have the biggest share," Saxton said pensively. "It's only fair, Ted." He looked imploringly at the CEO of PETRO-COMP and added, "My company stands to benefit the most from the demise of fuel cell technology—then yours." Finley glanced at Kennelly, unable to stop himself from beaming.

Kennelly looked away from both men in disgust and, with a grunt, nodded his concurrence.

A smile of relief came across Saxton's face. "So gentlemen, it appears we're in agreement: it shall be proportional. Now, the question is, how much?"

Again the room went silent. The three men looked at each other, each hoping someone else would be the first with a suggestion. Tiring of the stalemate, Kennelly rolled his eyes and snarled, "Fifty million."

Nervously, Wendell Finley said, "Ya know...what we'll be askin' Haggerty and his firm to do is highly illegal. If he's caught, he and many of his associates will most likely rot in prison for the rest of their lives."

"Fuck Haggerty!" Kennelly all but shouted. "What about us? If he's caught, what's to stop him from fingering us? He'll certainly plea bargain—do anything necessary to lessen his sentence." Then quietly he added, "Hell...I would!"

"Yes...it's clearly imperative that if Haggerty agrees to do this, he does a proper job of it," Saxton offered. "The stakes involved are tremendous, he'll certainly understand that.

"Whatever actions are necessary, his plan must ensure there can be no link to us. The trail of breadcrumbs, if you will, must lead to oblivion."

Almost offhandedly Finley blurted out, "One hundred million." Kennelly glared at him censoriously. "Offer him twenty-five million upfront to draw up a strategy for our review and approval." He stopped to puff on his cigar, savoring the interest the other two men were giving him. Presently he continued. "Give him the balance, seventy-five million, upon successful completion of the plan. That is, of course, should we decide to use it. And..." he took another quick puff. "I stress the word, *successful.*"

"How do we measure success?" Kennelly asked.

Finley continued to puff on his cigar as he considered the question. Kenneth Saxton chimed in. "In my opinion, success can only be measured one way. The leading fuel cell companies abandon all efforts to mass produce their product. Or preferably, their insolvency."

Wendell Finley nodded his head in agreement. Saxton locked his eyes on Kennelly. "Ted?" The CEO of PETROCOMP hesitated for a moment, frowned then nodded. "Alright then, we'll get together with Laurence Haggerty and set him to the task."

The twenty-five million couldn't have come at a better time. Struggling financially, Haggerty was worried about making payroll and even considered laying off some of his employees. Now he was glad he hadn't. There was a tremendous amount of work to do and he'd need every one of them.

But he was still a little on edge. He hadn't actually received the money yet. Due to the nature of the services provided, payment from all customers of Noble Consultants was laundered through several legitimate companies Haggerty had under contract. Normally, it took two weeks before funds were deposited in Noble's account at Capital Savings and Trust. He knew the money was coming, but he'd bite his nails until it actually arrived. Although they had never given him reason for concern, he didn't completely trust the guys running the front companies.

He was sitting at his desk staring blankly at the yellow legal pad before him. Laurence Haggerty's office was on the outskirts of Washington, D.C. and normally noise from traffic on 495 didn't bother him. Today it did. Frustrated, Haggerty carefully ran his hands through the thin, graying hair at his temples. More than once when flustered he'd knocked off his toupee; twice in the presence of his secretary. He was giving serious thought to getting rid of the damn thing.

Leaving PETROCOMP's boardroom the week before Christmas, he initially thought the task The Committee had presented would be relatively easy. The continuation of his contract instilled him with a confidence he hadn't felt in a long time; the moment he parted company with the CEOs he marched directly to Martha Putnam's office. Determined to ask her to dinner, he completely deflated when she wasn't there—she'd just departed for a dentist appointment.

The moment Saxton began outlining what The Committee wanted his firm to do, Haggerty realized that what was being asked of him wasn't his area of expertise—industrial espionage. Rather, it was industrial sabotage. But for a few days he didn't give their proposition much thought, he was too euphoric about meeting payroll and paying off several outstanding debts. Only later, after the exhilaration of the contract renewal had worn off did the enormity of the task hit him. Formulating a strategy seemed impossible. This wouldn't be the destruction of a single program or product, this would be industrial sabotage on a grand scale.

It was now mid-January; at the latest, The Committee wanted his proposal by the end of March. He began to rub his temples again, but thoughts just weren't coming. He threw his pen on the pad, leaned back in his chair and sighed. Sandra would be back in a week; he'd consult with her when she returned.

He'd given his most trusted confidant an extended Christmas vacation. Sandra, whose parents had died in a tragic car accident shortly after the New Year, was putting their affairs in order. Haggerty hoped that when she returned her grieving would be over and she'd be back with a clear head—he needed her now, more than ever.

It was a good decision. Although she didn't seem completely herself yet, her mind was sharp and she'd given him some excellent ideas for the proposal's framework. Actually, Sandra's cunning and complete disregard for ethics actually scared Haggerty a bit. He was glad she was on his payroll—he'd hate to face her as a competitor.

The plan he developed over the last two months was straightforward, but not without risk—that couldn't be avoided. Although he tried, he found it wasn't possible to sabotage an entire industry, its technology and numerous companies, not to mention the lives of thousands of people, without risk to Noble Consultants.

Painstakingly, Haggerty had formulated the plan so that there was virtually no danger to his clients; there was practically no way any member of The Committee could ever be connected with the operation. Should something go wrong and an investigation ensue, only Noble Consultants could be accused. Provided the scheme was executed properly, proving guilt would be difficult—even for the most seasoned prosecutor. Still, the risk was substantial; but so was the reward.

For his plan to be successful, Haggerty required a person with "*special*" talents. Someone who had experience in unconventional methods of persuasion and wasn't afraid to get a little dirt on his hands. Perhaps most importantly, someone who knew how to keep his mouth shut.

Part of the plan required a heavy-handed approach, something Haggerty wasn't exactly thrilled about. But he saw no other option. To bring down fuel cell technology—particularly now when it was at such an advanced stage—would require a bold approach. Fortunately, he knew someone with the necessary qualifications.

Question was, could he recruit this man? For seventy-five million he'd find a way!

Tomorrow, he and Sandra would present his plan to The Committee, and he was nervous—far more nervous than he'd ever been before. It wasn't only because of the money. At fifty-seven years old he would never be presented with a challenge of this magnitude again. This would be the crown jewel in an otherwise undistinguished career. Failure was not an option.

Regrettably, his efforts would be a detriment to mankind rather than a benefit. He shook his head in disbelief; ethics…they were seeping into his conscious thought again. *Thank God I'm no longer practiced law,* he thought. *I'd starve.*

To soothe his slightly guilty conscience he focused on his client; that was his only concern. *To hell with everybody else!* he thought to himself.

"I call the plan P3, and will refer to it as such from this point on," Laurence Haggerty said with a crispness he didn't feel. Last night, despite his best effort, he couldn't sleep. The presentation weighed heavy on his mind and kept running through his head. But how could it not? His firm's survival depended on it. Dressed in his best suit, he projected an air of professionalism that even impressed Theodore Kennelly.

"It's a three-pronged approach," he continued, "hence its name. The beauty of P3, in my opinion, is its redundancy. If one prong of the strategy doesn't work, one of the others will, ensuring we achieve our objective." With furrowed brows, the members of The Committee studied the document projected on the screen. Sandra Beach, dressed in a particularly provocative outfit, (in Haggerty's opinion) sat behind her laptop and subtly tried to get the attention of Wendell Finley.

The proprietor of Noble Consultants allowed the three men time to read each page of the document before signaling Sandra to proceed to the next. When she did, Haggerty would give a brief synopsis of the page's content, and then remain silent next to the projection screen with his hands clasped behind his back.

Saxton was the first with a question. "Laurence, would the three stratagem be implemented simultaneously, or in order of probability of success?"

Haggerty cleared his throat. "Ideally simultaneously. However, I'm not certain yet if that will be possible. As I'm sure you've ascertained for yourselves, a significant amount of covert investigation into the lives of the target individuals we'll be required prior to execution of the first two strategies. But...yes, it is my intention to put all three in motion at the same time.

"All three strategies will involve either intimidation, blackmail or bribery—not necessarily in that order." He took a few steps away from the screen. Like a professor lecturing to students he continued. "In detail, the first strategy, what I've code named "Larry," will first involve digging up dirt on Cynthia Klash of GFCT and Daniel Stallinger of UES. Of course, before we can consid—"

"You're working under the assumption that there *is* dirt to dig up on these individuals," Theodore Kennelly interjected.

Haggerty glanced down at the floor, an embarrassed smile forming on his face. He remained silent for a moment, then lifted his head and stared sheepishly at Kennelly. "No offense, but people in your position *always* have skeletons in their closets." Saxton smiled and nodded his head. Finley nervously shifted in his chair while Kennelly looked down at his folded hands. With a smug expression Haggerty asked, "Is that an accurate statement?"

"Please continue, Laurence." Saxton said, sounding eager to move on from the subject.

Haggerty solemnly nodded. "In any case, in the highly unlikely event we can't find anything of use on Mr. Stallinger or Ms. Klash, it can always be credibly fabricated." Haggerty turned and walked back to the screen. "As I was about to say, before we resort to blackmail we'll first attempt to bribe them. The carrot is always preferable to the stick. However, should bribing fail to achieve the objective—the financial ruin of their companies—then we'll turn to intimidation and/or blackmail."

"How do you expect them to bankrupt their companies before their boards intervene?" Finley asked. "And even if they do, the demise of a couple fuel cell companies won't solve our problem."

"You're quite right of course," Haggerty replied earnestly. "But we must not lose sight of the ultimate objective of P3—to completely discredit fuel cell technology as a viable source of energy for decades to come. How Klash and Stallinger covertly accomplish the bankruptcy—or collapse—of their company is going to be left up to them. However, a well-formulated statement either given to, or leaked to the press by someone in their position could conceivably cause a run on their stock.

"Also, to address your other concern, Mr. Finley, you must keep in mind that Global Fuel Cell Technologies and Unlimited Energy Systems are by far the leaders in the fuel cell industry—years ahead of their competition in going to market. Their failure will send shock waves through the entire industry. Their collapse will send a strong signal to Wall Street, investors, vendors and employees; not to mention Washington and the politicians sympatic to the industry." Finley seemed satisfied with the answer and nodded thoughtfully.

The head of Noble Consultants waited a moment for further questions. He glanced at Sandra who gave him a reassuring wink. So far the presentation was going well and he tried to relax a little. Relaxation was something he found difficult to do and lately, could only accomplish with a drink in his hand.

Silence signaled Haggerty to proceed. "Strategy two, or what we've code named "Moe", is essentially the same as Larry. The difference is we're targeting the executives of UES and GFCT's strategic suppliers.

"These vendors are of vital importance to the fuel cell companies. They depend on them not only for components, but much of their technical support as well. By bringing about their withdrawal from the fuel cell industry, we will effectively circumvent UES' and GFCT's efforts to go to market. Given what these two companies have invested up to this point, with the departure of their most important suppliers, UES simply won't have the financial means to develop and qualify new sources and I suspect GFCT's parent company would be reluctant to finance the effort as well." Kennelly nodded agreement.

"Why not?" Saxton asked.

"Yeah, what's so difficult about finding someone else to supply a given component?" Finley added.

Haggerty was not surprised by Saxton and Finley's lack of understanding. Unlike Kennelly, neither man had any manufacturing experience. Both men had spent their entire careers in one facet or another of the oil industry.

"It's not as easy as you might think," Haggerty began. "True, there may be numerous sources for any given component of a fuel cell and its support equipment—with the possible exception of the GDL and NAFION suppliers—but qualifying them as approved sources is both time consuming and very expensive.

"All vendors' products must be thoroughly tested both in the lab and in actual application. In many instances a listing, or accreditation, from UL, that's Underwriters Laboratory, or the Canadian equivalent, CUL, is required before the fuel cell component can be sold on the open market. Though not a federal requirement, it's a way for companies—particularly start-ups like our fuel cell friends—to cover their butts. By having their product listed through one of these agencies they can limit their liability should the product cause harm to someone and they litigate."

Haggerty stopped to take a sip of water. He let out a long, silent sigh and continued. "Also of note, GFCT is heading up the committee to write engineering and performance standards for the industry. Many vendors' products will be required to meet these new standards. No…" Haggerty shook his head; a dubious look came across his face. "Given how far along UES and GFCT are with their strategic suppliers, the loss of one of them at this point in time would be a deathblow."

"GDL, NAFION?" Kennelly asked.

"Two absolutely critical components for a PEM—PEM stands for Proton Exchange Membrane—fuel cell. It is the heart of the fuel cell. They are part of what the engineers call the "soft goods" package. GDL stands for Gas Diffusion Layer. It's a special fabric that, along with the NAFION, which is a Saran-Wrap type material for lack of a better analogy, is what separates the hydrogen atom's proton and electron to produce electricity.

"The NAFION is sandwiched between the GDL, and this soft goods package sits between the fuel cell's Anode and Cathode plates. The GDL, and particularly the NAFION, are still very expensive. To my knowledge there are only a handful of companies that can produce the GDL and only one company, Duplex Chemical, which can manufacture NAFION. Naturally, GFCT and UES' suppliers for these items are on our radar screen.

"It should be relatively easy to deal with the executives of the supplier companies. They've put a lot into these fuel cell companies and will be quick to panic if they catch wind that UES and GFCT are experiencing financial or other difficulties. As I reported earlier, they still haven't jumped into bed with GFCT and UES, but, they're certainly getting undressed."

Sandra Beach jumped at the opportunity her boss gave her. She giggled. It got Finley's attention. He stared at her for a long moment, his eyes eventually drifting to her cleavage.

Finley was still gaping at Sandra when Haggerty continued. "It's a safe bet they'd react like most of their competitors did early on. If they see no prospect of obtaining a return on their investment, they'll abandon the fuel cell companies."

Haggerty turned from the screen and took a few steps toward his seated clients. "It should be fairly easy to coerce the CEO's of a few select vendors to sever their ties with GFCT and UES. Persuade them to raise their prices to unacceptable levels for example, or eliminate the R&D they're conducting on behalf of their fuel cell customers. Steps such as these should be relatively easy to accomplish." He paused and looked at each member of The Committee. "Any questions on Moe?" The three men shook their heads. "All right, let's move on then.

"Lastly we have Curly. Here's where we target the fuel cell lobby and its congressional supporters. I'm confident we can succeed here by scare tactics alone because as we all know, politicians value self-preservation above all else. Political survival depends on money and votes and both flow from districts and states that are economically healthy.

"Recently, I received conformation that the fuel cell lobby is pressuring influential lawmakers sympathic to their cause to support the zero emissions bill Congressman Hanson of Vermont has drafted. You...recall the bill?" The three CEO's wore blank expressions. Haggerty grimaced and continued. "In a nutshell, if it becomes law, it will require all federal agencies in all states to have fleets of zero emission vehicles by 2008—with the exception of heavy trucks." The owner of Noble Consultants tried to put on an ominous expression. Slowly he said, "Frankly, I'm worried. The support pledged to the bill thus far is quite substantial." He paused a moment for effect, looking briefly at each CEO, then continued. "Of equal concern, I've also learned that the states targeted for a ten percent zero emissions law similar to California's, are New York, Michigan, Texas, Indiana, Georgia, Ohio and Illinois."

"Christ!" Kennelly spit out apprehensively, running a hand through his thick, white hair. For the first time the three men of The Committee looked genuinely concerned. This was good.

Haggerty acknowledged Kennelly's outburst with a nod and continued. "Although this proposed legislation is gaining tremendous momentum, it's not too late to stop it." The confidence with which her boss made the statement seemed to console their clients. Sandra sensed the three men breathing a collective sigh of relief.

"How?" Saxton inquired; a touch of skepticism in his voice.

The corners of Laurence Haggerty's mouth slowly inched upward. "Education," he replied as if the answer was blatantly obvious. "We simply educate the appropriate congressmen of the consequences of supporting these bills."

Haggerty dropped his head as if contemplating what to say next. He stood motionless for a moment then walked over to one of the empty chairs pressed against the boardroom's huge table. Placing his hands on the back of the chair, he stared intensely at the three members of The Committee for an uncomfortably long time. Then, with serious earnestness he asked, "Do you gentlemen have *any* idea how much of the U.S. economy revolves around the internal combustion engine?" Hands clutching the back of the chair, he peered intensely at the three men and waited for a response.

Fishing another cigar out of his coat pocket Finley said in jest, *"A lot?"*

Haggerty smirked and let out a huffed grunt. "Yeah…a lot," he replied almost sardonically.

What he was going to say next was important; he wanted to make sure he got his point across both in word and sentiment. He took in a deep breath, tightened his grip on the top of the chair and bent a little lower over it. He fixed his stare on the tabletop and in a looming voice he said, "The loss of the internal combustion engine would have nothing less than a catastrophic effect on the U.S. economy—not to mention the rest of the developed world." He lifted his head to look at his clients. "Think for a moment how many industries are dependent on engines that burn fossil fuel: Foundries, lubricants, rubber, steel, paper—filters, electronics, machining, plastics…the list is damn near endless. And that's just the beginning. Then there are the other businesses to consider: Repair shops, quick oil change shops, dealership service centers, auto parts stores and all the companies that manufacture aftermarket products for retail sale." Haggerty dropped his head and shook it. Lifting it he said, "No…if the internal combustion engine should suddenly disappear, the loss of jobs both here and abroad would be absolutely devastating. It would take decades for the world's economies to recover—if ever.

"The aim of Curly is to emphasize that point to lawmakers siding with the fuel cell industry. Loss of jobs in their district—and I can't think of a single district in this country that wouldn't be affected to some degree—would spell hard times for their constituents and their anger would be vented at the polls. Remember what I said earlier—a politician's first order of business is self preservation."

Saxton leaned back in his chair with a thoughtful expression. Rubbing his chin he asked, "Your point is well taken, Laurence. However, couldn't it be argued that the manufacture of the fuel cell drive train will create jobs, replacing those that are lost?"

Haggerty nodded. Pensively he said, "Yes. And clearly it will…over time. But this won't happen overnight. Even with a gradual phase out of the internal combustion engine there would be an immense number of people out of work for a very long time. More importantly, Mr. Saxton…that argument is *not* in your best interest."

Kennelly threw a pencil on the table and leaned back himself. "The politicians will listen. No doubt in my mind."

"How would you implement Larry and Moe?" Finley asked, quickly shifting his eyes from Sandra to her boss. "No offense, Haggerty, but the talent needed to successfully accomplish the objectives of those two plans—and actually get away with it—are a tad out of your agency's area of expertise. Wouldn't you agree?"

"You needn't—"

"I have some serious concerns." Finley quickly continued, cutting Haggerty off. The CEO of ENDICORP leaned forward and folded his hands on top of the table. He looked hard at both Saxton and Kennelly. "I was on the bandwagon, Ken, when you first proposed it—discrediting the technology and all. But what I've heard so far…" he shook his head, "Frankly, it scares the shit out of me."

Sandra Beach and Laurence Haggerty quickly exchanged concerned glances. He didn't expect an objection so early in the presentation. He had to move quickly if he was to cut off any concurrence with Finley's statement. The twenty-five million dollar retainer was dwindling fast. He needed this job both for his own personal gratification, and for the money. He had to get The Committee's attention focused back on the plan.

Stepping back from the chair Haggerty said louder than necessary, "You're absolutely right, Mr. Finley." That got their attention; Haggerty rarely raised his voice. Speaking normally again he said, "You lead me to a topic I must discuss with you gentlemen.

"As you've ascertained, Larry and Moe are out of my agency's core competence. However, I have someone in mind for this task. Someone who meets all the criteria required to carry out P3 successfully. However…" Haggerty paused a moment and shifted his eyes to Sandra as if looking for support. This was the one part of the proposal he was most apprehensive about. Particularly now that Finley had expressed doubt. One hundred million dollars was a lot of money—even for these three men. To ask for more seemed terribly presumptuous. Beach gave her boss an almost imperceptible nod of encouragement and he continued. "…he won't come cheap. Should you approve of, and decide to implement P3, we will be breaking more laws than I care to admit.

"As World Energy, PETROCOMP and ENDICORP will be shielded from any connection to P3, Noble Consultants and those it contracts to carry out this operation, if caught, will bear the wrath of our judicial system. This man I have in mind, Ms. Beach and I would most likely spend twenty-five years in prison...at a minimum."

"Mr. Haggerty, should the worst happen, what assurance do we have that we," Kennelly gestured to Saxton and Finley, "will not be implicated in this scheme?" The tone of the question was such that Haggerty wondered if Kennelly even heard what he'd just said about him possibly spending the next twenty-five years in prison. Heartless bastard!

Haggerty clasped his hands behind his back and turned to face Ted Kennelly. "To begin with, Noble Consultants has no relationship—on record—with ENDICORP, World Energy or PETROCOMP. That, as you know, is due to how compensation to my firm has been handled up to this point. Should something go wrong and Noble Consultants is indicted...and I talk—not that I ever would—there is absolutely no proof that you or your corporations had anything to do with it.

"P3 is and will remain, the only document outlining this plan. Neither you nor your companies are mentioned in it. Bottom line, gentlemen, is that there is no paper trail leading to your doorstep, no evidence linking you to this operation." He paused then asked Kennelly, "Does that give you the level of assurance you require?" The CEO of PETROCOMP studied Haggerty for a moment, grinned and bobbed his head a few times. Feeling he was gaining momentum, Haggerty continued pushing his point.

"This gentleman I need to contract, along with a few select individuals at Noble Consultants, will be taking all the risk. Consequently..." Haggerty could feel his knees begin to buckle; he locked them and cleared his throat. "I feel that payment for this man's services should be separate from that of Noble Consultants." His eyes quickly darted to each of the three clients. Noticing the incredulous looks on their faces he quickly added, "After successful completion of P3, of course."

"And...what will this person want for compensation?" Finley asked guardedly.

Haggerty swallowed hard; he prayed his voice wouldn't waver. Steeling himself, he replied with all the assurance he could muster, "I'll offer him ten million. But...for a job of this magnitude he'll demand fifty million...not a penny less."

The silence in the room was deafening.

The sudden appearance of wide eyes and furrowed brows confirmed Haggerty's worst fear—he failed to convince. The one thing he absolutely had to accomplish was proving that the severity of the threat justified the cost to eradicate it. As he watched the members of The Committee shoot each other concerned looks, he cursed himself.

But he didn't have a choice; he had to ask for the additional money. Paying this man out of his pocket would leave him with only twenty-five million and that didn't justify the risk to him and his firm.

The owner of Noble Consultants now heard his three clients begin to talk rapidly amongst themselves; there was no mistaking the anxiety in their voices. Laurence Haggerty turned to Sandra Beach; she was staring at him intensely. Her expression was an odd mixture of displeasure and encouragement. In that brief glance she clearly told him he was giving up too easily, he could still sway them—he had to try.

She was right, of course—she usually was. *You've worked too hard to get this far,* he thought. *You can still turn this around. Think man!*

But this type of thinking was difficult for him. In a courtroom, under pressure, laws, statutes and past rulings flowed through his mind effortlessly and he could easily pick out the information he needed for the given situation. But this wasn't a courtroom; this was selling. He never had to sell the services of Noble Consultants before—they always sold themselves. But this was a far different situation and Haggerty never considered himself a very good salesman, unlike his father. That man could sell sand to the Arabs.

The three men before him now appeared to be on the brink of arguing; and Haggerty didn't know about what. He'd been so lost in panicked thought that nothing they were saying registered. He looked at Sandra again. She let out a desperate sigh and was staring at him with pleading eyes. *For Christ's sake, Laurence, do something!*

He then remembered something his father said once. When Haggerty was about twelve-years-old his father came home depressed—which was not like him. He asked his dad what was wrong and he replied, "I lost a sale, Laurence. I couldn't show her the benefit." And he walked to the kitchen for a beer.

Selling was more than just convincing—where's the benefit to the customer?

"*Gentlemen!*" Haggerty bellowed politely. The three members of The Committee stopped shouting and turned to look at him. "I can't pull off P3 without him." The three men continued to stare at him. Good. He had their attention. Slowly, with all eyes locked on him, he walked up to the table, pulled out a chair and sat down. Folding his hands in front of him he gave his clients a thoughtful look. Melodiously he said, "Mr. Saxton, Mr. Kennelly, Mr. Finley, what is your industry worth to you—I mean to *you,* personally?" It was a rhetorical question.

He knew none of them would publicize their net worth. Haggerty immediately continued. "I know one-hundred-twenty-five million dollars is a lot of money. But is it? Really? Think about it. If that amount ended up being next quarter's profits, heads would roll." He paused a moment to let the words sink in. "Without P3, I can guarantee you that within several years, you'll be happy if *annual* profits reach that amount."

The room remained silent for several moments. He looked at Sandra who gave him a relieved look.

The CEO of ENDICORP was the first to speak. "Who...*is* this guy?" he asked with audible consternation.

"It's better you don't know, Mr. Finley" Haggerty responded smoothly.

"Laurence, you make a good point. However, I'm sure you realize that this is adding up to an appreciable amount of money," Saxton said with uncharacteristic trepidation. "The only way for us to come up with these kinds of funds is to essentially..." he grimaced, his face becoming lightly crimson. "...*God*, I hate to even say the word; *embezzle* it. Even split three ways between Wendell, Ted and I, the drain is likely to be noticed and questions asked."

"I appreciate that, Mr. Saxton. But I'm sure you can appreciate my desire not to spend what years I have left rotting in prison." Catching a hint of callousness in his voice, Haggerty took a deep breath and tried to relax. "If we are to go through with this, Mr. Saxton, I want the best. This man *is* the best." Haggerty's face turned contrite. "I, ah...I don't mean to be...insolent sir, but how you acquire the funds and cover the void in the balance sheets will be your dragon to slay."

Saxton turned to his two associates; no words were required. If they were serious about taking action to counter the common threat, they had little choice but to accept Haggerty's terms. Kennelly and Finley gave him a grudging nod of approval.

Saxton put on a paper-thin smile then turned back to face Haggerty. "All right, Laurence. I thank you for giving it to us straight. Should we," he motioned to his colleagues, "decide to put P3 into operation, we'll pay the additional fifty million. However, like your fee, we will pay the lion's share upon successful completion of the task. Fifteen million upfront for this 'mystery man,' thirty-five million when the job is done. Persuading this...*individual* to accept this arrangement is, as you say, *your* dragon to slay."

An immense wave of relieve washed over Haggerty. "Yes sir. I'm sure I can convince him to agree to those terms." He again glanced at his assistant who gave him an imperceptible nod of approval. "Are there any further questions with regard to P3?" He looked at his clients who remained silent. "Then gentlemen, I will conclude by recommending that you not wait too long to take action. The progress Global Fuel Cell Technologies, Unlimited Energy Systems and others in the industry are making is phenomenal. It may soon be too late to discredit the viability and reliability of fuel cells to the general public."

"Sandra, would you mind waiting for me in the lobby?" Haggerty asked as soon as they'd stepped out of the boardroom.

"No, I guess not. Why?"

"Just something I've been meaning to do. I'll be down shortly."

After his assistant disappeared in to the elevator, he turned and with a confident stride approached the door. Without hesitating he knocked and stepped into the office.

"Uh…Martha? I was…umm, I was wondering if you'd be free for dinner tonight?

CHAPTER 4

▼

Kenneth Saxton cordially escorted Laurence Haggerty and his assistant out of the boardroom, his requisite smile vanishing with the closing of the door. With downcast eyes he walked back to his chair and fell into it with a heavy sigh. Slouching, he stared blankly at the untouched cup of coffee before him, and then reached for it. With the tips of his fingers gently embracing the mug, he slowly spun it around, careful not to let any coffee splash over the rim. At a loss for anything to say, Saxton's two colleagues simply watched the superfluous rotation of the cup.

After a minute's silence Saxton shrugged and said, "The decision has been made for us. Wouldn't you agree? There's really nothing to discuss, it there?" Slowly, he lifted his head to look questioningly at Theodore Kennelly and Wendell Finley. Both men just grimaced.

"Over the last year," Saxton continued, "at various business and social functions I've heard countless conversations, comments and concerns about the technology from our contemporaries. Surely, you must have too?" His eyes darted between the faces of his two colleagues; no answer was necessary; their sour expressions confirmed that indeed they had.

The CEO of World Energy lifted the cup to his mouth and took a sip, wincing at its cold, bitter taste. He put the cup down and continued. "They're scared...real scared. GFCT's announcement back in April that they've successfully tested an SUV with a fuel cell powertrain has got everybody in the gasoline business pissing their pants—from major corporations like us, to the owners of retail outlets."

Kenneth Saxton was referring to Global Fuel Cell Technologies' recent announcement that back in February of 2000 they pulled the engine and transmission from a Nissan Pathfinder and replaced it with one of their fuel cell powertrains. Over the fervent objection of engineering, GFCT's marketing department was successful in convincing management to pay for testing of the retrofitted vehicle by one of the country's most influential automotive periodicals, Road & Off Road magazine. This turned out to be a real coup for the company.

The testing didn't give GFCT's engineers the hard data they were looking for, but the positive publicity propelled the company to the forefront of both automotive and national news.

Road & Off Road magazine was lavish in its accolades of both the vehicle's performance and its dependability:

- *"Almost on a par with GM's vaunted 3.8 liter engine. Zero to sixty in a respectable 9.3 seconds!"*

- *"Smooth and extremely quiet—almost too quiet—and with surprising power and torque."*

- *"With an operating cost 1/3 that of conventional gasoline powered engines, everyone from professionals to Soccer Moms will be demanding fuel cell powered vehicles. I predict that once on the market, dealerships will have a hard time keeping them in stock."*

- *"75,000 trouble-free miles! Fuel cell vehicles have come of age."*

Pensively, Kennelly said, "I've heard all the hoopla too. But when I think about it, our contemporaries can't be *that* concerned. I mean, for God's sake, it will take years for GFCT and its competitors to woo automakers away from the traditional car—to seriously consider manufacturing and marketing the damn things. Convincing public opinion will take even longer. It will take more than a simple article in a trade magazine to create demand for fuel cell cars." He emphasized his statement with a sour look, and then took a sip of coffee.

Wendell Finley was shaking his head. "I wouldn't be so sure of that, Ted," he remarked dourly. "How quickly we forget history once out of school! How long did it take for the automobile to replace the horse in this country? The airplane to replace the train? The word processor to replace the typewriter, then the computer to replace the word processor? No...I think they, along with us, have every reason to be deeply concerned."

"And it's not just the petroleum industry that's nervous," Saxton added. "All the hype about Unlimited Energy Systems' introduction of their first residential unit for both commercial and retail sale has got our friends in the coal industry losing sleep. I actually got a call last week from Vince Cambell, he's on the board of Consolidated Mining, asking my take on what's going on."

"What'd you tell him?" Finley asked.

Saxton let out a weary sigh. "I told him the truth…that he should be concerned. I also suggested that he and his board look closely into what's going on between UES, the residential division of GFCT, and some of the country's largest utilities. Overnight they might discover that the demand for coal is dwindling."

In Laurence Haggerty's last written report to The Committee, he outlined in considerable detail the negotiations taking place between the utility companies serving several large metropolitan areas, and Unlimited Energy Systems and Global Fuel Cell Technologies' residential division. In the report, both companies had offered to sell a limited, but substantial number of their units—at cost—to the utilities serving Detroit, Toronto, Hartford, Atlanta, Houston, Minneapolis and the greater Troy, New York area.

GFCT was offering to supply their new CP53 unit, a huge 250kw Solid Oxide fuel cell capable of supplying the energy needs of approximately twenty-five homes in a subdivision type setting. UES would supply units for individual homes, those outside of an electrical grid. These units were of special interest to the power companies since the cost of maintaining power lines to homes located in remote areas was very costly.

The fuel cell companies were wisely marketing their products to ensure future growth. Their strategy consisted of building the infrastructure needed for stationary units while at the same time convincing the public of the technology's safety and reliability. The utilities, interested in selling power and not particularly caring how it's generated, could only benefit by reducing their dependence on fossil fuels such as coal and oil. Although George W. Bush was trying hard to relax air pollution standards, he could never be successful enough. Meeting even the most lax emission standards was both tedious and expensive.

Another aspect of the deal attractive to the power companies was that they would maintain control of the stationary unit's fuel source. Initially, natural gas would be the hydrogen source of choice. The infrastructure for piping it was already in place and like the distribution of electricity itself they would control it.

Somehow, Haggerty had obtained a confidential internal memo from Southern States Power. In the report, the utility estimated that by 2004 they could reduce their demand for coal and oil twenty-two percent—at a minimum—by installing stationary units in just the Atlanta area alone. For this to be realized, installation in seventy-four new and existing subdivisions surrounding metropolitan Atlanta along with nine industrial parks would have to begin by third quarter of 2001. Provided contracts were signed soon, the report's author was clearly confident this timeline could be achieved. The only concern he expressed was the ability of GFCT to produce enough CP53 fuel cells. Due to the unit's ease of installation, he estimated only two months would be required to complete the task.

The Committee was alarmed by the memo—the third quarter of 2001 was only three months away.

Southern States Power's report was one of many Saxton had in front of him for referenced during for Haggerty's proposal. He plucked it from the pile, glanced at it and sighed. "Wendell, Ken…let's face facts—we're out of time. We no longer have the luxury of waiting to see if fuel cell technology will stumble on its own. We have to decide right now whether or not to implement Haggerty's plan."

"I'll admit I'm scared," Finley offered.

Saxton nodded in agreement. "I think we all are. But if we're to ensure the world remains dependent on crude oil—and other fossil fuels—we have to act."

"And…if P3 fails?" Theodore Kennelly mused.

The CEO of World Energy shrugged indifferently, "I can't see how we'd be any worse off than we are now; provided, of course, there is no official probe. Undoubtedly, the abnormalities that will occur with Larry and Moe will raise a few eyebrows."

"*Christ!* I need a drink and a cigarette and time to think this thing through," the CEO of PETROCOMP bellowed.

Saxton shook his head. "The drink and cigarette you can have, Ted, but not more time." Kennelly frowned and looked away.

Kenneth Saxton gave his colleagues a minute to think. Then, shifting his eyes between them asked, "Are we all in agreement then that fuel cell technology is a legitimate and imminent threat?" Kennelly dawned an uncomfortable expression and Finley began to squirm nervously in his chair. Saxton sensed that he wasn't going to receive a response from either of them anytime soon. He prompted, "Ted…Wendell?"

"No!…I mean…I mean, yes, and no," Kennelly replied, shaking his head in a futile attempt to clear it. He abruptly pushed himself away from the table, walked over to the window and began to gaze solemnly at the Manhattan skyline.

Making no attempt to hide his contempt for Kennelly, Finley grimaced in disgust while reaching in his pocket to pull out another Havana that he didn't bother to light. Presently, his eyes wandered over to and locked with Saxton's. They were clearly of the same mind; concerned by their partner's hesitation.

"Care to explain, Ted?" World Energy's CEO asked, his eyes still locked on Finley's.

In response, the head of PETROCOMP gave Saxton a detached look then clasped his hands behind his back and continued to look out the window. He allowed his mind to wander a moment and thought it a shame he didn't appreciate this view more often. It was a remarkably sunny morning and the newer buildings glistened in the bright sunshine. The sparkling buildings against the clear blue sky was a breathtaking sight.

Kennelly finally let out an audible sigh. "It's too risky, Ken. There's just too much at stake should something go wrong." He turned from the window to face the other two men and quickly added, "And something *will* go wrong—it always does with such schemes." He slowly shook his head. "Before jumping into this, have you given any consideration to the fact that it won't be just us personally who will suffer should P3 be exposed? Our companies will as well.

"Lawsuits brought on by the government will be like nothing ever seen before—the federal prosecutors will have a field day! Christ…our boards won't know what hit them." Kennelly went back to his chair and sat down.

"Ted, I don't think there's much pos—"

"*Assuming* we can believe Haggerty," Kennelly said, cutting Wendell Finley off. "I understand that the possibility of the plot being exposed is small, but the possibility *does* exist, we can't deny that. Should something go wrong and we're caught…well…I don't believe I need to belabor that point."

Finley and Saxton glanced at each other again. Then Saxton said, "I certainly appreciate your position, Ted. But I believe the precautions Mr. Haggerty has taken are more than adequate to ensure we'll never be implicated should the worst happen: A detail plan will only exist on his personal computer's hard drive—no paper hard copies. In addition, neither our names nor our companies are mentioned. Only two people from Noble Consultants will know anything about this. Only one contracted individual will have knowledge." The CEO of World Energy pursed his lips and shook his head. "I'm satisfied with security."

Kennelly gave Saxton a apathetic look. "Ken…it's not terribly difficult to access information on a hard drive. Ask your eight-year-old grandson."

"Yes, but I trust Haggerty on this one. By the time a search warrant is served he'd have ample time to delete the document. It only takes seconds. And he'd have every reason to delete it. After all, it would only make matters worse for him personally if some investigative body got a hold of the plan."

"Do you think for a minute, Ken, that Haggerty wouldn't offer us up in a plea bargain to reduce his sentence?"

Saxton smiled. "Let him. Where's the evidence?"

The CEO of PETROCOMP leaned back in his chair, folded his arms across his chest and nodded.

Wendell Finley was becoming impatient; he wanted to implement P3. ENDICORP had nineteen percent of the world's market and projected twenty three percent by 2006—mainly at the expense of PETROCOMP. Although they agreed to set aside competitive concerns when they joined forces, Finley couldn't help but suspect that his colleague of convenience was dragging his feet due to ENDICORP's projected growth. In Finley's opinion, Kennelly was a vindictive son-of-a-bitch. He knew damn well that a much larger percentage of ENDICORP's oil was refined into gasoline than PETROCOMP's. When fuel cell cars started taking to the road, Kennelly wouldn't feel the impact as quickly or as severely as Finley's company would.

Yanking the unlit cigar from between his teeth, Finley snarled, "For Christ's sake, Kennelly, get some fuckin' backbone!" Taken aback by the vulgar insult, PETROCOMP's CEO began to glare menacingly at his detractor.

At sixty-nine, Kennelly was thirteen years Finley's senior. The brash affront quickly filled him with rage and he began to rise from his chair. Not since he was a soldier in the Korean War had he been physical with another man, but the speed and intensity with which his disposition changed left no doubt an assault on Wendell Finley was imminent.

The sight of the small, white-haired old man with clenched fists and murderous expression took Finely by surprise. At six foot three, two hundred-ninety pounds he dwarfed Theodore Kennelly. He hoisted himself from his chair to face the enraged executive.

The scene was surreal. Saxon couldn't believe his eyes. He jumped to his feet. *"GENTELMEN!"* he shouted; the two men hesitated. *"TED, WENDELL*...please! For *Christ's* sake...you're acting like a couple of illiterate dockworkers! Sit down!" Neither man moved. Sternly he demanded, "I *saidddd* sit down!" His fist struck the table. Slowly, the two CEO's took their seats; angry eyes remaining locked on each other.

When the belligerent men were seated, the CEO of World Energy took his. He ran a hand though his light brown hair and let out a long sigh. "I...I know this is incredibly stressful—for all of us," Saxton continued. "This a monumental decision and to my knowledge nothing like it has ever been done before." Finley slowly let his menacing expression melt away; he put the cigar back in his mouth. Kennelly focused his attention on Saxton; his jaw taut and face crimson.

Slowly, the tension in the boardroom started to ease. "Ted," Saxton began cautiously. "Wendell and I are in favor of implementing P3. Apparently, you feel it isn't necessary. I fear this is an all-or-nothing pact. Either all three of us agree to execute the plan, or we shelve it and live with the consequences." He paused a moment to let his words sink in. He glanced at Finley he continued. "I'll rescind my earlier statement and give you a little time to think about it. But not too long…we simply can't delay the decision any further."

Kenneth Saxton pushed himself away from the table but remained seated. "Can we agree to meet again at the end of September—before the start of fiscal 2000—for final disposition?" Both Kennelly and Finley nodded agreement. "Smashing," Saxton responded dourly. He quickly stood up and left the board-room, leaving Kennelly and Finley facing each other.

Checking his voice mail, he wasn't surprised that he had another message from David Greene. And, as usual, he wanted to talk to Rick immediately. It seemed like his boss called him every two minutes and in Rick's opinion the man needed excessive hand-holding. He pulled into the ever-dependable Holiday Inn and told his guest he'd be back in a minute.

He had a cell phone but hated the damn thing. If at all possible, he only used it to check his messages. Constantly getting cut off, inability to get a signal or shitty reception, Rick thought they should have waited a few years and perfected cell phone technology before rushing it to market. If a hotel with a lobby phone were available, he would park his car and return the call from there.

Rick Miller and Don Beckster, Flexible Tubing Technologies' Director of Sales Engineering, were on their way to Global Fuel Cell Technologies. Rick enjoyed teasing Don about his fancy title because he knew Don despised it. The designation was forced on him by Donald Kampnel, FTT's owner, so he had to use it.

Don, a deeply religious and unpretentious man, was quick to point out that he was just an engineer, and had been for over thirty years. He was far too modest. There was no one in the industry as knowledgeable about hose design and con-struction as Don Beckster. Rick enjoyed calling on customers with Don because when he did, the sale always went through. With few exceptions, the components Don designed always saw production.

Rick liked and admired him despite his few quirks and thought Kampnel was right putting the word "Sales" in Don's title. Unlike most engineers Rick had worked with in the past, Don got along great with customers. The man lacked any vestige of arrogance, so typical in many engineers.

This morning they were going to meet with Brad Selmants, GFCT's Vice President of Automotive Engineering and his group of engineers to discuss the redesign of several critical hoses. Rick lamented that he was too late to participate in GFCT's fuel cell gasket requirements; one of Flexible Sealing Solution's many competitors got to the stack engineers before he did. His competitor's gasket design was well incorporated into the fuel cell stack now and there was nothing Rick could do get the business unless a major problem developed with the seal. And at this stage of development something like that was unlikely to happen.

Unhappy as he was by losing out on GFCT's gasket potential, Rick took solace in the fact that he had all the company's hose business—and this was no minor accomplishment. The hose requirements for GFCT, particularly for the automotive group, were staggering. Looking under the hood and chassis of GFCT's fuel cell powered Nissan Pathfinder, Rick counted no less than twenty-four separate hoses. Even if Brad Selmants and his team were eventually successful in designing out half the hoses currently used, there was still incredible volume to be had once the powertrain was in production.

"David…Rick. You wanted me to give you a call right away?" Rick glanced at his watch with concern; Greene tended to be a tad long winded. As they were still several miles from GFCT's corporate headquarters in Brookfield, Massachusetts, he'd have to move David along. Traffic around the Boston area in the morning was about as bad as it got.

"Yes," he replied in his thick, Scottish accent. Women just went crazy when they heard his boss speak—they loved the accent. But Rick found it irritating. Everything the man said seemed to have a touch of conceit to it.

Then there was a long pause, very untypical for his boss. "David?"

"Have you seen the backlog for next quarter?" his boss asked warily, referring to FSS' orders that were to be manufactured and shipped over the next three months. A company's backlog is a good indicator of its financial health. Some orders will be pushed out, some pulled in and some canceled; but a backlog should ideally always be at or above the forecasted figure for the months ahead.

Rick rolled his eyes. He immediately knew where the conversation was heading. "Yeah, I've seen it," he replied with a noticeable lack of zeal.

"Our sales are continuing to drop." Exasperation was now building in his voice. "We've got to increase them!" Rick stared hard at the pay phone in front of him and clenched his teeth. One of Rick's shortcomings was his inability to hold his tongue when he got mad, and listening to his boss whine never failed to make him angry.

"Unless we get an influx of orders in the next few days," Greene continued, "we'll be off our forecasted figure for the next month by over two-hundred thousand dollars!" There was now no mistaking the panic in his voice. "And at this rate, September will be over two-hundred-fifty thousand!. We'll end fiscal 2001 almost 1.8 million below forecast!"

Boo-hoo...pass the Kleenex! Serves you right, you stupid son-of-a-bitch! Rick had little sympathy for Greene, even though he had the unenviable task of facing Kampnel to explain the variation between forecasted and actual sales.

For the last three years Rick had supplied first John Gundermann, then David Greene with the most accurate sales forecast he could produce. Every year he would go through the pain-staking task of calling each customer to go over projected sales for each part FSS supplied. After doing the math he would produce the most precise report possible.

But his forecasts didn't show growth, they showed decline, and had since the acquisition. Rick often wondered just what the hell they expected. Kampnel bought a company that was rapidly decaying, and then totally mismanaged it.

But instead of facing the problem, of confronting the owner of FSS with the reality of the situation, it was easier and much more politically expedient to manipulate the forecast. Completely disregarding the figures Rick provided, Greene would inflate them to show growth where none could possibly exist. Then his boss would hope like hell the economy turned around and customers would order more product than forecasted.

The first year after the acquisition the gap between forecasted and actual sales wasn't too bad—only about half a million dollars. The economy in 1999 was still smoking, so it couldn't be blamed for the five-hundred thousand dollar deficit. Greene laid blame on Gundermann (behind his back, of course) who was managing FSS at that time. Rick had sold a job to a company by the name of Colonial Industries that, on second review, didn't have the required thirty-five percent gross profit margin. So, Gundermann ordered Rick to walk away from the opportunity. However, Gundermann kept the potential sales dollars of this job in the forecast. These dollars, that never materialized, created a sizable deficit. A deficit that David Greene inherited.

In 2000 the business climate began to sour; and the difference that year between forecasted and actual sales swelled to seven-hundred-fifty thousand dollars. Greene could, and did, blame the economy for the shortfall. Had Greene stuck with Rick's original numbers, he could have pointed out to Kampnel that despite a continued decline in sales, they did slightly better than the 10.3 million forecasted.

But for fiscal 2001 Greene had run out of excuses and was terrified at the prospect of confronting Donald Kampnel with the truth. Rick's boss had an ego the size of his native Scotland and considered himself a superb executive; it was simply inconceivable to him to consider laying blame for the shortfall on himself.

Restraining his temper, Rick sighed and said, "I know, David. What is it you're getting at?" He desperately wanted to say that being down 1.8 million put sales for the fiscal year within one-hundred-twenty thousand of where he had originally forecasted. Rick didn't think his estimate was too bad given a total forecast of 8.5 million.

"What am I getting at?" his boss barked. "I think it's pretty goddamn obvious what I'm getting at! You need to sell more product!" Scowling, Rick squeezed the receiver in his hand. He wanted nothing more than to tell this idiot exactly what he was thinking but fought to hold his tongue. He despised having to treat David Greene with kid gloves, but prudence recommended it.

His Scottish boss didn't have the authority to broom Rick on the spot, but given the influence the man had over Kampnel, approval for his dismissal would just be a matter of time if Rick chided him. The economy was bad now and getting worse. Rick didn't want, nor could he afford to lose his job. What a far cry it was from a couple of years ago when he'd receive two or three calls a week from recruiters trying to steal him away from FSS. Rick hadn't received a call from a headhunters in over a year. But he wasn't alone; neither had any of his friends in the rubber business.

What really perturbed Rick was that despite his best efforts to educate the man, Greene still didn't understand the product line—how it was sold and how to grow the business. Flexible Sealing Solutions manufactured a custom product. If their customers didn't have orders, FSS wouldn't have orders. It was that simple. Once a job was sold there was absolutely nothing Rick, or anybody else could do to influence its sale. The only way to grow the business was to keep current customers happy, and find new opportunities. This was exactly what Rick was doing; and had done successfully since 1988 when he gave up his job as a high school teacher and started his sales career with Tri-States Rubber Company.

His temper in check, Rick tried to be diplomatic. "Well David…I'm open to suggestions. How do you suggest I do that?"

There was silence at the other end of the line, bringing a little smile to Rick's face. Finally, his boss said calmly, "You're spending too much time at UES and GFCT. You need to spend more time with our existing customers."

"What good will *that* do?" Rick's voice took on a slightly higher pitch, as it always did when be became frustrated. Despite his best effort, he was starting to lose his composure. "We're not selling pencils out of a tin cup, David! My spending time with them won't influence their customers to place more orders with them so they can order more product from us!"

Again silence. Eventually, with more composure, Greene said, "You just need to understand that we're in trouble here, and we have to turn sales around." *What the hell do you think I'm trying to do?* Rick thought to himself. "I don't see the value in all the effort you're putting into those fuel cell companies, Rick. I don't think their product will ever see the light of day."

Rick took a deep breath and regained his equanimity. "David…as I've explained many times, UES holds the most promise of anything we've got going for fast and significant billing. And…as you're well aware, it's about the only customer we have where we're making an acceptable gross profit margin on the parts we supply."

"Yes, but it's all on prototype parts!" Greene shot back. "When is the volume coming? When will we begin to see a return on investment?"

This time it was Rick who was silent. He knew of UES' talks with the utilities, but to the best of his knowledge no deal had been reached yet. And though the volume from that agreement would be substantial, he knew it wouldn't please Greene. But at this point Rick didn't think anything would. So he decided to say, "No date has been finalized yet."

"That's because…*there is no date!* Goodbye!" Rick winced at the sound of Greene slamming down his receiver.

Rick did the same and stormed out to the car. Don Beckster was patiently waiting for him, reading a *USA TODAY* and sipping coffee.

"GODDAMNIT!" Rick cried as he slammed the car door shut. Don snapped his head around and glared at the angry salesman; his eyes a mixture of surprise and revulsion. "*Nothing* I do is fuckin' good enough for that asshole!"

"Maybe your choice of expletives is why," Don offered quietly. Rick gave him a curious look.

He was still getting to know Don Beckster and didn't realize how truly pious the man was. He should have caught on last night at dinner when Don asked Rick if he'd join in grace before they ate. Not wanting to offend him, Rick agreed, and uncomfortably endured the strange looks they received from the tables around them. Don remained oblivious to the onlookers. Only later, when re-telling the incident to Flexible Tubing Technologies' chemist, Tim Leigh, did Rick learn that Don was an ultra-religious Baptist.

"I don't believe that David Greene," Rick said with disgust as he started the car. "He just can't grasp what it is we do!"

Don nodded his head thoughtfully. Burying his face back into his *USA Today* he said, "The man's an idiot." Rick chuckled. A statement like that coming from such a prominent engineer immediately improved his mood.

"It's been *what*...almost a year and a half?" Laurence Haggerty complained bitterly to his trusted assistant, Sandra Beach. Leaning back in his chair, feet up on his desk and tapping a pencil against the palm of his hand he stared hard at the young woman after asking the rhetorical question. Having listened to the same complaint three times in as many weeks, Sandra knew the best thing she could do was just sit, listen and let him vent. Maybe say a word here and there to show that she's listening. Coffee cup in hand, she nestled in on the couch, crossed her legs and settled in to endure her boss' ranting. With luck, it would only last a few minutes.

The owner of Noble Consultants jumped to his feet and began to pace in front of his desk. "For Christ's sake...I presented P3 to them in March of 2000. *Fucking March!* And here it is, August. *Of 2001!*" he all but shouted. Haggerty stopped pacing; without thinking he ran a hand over his head only to find his toupee clutched in his fingers. Sandra giggled despite herself. She had known about his hair piece since the day she'd first laid eyes on him and had been subtly hinting that he get rid of it and just go bald. In vain, she'd tried to convince him that bald was sexy! He looked at the patch of synthetic hair in disgust, and then tossed it on his desk.

"Here it is, August of 2001 and I *still* no decision about its implementation!" Haggerty turned to face Sandra. "*Christ!* Didn't I sufficiently stress that they had to act quickly?" He strolled over to his desk and sat back down. "I expected it would take them a few months to make a decision—maybe six at the most! But..."

"Oh Laurence, you knew it would take time," Sandra replied in mild rebuke. "You've met with them many times since the initial presentation." Her boss just looked at her and grimaced.

In between visits Saxton would contact Haggerty, ask a frivolous question and explain that they just wanted a little more time to see what would transpire with the fuel cell companies before making a decision. And more than once the CEO of World Energy had hinted that they definitely would proceed with the plan. But Haggerty couldn't wait much longer. The firm's fiscal situation was bad. Partially out of embarrassment, he hadn't let on to his loyal assistant the severity of the financial problems he was now facing.

Today's tirade seemed a little different to Sandra; unlike the others, this one really came from the heart. The young woman looked at him and sighed. She wanted so much to tell him, but she couldn't. Instead, she just sat on the couch and feigned empathy. She suspected that there were other reasons than just money for his intense desire to follow through with the plan. She thought the firm was doing alright financially. Noble Consultants might be a little tight right now, but nothing catastrophic.

Since the presentation of P3 to The Committee, Noble Consultants had taken on several jobs. At first, Haggerty declined all new business thinking the CEO's would direct him to execute P3 at any moment; the plan would absorb every resource the firm had. But after outlining his strategy to the three men the days turned into weeks and the weeks into months. Resentfully, he finally accepted the fact that the activation of P3 would not happen anytime soon. But he never expected it would take this long. To maintain cash flow he reluctantly took on three new jobs—none of which generated much in the way of earnings.

Since presenting P3, The Committee would occasionally ask that he fly to New York and update them on the activities of Global Fuel Cell Technologies and Unlimited Energy Systems. When they called, Sandra noticed an anticipation in her boss that a simple updating of activities really didn't warrant. He also stayed in New York an extra evening or two. Although he never mentioned Kennelly's executive secretary, Sandra was fairly certain the woman was involved. He always returned to Washington D.C. in a good mood—albeit brief. She was happy for him.

Sandra Beach truly admired and respected her boss. She thought of him more as a father than an employer. He always treated her with respect and seemed to truly value her advice; he made her feel both important and needed. Perhaps what impressed her most about him (and, in an odd way disheartened her too) was that he never, even once, alluded to a desire to sleep with her. It was all business between them blanketed in a warm overtone of friendship. When home alone however, she sadly mused over the fact that the only relationship she had with the opposite sex was platonic. That was, until recently. There was now another man in her life. And, she reflected with immense satisfaction—not just any man.

The relationship was far from perfect, but it was improving. On several occasions she tried to induce him into opened up to her. When they first started seeing each other she inquired about The Committee, usually over drinks or dinner. But she always ended up where she started—nowhere. It wasn't a topic she wanted to talk about, but it offered commonality and broke the ice—it was a place to start.

Predictably, it wasn't until she'd slept with Wendell Finley that she started to obtain inside information on the activities of The Committee. She didn't start the affair for this purpose—she had another, more personal motive. She now had the information her boss wanted, and it was tormenting her that she couldn't share it. If Laurence ever found out about the affair he'd be livid. It might even jeopardize P3.

Although she was not terribly experienced sexually, Sandra Beach quickly perfected her technique of extracting information from the Chief Executive Officer of ENDICORP. Her method so far was successful in extracting almost every bit of information out of him except the one thing she really wanted to know. But she'd keep trying; it was crucial that she succeed.

Panting, he awkwardly rolled off her and onto his back. She exhaled an audible, satisfied sigh, turned on her side and smiling, gazed into his eyes. She then began to lightly run her hand over his sizable belly and through his abundant chest hair; moments later he was almost purring like a kitten. The time was right.

"So hon," she began, her eyes following her seductive fingers as they slowly danced through his chest hairs. "Is Kennelly still holding everything up?"

So absorbed in the feel of her touch, her lover didn't immediately answer. This didn't worry Sandra. She knew he eventually would; she had her technique almost down to a science. When he did answer this first question, it was a simple disdainfully grunted *"yes."*

She waited about a minute, pretending to concentrate on the physical task at hand. Presently she asked, "What's his problem anyway?"

"I don't know what the son-of-a-bitch's problem is," Finley mumbled. "It's all been clearly laid out for him." It was during these times that Finley would tell her virtually anything. So content was he with her touch, he almost sounded as if he were talking unconsciously. To her dismay, despite being completely tranquil, he was clearly cognizant of what he chose to answer.

Last week he'd told her about Theodore Kennelly's continued reluctance to cut Noble Consultants loose on P3. In the same breath he assured her that the idiot would come to his senses; he and Saxton were of like mind and anxious to get the plan underway. Kennelly would become a team player—it was just a matter of time.

There was mutual interest in the relationship, she could sense that. For her part it definitely wasn't physical—the man was a pig. Rather, she was enthralled by his money and power. If she played her cards right, she could become the fourth Mrs. Finley. And, if over time their marriage ended in divorce, (as she figured it surely would) she'd come out of it nicely.

She had no concerns about him demanding a pre-nuptial agreement. He had the money to hire the best attorneys. When they divorced, he'd be satisfied that she wasn't walking away with what he'd consider a lot of money—a couple of million maybe. For her, that would be plenty. She didn't consider herself greedy.

There was only one obstacle between her, vast wealth and the power that goes with it: his current wife.

In spite of her best efforts, Finley remained tight-lipped about one crucial subject. Although she tried at every opportunity, Sandra couldn't get out of him the state of his marital relationship; was it solid, falling apart or in limbo? Did he really love her? Did she him? Did she enter matrimony wealthy in her own right? Sandra hoped not; it would spoil her fall-back position.

In the two or three times he mentioned her, Sandra ascertained that his wife was young; maybe only a year or two older than herself. Apparently she was quite pretty too—obviously a "trophy wife."

Should he remain silent, she had a back-up plan. She'd have to begin convincing her lover that his wife was only after his money. A few dropped words here, a few suggestions there, and his mind should begin ticking. It would take a little time, but it should be a simple matter to eventually persuade him to divorce her. After all, what else but money could possibly attract a beautiful young woman to a repulsive man thirty years her senior?

She was worried however; her plan was far from perfect. The strategy would back-fire if Sandra couldn't convince Finley that unlike his wife, she truly loved him for himself. Also, she had to pray his wife didn't come to the marriage rich.

Laurence Haggerty's assistant felt absolutely no guilt over what she was trying to do. She wanted what Wendell Finley had: position, wealth, influence and power. She did however, feel a small amount of remorse for her employer; should she be successful, Laurence would be devastated.

Although she was making more money with Noble Consultants than she ever would as an attorney, even as a partner, what she earned now was just a drop in the bucket compared to what she'd walk away with from Finley.

Other than her inability to find out the condition of his marriage, Sandra was quite pleased with the progress of their affair. She limited their first three dates to drinks and dinner only. She didn't what to take him to bed too early; he might think she was easy. On the other hand, she didn't want to appear as if she was playing hard-to-get. It was a difficult balance, but she pulled it off.

They usually met at the Dulles Airport Sheraton. They'd have a few drinks at the bar, dinner at a local restaurant, and then proceed on to their suite. Typically, the process took about four hours. This wasn't enough time. If she was going to put an end to his marriage, she had to find a way to spend an extended period of time with him; perhaps two or three days.

Perhaps she could talk him into taking her to the Virgin Islands or Barbados? Sandra was certain his wife would never find out. He traveled so much, she probably didn't even bother to ask him where he was going any more.

It was difficult, but she forced herself to focus on the business at hand; she had the entire weekend to think about her next move. At the moment, she wanted to say something to her employer that would ease his anxiety. Leaning forward on the couch she said, "Laurence…don't ask me how I know, but I just have a feeling The Committee will call you soon and ask you to proceed with P3."

He smiled and lightly chuckled; touched by her attempt to cheer him up. "And how do you know that, young lady?"

"Didn't I just tell you not to ask me how I know?" she playfully reprimanded him. Haggerty continued to give her a dubious, yet warm smile. Sandra shrugged. "For lack of a better term, call it…woman's intuition."

CHAPTER 5

▼

Just as she had every morning for the last four years, Martha Putnam placed her purse in the bottom right hand drawer of her desk. As she slowly closed the drawer, a smile came to her face. Today was her work anniversary, and she was harboring the hope that her boss would give her the afternoon off. It was a beautiful day, not a cloud in the sky, and she wanted do a little shopping and buy Laurence a surprise gift.

But she wouldn't hold her breath. She had been working for the cantankerous old geezer four years now and he'd never even remembered her anniversary. But today it was Martha's intention to drop a few hints. She knew Theodore Kennelly both liked and valued her, and beneath the gruff exterior he was a softie. If he didn't take the hints she come right out and ask him; she was sure he'd give her the time off.

She caught a whiff of freshly brewed coffee. *Chad Whitman, God bless him!* she thought as she savored the fragrance wafting through the office. The charming young man was always the first to arrive in the morning and made the first pot. Martha was extremely fond of Chad, despite is many administrative shortcomings, she thought of him like the son she never had, but always wanted. She went to the kitchen and poured herself a cup.

Back at her desk, she glanced at her phone for the first time and saw the little red light blinking, indicating she had voice mail. *Already? So early?* Sighing, she dialed the code that gave her access to her messages. It was Mr. Kennelly. He wanted to let her know he'd be late this morning, probably not arriving until nine-thirty or so. Normally that would be good new as it would give her a chance to catch up on paperwork; but not today. She'd have to approach him as soon as he arrived—before he got too busy.

Martha went to the window and looked at the city spread out before her. She loved the view. She'd worked in a number of high-rise buildings across Manhattan over the years, but none with the panoramic view she had with this office—despite the narrow windows. It was a brilliantly sunny morning; brighter than most, she thought. The sky was so blue today. Holding her coffee cup in both hands close to her chest, she wondered when she'd see Laurence again. Up until he'd finally worked up the nerve to ask her out, her life had been so dull and repetitious. He made her feel like a schoolgirl again, young and vibrant.

She wished she could see him more often—and sometime soon maybe she would. He had asked her more than once to move to D.C. and work for him. Exactly what she'd do for Noble Consultants remained a mystery; he told her she'd do something other than administrative work. Laurence told her little about his company other than it was a consulting firm. But she suspected it did more than just make high-priced business proposals; she never push Laurence to find out more about what he did.

She did think it strange that Ted was associating with PETROCOMP's two main competitor, and that Noble Consultants was somehow involved. But she knew what to ask questions about and more importantly, what not to. If she needed to know, Ted would tell her what was going on.

Taking a sip of her coffee she thought again about Laurence's proposal. In her opinion, it was a little too early in their relationship to take such a big step. But she was fairly sure she'd eventually accept his offer; there was nothing holding her in New York.

"Hey, Marth!"

Hearing the familiar, chipper voice she smiled and turned around. "Good morning, Chad. Good coffee this morning."

"Thanks. Hey, have you seen the files on the Shreveport refinery? I can't seem to find them anywhere."

Oh, Chad! "Try looking under S."

"I did! They ain't there."

Martha furrowed her brow. "Really? Oh, ya know what, Jolene had them last. The girl just can't seem to remember that we file alphabetically and not by location. Look under Louisiana. If they're not there, ask her what she did with them."

The young man grimaced. "Ok, will do. How long are you going to keep her around as a temp anyway? Overall, she's not bad. Ya gonna make her permanent?" Martha just shrugged. Chad then gave his boss an enchanting smile. "Hey, congratulations. I un…der…..stand………that…………today………….." his speech slowed and then stopped. He was looking past Martha, out the window behind her. First, he appeared to squint, then, in an instant his eyes practically bulged out of his head. His face contorted in a surrealistic look of disbelief.

Martha gave him a concerned look, and then turned around to see what he was gaping at. Before she even had a chance to comprehend what she saw, she, and hundreds of others were vaporized.

"I was hoping you could pick Sean up after…oh…what the? *Oh my God!*" Rick Miller rolled his eyes. His wife, Terri, had one incredibly annoying habit. Almost every time they talked on the phone she'd blurt out an exclamation, and then leave him hanging—not bothering to tell him what she was so excited about. She wouldn't say a word for what seemed like an excruciatingly long period of time. It absolutely drove him crazy.

"*Wwwwwhat?*" he pleaded. Still, she said nothing.

"Oh my God!" she said again.

"Oh for God's sake, Terri! What the hell is it?" Rick almost shouted into the phone.

"I've…I've got the TV on. A plane just crashed into one of the World Trade Center buildings."

Rick frowned; the news didn't phase him. He thought it was probably just a little Cessna or something like that. It was not completely unheard of—private planes flying into tall buildings. He let out a long sigh. "You want me to pick Sean up at school after work?"

"Huh? Oh…yeah, Sean. Would you?" It was obvious her mind was elsewhere. "I'll ah…I'll call you back later," there was a soft click.

Rick looked at the receiver, shook his head and hung up.

Strange? Theodore Kennelly thought. Looking up from his *Wall Street Journal* in the back of his limousine, he noticed everybody on both sides of the street with their heads tilted back, staring up at something. Some were pointing, others were gaping in disbelieve, and a number of women had their hands over their mouths. He looked out the window and saw thick black smoke pouring out of the north tower as his chauffer made a comment about the unusually large number of people gathered in the street. Concentrating on what was ahead of him, the driver didn't see the smoke or notice the angle of the pedestrian's heads. His eyes locked on the building, Kennelly remained speechless.

With the traffic at a standstill ahead of him, the driver was forced to stop. Noticing for the first time that everybody was looking up, he uncomfortably leaned against the steering wheel and looked up through the windshield. In a stunned voice he whispered, "Holy mother of God."

Sandra Beach was in Los Angeles to screen a potential client. One of her more mundane jobs was to qualify potential customers so her boss wouldn't waste his precious time. Having trouble sleeping she'd awaken early.

Stepping out of the tub she thought about how much she hated hotel showers—they were so wimpy. After drying her body off she put on a robe and wrapped her wet hair in a towel. Strolling out of the bathroom she glanced at the muted television. At first, she disregarded what was on the screen, thinking it was a movie. Then she saw the face of her favorite network anchorman. Glancing at the clock she saw it was 5:48 A.M.

Peter Jennings? So early in the morning?

Curious, she picked up the remote and turned up the volume. Slowly, she sat down on the bed and continued to watch. For the next three hours she sat glued to the television, staring in disbelief at the horrible images coming from New York.

It was a day no one would ever forget; a day in which they would always remember what they were doing when the terrorists attacked on September 11th, 2001. Many lives were lost at the World Trade Center, Pentagon and in a field in Pennsylvania. Even more lives were inexorably altered. Anybody with a shred of human emotion wept that day. Some will never stop.

But Wall Street has no compassion; it only reacts positively or negatively to news or events. Closed down by the attacks, it opened several days later with shaken investors, their fingers on the sell button. Before the opening there was much speculation within financial circles as to how shareholders would react.

For the good of the economy—and the country—the Bush administration called on Wall Street to show restraint. But greed won out over patriotism; from the opening bell there was a massive sell-off.

After the first day's trading post 9/11, the analysts set to work. The bleak picture they painted of the country's economic future only served to accelerate the worsening situation. The economy of the United States was deteriorating even before Clinton left the White House. Fear that the actions of the Islamic terrorists would spark a Persian Gulf war and cut off Middle East oil helped fuel a growing recession.

Like most blue-chip companies, World Energy, PETROCOMP and ENDI-CORP lost almost half their value in less than three days. At the same time shares of alternative energy companies went through the roof. UES saw a 117% increase in value, GFCT 130%. Fuel cells and every other form of alternative energy were suddenly thrust into the public spotlight. The apprehensive CEO of PETRO-COMP called an emergency meeting of The Committee.

"I trust you've had this boardroom swept for bugs," Wendell Finley quietly asked an outwardly poignant Kenneth Saxton. With PETROCOMP's New York headquarters gone, meetings between the three were now held in London, at World Energy's corporate offices.

Saxton solemnly nodded, then turned to face Theodore Kennelly. "Ted...I want you to know how truly sorry I am about the tragedy. There...there are no words...."

"That goes for me too," Finley added.

Kennelly pursed his lips, gave one nod of his head then stood up. He had the requisite sullen appearance. Shoving his hands in his pant's pockets the CEO of PETROCOMP said, "*Christ*...I still can't believe it! Over seven million dollars of office equipment...gone. Countless files and documents...gone. Legal contracts—originals...gone. Furniture, Art, and many of my personal possessions...gone. And...I'll have to replace all those employees—damn near a third of my workforce." He paused for a moment to look at the callous faces of his two cohorts. "But I called this meeting to talk about the most important loss—that of our stock's value."

After making the statement, Theodore Kennelly's face froze and he eyed the two men sitting before him. He was pleased to see that his declaration had not invoked any kind of moralistic repulsion. The two CEO's returned his gaze with the same compassionless determination he was projecting.

This was good. If they were to turn their fortunes around, Kennelly believed it essential that their values have the same unscrupulous order of priority.

Up to this point there was no litmus test he could use to measure their true mettle. Kennelly didn't want to enter into a conspiracy with men he believed would crumble under pressure. He was now satisfied that the two men before him had the balls it would take to see P3 through.

"Alright then," the CEO of PETROCOMP continued sternly. "We've expressed our lament, let's get back to business." Saxton and Finley expressed eager acquiesce. "As you've probably guessed, I've changed my mind about P3. I now want to put Haggerty to work—and as quickly as possible." Smiles formed on the faces of the other two men.

"May I inquire as to what changed your mind, Ted?" Kenneth Saxton asked tentatively.

Kennelly returned to his seat. "Two reasons, actually. One I'll keep to myself. The other, gentlemen, is that I'm sixty-nine years old. Given what's happening in the market, I'm concerned by the amount of time it may potentially take to bring PETROCOMP's stock price back up to eighty dollars a share. Quite honestly, I was hoping to put the decision off a while longer; however, recent events have accelerated the fortunes of our new competitors. Something clearly must be done, and soon."

Saxton smirked and glanced down at the table as if embarrassed. He cleared his throat. "Ah, Ted...PETROCOMP has never been at eighty dollars."

"As usual, Ken, you're so very right," Kennelly replied serenely. "Let's just say I'm working under the assumption that it would eventually hit eighty had not this...this incident occurred." Kennelly sucked in his lower lip for a moment then sighed. "Also...that's the target the board set for me back in '97 when they enticed me out of retirement."

Saxton gave him a waxen smile then said, "Discrediting fuel cell technology won't necessarily increase our companies stock value, Ted. That was never the intended objective of P3. The plan's aim is to make certain the technology doesn't acquire a foothold in the marketplace and flourish. Its sole purpose is to ensure the world's dependency on oil for years to come. I thought you understood this?"

The CEO of PETROCOMP returned Saxton a knowing smile. "Mr. Saxton, how could it not? Where are investors going to put their money with the only viable alterative energy ventures gone? The market will respond favorably to our companies, I have no doubt about that."

"I tend to agree with Ted," Finley chimed in confidently. Saxton and Kennelly gave each other a sardonic glance. They were thinking the same thing—Finley's concurrence certainly lends credibility to Kennelly's reasoning!

Saxton pushed the slighted thought aside. He had been impatient to implement P3 and frankly didn't care what the reason for the man's change of heart. He decided to reinforce Kennelly's rationalization. "Of course...a rise in our share price—a significant rise—is inevitable. Particularly given the explosive growth in the Asian economy. Those countries—spearheaded by China—will soon require far more oil than they are now producing and importing."

Kennelly nodded his head in agreement. "Indeed. As much as I hate to admit it, Haggerty is right. The elimination of fuel cells will ensure that there will be no other realistic alternative to fossil fuels for decades to come."

The CEO of ENDICORP was bothered by the fact that he was the implicit junior partner—and treated accordingly. Feeling insignificant and needing to say something of consequence, Finley blurted out, "Well...for Christ's sake then, let's stop wasting time!" He gave Saxton a meaningful stare, "Give Laurence Haggerty a call."

To Finley's satisfaction the CEO of World Energy gave a quick nod and reached for the intercom. He glanced at his watch. "Catherine, would you be a dear and connect us with Mr. Laurence Haggerty of Noble Consultants at two o'clock?"

"Of course, Mr. Saxton," his secretary replied cheerfully.

Relieved that they were finally moving forward, the CEO of World Energy gleefully slapped his hands down on the table. "Wendell, Ted, you're welcome to join me for lunch. After which I'll ask Mr. Haggerty to meet us...?" he looked questioningly at the CEO of PETROCOMP.

"The sooner the better," Kennelly answered decisively. Saxton shifted his eyes to Finley and saw him nod his approval.

"Alright, I'll set up the meeting for first thing Monday. That should allow him ample time to prepare before he leaves for London."

Finley immediately wondered whether he should arrange a rendezvous with Sandra; undoubtedly, she'd accompany Haggerty to the meeting. He debated with himself a moment and decided against it. Even though there was little chance of them being seen together, it was still too great a risk. Should one of his associates discover their affair, The Committee would fall apart—all trust would be gone.

He suspected that Kennelly and Saxton may already be suspicious. Surely they must have seen him staring at her during previous meetings. But with a touch of jealously Finley realized he wasn't alone. More than once he' caught Saxton giving her longing glances. The CEO of ENDICORP briefly wondered if Sandra Beach was burning the candle at both ends.

Rick smiled at the computer monitor; but his grin soon turned into a tight-lipped grimace. It was finally happening, though he couldn't help but wonder whether recent events accounted for the better than expected sales he was now enjoying.

At long last UES' residential unit was now in production; all his hard work was beginning to pay off. Sales of stack gaskets and various hoses were going through the roof. All the traveling, all the hours spent with UES's engineers, all the arguments he had with his own engineers on the fuel cell company's behalf—

all worth it! How he would savor the moment he rubbed David Greene's nose in the figures.

Unlimited Energy System's ramp-up to full production was proceeding much faster than projected, and Rick was receiving calls from FTT's and FSS' plant managers complaining about the unexpected demand. Rick was tempted to tell them to quit whining. He had long since learned that there was no pleasing plant managers—they bitched when business was too slow and they bitched when it was too busy. Bitching must be part of a plant manager's job description.

The outlook was equally bright at GFCT. An excited Brad Selmants shared with Rick the confidential news that his company had signed contracts with two major automobile manufacturers. In six months, GFCT would begin supplying over fifty thousand fuel cell powertrains to each company. Rick did the math and realized that between the stack gaskets for UES and the hoses for both companies, this was going to be one of the biggest sales in the history of the rubber industry.

With immense satisfaction Rick recalled that not long ago, David Greene had all but told him to stop wasting his time at these two accounts. Now, management at both FTT and FSS were scrambling to meet the current demand, and prepare for projected future increases.

Rick was saddened by the fact that the sudden demand for these companies' products was the result of fear. Fear that September 11th would lead to war and the cut-off of Middle East oil. He knew it was naïve, but he hoped people would both advocate and purchase fuel cells for their environmental impact—or lack thereof. Rick believed that the wide-spread use of fuel cells greatly decreasing dependency on foreign oil was a secondary benefit.

From his very first meeting with UES, there was never any doubt in his mind that fuel cells would eventually become part of the world's arsenal for power generation. But he didn't think, nor expect, the product would be in such great demand so early on. Even though fuel cells weren't being purchased for the idealistic reasons he had hoped for, they were being purchased. And Rick Miller was exceptionally proud to be part of this energy revolution.

His first impulse was to say no—*hell no!* Laurence Haggerty was sorely tempted to tell Kenneth Saxton he didn't want to fly to London yet again to update The Committee on the latest undertakings of fuel cell companies. What was the point? They clearly didn't have the balls to take action, so why throw good money after bad for information they'd never put to use? *Fuck um!* Let the three buffoons dig their own graves.

"Mr. Haggerty...*are* you going to take the call?" Laura, his secretary queried guardedly. "Mr. Saxton has been holding for kind of a long time." The owner of Noble Consultants just stared blankly at his phone. He had his finger on the intercom button but had yet to push it.

He had worked extremely hard to formulate the P3 strategy, and after presenting it to his powerful clients was incredibly eager to put the plan into action. But that was then and this is now. Now, he no longer had Martha. The first woman he'd cared for in years was gone.

Given all the promise P3 had to offer both him and his clients, he couldn't understand how it was possible to lose all enthusiasm for it. Laurence Haggerty knew it was normal to mourn after a death, but what he was feeling seemed to go beyond a sense of loss. He could never have imagined that losing Martha could have such an affect on him; especially since he'd only known her for a relatively short period of time. But although their time together was brief, their blossoming relationship grew intense. He felt like he'd know her all his life.

After 9/11 Laurence Haggerty took stock of his life—as many Americans did. He had adjusted his priorities and everyday tasks; many of which he'd considered crucial to his life were now trivial. He no longer took life for granted.

Although he wanted to disregard his work, just ignore it, he pressed himself to keep going. Like millions of his fellow citizens after that fateful day, he pushed the feelings of loss, despair and anger aside. Letting out a heavy sigh he reached for the phone and pushed the button for line two.

"Mr. Saxton, how are you? Sorry to keep you waiting. As always, it's a pleasure to hear from you."

"Laurence! Doing well, thank you. And yourself?"

"Fine, fine. What can I do for you?" *As if I don't know.*

"For one thing, Laurence, we'd like another update. Do you think you could put one together for presentation next week?" Haggerty did not immediately respond. Sensing reluctance, the CEO of World Energy cleared his throat and continued; now with a great deal of deliberation. "Laurence...do you recall the proposal you presented to us back in March of last year?" It took several seconds for his words to sink in. When they did, Haggerty was caught completely off guard. So convinced was he that another useless update would only be asked of him that he utterly closed his mind to the CEO. *"Laurence...?"* Saxton prompted.

"Ah...ah, yeah, yes...of course. *Of course* I do, Mr. Saxton," he finally managed to mutter. He slowly rose to his feet. Still taken aback, he committed what he considered a grievous sin: putting his mouth in gear before his mind was in motion. "Frankly, sir, I'd written it off—thought you and your associates dismissed the idea. I mean…it's been so long—a terribly shortsighted decision in my opinion." He gritted his teeth and stuck his head with the palm of his hand. *You idiot! What a stupid thing to say to a man offering me seventy-five million dollars!*

If Saxton was offended by the comment, he kept it to himself. "On the contrary, Laurence. It's been foremost on our minds. We just had to wait for a time that…was convenient for all of us. We believe that time is now." Because of the very real possibility of electronic eavesdropping, when talking on the phone Saxton and Haggerty were both extremely careful to weigh their words. "My associates and I were hoping you'd be available for an immediate meeting here in London…say, Monday morning? Would that be too soon to discuss the immediate execution of your proposal?"

Haggerty's mind was dashing in a dozen different directions. *They're actually going to implement P3!! They had the balls after all! About fuckin' time! But how come…and why now?* he thought suspiciously. *I suppose that's rather obvious. I don't give a shit what the reason. Where the hell is Sandra anyway?*

To his surprise, Saxton's actual asking of the question instantly restored the enthusiasm Haggerty had for P3 when he'd first proposed it. In an instant he forgot about Martha and the self-pity he was wallowing in only a minute ago.

"*No!* Ahhh no, Mr. Saxton, Monday morning would be just fine. I'll make arrangements for Ms. Beach and me to fly into Heathrow. We'll arrive Sunday afternoon."

"Splendid! Catherine will handle your accommodations at the Hilton. As usual, a driver will be at your disposal for your entire stay. He'll meet you at the airport. Is that acceptable?"

"Yes…yes, of course."

"Alright then. Please email your schedule to my executive assistant so we can make the necessary arrangements. I look forward to seeing you Monday, Laurence."

"Likewise." Still stunned, Haggerty softly placed the phone back in its cradle. He stared at it for a moment then bellowed, *"LAURAAAAAA!"*

The young woman he'd recently hired as his secretary came flying threw the door; alarm pasted on her sweet, oval face. Her boss seldom raised his voice and had never screamed for her before. She panicked, thinking she'd made some colossal screw-up.

Panting she asked, "*Yes*, Mr. Haggerty?" Her boss took absolutely no notice of her flustered state.

"Where's San…where is Ms. Beach?"

Relieved, the young woman exhaled loudly. "I believe she's still in Seattle interviewing a potential client."

"Find her immediately! Get her back here!" he snapped. "I don't care what she's doing. Get her on the next flight to D.C.!"

His secretary rapidly nodded then quickly turned to leave. Haggerty stopped her mid-turn. "After you find her, book tickets for me and her to London. I want to arrive there Sunday afternoon. Understood?"

"Yes sir!" she said crisply, eager to dash out of the office.

"And this time, don't bother dinkin' around looking for the lowest fare," he yelled after her. "Just make sure we get there on Sunday—no later than 5:00 P.M. London time."

"Okay," came the distant reply.

With a groan the tired owner of Noble Consultants sat down and leaned back in his chair. Impulsively, he ran a hand through his hair; again knocking off his toupee. Picking it up off the floor he stared at it contemptuously. *"Fuck this!"* he whispered to himself. Frowning, he threw the hairpiece into the wastepaper basket. After the initial shock his employees would get used to seeing him without it. He then wondered what the point was of his vanity. Everyone knew he wore a toupee anyway.

Haggerty began to take mental stock of what he had to do. If indeed Saxton and the other two members of The Committee were serious about cutting his plan lose, there was much to do—including an extremely important phone call. He then thought of Nick Ragosta and began to bite his nails.

Back in March of 2000, right before he presented P3 to The Committee, he contacted Ragosta. Haggerty wanted to feel him out—see if he was receptive to doing a little dirty work. It was a crucial call. Without this man of exceptional talent, P3 simply wouldn't work. He could, of course, hire another agent to do his bidding if Ragosta declined, but Haggerty would be reluctant to do so. There was no equal to this man.

When he spoke with Ragosta he naturally made no mention of what would be expected of him, or what he could eventually be paid. Haggerty simply asked if he was still for hire and if he would be willing to make use of all his talents—if necessary. Ragosta briefly explained that he had his eye on retirement. He had a figure in mind and once achieved, he would hang it up. To hit this target, he would probably accept a couple more contracts—or one more if it paid enough. Currently, he was in negotiations with a potential client, but it was a relatively small job and he knew it wouldn't pay enough to allow him to exit the business. He told Haggerty to call him when he was ready.

Laurence Haggerty was scared. That brief chat was a year and a half ago and in Ragosta's line of work, that's an eternity. His talents were always in demand and Haggerty was sure they'd been put to good use several times since they'd last talked. He cursed himself for not keeping in touch with him during that time. What would he do if Ragosta made the money he wanted and retired? Could he talk him into accepting one more contract? He thought he knew the assassin well enough to know that persuading him to take the job would be difficult at best.

The atmosphere in World Energy's boardroom Monday morning was nothing less than apprehensive. All three members of The Committee seemed to have a hard time sitting still as the owner of Noble Consultants refreshed their memories on the mechanics of P3. As he spoke, the fearful expressions on their faces gave Haggerty the impression that at any moment, one of them would leap out of his chair and hysterically declare that they couldn't go through with it. They were terrified; that was certainly understandable—he was too. Thankfully, no one backed out.

In closing, he laid all the cards on the table and emphasized the need for an additional fifty million dollars to cover the cost of his vital contract employee. Haggerty was astounded when, without a second thought, The Committee authorized him to proceed with P3.

Sandra Beach remained quiet throughout the entire meeting, speaking only once. She instructed the three men to ensure the first installments for Noble Consultants and their special hire were filtered into the firm's account by the end of the week.

Haggerty thought his assistant seemed preoccupied, and this concerned him. Even on the flight over she seemed lethargic—not very interested or excited about the prospect of implanting the plan. She knew the big picture but not P3's finer points. A stickler for detail, Haggerty thought it odd she didn't ask about them.

Perhaps what he found most strange was the fact that she only asked who the contract employee was; nothing about the man himself. She inquired only about his name. Haggerty advised her she didn't know the man, but soon would. She, and he, would be the only two to know his identity.

Haggerty's concern stemmed from the fact that Sandra had to know the plan cold. The only detailed narrative of it would remain on the hard-drive of the computer that never left his sight. Should anything happen to him, she would be responsible for ensuring P3 was successful. Should he drop out of the picture for whatever reason, it was important to him that his firm see the job through to a successful conclusion.

Before anything could happen, however, she had to snap out of whatever state of indifference she seemed to be wallowing in. He couldn't afford to have his first lieutenant making careless mistakes, particularly now. It was vital that she remain sharp and pay close attention to all details.

Haggerty was slightly baffled, but none the less relieved by Beach's sudden mood shift once they departed World Energy's boardroom. She seemed to be her old self again. It was his intention to tell her during the flight back home about the responsibilities he'd be placing on her, and make sure she was willing and able to see the plan through. Because of her demeanor up to this point, he was afraid this opportunity would be lost. But he now felt comfortable enough to approach her.

They settled into their seats for the long flight back to Washington. Once airborne, Haggerty asked Sandra to join him in the first class lounge. The flight was rather full and he didn't want anyone around them eavesdropping on their conversation. Drinks in hand, they settled on the lounge's couch.

Staring into his drink Haggerty said in a fatherly way, "You seemed a little…a little restrained during the meeting this morning, Sandra." He turned to look at her. "Is everything alright?" Although she was clearly in better sprits, he still felt compelled to ask the question. He was going to place tremendous trust in her; if there was a problem, he had to know what it was.

Sandra glanced at him, quickly trying to decide how to respond. She knew she had been detached on this trip, which was very untypical for her. She was warmed by his concern for her—the question didn't really come as a surprise.

She couldn't tell him the truth, of course; that she was sleeping with one of their clients; and doing so because her ambition extended far beyond what he and Noble Consultants could ever offer her. During this presentation she deliberately remained subdued, hoping she wouldn't draw attention from Wendell.

When in the presence of others, remaining impassive in all matters other than business was an absolute necessity for Sandra Beach and her lover. Ordinarily, this was not difficult for them to accomplish, but Sandra worried that today's meeting might have been different because it had been longer than normal since they'd been together. She found it strange that he didn't call her before she left for London—he always had before. But she tried not to read too much into that, assuming that something must have prevented him from contacting her. Because of this, she was deathly afraid he might try to covertly signal her during the presentation. Perhaps indicate his desire to meet as soon as Laurence was finished speaking. By avoiding eye contact with all three men, staying silent and remaining aloof, she hoped to discourage any attempt by her lover to send a clandestine message. Thankfully, it appeared to work.

But how to answer Laurence? He looked at her patiently, waiting for her reply. Tightening the grip on her drink she said, "Yes…I know I haven't been myself these past few days. It's just that…well…" she shrugged, "I've been thinking a lot about my parents lately. That's all. I find myself missing them a great deal more than I thought I would." She gave him a smile and patted his knee. "But I'll be fine, Laurence, really. Thank you for your concern."

It wasn't a complete lie; she did find herself thinking about them occasionally. She regretted not spending more time with them when they were alive. But how was she to know they'd be taken from her so soon—and so suddenly? With an inkling of self-reproach she also wondered what her father would think of what she was doing. Would he be completely disgusted or would he understand, perhaps even be proud of her drive and determination? She felt more ashamed that she didn't get to know him well enough to know the answers to such questions.

But that was all water under the bridge—nothing she could do anything about anymore. Thankfully, she could see by the relief in her boss's face that her respond worked; his tense body relaxed. "Yes, your parents, of course." He grimaced, turned his eyes from her and looked at his drink. "No matter how much time passes the sorrow never really goes away. Does it? Particularly, I should think, when their departure is so sudden and unexpected, as it was in your case." *Yours too,* she thought. Sandra knew he was hurting too, and sensed that he made the statement for his own benefit as well has hers.

Her boss remained in a trance-like state for several moments. When he snapped out of it he said, "Well, I wanted to make sure everything was alright before I begin discussing with you a matter of grave importance."

She gave him a warm smile. "I'm perfectly alright, Laurence," she assured him.

He returned her smile, nodded, and then took in a deep breath. Abruptly his expression turned grave. "Sandra, it's…it's *extremely* important to me—for personal reasons—that P3 succeed."

"Personal reasons?"

"Reasons…I'd rather not divulge."

"Well, I have every confidence it will succeed, Laurence," She said cheerfully.

He ignored the comment and continued in a resolute voice. "With an operation of this magnitude, of…of this level of complexity, many things could go wrong—and undoubtedly will. However, with proper direction from the top," he gestured to himself "the problems that are bound to surface during the course of the operation can be swiftly dealt with and overcome."

Sandra, taking the cue from his demeanor said nothing and continued to listen attentively.

He dropped his eyes from his assistant and looked at his scotch and water. "Because it's so important to me that P3 achieves its objective, I want to make certain that the plan will proceed, uninterrupted, in the event something should happen to me."

"Nothing is going to happen to you, Laurence," Sandra said dismissively.

Haggerty gave her a side-glance. "Your parents probably thought the same thing." The words came out harsher than he'd intended. He frowned. "I'm sorry, Sandra. That was…inappropriate." His voice softened. "My point is, you *never* know! In the event something should happen to me, I want *you* to see P3 through to completion." Sandra straighten and looked at her boss soberly. Studying his drink again he added, "There is *no one* I trust more than you, Sandra. I know I don't say it often enough, but over the years you've done a hell of a job for me, and I've come to rely on you a great deal." He paused a moment. Placing his hand on her knee he implored, "I want…no, I *need* you to do this for me. Will you…Sandra?" He stared at her expectantly.

"Laurence…I'm, well…I'm honored," she replied, clearly stunned. She always knew her boss thought highly of her, but she never expected him to actually come out and say it. Despite what he believed, he'd never expressed any kind of gratitude to her. She didn't mind though, she knew he appreciated her. Truly touched she said, "Of course I'll carry the torch for P3…in the *very* unlikely event something should happen to you."

Haggerty gave her a warm smile and she thought she heard him breathe a sigh of relief. "Thank you, Sandra," he replied, clearly grateful. "That's a load off my mind." Slapping the tops of his thighs he said excitedly, "All right then, I need to begin filling you in on the details of the plan. It's a long flight; I should be able to cover most of it."

He began to instruct the young woman of how exactly his plan was going to work, including the absolute necessity of hiring Nick Ragosta. She was more inquisitive about him now and Haggerty was somewhat disquieted by her reaction to learning Ragosta's true profession. But her boss assured her the man's core competency would only be used if absolutely necessary.

"But I'm concerned that I won't be able to hire him, Sandra." He sighed. "It's crucial, absolutely crucial that we get Ragosta under contract. Without him," he shook his head, "it's over. We'll refund our clients their money and file Chapter 11."

Sandra looked at him inquisitively. "What's so special about this Ragosta guy? I mean, I now understand where he fits into the big picture, but there certainly must be other…individuals in his line of work we could hire…and probably for considerably less!"

"It's primarily a matter of trust and anonymity, Sandra. I've known Nick for a number of years, and he's worked for me on two other occasions. Once back in '86 when I was still an attorney, and shortly before I hired you.

"Nick doesn't exist—officially that is. He has no Social Security number, no driver's license, no tangible substantiation that can identify him. Somehow he managed to erase his identity with the federal government. Consequently, no governmental agency—the FBI, NSA, IRS—whatever, has a file on him. He could leave his fingerprints plastered all over a crime scene and they'd never be able to identify him. For his profession, that's priceless."

The founder of Noble Consultants paused thoughtfully for a minute, took a sip from his third Scotch and Water and continued. "And he's good, Sandra— damn good. The two contracts he carried out for me were completed quickly and efficiently. He's well worth the money."

Haggerty looked out the window, his face grew deeply solemn. Almost in a whisper he said, "With an undertaking such as P3, I can't put my trust in anyone else. The lives of too many people—including our own—will be ruined if a situation arises that can't be dealt with properly. Between Ragosta and ourselves," turning back to her he gestured to himself and Sandra, "I'm confident that the problems that do occur will be handled with the haste and discretion necessary to keep the plan on track."

Sandra nodded. "He sounds like quite the man. I look forward to meeting him," she said with a hint of sincere anticipation in her voice.

"I'm going to contact him first thing tomorrow, so keep your fingers crossed."

The plane was beginning its decent into Reagan National. Haggerty looked at his watch and said, "There's one last thing you need to know."

"And what's that, Laurence?"

"My password. Should something happen to me, you'll need to access the only detailed narrative of the plan. Currently, it's a living document. I'm continuing to add information on the fuel cell companies, their vendors and the various senators and congressmen targeted as it becomes available."

"And the password is?"

Haggerty frowned, turned from her and looked out the window again. "I changed it the other day," he said soberly. Sandra was startled when he turned back to her with tears welling in his eyes. Softly he said, "*Martha.*"

CHAPTER 6

▼

Before making the call to Nick Ragosta, Haggerty contacted Mike Swenson, a private investigator whom he'd hired on numerous occasions to work for Noble Consultants. The man was efficient, thorough, for the most part discrete and, unlike every other private detective he'd looked at, Swenson provided his services for a reasonable fee.

But Haggerty was still upset with him for recommending Grossmann for the break-in at Global Fuel Cell Technologies; even though he never bothered to share with Swenson exactly why he was so exacting in what he required in this particular individual. Granted, a burglar with a degree in electrical engineering wasn't easy to find—it's not like you can just turn to the Yellow Pages or consult an executive search firm. But Haggerty had trusted Swenson's recommendation and hired Grossmann, who turned out to be a far more competent burglar than electrical engineer.

When The Committee appeared to be wavering about extending Noble Consultant's contract, Haggerty decided to provide a small demonstration for the three men to prove his ability to influence events at GFCT and remain impervious to the consequences of any investigation. He hoped this would eliminate any doubt in the minds of the three men of his ability to successfully conduct an operation the size and scale of P3. This, in turn, would provide the tacit assurance The Committee apparently required before they'd open their checkbook.

Because Grossmann was a degreed electrical engineer, Haggerty didn't even consider the possibility that he couldn't do something as simple as rig a fuel cell to short-circuit. The night before Bob Hobbs and Terrance McChaffee were to demonstrate the latest revisions to the fuel cell powertrain, Grossmann was to break into the company's lab and wire the prototype vehicle so that it would malfunction during the short test-drive. Nothing extravagant; he just wanted the vehicle to stop running, maybe smoke a little in front of the GFCT executives.

But rather than producing a disappointing show for the company's royalty, their top engineer wound up dead. Luckily, a homicide investigation never took place, the incident was ruled an accident. What pissed Haggerty off the most was that it was all for not. He couldn't even use the incident for its intended purpose. To do so would be tantamount to admitting to murder.

It gnawed at Haggerty that he'd have to overlook this screw-up; he wanted nothing more than to reprimand Swenson for how his scheme to influence The Committee turned out. But he couldn't; he needed him too much.

He needed Mike Swenson to keep costs down and allow Ragosta to do his job as quickly and efficiently as possible. It was essential that he gather intelligence on these fuel cell companies and their key employees; to ask Ragosta to do his own spadework would be incredibly expensive. He could hire Swenson to do this for a fraction of the cost.

After Swenson finished his investigation on these people, Haggerty would set him to work on the executives of the vendor companies. All this information would be provided to Ragosta. At the fifty million he was expecting to pay the contract killer, Haggerty didn't want the man wasting his time doing the spadework.

When the time came to call Ragosta, Haggerty was aghast at how nervous he actually was. His mouth went dry, his hands became clammy and he actually felt butterflies in his stomach. He hadn't been this worried about rejection since proposing to his ex-wife Carrie back in '72.

On a personal level, he didn't know much about the assassin. Outside of the necessary interactions during the two jobs he'd hired him for, Haggerty had only had dinner with him twice. That was back in '93 when he was with Powers, Hancock, Trumble & Haggerty; the second in '95, shortly after the founding of Noble Consultants LLC.

In 1993, Nick Ragosta was hired for the relatively simple job of roughing up a few key witnesses to ensure cooperation when their time came to testify. Desperate to ensure the survival of his struggling company, Haggerty hired him again in 1995. He extracted vital information from several scientists that allowed Haggerty to successfully complete his first job for a major client. Since that time, he'd call the hit man occasionally just to stay in touch. Eventually, he would again require a man of his talents.

And now he did. More than ever.

The only personal information Ragosta shared with him was his desire to retire by the time he was fifty. He wanted a cabin in northern Minnesota so he could fish his life away; but he wouldn't pursue that dream until he had enough money. What the amount was and why he needed so much, Ragosta didn't say. But with considerable envy Haggerty thought that it really wasn't a bad goal.

What's the amount? Could he have made it by now? Haggerty thought as he slowly picked up the phone and dialed Ragosta's number. If he hadn't reached his financial goal yet, this job would most certainly do it for him. *Christ, fifty million had to—who the hell needs that much money?* The first ring hadn't even cycled before the phone was answered.

"Yeah." Haggerty's sprits soared; he didn't use his name; he must still be in the vocation.

"Ummm…Nick, it's Haggerty. Laurence Haggerty. How are you?"

"Ahhh Mr. Haggerty! It's been a while. Good. And yourself?"

The tension in Haggerty's body eased a bit. Ragosta sounded like he was in a good mood—that could only help. "Fine, fine, thank you. Am I catching you at a good time?"

"Good as any. I have a few minutes. What's on your mind, Laurence?"

"I'd like to meet you for dinner—discuss some business. Would you be available to get together with me anytime soon?" There was a long pause; Haggerty began to tense up again—terrified that Ragosta would say they had nothing to talk about.

Finally: "How soon?"

Haggerty slouched in his chair. Covering the mouthpiece he breathed a sigh of relief. "As soon as possible. Where are you?"

"Laurence, you know damn well that's a question I don't answer."

"I know…sorry."

The line remained silent for an uncomfortably long period of time. Stricken with anxiety, Haggerty tighten his grip on the phone and pressed it so hard against his ear that it began to hurt. He felt utterly foolish.

"Let's meet in Milwaukee," Ragosta finally suggested.

Relieved, Haggerty replied, "Milwaukee…haven't been there in a long time. There's this fabulous steakhouse in…ah," he had to think for a moment. "Somewhere around Delafield. Place has been there forever. Nino's I believe it's called. Can you meet me there?"

"Sure."

"That's great. I'll fly in tomorrow. Does seven o'clock work for you?"

"Make it seven-thirty," Ragosta replied.

"I'll see you then." Haggerty gently placed the phone back in the cradle and leaned back in his chair. A wave of enormous relief swept through him. The assassin was still in business and willing to talk. P3 would be a reality.

He called for Laura to book two tickets to Milwaukee and make reservations for three at Nino's. "When you're done with that, would you track down Ms. Beach for me?" The secretary nodded and went to work.

The place hadn't changed in twenty-six years. Good restaurants seldom do. Its décor was how he remembered it and they still kept their lights very dim in both the bar and dining area. It took some time for his eyes to adjust.

The last time Laurence Haggerty had been to Nino's was in 1975, ironically, when he was an attorney for the US Department of Energy. He didn't remember why he was in the Milwaukee area then; it was a long time ago. But he remembered Nino's distinctly. Ragosta should feel right at home here, he thought; the place was obviously mob run, no doubt used to launder money. Haggerty didn't mind that he was helping bolster the family operation; it had some of the best food he'd ever tasted.

As the waiter pulled out a chair for Sandra, it dawned on Haggerty that he'd probably made a mistake not mentioning to Nick that she would be joining them. But he'd cross that bridge if and when he had to.

To pass the time as they waited for Ragosta, Haggerty told Sandra a few stories from his days as an attorney. Sandra feigned interest. Their waiter came and offered to freshen their drinks; Sandra declined, her boss accepted. The young couple at the table next to them were clearly infatuated with each other and were not terribly discrete about proclaiming their love; Haggerty saw that they made Sandra uncomfortable.

He looked at his watch, seven forty-five. Not like Ragosta to be late. He'd give him a few more minutes then call his cell phone. He saw Sandra glance at the lovers next to them, then scan the area for the waiter; apparently she changed her mind about another drink. As Haggerty watched her look around for the waiter, he thought it strange that she wasn't seeing anybody.

As Sandra waved down the waiter, her boss reached for his cell phone. Then he heard voices coming from the atrium, the hostess was greeting someone. He couldn't see who the person was hidden behind the decorative drape partitions, but the low, gravely voice sounded like the man he hoped to hire. A moment later he saw Nick Ragosta following the perky hostess.

Haggerty's first thought was that the man hadn't changed much in the seven years since he'd seen him last. Ragosta was forty-six years old, five eleven and a muscular two-hundred-thirty pounds. His hair was short, styled and generously covered in mousse. He had a square face and jaw, and his nose was slightly askew from having been broken several times, but this didn't distract from his rugged good looks. His eyes were dark brown—almost black, like his heart, Haggerty thought. Although he couldn't see it, he remembered that the assassin had a rather large scar behind his left ear. Because of its odd shape, Haggerty had always wanted to find out how he got it. However tonight would not be a good time to ask.

The only change in appearance he noticed was a touch of gray at his temples; it gave him a rather distinguished look. Dressed sharply in a navy blue suit, Haggerty would have guess that the man was an extremely successful businessman if he didn't know him. He briefly wondered whether Sandra would find him attractive.

The hit man almost seemed to saunter to their table although his posture remained erect and dignified. His right hand remained flat against his stomach has he approached, as if he was holding down his silk tie. He radiated the kind of self-assuredness women typically find irresistible; the vivacious young hostess who was less than half his age gave him a desirous glance as she turned leave.

The owner of Noble Consultants stood and extended his hand. "Nick, great to see you again. And thanks again for meeting me on such short notice."

The assassin hesitated a moment before taking Haggerty's hand, suspiciously eyeing Sandra Beach. "Good to see you too, Laurence," Ragosta said as he took Haggerty's hand and shook it firmly. The two men looked at each other intently for a moment. Then, for the second time, the assassin guardedly looked at the young woman sitting at their table; his face turning to stone.

After they dropped their hands, Haggerty gestured to his assistant. "Allow me to introduce Ms. Sandra Beach. She's my partner." Noticing Ragosta trepidation, Haggerty added, "I trust her implicitly."

"Ms. Beach…it's a pleasure," the hit man said with little sincerity.

Sandra felt a cold chill run through her body; the man's icy eyes seemed to brutally bore into her soul. She swallowed hard. "Nice to meet you too," she managed to say; fighting to keep her voice even. After giving her boss a quick glance she dropped her eyes, shifted nervously in her chair and took a sip of her drink. Ragosta continued to look at her intently, his eyes eventually shifting to the young woman's ample cleavage.

Presently, the assassin took his seat. He apologized for being late, using the excuse that he had a little trouble finding the place. Their waiter came and took his drink order and they engaged in idle small talk until his cocktail arrived.

Guardedly, Sandra asked him what she thought was an innocent question about his family life. She fought the urge to recoil when Ragosta locked lifeless eyes on her and bluntly stated that he had none. Despite her best effort, she couldn't hide the revulsion she felt by the icy ingenuousness of the epigrammatic reply. She saw that Ragosta took notice of her reaction to him and it seemed to her that he was making a genuine effort to soften his features a bit.

He apologized to Haggerty's assistant for his abrupt answer, explaining he wasn't comfortable talking about family matters because he wasn't married, had no kids or siblings, and his mother and father were long deceased. This pulled at Sandra's heartstrings and she immediately warmed to him. No wonder the man seemed so detached, so unsociable. It must be terribly lonely having no family.

She managed a smile. "Well, Nick, could you tell me a little about yourself then?"

Ragosta glanced sternly at Haggerty for a moment, expressing his displeasure at having to talk about himself. He cleared his throat and was about to speak when his drink arrived. He thanked the waiter, took a long sip and then turned to look at Sandra.

In an even voice he told her that he was born in Chicago and that his parents were killed when he was twelve-years-old. He didn't offer to explain what happened to them and clearly didn't want to. A brief but intense look of anger flashed across his face when he mentioned their deaths—as if the event that took their lives shouldn't have happened. The Cook County Department of Child Welfare sent him to live with his alcoholic uncle and anorexic aunt in a small town in western South Dakota where he spent as much time as possible in school to avoid being around them.

To escape Provo South Dakota and his abusive relatives, he intended to enlist in the Marines as soon as he was old enough. But the school counselor took a shining to him and urged him to attend college. Having no money, he applied for and received an NROTC scholarship. He attended Iowa State University, graduating in 1976 as a Second Lieutenant in the Marine Corps with a degree in Criminal Science. He served in Naval Intelligence until 1980 then resigned his commission.

Ragosta ended the chronicle there. After giving the young woman across from him a nervous look, he scanned the restaurant hoping to see the waiter—he wanted another drink. Seeing him, he signaled for another round. Sandra stared at him incredulously, wondering why he ended the story at what was obviously the half-way point of his life thus far. After a moment of awkward silence, she was about to ask him what he did after the service when their waiter came to take their order.

As soon as he left the table, Nick Ragosta took the opportunity to change the subject. "So, Laurence, what's this business you want to discuss?" Locking his dark eyes on the older man seated next to him, the assassin took the last sip of his Sam Adams.

From the moment they agreed to meet, Haggerty struggled with the best way to approach Ragosta. If indeed he didn't need the money, a direct approach might prove disastrous. Having all he needs, Haggerty worried that he wouldn't take the time to consider his proposal from all angles; he'd just dismiss the offer because he wouldn't see the need to work.

Ultimately, Haggerty decided that sweetening the man's retirement nest egg would be the best approach. From what he gathered so far, retirement was Ragosta's only apparent concern.

After taking a sip of his drink, Haggerty shot Sandra a quick side-glance, then looked back at Ragosta and asked, "If I recall correctly, Nick, you wanted to hang it up by the time you were, what…fifty?" Nick nodded. "What are you now; around forty-five?"

"Forty-six," Ragosta corrected him.

"And how's that plan working out for you?"

Ragosta's looked at Sandra for a moment, then shifted his eyes back to Haggerty. He shrugged and said, "I could retire comfortably now…if I wanted to. But a little extra pocket change might come in handy. I might decide I want the speedboat rather than the pontoon." He looked back at Sandra and smiled.

Haggerty let out a forced laugh; Sandra smiled obligingly. No doubt the man had millions; but it was Haggerty's good fortune that Ragosta felt he didn't have enough to retire on yet. The prospects for contracting the man were looking brighter.

The waiter came with the round of drinks Ragosta ordered and told them their dinner should be ready soon.

After he left, Haggerty's face lit with confidence and he said, "You may not have to decide between them, Nick. Consider what I have to say and you might be able to buy them both. That is, if you're interested in another job." Before the assassin could make any kind of reply Haggerty leaned forward and added, "And if the job is pulled off properly, there will even be a little left over for an anchor— a good one—one that will stop your boat from drifting when it's windy."

It was Ragosta's turn for a forced laugh. He raised his beer to take another sip but stopped to studying the bubbling amber liquid trapped within the transparent goblet. As he concentrated on the tiny bubbles he said, "Those anchors are quite expensive, you know. And they have different levels of quality. Like anything else, you get what you pay for." He tossed down three large gulps, put the glass back down, and then stared at his host expectantly.

Laurence Haggerty was ecstatic; Nick Ragosta was still for hire. Under the table he reached for Sandra's knee and gave it a light squeeze. His assistant quickly glanced at him and returned a diminutive grin that confused him. He wasn't sure how Sandra was taking to the hit man—her flash of a smile could mean anything.

Haggerty found it hard to contain his exhilaration and fought to control his expanding smile. He looked around; with the exception of Romeo and Juliet at the adjacent table, no one else was within earshot. And the lovers clearly had ears only for each other.

His glee under control, he leaned forward again and was about to speak when their waiter arrived with salads. The interruption caused Haggerty to grimace in frustration. Ragosta used the time to study Sandra. She was so young. Other than her breasts, he wondered what Haggerty saw in her. He introduced her as his partner, but the assassin naturally speculated that she was nothing more than his mistress. But it didn't matter; he'd find out her role soon enough.

The waiter finished and left for the kitchen.

"If providence smiles on us," Haggerty began after taking a bite of salad and wiping his mouth. "Your job will only consist of intimidating several executives at various companies. At worst, you may have to…" he looked around quickly then leaned in toward Ragosta, "eliminate a couple of people to make your point." He grimaced, then pulled back from the assassin. "Hopefully, it won't come to that. If coercion doesn't produce acceptable results, we'll have to consider that option, but only as a last resort."

Sandra was horrified to see that Ragosta didn't even flinch at the word "eliminate." It was as if the word was a normal part of his everyday vocabulary. She wondered what kind of man he was. He could extract sympathy from her one moment, and repulse her the next.

"What kind of companies?" the hit man inquired.

"Are you familiar with fuel cell technology?"

With a mouth half full of salad Ragosta replied, "Yeah, I know what a fuel cell is; I have no idea how they work though."

"Well, it's not necessary that you understand how they work. If you want, I can fill you in on the technical details later—that is, if you agree to take the job.

The bottom line here Nick, is that I'd want you to help me discredit the technology; cause these companies—"

"Who's your client?" Ragosta interrupted.

Haggerty cringed inwardly; he had to somehow deflect the question. If Ragosta learns who the clients are before he agrees to a negotiated contract price, the cost of his services would soar. The man was no fool; he knew who had the deep pockets.

"Who my client is isn't important at the moment. What is, is that you understand what they want done."

Ragosta huffed, then produced a seriously smirk. "On the contrary, Laurence, it's very important to me. I won't work for just anybody."

"You'll be working for me."

Up to this point Sandra felt useless. She sensed that tension was beginning to build between the two men. She also saw that the assassin clearly wasn't satisfied with her boss's answer. Worried that he might offend Ragosta she said, "Laurence, perhaps if you finish explaining what's to be done, Mr. Ragosta's question will be answered."

The hit man nodded in acquiescence. "How rude of me to interrupt. Please, continue Laurence."

Haggerty gave his assistant an appreciative glance. "Don't mention it, Nick," he began with a quick, dismissive wave of his hand. "As I was saying, my client wants to discredit fuel cell technology; cause the leading companies to give up all efforts to bring their product to market. Our primarily focus will be two fuel cell companies. Unlimited Energy Systems produces stationary fuel cells that can produce enough electricity to power a residential home. Global Fuel Cell Technologies is focusing on automotive fuel cells that will replace the internal combustion engine. They also have a division that manufactures huge stationary fuel cells— units large enough to power a typical subdivision."

Haggerty paused to take a sip of his Scotch and Water. Ragosta used the break in conversation to wave down their waiter. He ordered another beer. Against her better judgment Sandra ordered another Tanqueray Tonic. She was buzzing already. Most likely, if tonight was typical, she'd take the car keys; Laurence would be too inebriated to drive.

After savoring the taste of his drink, Haggerty continued. "My plan also targets several of their primary vendors. This will be your job, Nick. I want you to have a heart-to-heart with the key executives of these companies. Explain to them in no uncertain terms why it's in their best interest not to do business with these fuel cell companies. While you're busy doing that, I'll be chatting with a couple of influential politicians who can help further my client's cause."

"It'll take some time to research the targeted individuals," Ragosta said. "It'll take time to obtain the information that will help me convince them to cooperate. And I hate doing that shit! It's tedious and time consuming."

"There'll be no need for you to do that, Nick," Haggerty replied, shaking his head. "I'll have all that information for you before I set the plot in motion. I'll put Swenson on it. He excels at finding skeletons in people's closets." Ragosta sanctioned Haggerty's intention with pursed lips and a nod of his head.

"Naturally," Haggerty continued, "it goes without saying that all this must be accomplished with the utmost discretion. The wrong people must *never* discover this conspiracy—God help us if they do.

"Should something go wrong, I've assured my client (he was careful to use the singular) that under no circumstances would he be connected with this plot. There will be no paper trial. This is one of the reasons I'd prefer not to tell you who my client is." The president of Noble Consultants shot a hopefully glance at his assistant and added, "So, Nick…you game?"

Ragosta sighed and looked at his glass of beer. Haggerty was troubled by the assassin's neutral body language because all indications from him so far were positive. Haggerty gave Sandra a worried look. To his dismay she had a concerned expression on her face. *Did she read something into the man I missed?* Haggerty thought to himself. *Have I been too optimistic by his responses so far?*

Gritting his teeth, Haggerty turned back to Ragosta. He waited a few more moments then said, "Nick…?"

The dark eyes of the assassin rolled up to meet Haggerty's pleading eyes. He took pleasure in the apprehensive look on the older man's face. Ragosta sensed that Haggerty was fraught with the possibility that he might be rejected; he clearly wanted and needed a hired gun. Ragosta decided to let him sweat a little longer; it might sweeten the offer. He remained silent. Slowly, the killer reached for his beer and took several long, slow swallows.

After placing his glass back down on the table, Ragosta leaned back, tilting his chair, and folded his arms across his broad chest. He stared at the empty glass before him with an expressionless face. A few moments later he shifted his eyes to Haggerty and responded to the question. "Laurence, it's not terribly difficult to figure out who your clients are—I'm sure there's more than one. Come now my friend…who will suffer most if there's a substantial drop in the sale of oil? It ain't Jiffy Lube. No, the client companies are a tad bigger—aren't they?" He ended the question with an arrogant smirk.

The owner of Noble Consultants shifted uncomfortable in his chair. The sour expression on his face told the assassin he was on the right track. Glancing at Sandra Beach, he saw that the young woman was also slightly taken aback. She had a better poker face than her boss, though. Perhaps Haggerty should let his young, busty assistant do the talking.

Concluding that he had them by the balls, Ragosta continued, "And no one oil company would go it alone, would they? I mean, why put your own corporate ass on the line for a scheme that would also benefit your competitors?" Haggerty couldn't help but be impressed. He knew Ragosta was intelligent, but he didn't expect him to fit the pieces together so quickly—and with so little information.

The assassin finished his line of reasoning. "I'd hazard to guess that your client base consists of the CEO's of the top three oil companies…at a minimum. Hell, I wouldn't be surprised if it comprised the top five." He paused and let his chair fall forward; but he kept his arms crossed. Intensifying his supercilious expression he then asked, "Well Laurence…am I on the mark?"

Haggerty grimaced; he struggled with what to say. He was saved by the waiter who was approaching with their meals. Placing their orders before them, the maître d' provided Haggerty with a few moments to think. As their server was accomplishing his task, Ragosta kept his eyes locked on Haggerty; he retained his triumphant appearance.

"May I get you anything else?" their waiter asked.

"Yes," Ragosta replied cheerfully. "I'd like another Sam Adams, please."

"Drinks all around if you would," Haggerty added sullenly. Their server smiled and briskly departed.

Ragosta's declaration frightened Haggerty. Not that he wouldn't take the job; on the contrary, concluding that big oil was involved probably enticed the assassin. Rather, his earlier concern that the cost of his services would skyrocket should he learn who Noble Consultant's customers were. He might not be able to afford him, and he certainly didn't want to ask The Committee for more money. To prevent further deterioration of his negotiating position, Haggerty smiled back at Ragosta and pointed to the killer's plate with his steak knife. "You're gonna love that, Nick."

Ragosta gave him a wan smile. "You're not going to succeed in dodging the question, Laurence." Raising an eyebrow he again asked, "Am I correct?" He cut into his Porterhouse. "Mmmm, you were right about the food here," he said in a muffled voice, all but chomping on the piece of meat, "this shit's great!" Sandra, rather put off by his table manners, noticed that somehow the man managed to maintain his grin while chewing. He continued to look at her boss expectantly.

Haggerty pursed his lips and let out a defeated sigh. Giving Ragosta a poignant look he answered, "Nick, I'm sure you can appreciate my client's need for anonymity and my obligation to maintain it." By the look on the assassin's face he apparently didn't. Disappointed that Ragosta didn't buy the pretext, the older man grimaced and said, "All I'll say is what I was taught to say in the army if asked about nuclear weapons on base. 'I can neither confirm nor deny the existence of nuclear weapons on this installation.'" Haggerty reached for his drink and added mellifluously, "You can read into that what you like." The tacit confirmation brought a smile to the younger man's face; Haggerty was relieved.

The waiter came with their next round of cocktails. Ragosta remained silent until he left the vicinity of their table. When he was far enough away the killer asked, "Do you remember my limits, Laurence?"

"Yes." Looking at his assistant he said, "But go over them for Sandra's sake."

Ragosta put down his utensils and wiped his mouth with his napkin. He glanced at Haggerty, and then shifted his eyes to Sandra. His face hardened and his eye narrowed, sending a chill through the young woman. His eyes seemed to pierce her soul. In a voice on the edge of malevolence he said, "You may find it hard to believe, Ms. Beach, but I have standards." Haggerty's assistant responded to the statement with a thin smile. "I don't take out anybody under twenty-one, or anybody who is mentally incapacitated. I'm also not particularly fond of taking out women either, regardless of age...call me old fashion." Ragosta flashed her a smug smile. Sandra Beach only continued to stare into his callous eyes. The statement caused her to feel oddly relieved until he added, "But I will if necessary." Sandra's eyes darted to her boss; his attention was on the killer. She then turned her attention back to the assassin. "And I will never, under any circumstances, harm a child. I'll not kidnap or threaten harm to anyone under eighteen. Insist that I break these rules and the contract between us is null and void. I keep my retainer." He raised his eyebrows and tilted his head, silently asking her if she understood. Sandra gave him a small nod.

He continued to stare at her and she began to feel self-conscious. She reached for her drink and struggled to keep her hand from shaking. How could a man kill people for a living and yet have ethics, she thought. Maybe it was his way of adding morality to an immoral profession. He continued to watch her as she took a sip of her Tanqueray and Tonic; she wished he'd focus his attention elsewhere.

She was relieved when her boss asked, "Okay, Nick...will you work for me? And what's your price?"

Ragosta turned to face Haggerty; out of the corner of his eye he saw Sandra's body lax and was pleased. He took his beer, seemed to study it for a moment then took several large swallows. His delay in answering caused an anxious look to come across Haggerty's face.

"Let me qualify my answer, Laurence, so you know exactly where I stand. I'm not far from retirement; the last thing I want to do now is put myself at risk. I'm past that point in my career. Though I don't know all the details yet, your job sounds risky, complex and dangerous. Anytime you fuck with politicians—as you mentioned you would—you open Pandora's box. The idiots begin to talk and eventually say the wrong thing. The press gets a hold of it and the next thing you know the accusations fly. Investigations ensue—sometimes congressional.

"I've spent the last twenty years doing my job efficiently, cleanly and anonymously. I've eliminated more people than I care to admit and have never even come close to getting caught; that's because I'm damn good and extremely careful. But...my luck can't last forever. I feel taking a job like this is tempting fate—and I'm superstitious."

The owner of Noble Consultant fell into denial. He refused to believe what he was hearing. All at once a million thoughts jarred his mind, some competing to bring him back to reality—to acknowledge the refusal—others trying to comprehend the implications of it. He gaped at Ragosta with wide, empty eyes; their hollowness emphasizing the only emotion he was feeling—utter disbelief.

Sandra was crestfallen; seeing her boss' reaction she dropped her head and stared at her napkin. Looking blankly at the white, crumpled cloth on her lap she decided she had to help Laurence out. But how? He made it perfectly clear to her that without Nick Ragosta, P3 wouldn't succeed. And the assassin's last words had a finality to them—it didn't sound like there was much room for compromise.

Ragosta's eyes were slowly swinging back and forth between her and her boss. The bastard seemed to be enjoying the torment he was putting Laurence through. For a brief second while he was looking at her, she saw his eyes drop to her breasts. Then it hit her.

"We certainly understand, Mr. Ragosta," Sandra said without emotion; she appeared completely composed and unconcerned. "We..." she gestured towards her boss and saw that he was gaping at her with a mixture of confusion, surprise and astonishment. She continued talking; under the table she quickly touched his leg with her foot. Thankfully he understood the message and immediately pulled himself together. "...appreciate your candor." She flashed a wisp of a smile. "And might I add that it's refreshing to find somebody in your trade who thinks of the client's best interest first."

Ragosta gave her a strange look then huffed. "I'm afraid you misunderstood me, Ms. Beach." Haggerty was now looking at her questioningly, trying to figure out what she was up to.

"Really?" she replied coyly, yet brazenly. "You're clearly not interested in the job. Can't say that I blame you. Why risk exposure now, especially when you're not sure you could pull it off. Can you offer the name of someone who could—a replacement?"

An annoyed look came over the assassin's face, but it was quickly changed, as if he were amused. Serenely he said, "I didn't say I wouldn't take the job, Ms. Beach. I was only emphasizing the risks to me personally." Harshly he added, "As for any inability on my part to do the job—successfully—I'm afraid you underestimate me terribly. And yes, I could give you several names, but they'll second stringers."

Haggerty's face brighten, as if a powerful spotlight had illuminated his face. Cautiously he asked, "You'll take the job then, Nick?"

Ragosta gave Sandra another menacing look and then answered, "Yeah, why not? One more job before I hang it up."

Sandra Beach was rather pleased with herself; she had managed to manipulate this conceited man. To her own surprise, one of the oldest tricks between the sexes had worked for her: challenging the man's vanity. But she was careful not to gloat; he could always change his mind.

Her boss gave her a quick, grateful glance; under the table he gently squeezed her thigh. Excitedly he said, "That's great, Nick. You have no idea how glad I am you're taking the contract."

The assassin smirked. "I think I do," he paused then added, "As you well know, I won't come cheap. In addition…I reserve the right to back out after I know all the details…and I will, if I feel your plan could jeopardize my best interests."

"Of course," Haggerty replied. "But I'm confident you'll not only be impressed by the plan, but also be as excited as I am to be part of it." He took a sip of his drink then added, "This will be the biggest contract you've ever been awarded, Nick. You'll be ending your career on a high note."

While her boss was talking, Sandra studied the man across from her and inwardly cringed. She wondered what kind of person killed others for a living. To take someone's life for money you'd have to have absolutely no conscience, no heart. She then thought how her own job lacked both ethics and morals, but there was no comparison. She admitted to herself that she was far from the most ethical woman ever to walk the face of the earth, but at least nobody was ever physically hurt by her line of work. Lives temporarily ruined perhaps, but that was business. She didn't put anybody in the ground.

She continued to tune the two men's conversation in and out. It was when she heard Ragosta use the word "terminate," that a spasm quaked so fiercely in her stomach that she flinched. She was suddenly struck by the realization that her participation in P3 might well make her party to murder. Strangely, the thought never occurred to her until now. It took the experience of sitting across from a paid assassin, listening to him callously explain who he would and would not kill, before the terrible nature of her boss' plan completely registered. Turning her eyes to Laurence Haggerty, she was beginning to see him, Noble Consultants and The Committee in a whole new light. And it wasn't a good light—she wasn't sure how she felt about that. Disillusioned, she began to pay closer attention to their conversation.

"I wouldn't expect you to," she heard her employer say.

She looked at Ragosta; he seemed to be contemplating something. He remained silent for a moment then asked, "So...what's your offer?"

Without batting an eye Haggerty spit out, "Ten." The "million" was understood. "Five upfront, five upon successful completion of the job."

Ragosta frowned and gave Haggerty a sour look. Sandra could almost hear the assassin say *You've got to be kidding!"*

A waxen smile formed on Haggerty's face, "Ok Nick, what will it take?"

"Fifty."

"Fifty!" Haggerty cried, trying to sound and look shocked. Perhaps it was because she knew him so well, but Sandra wasn't convinced by his act. She didn't think the assassin was either.

"Yes," Ragosta replied calmly. "And as this will be my sawn-song, if you will, I'll make it a bargain. My fee will remain fifty...regardless of the number terminated."

The coldness with which Ragosta made the offer caused Sandra's skin to break out in goose bumps. Even though her employer made it clear that killing anybody would be an option of last resort, the assassin was making it sound inevitable. *The man's not human,* she thought. He began to eat his meal in earnest. A wave of revulsion swept over her as she watched him; she thought she'd scream if she had to be around him much longer. She turned her head to look at the young couple at the nearby table.

Haggerty shook his head lightly while biting his lower lip. "Fifty's pretty steep, Nick. I'll need to pass that figure by my client."

"You do that. Call me if it's approved. If it isn't," he shrugged indifferently, "I won't be heartbroken. And don't bother to counter-offer. The price is firm."

Haggerty nodded his understanding and began to eat his meal. After a minute of silence Ragosta asked Haggerty about his children; they ate the rest of their meal engaged in polite conversation; at least Haggerty and Ragosta did. Sandra remained quiet and only picked at her food.

"I'm sorry, Laurence, I just don't like him!" Sandra said tersely while looking out the passenger side window. "I've no doubt he'll get the job done, but—" her voice trailed off.

"Really? I thought you'd be impressed by his show of ethics—not killing kids and so forth."

She turned to look at him. It was dark in the car and he was only illuminated periodically when they passed under a streetlight; the brief glimpses of his face made it difficult to gauge his mood. She didn't want to give him the impression she was second-guessing his decision to hire Ragosta. She decided it would be a good idea to lighten her tone. "Truthfully...I was impressed when I first met him. He seemed rather urbane enough, intelligent and...he certainly wasn't hard to look at." She had to admit to herself that the man was handsome.

Haggerty smiled. He briefly wondered if young women still considered him good-looking. "What in particular didn't you like about him?"

Without a second's thought she replied, "His cold-hearted attitude toward killing." She pulled her crossed arms tighter to her chest. "God...he gives me the willies!"

Her boss sighed then said, "As unsavory as it sounds, killing is what the man does. It's as natural to him as filling out a spreadsheet is to you. There's no emotion because it's an everyday thing."

"Yeah, I suppose so," she responded, giving her boss a side-glance.

They drove for a while with out speaking. As they turned into their hotel's parking lot she said, "By the way, Laurence, I was impressed you predicted the amount of money he'd want for the job. But one question."

"What's that?"

"Why didn't you accept his demand for fifty million right away? You've got the money. Why'd you appear hesitant when you want him so badly?"

Haggerty pulled into a parking space and threw the car into park. After turning off the engine he said, "I don't want him to think I have that much clout with my clients. I want him to understand that I'm working within restraints."

"Why?"

"Simply so he won't second my decisions or how I plan to implement P3 when he learns the details. I know him well enough to know that he'll want to alter my plans—do things his way. I don't want to deal with that."

Their rooms were across the hall from each other. Before they entered Haggerty turned to Sandra and said, "About your feelings for Ragosta...remember, you don't have to like him to work with him." Sandra smiled weakly, nodded and went into her room.

Laurence Haggerty waited two days, and then called Nick Ragosta to tell him the fifty million was approved by his client with the stipulation that payment would be fifteen up front, the balance upon successful completion of P3. He was sorry, but it was the best he could do. He became a little nervous again when the assassin didn't immediately accept the terms; but he figured Ragosta had to put on his own show of prudent reluctance. Several days later Ragosta called Haggerty and told him he'd accept the terms. The next week Sandra Beach, Nick Ragosta and Laurence Haggerty met at the offices of Noble Consultants for their first meeting.

The conspirators spent the next six days going over the plan and coordinating strategy. Starting at seven-thirty in the morning, they worked without a break until about six or so in the evening. Lunch, along with coffee, soda, snacks or any other item one of them might want during the day was catered. It was an exhausting ordeal.

Ragosta was impressed by the overall simplicity of the plan, and said so. As his new employer had pointed out, he soon came to realize that this would be the biggest and most intricate contract of his career. Never before had he been tasked with the coercion of so many people at the same time in so many different places. He didn't look forward to the tremendous amount of travel in store for him, but that was a small price to pay for this, his final and most lucrative job.

Once the assassin thoroughly understood the plan, Sandra was relieved to hear that he believed he might be able to pull off Larry and Moe without the need to eliminate anyone. However, before he'd have a high level of confidence that that was possible, he'd have to wait for Mike Swenson to complete his investigation of the targeted executives.

For the most part, the top managers at the fuel cell companies and their key vendors were ordinary, honest people. The intelligence Mike Swenson had dug up on these individuals so far was, for the most part, mundane: infidelity, drug and alcohol abuse, gambling problems, run-of-the-mill stuff. Ragosta kept to himself one small, but important detail. If a hit was necessary, complications were not likely to develop as a consequence. None of these people were celebrities—

there wasn't a Jack Welsh in the bunch. Nobody was associated with organized crime or a prominent political figure accused of corruption. If made to look accidental, their deaths wouldn't be investigated very vigorously—nowadays, investigators were always overwhelmed. The incident would bring nothing more than an obituary notice; at most, a small column in their town's newspaper describing what a wonderful citizen they were and how their death was so terribly tragic. But making a murder appear accidental was not easy, even for him.

Nick Ragosta would be responsible for both the Larry and Moe strategies of P3. Larry, the bribing, intimidation or elimination of UES' and GFCT's executives would begin November 1st, 2001. Moe—the coercion of their suppliers' top management—would begin on or about December 1st, 2001. As would Curly—Haggerty's attempt to influence congressional supporters and other important politicians. Although the optimal strategy would be to execute all three schemes at once, Haggerty explained that he wanted to hold off on the implementation of Curly until he saw the results of Larry. If the Chief Executive Officers of the fuel cell companies proved to be more obstinate than anticipated, it may be necessary to rethinking Curly.

There was a great deal of debate between the three conspirators as to what suppliers to target—there were many to choose from. In the end they agreed on three. The vendors were chosen for their strategic importance to the fuel cell companies, their company's public profile (the lower the better. A Dow or Parker were companies with too high a public profile) and the level of difficulty the fuel cell companies would experience trying to replace the purchased component.

Drextal industries, located in Lawrence, Kansas, molded composite material to produce GFCT's anode and cathode plates. It was a mid-sized company, about fifty million in sales, privately held and run by the daughter of the founder.

Rayonicx of Norcross, Georgia was their second choice. Annual revenues of approximately sixty-five million, the company supplied Power Conditioning Modules to UES.

The last supplier chosen was the only company all three conspirators immediately agreed upon. Flexible Tubing Technologies was a gem in that it happened to belong to the same man who owned the tiny silicone molding company Flexible Sealing Solutions: Donald Kampnel. This was a stroke of luck. Both GFCT and UES obtained products from these two companies that happened to be run by the same executives. Ragosta would be able to kill two birds with one stone. The hoses and gaskets supplied by these companies were not high tech by any means, but the product did require extensive testing. Replacing these items would be both time consuming and expensive.

Mike Swenson was still gathering information on the numerous targets of the plot. However, they had more than enough information to get started. After the final marathon meeting, Nick Ragosta, Sandra Beach and Laurence Haggerty treated themselves to dinner at Charlie's, one of D.C.'s more upscale restaurants. The next day, Ragosta flew to Troy, New York.

P3, the unprecedented effort to sabotage an entire industry, was about to begin.

Daniel Stallinger pulled into his reserved parking space near the main door to Unlimited Energy Systems' corporate office. For the last week he had felt a pang of guilt when he parked in front of the sign that said,

Reserved
Chief Executive Officer

He had purchased a new Mercedes E Class and thought some of his employees might consider the car rather opulent, a status symbol, a means for him to show off his wealth and position. No one had said anything about the car of course, but since purchasing the automobile he'd received a couple of spiteful looks; few employees at UES were paid enough to allow them to own one.

If indeed he was the recipient of a low-lying malevolence from some of his people, they'd get over it in time; he was fairly certain of that. As CEOs go, he believed he was fairly well liked. Instead of averting their eyes, most of the employees smiled and greeted him warmly when they passed him in a hallway or on the factory floor, and he insisted everyone call him Dan. Besides, he just couldn't imagine switching cars with his wife now, if only for the reason of eliminating a few nasty looks. He absolutely loved the car and couldn't wait to drive it every morning.

Stepping out of the car and gently closing the door, he pushed the button on the fob to lock his baby and heard the comforting chirp of the car's alarm system. But just to be safe he tugged on the door's handle; he didn't want to take any chances. Satisfied his E Class was secure he headed up to his office.

It was a typical day for him at UES. The morning started as they usually did, with the accountants. Sales of their residential units were beginning to take off. Provided they continued to meet their sales targets and keep costs in line, UES' operating deficit would only run four and a half million in fiscal '02—far better then projected.

Four corporations formed the joint venture that was Unlimited Energy Systems: American Electrical Corporation, PUC, Advanced Mechanical Concepts and his former company DPE Energy. Operational subsidies obtained from these companies in fiscal '03 would drop the deficit to three point one million. And a generous grant from the U.S. Department of Energy added another two point four million into the coffers. By fiscal '05, UES' earnings were projected at two point three million. From there, only their capacity to build fuel cells would limit their ability to make what many will consider obscene profits.

By the time this happened however, American Electrical Corporation, which was the majority share holder, would buy out the other three partners and own UES outright. When that day comes, Stallinger knew he'd be replaced. But that fact didn't bother him; CEO's—like professional football coaches—were hired to be fired.

Lately, there was a lot of negative press concerning CEO's compensation. It was too lavish, extraordinarily out of balance with what employees earned, unwarranted. But what most people didn't understand was that CEOs had to set themselves up with a golden parachute; their tenure at any one company was tenuous at best. However, he too believed that some packages went way overboard.

Naturally, both he and the board of directors were delighted with the steady climb of UES's share price; remarkable during this time of recession. Since their initial public offering in September 1999, the stock's value had increased over four hundred percent. Thanks to UES's initial sales success, the recession and the nose-diving NASDAQ had had little effect on the company's value. And this was good for him personally; his compensation package included ten thousand shares of company stock. Depending on what came first, his firing or June of '04—his five year anniversary—he'd be free to exercise his stock options. Given its current price, he toyed with the idea of intentional dismissal.

But he had no regrets about taking the position with UES. While he was being recruited by UES, Honda made him an offer to be director of North American Operations. It was a tempting offer. A far more prestigious position than CEO of a start-up company and certainly more lucrative from a financial standpoint. But he wasn't in it for the money. He truly believed in fuel cell technology and the benefits it had to offer. He had always wanted—at least once in his life—to work for a company that benefited the common good.

The rest of his day promised to be boring; production, sales and marketing and staff meetings. About the only highlight of the day would be lunch. The general manager and sales representative for ARCO, one of UES's smaller vendors, were in town and he accepted their invitation to lunch. The guys were unique. He'd dined with them on several occasions and it was always a pleasure; they seldom discussed business and never asked for preferential treatment.

At four-thirty that afternoon Stallinger walked out of the building. He was in the company of a junior engineer and was embarrassed that he didn't know the young woman's name. Fortunately, before she zipped up her coat, he managed a glimpse at the company identification badge hanging around her neck and then was able to address her by name.

Their conversation was brief and consisted only of how much each was looking forward to the upcoming Thanksgiving holiday. He normally didn't leave work this early, but he promised Melissa, his seventeen-year-old daughter, that he'd pick her up after drama club. Her car was in the shop, again, and she dreaded taking the activity bus. He found it incredibly difficult to say no to her.

Reaching his car he wished "Ann" a good evening. After unlocking the Mercedes he waved to another employee and then got in. *"What the hell?"* he mumbled to himself. Taped to the steering wheel was small, plain white envelope. *How could that get here?* he thought. He was absolutely sure he locked the car this morning.

He pondered the question for a moment and then a smile came to his face. Abby! Of course! She had a spare key to the Mercedes and obviously used it to gain entry sometime during the day. *But why would she leave me a card?* Today was no special occasion—not an anniversary or birthday. But then he thought how Abby didn't need one, God bless her. His wife would occasionally do special little things like this; leave him a card or note, cook him a special dinner or make a wonderful dessert. Not the type to express affection through physical contact, this was her way of expressing love. Every time she did it he felt a sharp stab of guilt—as he did now.

After the brief feeling of remorse passed, with a smile he pulled the envelope from the steering wheel and opened it. He froze. A cold chill shot though his entire body and the smile instantly vanished from his face. He couldn't believe what he was reading. *Was this some kind of a joke?*

After reading the short note he thought that maybe this was a prank, perpetrated by a disgruntled employee. But it couldn't be. How could one of his employees possibly know about that? What employee would have the nerve to break into the CEO's car in broad daylight?

Break into…?

HIS CAR!

He quickly jumped out and examined the car's door for the damage that must have occurred during the entry attempt. To his astonishment, there wasn't so much as a scratch on it. He ran his hand along the window frame and over the latching mechanism to feel for anything unusual; but he felt nothing. He was completely perplexed, but the feeling quickly gave way to one of fear as he got back in the car and read the note a third time:

My Dear Mr. Stallinger,

We need to have a little chat, you and I. We have much to discuss. I'm not a man who takes rejection lightly so I'll be crushed should you decide not to join me.

Meet me at the Holiday Inn Lounge on Bear Road, Thursday at 8:00 pm. Sit at an empty table near the back of the lounge and wait for me. I'll even buy you a beer.

Should you think this invitation lacks sincerity, perhaps it would interest you to know that one of the topics to be discussed Thursday night is Rhonda Beattie.

And do not even think of telling anybody about this note and our meeting—especially the police. If you do—and I assure you I will know if you do—I will kill Brett.

Have a nice day.

Stallinger's mind began to race, who would do this and why? Did this person want money? He and Abby were well off, but not rich, not by any stretch of the imagination. Anybody who knew about Rhonda would know this. But if it was money this person wanted, why didn't he or she just say so and demand he drop it off somewhere rather then go through the ritual of a meeting—where he'd allow himself to be seen. If it wasn't money, what could he possibly possess, control or know that was so valuable they would threaten his son to obtain it? One thing was certain, he would do as he was told and not go to the police.

Stallinger put the card back in its envelope and shoved it in his coat pocket. He sat behind the wheel of his car, stone-still and expressionless. He bit his lower lip and his eyes stared straight out the windshield, seeing nothing. *How could this person know about Rhonda? It was so long ago!*

Because his hands were trembling, it took a few tries to actually get the key into the ignition. Backing out, he almost hit another car because he failed to look behind him. The thought that he could have damaged his precious car didn't even cross his mind. He'd never experienced this kind of emotion before; a mixture of fear, anxiety, bewilderment and anger. Thursday night. It was only Tuesday. He'd have to wait an entire day before he met his tormentor and got some answers.

"Thursday night!" he cursed to himself while throwing the Mercedes in drive. *Abby and I are having dinner with Rick and Betty Bergman.* How could he get out of it without Abby asking a lot of questions? This dinner get-together had been planned for weeks, and his wife had reminded him several times not to plan any-thing for that evening. Well, he'd think of something—he'd have to—there was no question of blowing this off.

This was a legitimate threat. Should Abby ever learn about Rhonda, Stallinger knew it would be all over, regardless of how long ago it happened. More than once he'd thought of telling his wife about the affair; come clean and get it off his chest. But he just didn't have the heart to do it. Abby would be devastated, even though the only consequence of the affair was to make him appreciate his wife even more.

When he pulled into Stockdale Senior High to pick up his daughter he'd thought he'd composed himself—but he hadn't. Half-way home he knew his attempts to make conversation with Melissa failed when she disregarded what he'd just said and asked, "Daddy, what's wrong?"

By the time Stallinger was reading his summons, Ragosta was already in Brookfield, Massachusetts. It was less than a three-hour drive from Troy, New York to the Boston area where Global Fuel Cell Technologies was headquartered. He'd always enjoyed driving the Mass Turnpike; too bad most of the leaves were already off the trees. Nothing like the fall colors in New England.

The assassin looked forward to tomorrow. He'd pose as a florist and deliver a beautiful bouquet of flowers to Cynthia Klash, CEO of GFCT and closet lesbian. He'd enjoy tormenting Ms. Klash. Ragosta detested homosexuals. And he'd have no problem killing her either; he didn't consider lesbians women. Although play-ing the role would be fun, he wasn't looking forward to going through all the trouble of posing as a deliveryman—but he really had no choice. He couldn't call in a delivery of flowers because the person taking the order would no doubt ques-tion what he'd want written on the greeting card. In the greater scheme of things, play acting was a minor inconvenience.

After the delivery, he'd drive back to Troy and wait for his meeting with Stall-inger. He'd have plenty of time to kill. He could have planned it tighter from a timing standpoint, but he wanted to leave sufficient time for Stallinger and Klash to sweat. He'd learned long ago that people are easier to manipulate when they're unnerved. Maybe he'd take in a movie or see the local sights—whatever the hell there was to see in Troy, New York. And after he'd had his chat with Stallinger, he'd spend the night in the area and leave for Brookfield the next morning to meet with Klash Friday evening. *Haggerty's contract certainly wasn't taxing*, he thought to himself.

It was a cold, rainy, dreary morning when Cynthia Klash finally made it into work; the weather mirrored her mood. Normally Lenny, her husband, handled the task of taking their children to the doctor, dentist, school, or any other domestic chore. He loved doing it. But this morning he had to meet with his publisher concerning the latest problem they had with his new book. The inconvenience annoyed her. It would be different if his books were literary novels or works with some historical or otherwise intellectual value. Instead, the man wrote children's books, which to her was akin to selling finger paintings to the fine arts market.

She'd never let Lenny know her true feelings about the area of writing he'd chosen to specialize in; how he could make respectable money if he'd change his genre. He certainly had the talent. She'd kept her opinion to herself because his writing of mind-numbing children's books allowed her to remain the breadwinner of the family, releasing her from the more mundane aspects of day-to-day child rearing. She had to admit that her husband did a pretty good job of taking care of the kids, and she was happy to allow him to do it.

Shifting her mind to matters of work, she hurriedly sat down behind her desk and turned on her computer. As she did every morning, Cynthia Klash reminded herself to keep her eye on the big picture. GFCT was only a stepping-stone, a launch platform to bigger and better companies. Two more years, she figured, provided everything went as planned—which, in manufacturing it seldom does—and she'd be out of the trenches. One way or another, she'd ensure everything went as planned.

She had received her BS in electrical engineering from the University of Southern California in 1978 and had worked in defense related industries as an engineer for several companies. During this time however, she discovered that she much preferred business; she also found that she had a knack for it. She received her MBA in 1993 from Berkley and according to her trusted recruiter, she was on the road to becoming the youngest CEO of a fortune five hundred company. He figured two more years and she'd be on the short list of potential candidates. Accepting the position of CEO for Global Fuel Cell Technologies made her resume complete. And if the company is successful, well, that would just be the icing on the cake. Her future looked bright.

All major engineering obstacles had been overcome and she saw nothing in the balance of GFCT's long-term plan that could pop up and become a showstopper—for her or for her company. Under her tenure GFCT had developed a functioning, reliable automotive fuel cell powertrain and was the first company to do so. Now it was only a matter of working out the details of its manufacture and driving down costs before the product would be ready for market. Conservatively, this also would take about another two years. She couldn't have timed it better. Any problems that did arise now should be easy to handle. And when the time came for the successful unveiling of their product, she undoubtedly would have her pick of companies.

Cynthia Klash was on the corporate fast-track. The speed with which she'd climbed the corporate latter surprised even her and she was quite pleased with what she'd achieved up to this point. Her career goal now was to be the youngest woman CEO of a fortune 500 company; and the prospect of realizing that dream was looking better everyday.

Being the CEO of the first company to successfully develop and market a fuel cell powertrain was impressive enough. The fact that she was only forty-five years old, and a woman, made her look like a prodigy. Her recruiter had assured her the boards of the corporate giants would come knocking as soon as GFCT went to market.

She doubted she'd make up the time she'd lost this morning taking their youngest, Bridget, to the doctor. As she logged on to her email she briefly wondered again why she'd bothered to get married and have children. She knew the answer of course; at the time she felt having a successful marriage and family was necessary for her career. More importantly, it would mitigate the legitimacy of any rumors that might emerge concerning her actual sexual preference. In the corporate world today, the marriage aspect was no longer relevant, but homosexuality was still taboo—despite what some may say.

It was going to be an exceptionally busy day. Along with several meetings this afternoon she had to prepare for her trip to Los Angeles. Tomorrow, she'd meet with Enterprise Media, the company she'd contracted to produce the television commercial that would air when GFCT officially unveiled their product to the general public.

Use of an advertisement was her brainchild and pet project. Tier one companies—companies that supply direct to automotive manufacturers or OEM's, Original Equipment Manufacturers—seldom advertise. But when fuel cell powered cars hit the market, it would be an historical moment. She wanted GFCT to share the spotlight.

Advertising would also be smart business. Because companies such as Global Fuel Cell Technologies typically don't advertise to the general public, GFCT's board of directors initially resisted the idea. Cringing at the five-million-dollar price tag, they considered her proposal nothing more than free advertising for their customers. But Klash pointed out that GFCT currently had a corner on the market—no other company was in a position to mass produce fuel cell power-trains. However, she warned, this was a situation that wouldn't last forever. They had to capitalize on the opportunity while they had the chance. The board wisely gave in.

Cynthia Klash couldn't have been more pleased with how she'd positioned her company in the automotive market. GFCT had a monopoly, and was already talking with several of the larger manufacturers—both domestic and foreign—about long-term contracts. Agreements would probably be reached within the next eighteen months.

She was delighted, yet somewhat surprised with how well the automotive manufacturers were embracing the new technology. With so much invested for so long in the internal combustion engine, she thought resistance to fuel cells would be far stiffer than was the case. But with an American public outraged by ever increasing gasoline prices, the alternative energy industry had little difficulty reading the writing on the wall. The public was ready for hydrogen powered cars.

She let out a resigned sigh when Outlook opened up and she discovered thirty-four e-mails messages in her inbox since 6:00 pm yesterday. Scanning the titles, she only looked at those that sounded crucial. She had just opened a message from Nash at Enterprise Media when she heard a knock at the door. Standing in the doorway to her office was Tanya, the receptionist. A large bouquet of flowers accompanied her wide, excited grin.

The possibility that the flower could be for her never crossed the CEO's mind. Annoyed by the interruption she curtly asked, "What is it, Tanya?"

The brusque greeting immediately turned the receptionist's brilliant smile into a disenchanted frown. Slightly crestfallen with her boss's lack of comprehension, she held out the flowers and said, "Cindy...they're for you!"

"Me?" Cynthia quipped incredulously, her eyes dropping to the huge bouquet in the receptionist's hands. "Who the hell would send *me* flowers...and why?"

Slightly exasperated Tanya said, "Your husband maybe?" as she strolled into the office and set them on the chief executives' desk. She stepped back and admired the arrangement. "Aren't they beautiful? They must have cost a fortune!"

"Couldn't possibly be my husband," Klash responded with a dismissive wave of her hand. "In our twenty-one years of marriage he's never given me flowers."

"Secret admirer perhaps?" Tanya said teasingly.

The CEO huffed and said sarcastically, "Yeah...I'm such a babe!" She remained silent a moment then serenely added, "They really are quite beautiful, aren't they, Tanya."

"I'll say. I wish my boyfriend would send me flowers—just once." She turned to leave the office, froze, and then turned back to face her boss. Nodding toward the envelope wedged between the stems she asked excitedly, "The card. What's it say? I'll bet they're from your hubby—there's a first time for everything ya know!"

Flashing Tanya a dubious look, Klash reached for the card. "It's awful big for the kind of card that usually accompanies flowers. It's regular size."

"It is, isn't it?" the receptionist agreed. "Must be a Hallmark or something. How sweet!"

Cynthia Klash stared at the flowers a moment longer. She would never admit it to Tanya, or anybody else for that matter, but she'd never received flowers from *anybody* before. Reaching for the card she assured herself that they couldn't have come from Lenny. But if not her husband, then from who? *They couldn't—they'd better not—be from Alexis,* she thought. Her young lover was certainly the type of person who'd send flowers, but she wasn't stupid. They were extremely careful to safeguard the secrecy of their love affair.

She pulled the card from the envelope and opened it.

Dear Ms. Klash,
It is my pleasure to inform you that you're going to make some changes at Global Fuel Cell Technologies.

The CEO's brow furrowed and she narrowed her eyes. "Huh?" she said out loud. The opening line threw her for a loop; she was genuinely puzzled.

I trust this will not be too difficult a task. I'm aware of your lofty ambitions; if you want them to be realized, meet me Friday evening, 7:00 pm at The Happy Tap. Alexis Kostreva will be a topic of discussion.

Her head snapped back in shock; her stomach felt as if it had dropped ten stories in an instant. She glanced at Tanya and saw a concern expression on her face.

What the hell's going on? Klash thought. *How could this person possibly know about Alexis, or my ambitions for that matter? Alexis would never tell—would she?*

A chill went down Cynthia's spine. For the first time she wondered if the young mechanical engineer would try to benefit by publicizing their affair. *Alex had nothing to lose, but what could she possible hope to gain?*

Alexis was half her age, had little material wealth and could be easily bribed. *But how could she?* Cynthia truly loved her and was sure the affection was mutual. *Surely,* Klash thought, *Alexis would come to her if she were in financial straights. She wouldn't need to resort to bribes from people out to destroy me.* She continued reading:

I want you to keep our get-together to yourself; it will be our little secret. If you tell anybody—and I mean anybody—I'll know. And I'll be very angry. You wouldn't want anything to happen to that handsome young son of yours. Would you?

One more thing, Cynthia. Don't be late. I do so hate to wait.

She felt herself start to sway and reached for the edge of her desk to brace herself. It took several seconds but the light-headedness eventually ebbed. She closed her eyes and took a couple deep breaths. It didn't seem to help.

"Cindy...?" Tanya said with cautious concern while placing her hand on Klash's shoulder. Her eyes darted between the CEO's pale face and the card she was clutching in her hand.

Klash gently removed the receptionists hand from her shoulder and staggered back to her chair. "Tanya, I'm...I'm, fine," she said almost in a whisper. "Thanks for bringing in the flower? I've, ahhh, got a lot to do." She sat down. The receptionist said nothing. Slowly she walked out of the office, glancing back several times as she did. Klash could see bewilderment written all over the young woman's face.

Once Tanya had left, she read the card again. She couldn't believe what she was reading. *Is this person serious? This can't be happening? I must be dreaming!* But of course she knew she wasn't.

Friday night, 7:00 sharp!

Nice touch, she thought, *meeting at The Happy Tap—a gay bar.*

She dropped her hands to her lap and stared blankly at the flowers. She was being dictated to—and threatened! *This son-of-a-bitch threatened my oldest son!* Anger began to well up inside her but quickly ebbed. *Why the hell couldn't this bastard do me a favor and threaten Lenny?* As far as she was concerned, it would be no big loss if he was out of the picture; the only drawback would be that she'd either have to be more of a parent to Steve and Bridget, or hire a nanny.

Her son Bruce was a junior at Boston College and really didn't need parents any more. Steve, a junior in high school, could probably get by with out parental guidance. But Bridget still needed her; she was only thirteen. Having lived with Lenny for over two decades she felt affection for the man, but she loved her children. She loved them with an intensity only mother's experience.

She stood up, shut the door to her office then sat back down. Her phone rang several times but she ignored it. She was tempted to call Alexis and confront her, but decided not to. Their number one rule was never to show any familiarity toward each other at work. That's how rumors start.

When she'd calmed down she read the note one more time then shredded the card. *So much for my trip to L.A.,* she thought as she marked her date book. She tried to think of what she possessed, or knew, that was of such value someone would resort to blackmail to obtain it. Nothing came to mind.

From the bar, Nick Ragosta watched him walk into the darkened lounge. The assassin slowly took another sip from his bottle of beer and followed the man with his eyes. The place was rather busy; mostly with salesmen away from home who had no better way to kill time. Ragosta knew he'd look like just another patron should his quarry start scrutinizing everyone in the bar. But that didn't happen; he barely looked around at all. A small smile came to the hit man's face as the chief executive did as he was told and sat at an isolated table in the back of the tavern. This was a good sign.

Swenson's description of Daniel Stallinger wasn't terribly accurate, Ragosta thought. The private investigator reported him at six-feet-two inches, but Ragosta put him at six-five—minimum. He also seemed awful skinny; he couldn't weigh much more than one-hundred-sixty pounds or so. The guy was probably one of those health nuts who jogs ten miles a day. Swenson needed to get his eyes checked—the man wasn't even close to one-hundred-ninety pounds.

Stallinger was nervously looking around; he didn't seem to know what to do with his hands—they kept moving between his lap and the table top. He was searching, but not for the person he was supposed to meet. Not staring at anyone in particular he was clearly hoping to flag down a waitress. That was another good sign—he drank to calm his nerves. Ragosta had learned long ago to be wary of men who didn't drink.

He was still dressed in a suit and tie, so Ragosta assumed he didn't bother to go home after work even though he lived only a few miles away. Glancing at his watch, Ragosta saw it was seven-forty-five. The man came early. The assassin remained seated at the bar. He ordered another beer, lit a cigarette and occasionally looked at the apprehensive chief executive of Unlimited Energy Systems. He'd let him sweat for a while; should make his job a little easier.

After eight o'clock, Daniel Stallinger began glancing at this watch every thirty seconds and kept anxiously looking toward the doors of the lounge. Grinning, Ragosta took one last drag, blew the smoke out of the side of his mouth and crushed out the cigarette. Bottle of beer in hand, he approached the chief executive.

Stallinger was looking off toward the door when Ragosta came into his peripheral vision. Snapping his head around, the CEO froze at the sight of the ominous figure approaching him. His black turtleneck sweater, ebony leather sport coat and black slacks accentuated his cold, dark eyes and massive chest. With his clean-shaven expressionless face, the man seemed the embodiment of all that was evil. Stallinger straightened in his chair and with a trembling hand, reached for his liquid courage.

Nick Ragosta could see the color drain from the man's face; he looked as if he would fall to pieces. When he reached the table, the hit man hooked his foot around the leg of a chair and pulled it out. "Mind if I join you?" he asked derisively. He sat down, casually took a sip from his bottle, stared at the CEO for a moment and then said, "My, my, my, Mr. Stallinger. You look as nervous as a whore in church." He then flashed the man a disingenuous smile. According to Swenson, Daniel Stallinger was a Methodist; a very religious man—at least outwardly. Ragosta was hoping the statement would rattle him a bit. It didn't appear to.

Swenson said he was a very intelligent man—that was obvious. He was also quite conservative; reportedly, not much of a risk taker when it came to business. And with the exception of the year 1991, he was a devote husband and father. Ragosta pegged him as a man with all brains and no balls; he should be easy to handle.

Slowly, the assassin's smile melted away and his face turned to stone. As intended, he was clearly intimidating Stallinger with his piercing eyes. This was a tactic Ragosta used on first encounters; it was intended to let the other party know who was running the show.

Stallinger broke eye contact and quickly looked around. Satisfied no one was within earshot he demanded in a hushed, but firm voice, "What the hell is this all about? Who are you?" He tried his best to sound authoritative in the hope that he wouldn't appear frightened. But in truth he was scared to death. Having now met his antagonist, he was certain his attempt at bravado was coming up short.

"Please, relax Mr. Stallinger," Ragosta said calmly.

"Don't tell me what to do!" the executive snapped.

Ragosta gave him an icy stare, smirked, then tilted his head and studied the executive for a moment. After taking a long sip of beer he said in a menacing voice, "Oh, I'll tell you what to do, Mr. Stallinger—and you'll do it." He leaned back a little in his chair, his eyes drilling into the older man. "You best become accustomed to being told what to do by me. Failure to do so will have...*dire* consequences."

Stallinger grimaced and remained silent; he wasn't really sure what to do next. Ragosta continued. "No doubt you're curious as to why I've requested you presents here this evening?"

The executive's face turned sour. "It didn't sound much like a request."

Stallinger had finished his beer and wanted another—his mouth was incredibly dry. He scanned the bar for the waitress but didn't see her. He let out a disappointed sigh.

"Before I get into that, would you like to hear—"

Suddenly, a determined look came across Stallinger's face. He bent forward over the table and bellowed, "Look—whoever you are—let's cut to the chase! What is it you want...money?"

Ragosta let out a burst of laughter. "Money! Ha!" He stared at the executive and smiled mockingly. "You can't give me what you don't have." The CEO visibly deflated. He pursed his lips together and averted his eyes. "*Money*," the assassin quipped sardonically. "*Christ*...a man in your position, you ought to be embarrassed by the condition of your personal finances. How the hell did you become a chief executive anyway?" he added rhetorically.

Stallinger continued to look embarrassed. He crossed his arms over his chest and kept his eyes on his empty bottle of beer. If the man across from him knew about Rhonda, he'd certainly know about the status of his wealth, or lack thereof.

He was nowhere near personal bankruptcy, but given his income history he should have more than half a million in assets and five thousand in the bank. Putting Brett through Yale had taken a devastating toll on his pocketbook. He was further drained by his daughter Kim, who was a senior at Brown and apparently on the seven year graduation plan. To top it off, Melissa, now seventeen, had her heart set on Princeton. And despite his numerous subtle hints, Abby refused to get a job. What the hell *was* he thinking when he purchased the E Class?

If the son-of-a-bitch doesn't want money, I sure as hell don't want to talk about it. "So...what is it you *do* want then?"

Ragosta studied Stallinger somberly for an unnervingly long period of time, causing the executive to shift uncomfortably in his seat. Finally, the hit man narrowed his eyes, leaned forward slightly and said, "It's simple, Mr. Stallinger. I want Unlimited Energy Systems to fail."

The executive gave him a bewildered look; clearly not comprehending what was said. He shook his head and asked incredulously, "You want...*what?*"

The assassin scowled. "Get the shit out of your ears, Stallinger. You heard me. I want UES to fail."

The CEO's jaw dropped and he glared his antagonist in disbelief. Finally he said evenly, "You…want my company to go bankrupt?"

Ragosta sat back and crossed his legs; he looked totally at ease. Calmly he said, "Allow me to clarify, Danny. The bottom line here is that I don't want you to go to market with your product." Seeing the waitress, Ragosta flagged her down. Shocked by the declaration, Stallinger had forgotten about wanting another beer and just continued to stare in disbelief at the malicious man across from him. "Two more please darlin." After the woman acknowledged his order he turned back to the CEO and continued. "Actually, it's not so much UES I want to see fail, but rather its product and the technology behind it." He shrugged indifferently. "I suppose however, if the product doesn't make it, the company's bound to go down with it."

Stallinger sat dumbfounded. Several moments passed before he asked the obvious question. "Why? I…I mean, how could my company's collapse possibly benefit you?"

The waitress came with their beers. She set one in front of the executive, but he was staring so intensely at his antagonist he didn't even notice her or the beer. Ragosta gave the waitress an enchanting smile. "Thank you, sweetheart." He watched her walk away, then turned back to Stallinger and said, "That I won't share with you. All you need to know is that this is what I want. And I want it done clandestinely, slowly—over the next two years or so. I don't want you to raise suspicion within your company, or the industry for that matter."

A flood of questions raced through Stallinger's head, but all he could manage to say at the moment was, "That's impossible…I mean, we're already selling units."

Ragosta let out a patient sigh. "It's far from impossible, Mr. Stallinger. But even if it was, it'd be your job to figure out how to do it. You know your employees, board, customers and investors. You're bright enough to work around them, make the failure look like it's the result of unfortunate events." Ragosta took another sip of beer then added forebodingly, "For your sake, sir, you *will* pull this off successfully. And within the time frame I've outlined. You'll see to it that there will be no investigation as to why UES dissolved, and you'll also ensure that the Security and Exchange Commission doesn't get involved. Your company's demise will be obvious and accepted as legitimate by all concerned. Understood?"

Stallinger looked blankly down at the table and began to shake his head. "I…I," he stammered.

"You what?"

"I can't believe this is happening," Stallinger said to himself.

"Oh, believe it, Danny boy! And one more thing—this is very important" Ragosta locked his dark eyes with the executive's. "Are you paying attention?" Stallinger nodded. "Good. Like I mentioned in your invitation to this evening's little chat, should I learn that you've gone to the police, or even eluded to anybody that you and I have this little scheme going, or drag your feet," his voice turned frighteningly ominous, "the consequences for you will be…most dire." Stallinger's throat went dry; he tried to swallow but couldn't. "I'll be keeping very close tabs on you. If you do what I want, you have nothing to worry about. If you—"

"Wait a minute, I—" Stallinger abruptly stopped. He was so shaken he forgot what he was going to say. He blurted out the first thing that came to mind, "What the hell is your name, anyway?"

Ragosta gave him a condescending look. "You're an idiot! You really think I'd give you my name? You may refer to me as Mr. R."

The CEO then remembered what he was going to say. "Mr. R." He rolled his eyes; the name sounded ridiculous. "Surely you must realize that if UES starts to fail, I'll be booted out—in a New York minute!"

"You'll have to prevent that from happening," Ragosta replied matter-of-factly.

Stallinger didn't acknowledge the remark, he only quickly added, "You said you wanted to see the technology fail. We're not…UES is not, the only company pursuing this technology for commercial gain. There are dozens of companies working on it. Why single out my company?"

Ragosta gave him a slow, calm nod of concurrence. "True…but only two companies are of any real consequence. You let me worry about the competition."

Then, mustering all the courage he could, Stallinger defiantly said, "And if I refuse to cooperate? If I go to the police?"

The assassin gave him a cold smile. Petulantly he retorted, "Ohhhh, Daniel. I can't believe you'd even ask the question. But to satisfy your curiosity I'll tell you. I'll start off slow; make your life miserable. I'm sure Mrs. Stallinger—Abby— would be interested to learn about your affair with Rhonda Beattie back in 91. From what I know about your charming wife, I'm quite confident your marriage would end as a result. And, you know as well as I do, that she'd get custody of Melissa along with generous alimony and child support.

"After that, I'd begin to kill off your family, starting with Mrs. Stallinger. Of course, I'd get to know her much better before I slowly strangle her. Brett would come next, then Kim and Melissa. I must tell you, I'd look forward to the pleasure of intimately acquainting myself with your lovely daughters." Blood began to drain from the executive's face.

"I'd save you for last, of course." He shrugged, "Hell, I might not even kill you. I'd want you to live with the consequences of your foolish decision for as long as possible."

By this point Stallinger had turned completely white. He could actually feel the sweat trickling down the back of his neck.

"There is something you should know about me, Mr. Stallinger. This is what I do for a living, and I'm exceptionally good at it. I've eliminated over thirty people in my career, many of whom were far more important and prominent than you and your family. Most had professional bodyguards. The police, nor anybody else for that matter, could prevent the deaths from happening. Your family would be helpless. And rest assured, I will never be caught." He kept his malicious stare locked on Stallinger then added, "Does that answer your question?"

The Chief Executive Officer of Unlimited Energy Systems nodded and simply replied, "Yes."

With incredible speed Ragosta shot up from his chair and slapped his hand over Stallinger's mouth. Simultaneously, he grasped his right index finger and bent it back until it touched the back of his hand. There was a loud crack followed by Stallinger's muffled scream. Ragosta signaled him to stop yelling by squeezing hard on the man's cheeks.

As quickly as he got up, Ragosta sat back down, scanning the lounge as he did. Executed with such swiftness the brutal act attracted no attention from any of the other customers; the muted cry blending in with the noise of the boisterous patrons. Tears were beginning to stream down Stallinger's face and he gently cradled his wounded hand. His knuckle was shattered, causing him incredible pain. He had to struggle to keep from whimpering.

Completely ignoring Stallinger's agony Ragosta leaned forward, his face forewarning of implacable consequences. In a low growl the assassin said, "You're damn right you're going to cooperate, Mr. Stallinger. You're going to do *exactly* what I say, when I say it. And God help you should I never suspect the slightest amount of hesitation on your part." His visage and intonation with which the warning was delivered was so terrifying that for a moment Stallinger forgot the searing pain in his hand.

Ragosta sat back in his chair with a content expression. He took a few more languid sips of beer then set the bottle down and got to his feet. He threw a twenty on the table and said flatly, "You know what you need to do. I'll expect initial results within the next few months." Gesturing to the executive's finger he added, "You might wanta get that looked at." He smirked, turned and walked out of the bar; leaving the disillusioned CEO of Unlimited Energy Systems holding his painfully deformed hand.

He thought the tulip was a nice touch. When he saw Cynthia Klash walk into the establishment, he donned an disingenuous smile and began to twirl the flower between his thumb and forefinger. Unlike the meeting with Daniel Stallinger, Ragosta made a point to wait until the last minute to enter The Happy Tap; coming in only when he saw Klash's Lexus pull into the parking lot. He was glad he did; the looks he was receiving from some of the male patrons made him sick. He thought about how he'd love to pull out his .44 and end the lives of these miserable, disgusting creatures.

Klash slowly walk into the bar and came to a stop when she saw a man smirking at her and twirling a Tulip. She hesitated for a moment, then frowned and strode defiantly toward the sneering man's booth. Ignoring him, she sat down and using both hands, tucked loose hair behind her ears. She then looked hard Ragosta and said, "So, what are you—some kind of sicko?" Unlike her current temperament, Ragosta thought her voice was surprisingly feminine.

Sill wearing his insincere grin, the assassin extended his arm and offered the CEO of Global Fuel Cell Technologies the flower. She only scoffed at it. He looked around the room for a moment, grimaced menacingly, and then smelling the Tulip said, "I'd say *you're* the sick one, Ms. Klash. You're the one who performs unnatural acts that go against the laws of God and nature, not me."

"Spare me your homophobic rhetoric," she sneered. "What is it you want, Mr...?"

"You may call me Mr. R." Like Stallinger, she rolled her eyes. Ragosta quickly wondered what was so dumb sounding about Mr. R.

"I don't want to call you *"Mr"* at all. You're no gentleman!"

"And what would you know about gentlemen, Ms. Klash?" Ragosta responded playfully.

"I'm married to one," she shot back, then looked around the bar to avoid having to look at him.

"I'm sure it's been twenty-one years of wedded bliss!"

This got her attention. She jerked her head back slightly and gazed at her tormentor with narrowed eyes. *What else did he know?* she wondered. "Yeah, it's been fuckin' great," she said flatly. "What is it you want?"

Like her counterpart at UES, she wasted no time getting to the meat of the matter. All the better for him. He wanted to get the hell out of there and back to

Minnesota for the weekend. He was rather upset that he'd missed the opening of deer hunting. He had no license, but that didn't concern him.

Ragosta was about to answer when a waiter appeared at their table. "Hi, my name is Bruce," he said with the stereotypical lisp. "And I'll be serving you this evening. Can I get you anything?"

"I'll take whatever you've got on tap," Klash replied.

"Gin and tonic," the assassin said.

The waiter jut out his hip. On the verge of insolence he said, "This is a tavern, man. We only have beer and wine."

Ragosta wanted to slap him. "I'll just take a tap—whatever you got," he answered brusquely. The waiter raised his eyebrows apathetically, jotted down the order and walked away. Ragosta watched him leave with revulsion. He then turned back to Klash and continued. "Like I mentioned in the card…" he paused; a charming smile lit up his face. "Did you like the flowers, Cynthia? I thought they were quite beautiful. Expensive too!"

"You were saying?" she replied impatiently, clearly annoyed.

"Last time I send *you* flowers!" he said, playfully feigning wounded feelings. But a moment later he dropped the spurious façade and became gravely serious. "It's quite simple, Ms. Klash. I don't want to see Global Fuel Cell Technologies manufacture and sell fuel cell powertrains. In addition, I want your product discredited—categorized as unfeasible. I want you to foster the belief that fuel cell powertrains are a technology and product that won't be feasible for the next twenty years or more."

She just stared at him blankly for several moments, mouth agape, and then bellowed incredulously, ***"You're joking?"***

"I assure you Ms. Klash, this is no joke," he replied placidly. "I want to see GFCT fold—but not instantly. It must be done gradually, over the next two years. I don't want any investigations sparked by a sudden, dramatic incident."

"Anything else?" she asked mordantly while snatching up her coat and purse. Then, as she began to slide across the vinyl-covered bench to leave the booth she snapped, ***"Fuck you!"***

With astonishing speed he reached across the table and grabbed her right arm. He was incredibly strong. Violently, he pulled her back down with such force she thought her shoulder would pop out of its socket. "Sit down, *bitch!*" he snarled maliciously. "I'm not through with you." Several people in the tavern looked in their direction but apparently thought nothing of the disturbance; they quickly went back to their conversations. Luck was on his side today; for a Friday night the bar was not very crowded.

Ragosta fixed her with a terrifying stare and remained silent for almost a minute. After several moments Klash couldn't stand looking at his cold, dark, lifeless eyes any longer and timidly looked away. She continued to rub her throbbing shoulder and shifted several times in her seat waiting for the man across from her to say something.

Unnerved by his continued silence, she slowly turned her eyes to her tormentor and was shocked by his expression; it lacked any trace of humanity. When he finally spoke, his low, quiet voice was incredibly vicious. "Don't fuck with me, Ms. Klash. We're talking about your life here, and the life of your family. Do as I say, and you will all live. Dismiss me, go to the police, or alert someone who you foolishly think could help you against me, and I assure you retribution will be swift and savage. After your husband and children learn that you're a dike, I'll kill Lenny, Bruce, Steve and Bridget—in that order. I might have some fun with your little girl before I slowly strangle her."

Petrified, Cynthia Klash sat gapping wide-eyed at the fiend threatening her. She couldn't believe this was happening; this wasn't possible. Nothing even remotely like this had ever happened to her. She started when their waiter placed a beer before her; snapping her head up she looked at him with a perplexed expression. But the assassin's eyes never hers. After the waiter left—in a huff because he didn't get so much as a thank you from the couple—Ragosta continued.

"I've done this before—many times, Ms. Klash. It's what I do for a living and I do it exceptionally well. There's not a police precinct in the country or federal agency that knows who I am. I've killed, and will continue to kill if necessary with impunity." As he did with UES's CEO Daniel Stallinger, he lied. He'd never kill or in any way harm a child, but his contracts didn't know that. If he was dealing with a rational person, merely mentioning harm to their children would produce the desired results.

Klash wet herself. All at once her idyllic little world came crashing down around her. Any defiance she harbored instantly vanished as the implications of what she was hearing sunk in. Her mind became a mass of jumbled thoughts and she struggled to concentrate; it took several moments for coherent thought to return.

As he watched her trying to come to grips with the situation, Ragosta thought she'd never get around to the one inevitable and logical question; but finally she did. In a meek and quivering voice she asked, "Wa…wa…why are you doing this?"

"The reason is none of your concern," he replied evenly. "The only thing that matters to me is that you do it, and do it right." The assassin sat back and rested his right arm on top of the booth's backrest and allowed her another minute of thought. He then cheerfully asked, "So, Ms. Klash…I can count on your cooperation then?"

The CEO of Global Fuel Cell Technologies picked up her beer and to Ragosta' amusement, chugged half of it. The alcohol instantly calmed her nerves and she quickly became more loquacious. After guzzling the rest she said, "This will not only ruin GFCT you know…it will ruin me!"

"Not necessarily," her antagonist replied. "It all depends on how you handle it. And how you do I leave up to you; as long as it's accomplished within the guidelines and timetable I'll give you."

Heatedly she replied, "It doesn't matter what I do, you son-of-a-bitch! The end result will be the same. GFCT will have collapsed during my watch."

Ragosta shrugged indifferently. "Then think of it as sacrificing yourself for the greater good."

"Whose greater good?" she shot back.

"Why…*mine*, of course," Ragosta replied arrogantly.

Hearing his reply she scowled, and then gave at him a puzzled look. "You said in the card that you were aware of my ambitions. How do you know what it is I want to do? Did my recruiter talk?"

"He did, but unwittingly I might add. Suffice to say it's also not too difficult to tap land lines or intercept cellular transmissions." He then leaned forward and folded his hands on the table. Impatiently he said, "You still haven't answered my question Ms. Klash. Are you going to cooperate…willingly?" Then looking around he added, "Answer the fucking question, will you. I want to get the hell out of this…cesspool."

Sadly she asked, "What choice do I have?"

"None!"

"You promise not to harm my family…or reveal my secret?"

"I assure you, Ms. Klash, you do as I say and you'll have nothing to worry about from me. But rest assured that I'll be watching you very closely. *Very* closely. I'll be monitoring everything you do. Don't try anything cute, or all bets are off." With that, he got up and quickly walked out of the bar. Klash flagged down the waiter and ordered another beer. As he turned to leave, she changed it to a boilermaker.

"Christ," Ragosta said nonchalantly with a wave of his hand, "they folded like a cheap card table." Reclining on the couch in Haggerty's office, he stretched and scratched at the four-day's worth of stubble on his face. If he hadn't bagged a deer over the weekend he would have been furious at having to fly back to Washington D.C. to report on his contact with Stallinger and Klash. But he'd agreed to the protocol before taking the job. Like communicating with The Committee, all interactions between he, Haggerty and Beach would be done face-to-face and at a secure location. As a consequence, he'd flown to the nation's capital this morning having put forth little effort to clean himself up—much to the consternation of those around him in the first class cabin.

"I trust we can expect no trouble from them then? They will do as you instructed, and in the time required?" Haggerty asked, seated behind his desk with a coffee cup clasped in both hands. It was a bright, sunny day and late morning sunshine poured through the window behind Haggerty causing Ragosta to squint.

The assassin got up off the couch and dropped the shade. "No doubt in my mind, Laurence," he replied as he went back to the sofa to resume his reclined position. Rubbing his eyes he asked, "Who will you have watching them in case they do decide to wander off course?"

"Two men named Pascheck and Maltese," Sandra answered. "They both come highly recommended by Mike Swenson, our P.I." She was sitting on the edge of Haggerty's desk, one leg wrapped behind the other with her arms folded across her chest. Despite the amount of time she'd spent with him, she still was not comfortable around the hit man.

"Competent?" Ragosta asked.

Haggerty frowned, but said nothing. Sandra gave her boss a quick glance; she was aware that Haggerty wasn't terribly keen on any recommendation from Swenson. She nodded affirmation to the assassin. "Swenson vouches for them and I interviewed them myself. They seem pretty sharp. Both experts at electronic surveillance. They'll work off existing taps on GFCT's and UES' lines, ready to remove and replace them at a moment's notice."

"What about their residences?" Haggerty asked.

Sandra nodded. "Both covered, including their cell phones and those of their spouses."

Her boss took a sip of coffee and added, "Of course, these two guys don't know why they've been hired to monitor these two executives, but they know what to listen for." If in doubt, they'll tape the conversation and we'll have it in our hands within an hour."

With a grunt, Ragosta switched from a reclining position to a sitting one. Leaning forward with his forearms on the top of his thighs he turned his head toward Sandra and asked, "Who is handling whom?"

"Maltese is watching Klash and Pascheck, Stallinger. Both know to contact you immediately should they suspect their charge is trying to pull something."

"Good," Ragosta said with a nod of his head.

Haggerty set his cup of coffee down, stood up and walked around to the front of his desk. Like he always did before making what he considered an important statement, he clasped his hands behind his back. Raising his eyebrows and clucking his tongue against the roof of his mouth he said in a slightly elevated tone, "Well, the game is on and there's no turning back now. Larry has been executed flawlessly...thank you." Sandra smiled but Ragosta remained impassive. "Let's all head home and have a nice Thanksgiving. Plan on meeting back here on December first for the execution of Moe and Curly."

The thought of going home for Thanksgiving only appealed to Haggerty; he'd be spending it with his daughter, Julie, and his son-in-law Steve in Cheyenne, Wyoming. Recently married, Julie told her father they'd also intended on inviting her mother and her little brother Ted. Haggerty wasn't thrilled with the prospect of seeing his ex-wife again, and suspected this was his daughter's way of trying to make peace between them. It wouldn't work, of course, but he and Carrie could be civil to each other for a day or so.

But Sandra Beach and Nick Ragosta had no one to spend the time with. Ragosta had been alone for so long the holidays no longer made him melancholy. He'd spend the time in Las Vegas gambling and partaking in his favorite hobby other than fishing and hunting—trying to bed rich, lonely women.

Sandra longed to see Wendell during the holiday; she knew she'd be terribly lonely. He said he wanted to see her too, but naturally had to spend it with his family. She understood, but she was also becoming frustrated by the lack of progress she was making in creating a rift between him and his wife. Subtle suggestions that she would be a better all-around mate weren't working, even though she'd flatly pointed out several times that as he had a prenuptial agreement with his wife, he had nothing to lose. He wasn't biting. It may be time for a more aggressive approach.

CHAPTER 7

▼

"How soon do you think you could arrange a meeting?" Haggerty asked his old friend Senator Pat Wheeler. He'd called Pat and offered to buy him lunch, and didn't conceal the fact that he had a favor to ask of him. Pat could arrange an audience with the one senator and two congressmen targeted for Curly far more expeditiously than the owner of Noble Consultants could going through normal channels. A veteran senator, Wheeler was well-respected and liked on the hill, and was known for his cordial relationship with members of Congress on both sides of the aisle. If he asked, most lawmakers would clear their schedule to accommodate a visit by him or one of his friends.

"What's this about, Laurence?" Wheeler asked after swallowing a mouthful of Cobb Salad. Pointing his fork as Haggerty and twirling it around in little circles he added, "I mean, they will want to know the topic of discussion so they can be prepared and all."

Haggerty hesitated. He wasn't sure how best to answer the question. Pat knew what Noble Consultants did; as a matter of fact, Haggerty had the senator to thank for his current lot in life. It was Senator Pat Wheeler who gave him the idea for his specialized firm. However, what the lawmaker didn't know was how diversified Noble Consultant had become, progressing from industrial espionage to industrial sabotage. Adding to his concerns, Wheeler was a senator from New York. Haggerty didn't want him to know that one of the targets, a company with incredible potential to create thousands of jobs and generate huge tax revenue, was located in his state.

Haggerty cleared his throat. "It has to do with saving jobs for their constituents." He was pleased with the answer he'd just thought up; in his mind it was a truthful statement. "I've learned of several companies in their districts that are in the process of outsourcing. There're only in the initial planning stages now, so it's not too late to act."

"Where are the jobs going be outsourced?" the senator asked.

"Mainly India and China," Haggerty replied. "I want to make a pitch for my services. Offer to develop arguments for keeping the jobs in the United States; give them ammunition to approach the corporation's influential board members; perhaps persuade them to reconsider."

Wheeler accepted the answer with a nod of his head. "You think these three representatives will be able to come up with enough money to hire your firm?"

Haggerty smiled. "I intent to show them that they can't afford *not* to hire me. Not if they want to be reelected that is."

Wheeler pursed his lips and gave Haggerty a slight nod of his head, then took another bite of his salad.

"So, Pat...when can you arrange the first meeting?"

The senator wiped his mouth and placed the napkin back on his lap. "Well, I know Senator Plecha is still on vacation, but I think he's back next week. He'll probably be the most amicable to your proposal. Christ, jobs are vanishing from Michigan at an alarming rate. This is going to make reelection for him pretty goddamn tough—and he knows it. Particularly since he's being labeled by the opposition as tight with the Bush administration. If he can stop even one company from outsourcing, he'll look like a hero."

Haggerty looked at his Franklin Planner. Laura, his executive assistant, had been trying to convince him to dump the prehistoric spiral notebook organizer and switch to a modern electronic Palm Pilot. But he refused; arguing that if he threw his Franklin Planner against the wall, it would still work. "See if you can arrange for me to meet with Senator Plecha on Tuesday, December eleventh." Wheeler nodded his head and entered the date in his Palm Pilot. "What about Congresswoman Zwart from Ohio?" Haggerty added.

The senator shrugged. "Don't know. But I'll give her office a call later on this afternoon and let you know." He added another note to his Palm Pilot and stuffed it in his shirt pocket. "However, I'm meeting with Congressman Radakovich after lunch. I can probably arrange for you to meet with him in the next day or so. Want me to set it up that soon?"

"Absolutely," Haggerty replied. "The sooner the better."

"Fine. I'll give you a call after I meet with him." Pat Wheeler stood up and extended his hand. "I've got to run now, Laurence. Thanks for lunch."

"No. Thank you, Pat!" Haggerty stood and shook his friend's hand. "I really appreciate your help." The senator waved him off as if it were no trouble at all and left the restaurant.

Haggerty sat back down and placed his credit card on the table. As he waited for the waiter to close him out, he reached in his briefcase and pulled out the extensive information Sandra, with the help of Mike Swenson, had compiled on Congressman Richard Radakovich of North Carolina.

What a shitty little town, Ragosta thought to himself as he drove into Lake Rapids, Michigan. He was in a foul mood. His flights were late and his car rental reservations were lost. He'd requested a Lincoln Town Car, but at this time of night all they had left was a Ford Mustang. He wasn't tall, but he still felt terribly cramped in the little sports car. All he'd need now to top off the day was a crappy hotel room. Given what he observed as he drove down the main street of Lake Rapids, that was a certainty. The most modern building must have been erected before the stock market crash of 1929.

He'd given it quite a bit of thought and decided he'd handle UES' and GFCT's vendors differently than he handled the CEO's of the two fuel cell companies. He didn't know a lot about how business was conducted, but reasoned that CEO's—like military officers or even paid assassins for that matter—shared common bonds amongst their peers. Given the critical relationship at this point in time between the fuel cell companies and their vendors, the CEO's must talk occasionally. Working under the assumption that this theory was correct, why take the risk that something might inadvertently be said when they talked? Something that would trigger recognition of a common dilemma, leading to a desire for deeper probing? Although he was confident that he'd sufficiently frightened Klash and Stallinger, it's only human nature to think you can outsmart an adversary. The sequence of events that could occur with a slip of the tongue might be beyond his ability effectively control.

Mike Swenson had compiled the report on Flexible Sealing Solutions and its parent company, Flexible Tubing Technologies. Reading the information, it was clear whom to target. A gentleman by the name of David Greene appeared to be the perfect choice. He had both the ear and trust of the owner, Donald Kampnel, and substantial influence over the general managers of both FSS and FTT.

Laurence Haggerty trusted Mike Swenson and obviously thought him competent. But for reasons unknown never had many good things to say about the private detective. Since taking on this job, Ragosta had come to admire the man's work. He provided fact along with gut instincts that were proving to be damned accurate. Ragosta had only talked with Swenson a couple of times; there usually was no reason to contact him because the private investigator's written reports where so complete and detailed no question was left unanswered.

However, out of professional curiosity he did ask the P.I. once how he obtained his information so quickly and accurately. He was surprised to learn it wasn't through surveillance, research, or any other method Ragosta would have consider standard practice. But rather through money. Swenson commented that even he was astounded at how effective simple bribes could be. Wave money under someone's nose, tell them you need the information for a potential lawsuit against the company, and for the price of a tank of gas most employees were more than willing to spill their guts. This method of intelligence-gathering was particularly effective in a podunk little town like Lake Rapids, where the preferred past time for most residents was drinking tap beer at one of the town's two dilapidated bars.

Swenson obtained most of his information on Greene from Donald Kampnel's executive secretary, Judith McCandish. A divorced mother of two, Ms. McCandish voluntarily supplied far more information than Swenson asked for. She apparently was venting frustration over the fact that like most companies, FTT was cutting back on employees and those left standing were required to take on more work. Of course, they weren't paid for it. With few other employers in the area, she had no choice but to, in her own words, "Bend over and take it in the ass." Reading that in the report, Ragosta chuckled; Judith was his kind of woman.

To collaborate and verify the accuracy of the information supplied by the animated executive secretary, Swenson also spoke with an accountant by the name of Gordon Gallup. Like McCandish, the young controller wasn't terribly impressed with Green's style of management. The private investigator wrote that at the mention of Greene's name, the first thing the accountant did was scowl bitterly.

The picture the two FTT employees painted of Greene was not flattering. An arrogant, self-important micro manager who, in the words of Gallup, "Doesn't know half of what he thinks he does." They did however, give him credit for being very intelligent, silver-tongued and a master of office politics.

Reading between the lines and based on his employment history, Ragosta pegged David Greene as a survivor. He'd held numerous managerial positions for a variety of companies over the years, his tenure at any one company only about two to three years. But with FTT it looked like he was setting a longevity record. It was Ragosta's guess that Greene had struck pay-dirt with Flexible Tubing Technologies. He'd finally found an owner who wasn't catching on to him—one that wasn't bright enough, or refused to believe that he was being manipulated; and Greene was milking it for all it was worth. And why not? At fifty-three years of age he still had considerable time to put in before retirement.

Because he still had two other vendors to manipulate, Ragosta didn't want to spend any more time in Lake Rapids than was absolutely necessary. With Greene, he was going to take a direct approach. Tomorrow, he'd wake early and drive to Greene's home outside of Muskegon. He'd then follow him to his office at FTT, and back home again in the afternoon. If Greene used the same route both ways—like most people he probably would—an area would be chosen for contact. In a couple of days, he should be on his way to Lawrence, Kansas.

He closed his eyes and forced himself to take a deep breath. He hadn't felt this apprehensive in years. *Why am I so nervous?* Haggerty silently asked himself. "I'm ready," he mumbled. "I'm ready!" He had gone over the statistics more times than he cared to admit. He wanted to be prepared and sound indisputably credible when he made his case to the congressman from North Carolina. He also had to be concise. Pat Wheeler informed him that Richard Radakovich was happy to meet with him, but because of a number of pressing commitments, could only spare the president of Noble Consultants thirty minutes of his time. But that should be enough.

Waiting outside the congressman's office and poring over the figures yet again, Haggerty shook his head and thought how the data even frightened him, and he couldn't care less about the economy of North Carolina. If he laid out his case properly, he couldn't imagine Radakovich not supporting him.

The office door opened and a pretty young woman with a lovely southern accent peered around the door. "The congressman will see you now, Mr. Haggerty."

Immediately, his anxiety caused a sharp, but brief cramp to shoot through his stomach. "Thank you," he replied, stuffing the documents he was reviewing back into his briefcase. He stood and smoothed out his suit jacket. The secretary held the door open for him and gave him a smile as he passed her. He had to appear confident, he thought to himself as he approached the congressman's desk.

By congressional standards Radakovich's office was small, reflecting his status as a junior member of congress. Not surprisingly, it lacked a window. But the congressman made good use of his walls, tastefully covering them with a mixture of personal and professional pictures. Like all institutions with history and tradition, congress had its protocols, Haggerty thought. First term lawmakers didn't get the perks until they paid their dues.

"Congressman Radakovich, thank you for seeing me on such short notice," Haggerty said with sincere gratitude while extending his hand. He was a little surprised at how youthful Radakovich looked. He knew the lawmaker was young, but he looked far younger than his thirty-nine years.

Rising from behind his desk, the congressman smiled, grasped Haggerty's hand firmly and said, "I regret that I don't have a great deal of time to give you, Mr. Haggerty."

"I understand that, congressman. I appreciate any time you can give me."

Radakovich sat back down in his chair, leaned back a little and interlaced his fingers over his stomach. "So, Mr. Haggerty, what can I do for the president of Noble Consultants? I understand this visit has something to do with job retention in my district."

"Yes, it does," Haggerty replied uneasily; he was surprised at how nervous he still was. The success of this meeting was crucial. If he failed, he'd most likely fail with Congresswoman Zwart and Senator Plecha also. He had to convince the lawmaker from North Carolina that the fuel cell threat was both real and imminent. "Your district and those of several of your colleagues."

The congressman looked away from Haggerty and sighed. Turning back to his visitor he said with a sad expression, "I'm doing everything I can to stem the loss of manufacturing jobs from my district, but it's an extremely difficult situation— as I'm sure you know. Hell...I'm practically begging the board members of some of the largest employers in my district to reconsider what they're euphemistically calling *reorganization.* Promising tax cuts, infrastructure improvements and other incentives I doubt I can actually provide.

"But," he shrugged, "I certainly see their side of the story. If company B moves to a country with drastically lower labor rates, no environmental or safety regulations and in particular no unions, and company A doesn't, in a relatively short amount of time company A will not be able to compete with company B.

"End of story; company A ceases to exist. And if company A goes bankrupt, it will fold with the loss of *all* jobs, both blue and white collar. Moving manufacturing to say, China, and keeping corporate functions here in the United States, we at least save some jobs." Lifting his thumbs from the locked hands on his belly he added, "That's the way I see it." He looked at something on the floor for a moment, then continued. "I...I know that's little comfort for those out of work—but we have to face reality."

Before Haggerty could respond, Radakovich said, "Amazing, isn't it? Back in the eighties, manufacturing companies—particularly automotive—were flocking to the south. Ostentatiously, they admitted it was for the lower labor rates and to escape demanding and unreasonable unions. Shit, I paid my way through college by working third shift on an assembly line making car lights. Ten short years later they ran to Mexico," Radakovich shook his head in dismay. "Now, even Mexico is considered an area with high labor costs. Where does it end?"

Haggerty shook his head in empathy. "I don't know, congressman. But what I'm here to talk to you about is the loss of jobs on a massive scale. So large in fact, that the loss your district has experienced for the last few years will seem like a trickle."

The lawmaker sat forward and folded his hands on his cluttered desk. "I'm listening," he said; his expression turning intense.

Haggerty's eyes, locked with the congressman's, they narrowed a bit as he prepared to deliver his next statement. It had to be put delicately, so he'd rehearsed it many times. It was imperative that he come across as neutral in both voice and expression, or he ran the risk of alienating Radakovich. Unpretentiously he said, "It's my understanding, congressman, that you're an advocate of fuel cell technology."

Radakovich nodded his head. "Yes...of course I am," he replied with a touch of enthusiasm. "So is everybody who understands the technology. Anybody in their right mind can see that fuel cells hold incredible potential for this country—and everywhere else for that matter. As I see it, there's no down side to a hydrogen economy."

Haggerty grimaced and shook his head gravely. "Oh, but there is, Mr. Radakovich. A very big down side."

The lawmaker scratched the back of his neck. "*Really?* How so?" he asked earnestly.

Haggerty was relieved by the tone of the congressman's reply; he appeared open-minded. *School's in session*, he thought to himself. "Congressman..." he began soberly. "Have you given any thought to the ramifications of this technology? The short or long term effects?"

Radakovich shook his head. "No, not really...because everything I've heard or read about it is positive—both from an economic and environmental standpoint."

"I'd hazard to guess that most of the information you've received is from the industry's lobby?"

The congressman nodded, "That, and various scientific journals. However, I admit I've been out of touch with what the industry's been up to lately."

Cautiously, Haggerty said, "Surely, you realize that the information you've received is biased; slanted in favor of the fuel cell industry." He hoped he didn't sound too baleful.

Radakovich looked conspicuously at his guest. "The thought had occurred to me, Mr. Haggerty. I'm really not that naive."

"Of course not," Haggerty quickly replied in apologetic concurrence.

"But the scientific data I do take at face value."

Haggerty hesitated for a moment, and then decided it was time to jump in with both feet. "Congressman Hanson's zero emission bill currently on the floor…you may want to seriously consider dropping your support for it. As a matter of fact, it's imperative that you do. You'll also want to encourage as many of your fellow lawmakers as possible to drop their support."

As he said this, Haggerty watched Radakovich's expression flashed from shock to skepticism to incredulousness. He finally settled on a look of amused curiosity. Peering at his guess with unfeigned interest he asked, "And why would I want to do that, Mr. Haggerty?"

Laurence Haggerty dropped his head to give the appearance of deep deliberation. A few seconds later he looked Radakovich in the eye and said with grave seriousness, "Have you ever given any thought, sir, to how dependent your constituents are—and for that matter literally everybody else in this country—on the internal combustion engine? What would happen to the economy of your district, North Carolina and the United States should the internal combustion engine disappear in a matter of a few short years?"

The congressman stared solemnly at the consultant who could clearly see the wheels turning in the lawmaker's head. Haggerty reached into his briefcase and pulled out several documents. Looking at one of them he said, "In your district alone, Mr. Radakovich, there are twenty seven companies that supply engine related components to the automotive industry: Raleigh Coil, Zender Industries, Tashman Automotive, Ale LLC, Stonebridge castings, Precision Seal and Gasket, and twenty one others. These companies alone employ over thirty thousand people, or approximately twenty eight percent of your constituents."

The intercom cracked with the pleasant voice of Radakovich's secretary. "Excuse me, Congressman. Governor Touton is on line two."

Without taking his apprehensive eyes off Haggerty he said, "Tell the governor I'll call him back."

"He say's it's urgent, sir."

"Trisha, *tell* him I'll call him back," the lawmaker responded irritably.

"Ahhh…yes, sir," the young woman replied timidly.

Haggerty's confidence soared. He had Radakovich concerned enough to defer an urgent call from North Carolina's governor. He continued as if the interruption hadn't taken place. "But there's more...much more, congressman. Now, think about the other industries affected by the internal combustion engine. Lubricant, coolant and additive manufacturers, of which your state has three—four hundred and eight people. Belt manufacturers—two, one in your district—fifty eight people. Three manufacturers of fasteners, nuts and bolts, one in district 4A—twenty four people. Pulp fiber manufacturers, four in North Carolina, one in your district—six hundred and ninety people. Distributors—sixteen statewide, two in district 4A—forty seven people.

"As we continue to look down the chain," Haggerty continued without taking a breath, "we have the quick oil change establishments, tire and repair shops, auto parts stores. Not to mention all the other people within your district whose livelihoods depend on the employees of these businesses: Dry cleaners, retail stores, restaurants, gas stations, health care professionals, convenience stores...I could go on, but I believe you get the picture. As you see, this is an *enormous* economic food chain."

The congressman was clearly taken aback by what he was hearing. Haggerty knew Radakovich, like most people, had never given much thought to the true impact the internal combustion engine—the automotive industry in general—has on the entire economy. Deep in thought, the congressman sat motionless, looking blankly through the consultant on the other side of his desk.

"All told," Haggerty continued, "I calculate over seventy-seven percent of your constituents are totally dependant on these industries—sixty four statewide." He paused for effect. "When you give it some thought—of how much of our economy is centered around the internal combustion engine—it's..." Haggerty shook his head. "Well...it's nothing less than staggering! Frightening really."

Radakovich remained in silent contemplation; sucking in his lower lip and looking off into the distance. Some moments later he said with a trace of astonishment, "*Shit!* I ah...I never considered fuel cell technology's impact from that perspective."

"Most people wouldn't," Haggerty replied bluntly. "I assume, sir, that you have political ambitions that extent beyond congressman for district 4A?" Radakovich said nothing; he didn't have to; his expression answered the question. "What do you think your chances are for re-election with over seventy percent of your constituents out of work?" Drolly he added, "I'm going to go out on a limb and say...not good."

The congressman's embittered face lightened a bit and he shot back, "But the fuel cell industry will *create* jobs! Jobs that will stay in this country long after you and I are dead." His face soured again at the statement's lack of conviction—Radakovich realized he couldn't even convince himself.

"True," Haggerty replied evenly. "But, most likely they'll be created where the fuel cell manufacturers are located now—at least initially—Massachusetts, New York, New Jersey, Connecticut, basically the northeast. And it's important to keep in mind that the industry will only create a fraction of the jobs. Unlike the internal combustion engine, a fuel cell is a relatively simple device with far fewer components.

"Of course, like the fuel cell manufacturers themselves, the component suppliers could possibly unionize and create an incentive to move operations elsewhere, like they moved to the south in the eighties. However, I have a feeling the unionized people in the north have learned their lesson. Starting out in what will essentially be a new automotive industry, I don't think they'll have that union mentality of *the world owes me a living*. They'll be much more reasonable to work with."

The lawmaker was silent again, his mind racing while his eyes remained fixed on Haggerty. He suddenly took on a defiant look. He leaned over his desk a little toward his visitor. Slowly shaking his head he said, "This is all hypothetical...academic, Mr. Haggerty. What you say may well be true, but fuel cell vehicles aren't going to appear on the streets overnight. It will take *years* before they begin to replace conventional automobiles in significant numbers."

"I wouldn't count on that, congressman. The fuel cell manufacturers are farther along—much farther along—than they've let on. As we speak, they're negotiating contracts with the big three, along with two Japanese and one European car maker. The automotive companies aren't stupid—they see the writing on the wall. Already the press is starting to criticize the gluttony of SUV's and gas prices will only continue climb in one direction. And, thanks to Congressman Hanson's legislation, once the general public sees a lot of these vehicles on the road—running cheaply and dependably—interest will skyrocket; no question of it."

Radakovich sat tight-lipped for a moment. Then, still trying to sound skeptical he asked, "What about the infrastructure to support these vehicles; where are people going to purchase hydrogen fuel?"

Haggerty was prepared for that question. "Hanson's zero emissions bill proposes that the automotive fleets of all federal agencies be powered by fuel cells no later than 2008, correct?"

"That's right," the lawmaker responded with a nod.

"As you may recall, there's been an amendment added—little publicized—requiring state-run garages to install reformers. Reformers take natural gas, propane, whatever, and convert it to pure hydrogen fuel called refromate The same idea is being proposed for supplying refromate to the general public; installing reformers at existing gas stations. So...an infrastructure can quickly be put in place—easily and at little cost.

"Are you aware of the fact that there's a company developing what's called a Home Energy Base?" The lawmaker shook his head. "This particular company has teamed up with a Japanese automaker to develop a duel-purpose fuel cell system. One that will supply electricity and heat to a home along with the hydrogen refromate needed for the family fuel cell car. The owner will be able to fuel his car at home. I've got to give um credit; it's quite an ingenious idea."

Congressman Radakovich leaned back in his chair again and eyed the consultant suspiciously. With a slightly tilted head and narrowed eyes he asked guardedly, "Why are you telling me this, Mr. Haggerty? Pat Wheeler told me you're not affiliated with any lobby or special interest group, and represent no client. But I'm finding that hard to believe. Have you an axe to grind with the fuel cell industry or something?"

Slightly frowning, Haggerty slowly shook his head to indicate the statement couldn't be further from the truth. "Not at all, congressman. I'm also hoping to make this same pitch to Senator Plecha and Congresswoman Zwart. Like you, Zwart represents constituents who are highly dependent on the automotive industry—internal combustion engines to be precise—for their livelihood. As you know, Plecha represents Michigan in the Senate. I trust that by the time I leave, you'll be convinced of the threat this industry poses to your district, and...your political career."

Radakovich put on a sinister little grin and said light-heartedly, "You'd make a good politician, Mr. Haggerty. You dodged the question quite well."

Haggerty forced a chuckle. "I assure you congressman, I have no political ambitions."

Gesturing with his hands the lawmaker said, "The question still stands, Mr. Haggerty. Why are you telling me, and eventually Mr. Plecha and Ms. Zwart this? What have you possibly to gain? I know I'm relatively new to congress, but I wasn't in Washington two minutes before I learned that nobody in this town does anything for anybody for nothing." He leaned forward in his chain again. "So...what is it? What's in it for you, Mr. Haggerty?"

The congressman's intense eyes were burning into Haggerty; causing the consultant to feel apprehensive again. He cursed himself; with all his preparation he should've anticipated being asked about motive and was now astounded the thought never once occurred to him. It took a moment for him to brush aside his anxiety and formulate what he hoped would be a plausible response. Donning his most sincere smile, he sighed, shifted in his seat and replied, "You're right, of course. I do anticipate profiting by providing this information to you and the others. But it will not be financial gain—at least not at this point in time.

"In this business—like so many others—success rides on who you know and your capability to network." He shrugged. "Who knows what the future holds?

"I'll be frank, Mr. Radakovich; what I hope to obtain from this is your friendship. By now you must realize that the information I've just provided you is of great value. It's of absolutely of no importance to me. But it can—and *will* if you act—enhance your political fortunes. Whether you stay in the house, run for senate or governor of North Carolina, the loss of so many jobs so quickly will end your political career. By providing this information to you I'm doing you a favor; hopefully winning your trust and amity. Someday, I may ask you, or need you, to return it. When in business for yourself, the benefit of having friends in political office can't be underestimated. The fact that I'm here now is testimony to that."

Congressman Radakovich said nothing and only stared at the president of Noble Consultants for an uncomfortably long period of time. Haggerty was pleased with his impromptu response and tried to show his conviction by keeping his eyes locked with those of the congressman. But the man's face was beginning to show doubt, and the ex-attorney briefly feared that his answer didn't convince the young politician.

Eventually, any misgivings Radakovich was harboring seemed to fade away. Stroking his chin he said, "Had you come here of your own accord, Mr. Haggerty, I would be hard pressed to believe and trust your motives. But the fact that you have the endorsement of Pat Wheeler, that gives me the comfort level I need."

A wave of relief wash over Laurence Haggerty; and for the first time since he'd sat down he felt relaxed enough to lean back in his chair and crossed his legs. Trying to sound indifferent, Haggerty cautiously asked, "So…I assume you'll withdraw your support for the zero emissions bill?"

Radakovich grimaced. "I'm not prepared to say that…yet. But if what you say is true—and I'll want to verify your data—then yes, without a doubt. I'll not only drop my support, I'll lobby hard to persuade others in the house to do the same."

Haggerty leaned forward; eagerly he handed his documents over to Congressman Radakovich. "I'm confident you'll find my data accurate. I, and my assistant have double-checked everything." He stood and extended his hand. "I've taken enough of your time, congressman. Thank you."

Radakovich stood and took his hand. "If this data pans out," he raised the documents in his left hand, "you can call me Rich."

Haggerty flashed him a smile and left the office.

Ragosta cringed and spit the coffee back into the cup. He should've stopped at McDonald's. He didn't understand why everybody raved over Starbuck's Coffee; it was expensive and tasted like shit—regardless of how much sugar was poured into it. Setting the coffee aside, he looked at the majestic house about a block away.

David Greene and his family lived in Muskegon's only exclusive neighborhood. Located on a beautifully wooded cul-de-sac, Ragosta thought the picturesque two-story colonial couldn't have been built more than a few years ago. With his retirement looming, Ragosta was beginning to think of the features he'd like to build into his retirement home. He would've loved to take a walk-through Greene's house for ideas. Very shortly, he and the FTT executive would become acquainted; but somehow the assassin didn't think an invitation from Greene to stop by for tea and crumpets would be forthcoming.

Parked down the street and just around a corner, Ragosta couldn't miss seeing Greene's light gray BMW back out of the driveway. Both his quarry and the geography of Western Michigan were making his job easy. Following the executive yesterday, Ragosta had spotted several locations that would serve his purpose nicely. Most of Green's commute was rural, and these back roads had little traffic.

A few minutes before seven-thirty Ragosta saw Greene's garage door begin to open. The BMW emerged and slowly drove out of the subdivision. Hardly touched, Ragosta gladly dumped his coffee out the window. He didn't want to risk staining his cloths should the coffee bounce out of the cup holder. Keeping about a quarter-mile distance, the assassin began to follow Greene. The area he'd chosen for contact was only about ten minutes away.

Because of the distance between them, on two separate occasions another car got between the pursued and the pursuer, but luckily the vehicles quickly turned onto other roads. Those cars wouldn't have prevented the assassin from completing the contact, but they certainly would have complicated his task.

After crossing a small bridge and turning a sharp corner, Ragosta put the Mustang's accelerator to the floor. Predictably, the rental car's acceleration left much to be desired. For cost and safety reasons, rental fleets equipped the little sports cars with smaller, almost wimpy V6 engines. Ragosta couldn't understand why

Ford would denigrate one of their showcase vehicles by providing the option of such a derisory powerplant. But this wasn't a problem; he had taken the car's lack of muscle into consideration when working out timing.

Thirty seconds later he was passing Greene, who, being the courteous driver he was, pulled slightly to the right to allow the rapidly approaching vehicle to comfortably overtake him. The instant he passed Greene, Ragosta pulled in front the executive's BMW and slammed on the brakes. To limit the damage to Greene's car, Ragosta, watching from the rear view mirror, let up on the brakes as soon as he saw they were about to collide.

Ragosta smiled; he could tell by the gentle jolt that any damage to Greene's car should be minimal. He pulled over to the side of the road next to a heavily wooded area and watched through the rear view mirror as the light gray BMW pulled up behind him. The moment the car came to a stop the driver's door flew open and Ragosta's eyebrows arched in alarm. David Greene looked a hell of a lot bigger than reported; for a moment the assassin wondered if he had the wrong man.

Through his side view mirror, Ragosta saw a figure that was at least six-three, two-hundred-fifty pounds. He breathed a little easier when he saw a sizeable paunch at the beltline. Nevertheless, this guy could cause him more trouble than anticipated. He made a mental note to have a chat with Swenson—this was the first time he was really off the mark. Steeling himself, Ragosta put on a malicious face and stepped out of his car.

"WHAT THE HELL DO YOU THINK YOU'RE DOING?" Greene screamed as he stormed up to the Mustang. His Scottish accent almost made his angry outburst sound comical. The assassin shoved his hands in his pockets and stood next to his car, emotionless. The large man stopped several feet from him, and then spun to look at the damage to his BMW. Ragosta glanced at it too and was surprised at how extensive it was—far more than he'd intended. But the BMW was certainly drivable and that's all he really cared about.

Enraged, Greene turned back to the man in the black turtleneck and sport coat, the lapels of his suite and his shinny blue tie gently swayed in the breeze as he bellowed, *"WHY THE FUCK DID YOU HIT YOUR BRAKES?"*

Ragosta remained silent; he shot Greene a supercilious look then turned to watch a car slow down, stare at them, and then speed up. No blood, no gore, no reason to stop. Rubberneckers—he hated them with a passion.

Maddened by the lack of response, Greene clenched his teeth, stepped up to the arrogant son-of-a-bitch and grabbed his arm—he'd get the bastard's attention. *"I ASKE—"*

With incredible speed, Ragosta seized Greene's wrist in a vice-like grip, twisted his arm and spun him around, ramming the limb up past his shoulder blades and almost lifting him off his feet. Greene let out a cry as much from surprise as pain. As he shoved the executive against the side of the Mustang he pulled out his .44 and thrust it against Greene's temple.

"Know what that is against you head?" the assassin whispered into the big man's ear. Greene was so shocked all he managed to do was nod his head with a grunt. "Good! You're a smart guy. Now, start walking quickly into the woods. Make a false move and I'll blow your head off. Compendia?"

"Yeah," the executive cried out in pain.

Ragosta yanked on his arm, pulling him off the car. He then turned the big man toward the woods and shoved him hard. Greene stumbled forward a few steps. "Start moving!"

The executive almost tripped twice while cutting though the underbrush. The hit man prodded him a few times with the barrel of his pistol, telling him to speed it up. When they were about fifty yards into the trees they came to a small clearing and Ragosta told him to stop and turn around. Keeping the .44 pointed at his captive, he studied David Greene for several moments. He then quickly covered the distance between them, shoved the pistol under the executive's chin and pushing him up against a tree. Greene's eyes, filled with terror, darted up and down between the gun against his neck and the black, lifeless eyes drilling into him. He was beginning to sweat profusely, from both the short hike to the clearing and fear—he was petrified.

Beginning to hyperventilate and tremble, Greene cried out in a shaky voice, "Oh God…please, please don't kill me! *Please!* I'm…I'm sorry I hit you!"

"Shut the fuck up!" Ragosta snapped irritably. Greene immediately complied; his wide, frightened eyes locked on his tormentor. "Listen up, *David*," he snarled the name with contempt. "I'm only going to say this once. You, your wife…and your daughter are dead. You're all going to die if you don't do as I say." Keeping his pistol presses hard against Greene's neck, he quickly scanned the area around him. "I don't have time to talk now, but I'm going to call you. I'm going to call you this afternoon at your office, precisely at two. You'd better fucking pick up the phone on the first ring." Ragosta pushed the .44 even harder into the soft tissue of the executive's neck. "After you pick up the phone you're going to listen, and listen closely because your life, and the life of your family depend on it. Do I make myself clear?" Greene swallowed hard and nodded. "Good. And one more thing, *David*; if you do anything foolish like call the police, tap the phone or tell anybody, and I mean *anybody*, about our little chat here, you and yours will die. It's that simple. Are you still with me?"

"Y…y…yes," the executive stammered weakly in a dry voice.

The assassin slowly dropped his gun but continued to hold Greene firmly against the tree. The big man mumbled a *"thank God"* when Ragosta put the pistol back in his shoulder holster.

The tension in the executive's body began to diminish some as Ragosta gradually pulled his arm off David Greene, who closed his eyes and let out a sigh of relief as soon as he felt the arm leave his body. Then, without warning, the assassin grabbed the big man by the shoulders and with tremendous force, pulled him forward. Ragosta then savagely slammed his left knee into the executive's groin. Greene cried out from the sudden, horrible pain and buckled over, falling on all fours onto the leaf-covered ground.

Greene grasped his crotch with both hands, fell on his side and began to vomit violently. Ragosta looked at him callously for a moment then said, "Make damn sure you pick up the phone on the first ring." He then turned and began to walk back to his car. After taking several steps he shouted over his shoulder, "Two o'clock, *Davie!*"

Shortly after he drove off, Ragosta felt something cold on his left leg. Looking down, he saw his pants were stained around the knee. *Jesus Christ,* he thought, *the fat bastard pissed his pants!*

When his assailant was out of sight, David Greene slowly got back on all fours and with his head hanging down, panted for a minute. A mixture of blood and saliva drooled from his mouth. Once he was able to breathe again and the pain subsided a little, he wiped his mouth with the back of his hand and got to his feet. He'd never felt pain like that before; he stuck his hand down his pants and gently rubbed his throbbing testicles. He cringed in embarrassment when he realized his briefs and pants were saturated. The tears in his eyes made the surroundings area bleary and he squinted to force out the moisture. When that didn't work, he resorted to knuckling the sockets.

What in God's name just happen? he thought to himself. It was all so…so, incomprehensibly surreal. Here he was, battered, threatened, and left standing in the woods. *Why?* He took a few staggered steps then stopped; the pain was still too much and he leaned against a tree. *Who…or what was this…this man anyway? Some kind of…of mugger?* Greene shook his head. *Not a mugger, no. I wasn't robbed of anything.* Still leaning against the tree the incident began to replay in his mind and the assailant's words came back to him with perfect clarity. *He may not be a robber, but something would be demanded of me this afternoon.*

The pain in his groin finally subsided and with effort, the executive pushed off of the tree. He took a few steps and fell to his knees; he began to sob lightly. Disgusted with himself, with his lack of masculinity, he took a deep breath to steel himself, got up and stumbled back to his BMW.

As he opened the door he became conscious of his appearance. He was a mess and couldn't possibly go to work looking like this. By the time he got home to change, his wife will have left for work; she wouldn't be there to ask what happened to him. He would be late for work, but so what?

With a trembling hand he reached for the key he'd left in the ignition then quickly withdrew it. His entire body shook uncontrollably. He began to wonder why he was threatened. *What does this bastard want from me? This deranged son-of-a-bitch caused the accident. The damage was bad, but not bad enough to cause anybody to go crazy. At...at least I wouldn't think so. And he had a gun! Jesus Christ! He had a gun and put it to my head! Why did he have a gun?* He buried his face in his trembling hands and shook his head in an effort to try and gain control of his thoughts. *Did I hear him correctly? Did he threaten to...to kill me...me and my family? Two o'clock, I must remember two o'clock.* Five minutes later he felt calm enough to drive. He started the BMW, turned around and headed back home at a very slow speed.

David Greene didn't make it into the office until almost eleven o'clock. As he entered from the lobby, Judith McCandish gave him a double-take. He was arriving so late and looked so pail that she asked him if he was feeling alright. Walking quickly past her desk the executive assured her he was fine and demanded that he not be disturbed. As the door to his office closed, Judith turned and gave Katie, the receptionist, a confused look. The older woman just shrugged indifferently and went back to her typing.

The three hours between the time he'd arrived and the time he expected the call were sheer hell for Greene. He tried to do some work, but couldn't concentrate. His phone rang several times after he'd arrived, but he didn't answer it; he'd return the calls later. Undoubtedly one of those calls was Donald Kampnel. Though he was on vacation he called in twice a day—the son-of-a-bitch could never relax.

His daughter lived and Ann Arbor and was attending the University of Michigan. He knew she'd be in class, but he called her anyway. He left a message asking her to call him tonight. He just wanted to talk to her—make sure she was all right.

Starting at five minutes to two, David Greene never took his eyes off the clock and rested his hand on the phone for good measure. At two minutes to two he was startled by a knock at the door. Incensed, he watched Rick Miller casually enter. The fury with which he was greeted literally hurled the confused salesman back out the door. Even though she was in the lady's room down the hall, she heard her boss screaming at Rick. Judith McCandish cursed the receptionist for not stopping him. Katie was there! She heard Greene say he didn't want to be disturbed! But she let Rick enter anyway. Judith knew the receptionist—like most everybody else in the company—couldn't stand David Greene. But her little prank to piss him off would cause Judith grief—she'd be the one to catch hell later. And it would be hell. The executive secretary had never heard her boss verbally assault anyone like that before.

Given the choice, Nick Ragosta would've liked to finish his business with David Greene in the woods, then head to the airport and out of this godforsaken part of the country. However, he didn't want to leave their cars on the side of the road too long. Some nosey county mounty might come along and cause problems. He'd killed a cop once and didn't want to do it again. The officer had shown up at the wrong place at the wrong time and that was the only occasion he'd ever come close to being identified and possibly caught. When it came to their own, the police were relentless. No. It was better to let that weasel of an executive know he was serious so he could have his complete and undivided attention when he called. Based on the man's composure in the woods, Ragosta was sure he would.

He called from one of the Hilton's lobby telephones; this was the type of call where it was inadvisable to use a cell phone. He smiled when the receiver at the other end was plucked up before the first ring even ended. A good sign; the man could follow directions.

"David Greene." There was no mistaking the anxiety in the voice.

"Mr. Green, this is your new friend...the one you ran into this morning." He smiled at his unintended pun.

"Look...it was just an accident. I...I don't understand why—"

"Mr. Green, just shut the fuck up and listen," the assassin replied calmly. "This has nothing to do with the accident you idiot."

"It...it doesn't?"

"No."

David Greene's brow furrowed in surprise and he gave the receiver in his hand a confused look. For the first time since their encounter he forgot his fear; it was replaced by genuine curiosity. "Oh," he murmured.

"Are you listening *very* carefully, Mr. Greene? Because I don't want to repeat myself." The executive from FTT didn't even notice he was being spoken to as if he were a child.

"Yes. I'm listening."

"Good. You have two customers I want impaired. I want you to cause damage to them…irrevocable damage. But it must be done slowly, incrementally, so as not to appear blatant and arouse suspicion. And this must be done by you, and you alone. No one at your company must ever learn that you're doing this willfully. With me so far?"

"Ah…yeah."

Keeping the patronizing tone, Ragosta continued. "If you fail to do this, or fail to do it within the time frame I'm going to give you, the consequences will be…well, they won't be pleasant." He paused a moment for effect then said, "Still with me?"

"Yes. Yes, I am," Greene replied hurriedly.

Dropping the condescending timbre the assassin said, "We haven't had much of a chance to get acquainted yet, Mr. Greene. I apologize for being in such a hurry this morning. But I'm sure you're wondering who I am and why I'm doing this?"

"Well…yes. Of course."

"Why is none of your concern," Ragosta snapped back immediately. "The fact that I want it done is all you need to know. *Who* I am is of more relevance to you. I know everything about you, Mr. Greene, from your family to your finances—$6,751.40 in savings, current checking balance of $955.02, and a monthly mortgage of $3,980.60—to the fact that you don't particularly care for asparagus and have a cat named Precious." Greene's eyes widened at the factual statement. "*Precious…?* Come on!"

"It's ah, my wife's cat," the executive replied timidly.

Ragosta grunted. "The point I'm making is this: I can not only make your life a living hell…I can end it. Yours, along with those you care for most. And this is what I do for a living, Mr. Greene. I've done it for many years and am pretty goddamn good at it. Go to the police, or anybody else you think might help you, and I'll know. And retribution will start with that pretty little daughter of yours living in the dorm at the U of M, Ann Arbor. Centennial Hall, room nineteen if I'm not mistaken."

The fear Green had experienced earlier this morning instantly took hold of him again. His mouth went dry and he had to make a conscious effort not to wet himself again. He gripped the phone tighter and pushed it hard against his ear.

"I'll…do anything you say." His voice was weak and raspy. "Just don't harm my family."

"Excellent David! Excellent!" the assassin bellowed. "Follow my orders and you have nothing to fear, I assure you." Ragosta could here an audible sigh at the other end.

"Umm…what two companies do you want…ah…sabotaged?" Greene inquired cautiously.

"Unlimited Energy Systems and Global Fuel Cell Technologies."

Greene's eyebrows shot up and he straightened in his chair. *"UES and GFCT?"* he all but shouted.

"Yes."

Greene was dumbstruck. All he could manage to do was stare blankly at his desk.

Annoyed and a little concerned by the silence, Ragosta asked harshly, "Is there a *problem*, Mr. Greene?"

A small smile formed on the executive's lips. "No. No problem at all Mr…?"

"You can address me as Mr. R."

David Greene cleared his throat and let out an almost demonic laugh. At the other end of the line Ragosta's brow furrowed as he dawned a perplexed expression. Making no attempt to suppress his budding elation Greene said, "Ahhh, Mr. R…I'm, ah…I'm not quite sure how to say this, but…" he snickered again, "but you don't need to, ah…to coerce me to eliminate these customers." There was short pause after which he added gleefully, "I'm happy to do it!" Ragosta was completely taken aback by the executive's response. He opened his mouth, but nothing came out. "I'm no fan of the fuel cell industry, Mr. R. I assure you. If anything, I consider them a tremendous detriment to our business."

Ragosta remained speechless for a moment. When he recovered he replied flatly, "That's…good to hear, Mr. Greene. I can count on your full cooperation then?"

Since hearing the two company names, Greene's trepidation of the situation and the person at the other end of the line had almost vanished. "Absolutely!" he replied resolutely. "You'll have my compete cooperation." Boldly, yet guardedly he added, "Mr. R…there really is no need to threaten me."

"The threat *will* remain, Mr. Greene," the assassin quickly retorted. "If for no other reason than to keep you honest." The executive was crestfallen; he slumped in his chair. "This must be done correctly and gradually, and that will be *your* responsibility. Fuck it up, *Davie*, and I'll follow through with my threat."

Greene swallowed hard then asked sullenly, "What is the timetable?"

"Between eighteen and twenty four months," the assassin replied crisply. "How you accomplish this is up to you—just get it done! I'll be keeping a very close eye on you, Mr. Greene. Very close. Good-bye."

"What about—" but the line had already gone dead. Greene kept the receiver to his ear for a few more seconds then slowly hung up. He stared at the phone blankly for about a minute until his mind slowly began to digest the conversation. *UES and GFCT...how fortunate*, he thought. He leaned back in his chair and covered his face with hands that were still slightly trembling. *This should be relatively easy.* He dropped his hands to his lap and spun his chair to face the window. *Christ, what if it had been Airbus or Ford, our two biggest customers?* He pondered the unpleasant thought for a moment then decided not to dwell on it—there was no point.

Global Fuel Cell Technologies and Unlimited Energy Systems! The names of the two fuel cell companies shot through his mind again and he smiled. Rising from his chair to visit the men's room—something he'd painfully put off for the last two hours—he said to himself, "Hell, this might even be enjoyable!"

The meetings with Senator Landon Plecha and Congresswoman Amanda Zwart went as well as the discussion with Richard Radakovich—perhaps even better. Haggerty used the same logic with them that he did with the congressman from North Carolina and the statistics he used to back up his argument effectively eliminated any misgivings the two lawmakers may have harbored.

He was surprised at how little the politicians actually knew about the economics of their constituency; but that definitely worked in his favor. And, as his friend Senator Pat Wheeler had predicted, of the three elected officials P3 targeted, Senator Plecha was clearly the most appreciative. With a perverse satisfaction Haggerty recalled Plecha's parting comment: "Although, Mr. Haggerty, you've made clear you'll expect some type of...quid pro quo in the future, I'm nonetheless grateful to you for your genuine concern for the well being of my state...and the overall economic well being of the nation, of course."

Yes. It definitely was the right strategy to focus on the one thing most important to all three lawmakers—to all politicians for that matter—political survival. Strike a chord that questions their continued existence, and you'll have their full, undivided attention; not to mention cooperation.

After meeting with the three politicians, he mildly admonished himself for being so nervous before his first meeting with Radakovich. He hadn't felt such anxiety since he was a young attorney for the U.S. Department of Energy arguing his first case back in 1969. His apprehension could have shown, causing the congressman to become suspicious, possibly jeopardizing the Curly stratagem of P3. Having worked in and around Washington for so long, he should have trusted his instincts. The years spent in the nation's capital had given him knowledge and experience no amount of formal education could provide. Should he find himself in a similar situation prior to the completion of P3, he wouldn't second-guess his intuition.

Curly's objective was to show the three influential lawmakers the clear and imminent threat posed by their support of fuel cell technology. To that end, Curly was successful. In a matter of days he would be reading in the *Washington Post* of Radakovich, Zwart and Plecha's withdrawal of support for the zero emissions bill; and Haggerty was sure other lawmakers would soon follow.

Like any other profession, politicians talked amongst themselves. Eventually, Zwart, Plecha and Radakovich would informally meet with their fellow lawmakers and regurgitate the gloomy data graciously provided by the president of Noble Consultants. It wouldn't take long for the other politicians to see the light, and Haggerty was sure it would only be a matter of months before the zero emissions bill would wither and die. Odds were it wouldn't even make it to the house floor.

The demise of Congressman Hanson's bill would confirm Curly's successful completion. But of the three separate strategies of P3, Curly, Haggerty knew, was the least significant. Loss of congressional support would be a major blow to the fuel cell industry, but far from fatal. In time, the industry's lobbyists would eventually find other champions in congress and similar legislation, helped along by the environmental lobby, would inevitably be presented. And in the meantime the technological progress and appeal of fuel cells would march on, posing an ever-mounting threat to the interests of Noble Consultants' largest client, The Committee.

Laurence Haggerty had spent more than one sleepless night tossing and turning, worrying about how he should have formulated P3 to address the threat posed at the state level. Support and passage of zero emissions laws by several major states would most certainly provide an incentive to the fuel cell companies to continue their efforts. But could he have really addressed the issue of state legislation in P3? If he had, the potential existed that the plan would have become unmanageable; too big, too cumbersome, with too many people becoming involved. Too many things could go wrong leading to the unthinkable.

Later this year, 2002, New York, Georgia and Michigan's legislatures would be voting on their states' zero emissions bills. So what if the proposals pass and become state law? Sandra was right: the laws aren't worth the paper they're written on if there isn't a product on the market that will allow compliance! And

GM's EV program was proving that the concept of the hybrid car wasn't catching on yet.

He kept them to himself of course, but initially Haggerty had his doubts. But as he, Sandra Beach and Nick Ragosta became more deeply involved in P3, the more he was convinced that success really did lie in discrediting the technology or making it economically unfeasible for years to come. Consequently, it was critical that Larry and Moe be successful. And unfortunately for those strategies to be successful—for GFCT and UES to appear to fail from management incompetence and/or the fortunes of market forces—they couldn't be rushed.

He tried hard not to let on, but Laurence Haggerty was deeply troubled by Ragosta's report. Sandra Beach could clearly see that. Larry, the focus on GFCT's and UES's executives was going well, but the implementation of Moe, the crippling of the fuel cell companies' vendor base, was clearly running into trouble. Ragosta claimed it was necessary to eliminate Robert Love.

Early in March, Nick Ragosta flew to Washington to meet with Haggerty and Beach. As they had not seen Ragosta since the execution of Curly and Moe in early December, they were anxious to get an update from him. Haggerty almost dropped his coffee cup when the assassin flatly told him that he'd killed the owner or Rayonicx.

Plopping down behind his desk Haggerty appeared despondent, then angry. "Goddamit Nick, you should have consulted me before taking that kind of action!"

"It couldn't be helped," Ragosta said indifferently, pouring himself a cup of coffee with his back to Haggerty. "And I wouldn't of had time to call you and we wouldn't want to discuss it on the phone anyway!" Full cup of coffee in hand, the assassin turned to face Sandra Beach and her boss with a remorseless expression.

Haggerty tried not to show his disappointment, but he was clearly crestfallen. Turning a disgusted face away from the other two he said sullenly, "I'd really hoped we could pull this off without any bloodshed."

"What about the executive from Flexible Tubing Technologies?" Sandra Beach asked while rubbing her eyes. She was sitting on the couch looking uncharacteristically unkempt. Besides appearing as if she hadn't slept in two days, her hair—which Ragosta noticed she always tried to keep styled in some fashion—was flat, almost matted to her skull.

Ragosta took a sip of coffee and said, "I had no trouble with David Greene." He let out a light huff. "Hell, he sounded like he'd almost pay me to do it. He's apparently no fan of these two fuel cell companies."

The assassin walked over to the couch, sat down and flashed Sandra Beach a brilliant smile. She returned the affable gesture with a mild look of revulsion. Reducing his toothy grin to a smirk he continued. "As for Patricia Pennington, owner of Drextal Industries, she put up a little fight at first. But thanks to the thorough work of Mike Swenson she quickly caved in."

"Just out of curiosity, what'd we have on her?" Haggerty asked.

Ragosta shrugged. "Not a lot, really. They have no kids so I threatened to kill her husband if she didn't cooperate. Outside the company, he seems to be the only thing in her life."

"The only reason Pennington is in the CEO's chair is because she's the founder's daughter," Sandra offered while looking at a file. "From Swenson's profile of her, she's running the show, but her father keeps his nose close to the affairs of the company." She turned to Ragosta and asked, "Why didn't you threaten go after the father? Typically, daughters love their daddies far more than their husbands."

Ragosta didn't like anyone questioning his judgment. Narrowing his eyes he shot back, "Is he the CEO?" When Haggerty's trusted colleague didn't respond he said, "I read the report...*Sandy*," using that name because he knew it annoyed her. "I know what's going on. At the moment I don't see the need to rough-up a frail, eighty-three year old man." Then, turning his expression icy cold he scathingly asked, "*Do you?*" She winced and turned away from him.

Haggerty didn't like the way the tension was mounting between his two associates. To divert Ragosta's attention from Sandra he quickly, but calmly asked, "Nick, what happened with Love? Why'd you find it necessary to remove him?"

Ragosta continued to stare at Beach for a moment, then slowly turned his head to reply to the question. The anger that remained on his face caused a shiver to run down Haggerty's back, and made him wonder briefly whether he'd made the right decision retaining the man's services. He clearly had the potential to become a loose cannon.

"You read his profile, Laurence," Ragosta said flatly, "the man was squeaky clean." To Haggerty's relief he saw the assassin's expression finally soften. Ragosta let out a sigh and continued. "Swenson—who I might add up to this point has done an exceptional job compiling information—dropped the ball on this one. After I told Love what I wanted he almost laughed at me—told me I was wasting my time. Rayonicx had just been sold. As a matter of fact, it turned out I was speaking with him not long after he'd left his attorney's office—he had just signed all the necessary papers.

"Love hesitated when I asked him who bought the company so I slapped him around a bit. He finally told me some German firm acquired it. He told me the name, but I didn't write it down and forgot it." The assassin gave a dismissive wave of his hand. "It's irrelevant anyway. Some guy named Hans Gluklich is now running Rayonicx."

"Christ!" Haggerty mumbled, shaking his head. Looking at Sandra he asked, "How the *hell* did Swenson miss that?" She only shrugged in reply. "What a shitty stroke of luck!" He paused a moment then looked at Ragosta and placidly said, "You did the right thing, Nick." The assassin pursed his lips and nodded his agreement.

Stunned, Sandra Beach stared at her boss and exclaimed, "*He did the right thing?* What do you mean?"

Haggerty frowned. "Robert Love had to be eliminated, Sandra. Nick had told him too much."

"Regardless of the consequences he would've warned Gluklich and went to the police." Ragosta added, his earlier annoyance with her apparently gone. "He was that kind of guy."

Sandra looked solemnly down at her lap. "Oh…I see."

"Let's get Swenson to profile this Gluklich guy," Ragosta said. "If necessary, I'll go after him. But I think it would be best if we didn't—at least for a while. The ex-owner is dead; the police will be poking around Rayonicx for the foreseeable future."

Haggerty nodded. "I agree." He then leaned back in his chair and sat in silent reflection, staring at the coffee cup in his hands. A few moments later he said, "Since we've such a willing accomplice in David Greene, and the cooperation of Ms. Pennington, I wonder if it's really necessary to mess with Rayonicx?"

"I don't think it is, Laurence," Sandra offered. "We can always go after them later if necessary. Or, choose another vendor."

Haggerty nodded thoughtfully then stood up. "All right, we'll work with what we've got for now. Nick, I'd like you to meet with me whenever you feel it's necessary, but at a minimum once every three months. I'll need to update The Committee periodically. Any problems, I want to know about them." Ragosta nodded. Haggerty continued to look at the hit man. "Except for the occasional motivational pep talk I'm sure you'll find necessary to give Stallinger, Klash and Greene, I guess there's not much more we can do at this point but monitor what should be the slow, steady decline of the fuel cell industry."

CHAPTER 8

▼

"What do you mean it's on hold?" Rick Miller asked incredulously while tightening his grip on the receiver. Despite his best effort, he couldn't keep the frustration out of his voice. But he was glad he was on the phone and not actually meeting with Jim Daily; he wouldn't want the engineer to see just how mad he was. Along with several other project engineers, Rick was working with Daily on UES' next generation stationary fuel cell system, the US3.

Between his two fuel cell customers, this was the fifth project in the last two months that was either put on hold, had its funds diverted, or was outright cancelled. Although it wasn't uncommon for new programs to be delayed and occasionally canceled, these last five were—according to many of the engineers—critical for the continued improvement of the fuel cell system's performance and manufacturability.

Just as important, Rick knew, the new designs were friendlier to his company's manufacturing processes. This would significantly reduce the cost to produce the hoses and gaskets FTT and FSS supplied, and widen the companies' profit margin. GFCT and UES would soon have become very profitable customers, even during the limited quantity initial production runs.

"It's on hold, Rick. That's all I can tell you. I don't know why yet," Daily replied glumly. "Pisses me off too…I've got a lot of hours into this design!"

Rick closed his eyes and hung his head. After letting out a despondent sigh he asked, "Any idea when it will come off hold, Jim? *Will* it come off hold?"

"At this point Rick, your guess is as good as mine. But I've gotta believe it will come off hold soon. If we're gonna keep to the timetable, we've gotta get the goddamn thing on validation testing."

"Alright Jim, thanks," Rick said dolefully. "Anything else I can help you with?"

"Nah. I'll give you a shout if there's any change. Take it easy, Rick"

"Yeah, you too." Rick slowly hung up the phone. Drumming his fingers on the desk he began to think how peculiar this was. First, it was a revised hose design that was put on hold by GFCT. They quickly followed that decision by halting the testing of a new nitrile material Tim Leigh, FTT's chemist, had developed for them. The freeze in testing hurt Rick personally. He was determined to drag FTT and FSS—kicking and screaming if necessary—into the processing of polymers other than just silicone and fluorosilicone. The freeze would provide David Greene with more justification to drop their development efforts.

Tim Leigh was an outstanding polymer chemist who in Rick's opinion was under appreciated by FTT's management. He had developed a nitrile rubber compound that had the potential to replace stainless steel, which was currently the only material approved to pipe hydrogen.

Smiling suddenly, Rick remembered how Tim just laughed at him when Rick challenged him to develop a rubber material that would be impermeable to hydrogen—the smallest of all molecules. But Tim took the challenge and three months later came up with a recipe. Replacing all the incredibly expensive stainless steel pipes currently used in GFCT's fuel cell powertrain with rubber hoses made from this compound would provide Global Fuel Cell Technologies with tremendous savings while at the same time reduce the vehicle's weight. The potential of Tim's formulation was staggering. Once approved by GFCT, Flexible Tubing Technologies would have no choice but to process this non-silicone compound—the sales potential would be just too big to ignore. Just as important as far as Rick was concerned, successful testing would give him something else he could rub Greene's nose into. Given the incredible potential of hoses made from this material, it completely baffled Rick why GFCT would suspend testing; it made absolutely no sense whatsoever.

A few weeks after learning of GFCT's suspension in testing, Unlimited Energy Systems canceled its program to redesign the US3's manifold. The new manifold would have required a revised seal designed and prototyped by Flexible Sealing Solutions. Had UES followed through on this program, the number of seals required for this part of the system would have been reduced from six to two. In addition, the manifold would have become far less complicated and its assembly more efficient. Rick wasn't upset by the cancellation of this program as UES would continue to require more seals from his company. But like GFCT's abandonment of the nitrile testing, Rick found the termination of this cost savings program perplexing.

But Jim Daily's news was the most disturbing of all. Delaying the development of the US3 stack gasket was an ominous development at best. As was the case with the US1 program, testing would undoubtedly prove that the US3's stack gasket would require several modifications before the design was finalized; and these changes took time. The fuel cell company's current timetable called for the US3 to begin production beginning the first quarter of 2004. If validation testing wasn't completed by the third quarter of 2003, there was no way this could happen. It was Unlimited Energy Systems' plan to sell the US3 commercially; the volume of stack gaskets required from Flexible Sealing Solutions for this program would be fifty times that of the US1. Rick shuddered when he considered the repercussions of this program being delayed, or worst yet, canceled.

Anxiety ridden, Rick let out a small groan and ran a hand threw his rapidly graying hair. It was then that he remembered he had a meeting with David Greene at two o'clock this afternoon. Slightly panicked, he looked at his watch and was relieved to discover it was only one-forty-five—he prided himself on his punctuality and hated to be late for anything; even a meeting with David Greene.

It still bothered him that he didn't know what his boss wanted to talk about. But whatever the topic, it promised to be unpleasant—their last few chats certainly were. Yesterday, when Greene called to set it up, Rick naturally asked what the meeting would be about so he could be prepared, but his boss skillfully sidestepped the question—not a good sign. Rick tried to convince himself that it really didn't matter; regardless of the initial topic, Greene always managed to turn the conversation around so he could bitch about the fuel cell customers.

Let him bitch! Rick thought to himself. If the conversation turned ugly, he had something he could throw in Greene's face: the fact that the sale of US1 stack gasket were taking off—significantly better than projected—and UES was just selling these units to several New England utilities and a couple of government agencies. Because of his boss's contempt for their fuel cell customers, Rick took great pleasure in rubbing his nose in the sales figures, and did so every chance he got. Even better, the volume of business his company was now doing with UES and GFCT was getting Donald Kampnel attention. Gone were his occasional sarcastic gripes about the amount of charity work his companies were so graciously providing these two customers, and how he'd never live to see a return on investment. As Rick knew it would, all the support he and his companies had given UES was beginning to pay off—but the US1 program wouldn't last forever.

He rapped on the door and opened it; Greene was on the phone but waved him in. A much warmer welcome than the last time he'd entered his office—he thought his ears were still ringing from Green's hysterical screaming.

Rick quietly sat down in one of the two upholstered chairs in front of Greene's desk. He studied his boss for a moment, attempting to get a feel for his frame of mind. Rick thought he looked a tad more tense than usual, but maybe that was normal. Lately, the man always looked like he was in a perpetual state of constipation.

"What's up?" Rick asked insipidly when Greene hung up, noticing the scowl that was starting to form on his boss' face.

"Have you read the margin report lately?" Greene asked irritably.

"No," Rick replied flatly. He seldom did because he felt it a waste of time. Short of a price increase—which typically is the fastest way to loose a customer—there wasn't a damn thing he could do about a part's low or negative profit margin. That responsibility fell firmly in the hands of manufacturing.

Greene stared at him incredulously for a moment then said, "Well, I suggest you do. Something has to be done about Unlimited Energy Systems and Global Fuel Cell Technologies."

Rick's eyebrows shot up, the statement caught him off guard. He fully expected to hear the names of those two companies in this meeting, but the fact that their profitability would be called into question totally took him by surprise. "W…what do you mean? Last time I checked, those jobs were running just fine!" he replied while thinking that maybe he'd better start looking at the margin report.

"That's were you're wrong, Rick," Greene said almost serenely. "If you'd bother to review the margin report periodically you'd know that!" Rick silently questioned that. If a job was running poorly, he heard about it. The people on the floor never hesitated to tell him when they were having trouble with a part.

He'd heard plenty of complaints about the US1 stack gasket when it first began production. Made from very expensive fluorosilicone rubber and designed with numerous thin contours, the part was over a foot in diameter. Because of its size, material and design, the gasket was an extremely difficult part to produce, even for the most experienced of molders. When production began, the initial scrape rate—parts that had to be thrown away because they were defective—was alarming. Flexible Sealing Solutions' plant manager, responsible for the plant's overall manufacturing efficiency, was howling about the situation. But Rick continued to plead with her to continue testing different process parameters; because she was fond of Rick, she did—and it paid off. After three weeks of experimentation, they eventually found the optimal temperature, pressure and cure time; the scrap rate plummeted. Last Rick heard the part was still running smoothly and at $5.37 apiece, FSS was making a little more than the required thirty-five percent gross profit margin.

Rick grimaced. "Which part has the low margin?"

"Most of them."

He gave his boss a skeptical look. "That's *bullshit* David!" he wailed dubiously. "I haven't heard a word of complaint from anyone on the floor or the plant managers."

Lips tightly pressed together, Greene diverted his eyes from the salesman, who was staring hard at him in disbelief. The executive cleared his throat and said, "Well, the numbers don't lie." He now looked Rick in the eye. "FTT is having a hell of a time with the mandrel wrapped hoses and our scrap rate at FSS on the stack gasket and manifold seal is unacceptable."

"*If true*, then manufacturing has its work cut out for them," Rick replied dismissively. There was also a touch of arrogance in his voice his boss found irritating. He would enjoy putting this salesman in his place.

David Greene shook his head. "Not this time, Rick. We've wasted enough time and money on these parts…on these customers. There are other parts with issues the plants need to concentrate on—parts we ship to our largest, *profitable* customers. We simply don't have the resources to deal with all the problem parts at this time."

"So…what are you driving at?" Rick asked guardedly.

Greene smirked and let out a little laugh. "You know damn well what I'm driving at, Rick! Your fuel cell customer's parts need to have a satisfactory margin—plain and simple. If we can't improve the process, there's only one way *I'm* aware of to achieve an acceptable margin."

Immediately, Rick's temper flared. ***"You're not serious?"*** he cried. "We can't give them a price increase! Not now! *Christ*, David, that will…that will *kill* them!" Greene shrugged apathetically, leaned back in his chair and folded his arms across his chest.

"I'm quite serious, Rick," he said unequivocally. "Look at the report, then get back to me with revised pricing to bring the margins in line." The executive picked up the report and tossed it to his salesman.

"The report's wrong—it's got to be!" Rick said skeptically, flicking through the pages of the thick computer printout.

The Rick Miller's last statement caused David Greene to momentarily shudder. The report was wrong—because he was altering the data. Doing so, he only worried about the plant managers questioning the figures. But Greene knew he could get away with it as neither Kampnel nor Gundermann reviewed this particular report. When the plant managers called him to complain, he had the authority to tell them not to worry about it—it's being taken care of. He'd advise them to concentrate on putting out other fires; something he knew they'd gladly do.

"There's nothing wrong with the report." Greene replied facetiously in an attempt to sound casual. Then, in a stricter tone of voice he added, "Get back to me in a week with your recommendation."

Scowling, Rick huffed and stormed out of the office, to the amusement of his boss.

How long would she continue to see me like this? Wendell Finley asked himself as he rolled off Sandra Beach. It was a question he always asked himself after he'd slept with her. He didn't know the answer, but he knew the affair couldn't go on like this forever. He wanted it to of course, for as long as possible. But he was a realist and knew that eventually, Laurence Haggerty's assistant would want something more. Women always did.

He'd thought of ending the relationship several times but couldn't bring himself to do it. There was something about the woman he found irresistible. He couldn't put his finger on it, but it was there. She was far from the most beautiful woman he'd ever taken as a mistress, and next to his wife she paled by comparison. But she had a gift that more than compensated for her lack of superficial beauty.

Perhaps it was the skill with which she combined her body and soul. She differed from the other women he'd been with—and there had been plenty of other women. The energy and passion in her seemed to flow through every pore in her body, filling him with an amazing sensation that lasted long after their coupling. He couldn't describe it; it was a feeling that satisfied both his body and mind. Whatever it was, it was like a narcotic; he always wanted it again.

They had been seeing each other for close to a year now and although she had yet to say anything, he knew Sandra wanted some kind of commitment from him. He was foolish to complain so much about his wife early on in their relationship; it gave her the wrong idea. However, he decided he could use that impression to his advantage. He'd throw her a bone tonight; something that would make her believe he was eventually going to leave his wife. That should create the elusion in his lover's mind that she stood a chance of marrying him someday, and this, in turn, would buy him more time to enjoy the incredible experience of making love to her.

Of course he'd never leave Mindy, his third and by far most beautiful wife. Even if he wanted to, leaving her was completely out of the question. Besides, he was actually fond of the thirty-year-old ex-Miss Texas and truth was, compared to his first two wife's, she was rather easy to live with.

It wasn't a matter of losing money, property or possessions in a divorce settlement with Mindy, rather, it was the possibility of losing everything and spending the next twenty years in jail. He'd never told Betty, his first wife or Terry his second, but in a moment of drug-induced blissfulness he told Mindy his deepest, darkest secret. And he told everything—in detail: names, dates, location, et cetera. He knew Mindy wasn't above using this information if he'd ever tried to leave her; separating her from the money she had become so dependant upon and social standing she cherished.

Wendell Finley thought his wife knew, or at least suspected he was cheating on her. Surprisingly, that didn't bother the woman so long as he was discreet. But leaving her—especially for another woman—would completely humiliate her in the eyes of her high-society clique. If she was nothing else, she was vindictive, and he knew she wouldn't rest until she got even with him. He had never found the nerve to discuss it with his attorney so he didn't know if there was a statute of limitations for the actual crime. But he knew there wouldn't be for his standing in both society and business. Even if he didn't serve prison time, no amount of wealth could compensate for the shame public revelation of his crime would bring.

Shortly after leaving Texas A&M he'd raped two women—girls really. Having been raised in a family with wealth and power, he was terribly spoiled and used to having his own way. But all his money and status couldn't win the affection of a girl he worshiped from the moment he'd laid eyes on her. When he asked her out he was stunned by her refusal. What girl wouldn't want to date one of the richest bachelors in the country? She apparently didn't know that nobody says *no* to a Finley. Outraged, he exerted the governance upon her that was his birthright. Becoming embittered with women after the heinous act, two days later he raped another girl from his Political Science class because he considered her a stuck-up bitch.

Thanks to his father's power and connections, and an enormous about of hush money paid out to the families of both girls and the police investigator involved, the episode faded away. To ensure the incidents were quickly and completely forgotten, his father thought it prudent to get Wendell out of town for a while. He forced his son to join the Navy. Junior protested of course, but his father made clear that if he wanted to run ENDICORP one day and acquire his inheritance, he'd best shut up and do as he was told. Boot Camp, A school and three years as a signalman aboard an old Fram destroyer were intolerable.

Completely spent from the vigorous love making, he laid on his back and stared at the ceiling. Some moments later, Sandra snuggled up to him and slowly began to run her fingers through his thick chest hair. The wonderful feeling of her touch only strengthened his resolve not to lose her, and he hoped that what he was about to say would give him the additional time he desired while delaying any demands for a commitment she might be considering.

Just as he was about to open his mouth Sandra rolled on her side, propped herself up on her elbow and softly asked, "Sweetheart…" her sultry eyes dropped from his and concentrated on the finger she was twirling in his chest hair. "Can we go away somewhere for a week? Just you and I? I really feel the need to get away."

"Where would you like to go?" he replied softly, keeping his eyes fixed on the ceiling.

"I don't care…anywhere," she said. She laid her head on his shoulder and stared at her hand now gently running through his forest of chest hair. "Ever since we killed Robert Love, Laurence's plan has got me all wound up. I need a break—to go somewhere that will take my mind off it…even if it's for a short time." She stopped rubbing his chest and rolled onto her back. She let out a sigh and said, "I don't know…maybe Nassau or the Keys."

Finley was also disturbed by the news of the slaying. His affair with Sandra had benefits other than just physical gratification; his knowledge of P3's progress was far more detailed than anything Kennelly or Saxton would ever learn from Haggerty's periodic briefings.

The elimination of Rayonicx's former CEO was something the president of Noble Consultants didn't bother to share with his three clients. The omission greatly concerned Finley and caused him to silently question Haggerty's judgment. From the start, Finley wasn't keen on the idea of using assassination as a means to an end, and Laurence Haggerty's repeated assurances that The Committee could never be connected with the scheme did little to comfort him. No matter how far he and his two associates were supposedly distanced from P3, in Finley's opinion, they could never be distanced enough. Particularly now that murder was involved.

The CEO of ENDICORP turned his head to look at his mistress. "Sounds good to me, babe, I'll see what I can do." He paused a moment, ran the line through his head one final time to make sure it had the intended ambiguity and said in a jaunty voice, "As a matter of fact, Sandra my dear, you might as well get used to the idea of spending more time with me. I think that maybe soon, we'll be seeing a lot more of each other."

Sandra Beach instantly sat up and smiled amorously down at her lover; but she said nothing—she was too excited to speak.

Rick had been formally introduced to her—twice as a matter of fact—but not surprisingly she didn't recall their previous meetings. This didn't bother Rick in the least. If, several months from now he was introduced to her again, Cynthia Klash wouldn't remember him. Rick had dealt with this type of person many times before; important executives that only remembered important people, and to a CEO, preeminence was not synonymous with sales representative. Consequently, Rick debated whether or not he should approach the woman and greet her.

He was somewhat surprised to find Cynthia Klash here; McDonald's is not the place Rick pictured a woman of her status lunching. But she didn't appear to be eating; the only thing in front of her was a soda. She also appeared to be completely focused on her conversation; her face was taut and serious, her body rigid, and when she spoke, she looked as if she was quietly barking orders into her cell phone. After several moments of internal debate, Rick decided to greet her once she was finished with her call. It never hurt to be cordial to a customer's top executive. Besides, he rather admired her. A few years his junior, she had achieve career success he could never image himself attaining.

Approaching her from behind, Rick decided to sit in the booth behind her and wait for her to finish the call. If she talked too long, he'd get up, order his food and leave.

The booths had rather tall backrests and all Rick could see of her was the back of her head. He noticed that she was constantly looking from side to side, as if checking to ensure nobody was within earshot. Given her apparent concern for privacy, he found it odd that she didn't turn around and look to see if anybody was behind her.

Realizing that he was inadvertently eavesdropping, Rick began to feel uncomfortable and thought it best to leave. With no food in front of him, she could only conclude that he was listening in on her conversation should she suddenly stand up, turn around and see him sitting there. And considering his recent run of luck, this would be the one time she'd remembered him.

Rick started to slide out of the booth but then stopped when he heard her say, "*Oh God*, Alex. I'm, I'm *so* scared!" After sniffling several times she added, "No! No…I'm not alright," and started to cry.

Rick didn't move; he couldn't. Though guilt surged through him he felt compelled to continue listening. Keeping his back flat against the bench he slid down a little and turned an ear toward Klash.

"I know it's been a long time since we've seen each other outside of work, but.........what?.........Over seven month, has it been that long?.........No, I...I can explain, but not now."

Alex? Must be her husband, Rick thought. *I didn't know he worked at Global Fuel Cell Technologies? How could she possibly not have seen her husband in over seven months?*

"What?.........Yes, I'm scared. I'm terrified, Alex. I've *got* to talk to someone," she sniffled again. "I love you too, Alex. You're the only person I can trust." Rick heard her paused for a moment then add, "I...I *can* trust you, can't I?" Somehow, Rick could sense that her husband was offended by the question.

"I'm sorry darling, that was a stupid thing to ask. I know I can.........What?.........Yes, but you should know that I'm taking a real risk talking to you; I'm...I'm risking my life.........No, I'm not kidding! *God,* how I wish I were."

Rick's eyes widened in surprise. *Risking her life? What the hell is she talking about? What the hell is going on?* If she hadn't sounded so genuinely terrified, the salesman would have thought she was playing a practical joke on her husband.

"Alex, I...I might be risking yours as well.........Huh?.........I don't know. But I know I'm being watched."

She paused for a long time. Obviously her husband had a lot of questions; Rick knew he would if he were at the other end of the line. Clearly, the guy must be confused and concerned. It still struck Rick as odd that Klash hadn't seen him in such a long time.

She hadn't spoken for so long Rick was worried that maybe the call had ended and he didn't catch it. He was just about to try and peek over the bench when he heard her say, "I'll explain everything later, Alex, when we meet. All I can tell you now is that I'm being pressured; that's one of the reasons I've had to avoid you all this time. Also, I might as well tell you—" She sniffled again and blew her nose. "My...my career is...is, over!" She started to cry again, this time intensely. Rick noticed several people in the restaurant gazing in her direction. It took her some moments before she could compose herself and resume talking quietly. "Why? Because I'm being forced to—" she stopped to sniffle again. She was speaking so softly now that Rick was straining to hear her. To make matters worse, two boisterous teenagers sat down in the booth adjacent to his and began talking loudly. Panicked, Rick cleared his throat loudly while giving them his nastiest look. It worked. Perplexed, the two boys looked at him strangely and stopped talking long enough for Rick to hear her say, "Forced to destroy my company!"

The two adolescents didn't know what to make of the strange man across the aisle whose malicious face instantly turned blank with astonishment. They gazed at him as if he were a nut, then looked at each other, shook their head and went back to their conversation as they unwrapped their burgers.

Rick slowly turned his somber face from the two raucous kids to the empty table before him. *Destroy the company? Being forced to destroy GFCT? Why?* he thought. Suddenly, the recent program cancellations came to mind. *Is this the reason why so many of my recent programs have been eliminated? My God!*

He heard her begin talking again; now loudly; seemingly oblivious to the possibility that someone might overhear her. Despite the gabby boys next to him Rick could clearly make out what she was saying.

"Oh…I might as well tell you. He threaten to kill them all if I don't. My husband, the kids—" she sobbed some more.

Husband? She's not talking with her husband? Who the hell is this Alex? Shocked, Rick remembered what he'd heard Klash say earlier, 'I love you too, Alex. You're the only person I can trust.' He could only conclude that Cynthia Klash was having an affair.

"That's all I'm going to tell you…I've talked too much already. I'll tell you the rest tomorrow night. Should we meet at the usual place?..........Eight o'clock?..........Good."

The conversation was clearly winding up; Rick looked around for the best escape route. If possible, he didn't even want Klash to see him leave, let alone sitting in the booth behind her. He began to slide off the bench. Mouths full of food forced the two teenagers next to him to temporarily stop talking and Rick heard her whisper, "I love you, Alex…I love you like I've loved no other woman."

Rick had one leg out of the booth when he came to an abrupt stop. **Woman!** His eyes nearly popped out of his head. He was so taken aback, he momentarily forgot he didn't want to be seen by Klash and reflexively twisted around to look at her. But like before, all he could see was the top of her head. He then realized what he was doing and quickly turned back around, pressing his back up against the bench.

Rick then noticed the two boys were watching him; as they solemnly chewed, their eyes darted between him and the woman in the booth behind him. They were well aware of what he was doing; the disgusted expression on their faces was unmistakable. Rick flashed them an embarrassed smile, shrugged, and briskly headed for the exit. The two boys rolled their eyes and went back to eating.

Sitting in his car he saw Cynthia Klash leave the restaurant. As he watched her walk toward her car, he wondered why he found her being gay so surprising. After all, one of his closest friends recently confided in him that his wife of nearly twenty years just confessed to being a Lesbian. Situations like this were probably more common then most people think.

She was quickly approaching her car, dabbing at her eyes along the way. Before she reached her Lexus, she stopped to pull a Kleenex from her purse and blow her nose. As Rick watched her, the magnitude of what he'd heard her say began to sink in—it was a sickening sensation he could almost physically feel. The realization struck him that this woman was in real trouble. Rick shook his head at this almost surreal situation, thinking how things like this only happened in the movies.

At the door of her car, he watched the CEO of Global Fuel Cell Technologies dig into her purse again and pull out her keys—cursing as she dropped them. As soon as she was seated behind the steering wheel, she dropped her forehead on it and began to sob fiercely. Rick's face softened; he couldn't help feeling sorry for her. A few moments later she wiped her eyes with the back of her hand, started her car and drove off. As he put his key in the ignition, Rick wondered if he could help her. *But should I get involved? Get involved in what? What the hell was going on anyway? Would she even what my help? And if I did get involved, could that endanger her…or* me? He turned the key and threw his car into drive. *She wouldn't ask for my help. Hell, she doesn't even know who I am!* Stymied, he drove to his next appointment.

What he'd heard Klash say ate away at Rick for several days. He had trouble sleeping and concentrating on what he considered trivial matters. Things like Sean's poor grade in English or the fact that Bobbie came home late last night, again—things that normally upset him. His apathy did not escape the notice of his wife, Terri. After his third evening of complete indifference she confronted him as they got into bed.

Terri was Rick's second wife. He'd left his first for the same reason Terri left her first husband: alcohol. The only discernable difference in their past relationships was that her ex-husband was both physically and mentally abusive when he got drunk. Rick's alcoholic wife only blacked out. When she did so behind the wheel with their twelve-year-old daughter, it was time to change the situation. Refusing treatment, Rick was left with no choice but divorce. Her illness made getting custody of Marie a simple matter in the settlement.

Terri's story was pretty much the same as Rick's. However, it took a restraining order to get her abusive husband out of her life. She brought two boys to the marriage and Rick loved them as if they were his own.

Terri got up on her elbow and looked down at her husband who seemed to be engrossed in a book. "Honey...what's wrong?"

"Nothing," he replied, his eyes never leaving the book.

"C'mon...you've been really absent minded for the last few days. It's like you've...oh, I don't know; like you've tuned out or something."

"Nothing's wrong, Ter...really." He keep looking at his book. "I guess I've just been absorbed with work lately."

A dubious look came over her face. "I've seen you absorbed by work before; you've never been like this!" She sighed. "You didn't even bat an eye when Sean broke the window yesterday. Normally, you go ballistic over something like that. I don't think it's just work. It has to be something more."

Rick kept his face in the book a moment longer, and then dropped it on his chest. He turned his head to look at her. She was right of course, but he couldn't tell her the real reason why. It would only open up the door to an avalanche of questions, and she'd become terribly worried. Rick heaved a heavy sigh. "No, it *really* is work hon." He paused a moment, puckered his lips then said, "You know I've been busting my ass to develop two accounts, UES and GFCT." She nodded her head. It seemed to her that Rick couldn't talk about work without mentioning those two companies. "Well...everything is going to shit! And that asshole Greene isn't making it any easier."

He went on to explain that yet another program was canceled at Unlimited Energy Systems, and Global Fuel Cell Technologies was dragging its feet with testing and approvals. He was becoming extremely frustrated. The work he'd put into these accounts was tremendous, and if things kept going the way they were it would all be for not. The worst part of it was David Greene. The price increase Rick was being forced to give those two customers would probably be the nail in the coffin. Should the two accounts amount to nothing, his boss would gloat like a guy dating a supermodel. He might even use it as justification to fire him.

"*Fire you?*" his wife said skeptically. "Why would he fire you, Rick? You've lost accounts before."

"Yeah, but not accounts like this, Ter. Management is under the impression that they've put a tremendous amount of time, effort and money into GFCT and UES." Rick's face became angry. "That fucker Greene has Kampnel believing we've poured hundreds of thousands of dollars into supporting those two companies."

"Have you?" his wife asked with interest.

"*Hell no.*" Rick replied in disgust. "Between the two we've probably poured, or should I say invested, about forty thousand total over the years. Considering the potential of these accounts, that's a fucking bargain." He paused a moment and then added, "Besides, billing with UES is taking off. You'd think Kampnel would at least have the brains to see that."

Terri laid back down and stared at the ceiling. "Well honey, let it go. Try and get some sleep." She rolled over on her side. "If those idiots want to fire their best salesman, to hell with them! It's not worth getting an ulcer over."

Rick grimaced, put his book on the nightstand and turned out the light. He spent another sleepless night thinking about Cynthia Klash and what she had said.

The decision to get personally involved was settled the next day. Calling to talk about the discharge hose program with Brad Selmants, GFCT's Vice President of Engineering for the company's huge stationary power plant division, Rick was informed by the receptionist that, "Mr. Selmants is no longer with the company."

Rick was shocked. Brad was both an outstanding engineer and manager. When Rick had problems with other engineers he could always count on Brad to discreetly make the person in question cooperate; the engineer would never know it was Rick's idea to ask their boss to intervene. The man made his job so much easier, and Rick genuinely liked him.

Having worked so long at GFCT and with so many of its employees, Rick couldn't escape a certain amount of involvement in the company's internal politics. If Brad had been walking a thin line, Rick certainly would have heard about it. But it was just the opposite; he had heard nothing but praise about this particular vice president of engineering. And if he was considering taking a position with another company, Rick was sure Brad would have mentioned it to him at some point before leaving.

If there was ever any question in Rick's mind about the sincerity of what he'd heard come out of Cynthia Klash's mouth, there was none now. Only she had the authority at GFCT to fire Selmants. All the programs that had been canceled, all the personnel changes, all the poor decisions or bad luck, all these things had to be on account of her.

Since listening in on Klash at McDonald's, in his heart of hearts, Rick desperately didn't want to believe what he'd heard. He'd theorized a number of different scenarios since that day, like maybe she was just trying to get rid of her lesbian lover, or obtain sympathy from her? Maybe Klash was just strange and living in a delusional world? But he could no longer ignore the facts. For whatever reason, she was indeed out to destroy her company. The question now was, why?

Rick couldn't believe she'd do this of her own accord; career suicide would be the least of the possible ramifications facing her should she be found out. With all the money involved, she'd be in a world of legal trouble. No, given what he'd heard—her distressed frame of mind—she was clearly being forced into doing it. He did hear her say he'd threaten to kill them all if she didn't. So who was behind this? Who was threatening her? And why? He had to know.

But he didn't have a clue where to begin or even how to go about it. This would be an undertaking that was far out of his league. But doing nothing wasn't an option. He'd worked too hard and come too far just to sit on the sideline let all his efforts fall apart now. He was determined—if he could do something, he would!

Rick laughed at the idea of going to the police. What evidence did he have that an actual crime was being committed other than his suspicion? And even if they believed him—which he was sure they wouldn't—what could they do? Besides, an investigation by the police would most likely become public knowledge and he'd heard what Klash said—he'd be responsible for putting her in danger. Rick didn't want that on his conscience. No, any incursion into this situation had to be handled with the utmost discretion.

Then it hit him. Rick hadn't thought of him for many years—more years than he cared to admit—but he remembered him well. How could he possibly forget him? If memory served, he once told Rick that after his tour was up he wanted to become a private investigator. If he'd actually followed through on that ambition, Rick knew he'd help him out—he owed him one.

The date was October 30th, 1972; a date Rick would never forget. On their way back to base, his rescue helicopter was diverted and vectored to an area northwest of Da Nang. Certain of trouble, he put a fresh belt in his .30 caliber machine gun. Having an interest in electronics, when Rick joined the navy he wanted to become an ET, Electronics Technician. How the hell he ended up becoming a door-gunner aboard a SH-3 rescue helicopter he never did figure out. But there he was, flying fifty feet over the jungle looking for downed airmen, or any other "good guys" in distress.

Over the intercom the pilot told Rick they were looking for a Navy SEAL who got separated from his unit. There were no front lines in Vietnam, but the area they were going to was controlled by the Viet Cong. It went without saying that the guy didn't stand a chance if he wasn't pulled out.

As they neared the last known coordinates of the SEAL the pilot saw three quick flashes of reflected sun and turned toward it. Rick began to ready the wench and harness that would be lowered to pick the man up. As they approached the spot Rick was relieved to see the man in a small clearing; that made rescue much easier. But Rick's relief was short lived; he noticed that the sailor wasn't standing; he was lying on his back with an M16 rifle across his chest. As they got closer, Rick could see that the SEAL was wounded and clearly in pain.

A nauseating feeling came over Rick when he saw flashes of black creeping through the underbrush towards the wounded man. As the pilot dropped to hover over the area, Rick jerked back the breach of his .30 caliber and aiming at the shadowy figures, let loose with several bursts. The action had the desired effect; the VC began to retreat.

A hail of small arms fire began to slam against the chopper; the pilot screamed something unintelligible, but Rick clearly understood the essence of what he was conveying. The pilot wasn't going to hang around a second longer than necessary.

Lowering the harness, Rick's heart sank when he realized the man was too badly wounded to pull himself into it. Instinctively, he waived Cafferty, the other crewman, over to work the winch then grabbed onto the harness and rode it down twenty feet to the wounded sailor.

As soon as he hit the ground, Rick unhooked the harness from the cable. Being raked by gunfire the pilot rapidly moved away from the area. He would soon return, repositioning the aircraft to return fire and hopefully buy enough time for his crew to hoist the two men up.

Rick winced when he saw the man's legs—they were all shot up. He'd also taken a round in the shoulder. He'd lost a lot of blood but was still conscious and coherent. But Rick knew that if the man didn't get medical attention soon, he'd surly die. Glancing over his shoulder he saw the chopper was well out of small arms range and turning around.

As he was assuring the wounded SEAL that he was going to get him out of there, Rick saw the man's eyes suddenly shift and glance behind him. Without thinking, Rick snatched the weapon off the sailor's chest, spun around and fired a long burst into the thick underbrush. A hand fell out of the tall grass and landed palm up, twitching.

The helicopter was now approaching to hover. Cafferty fired the .30 caliber in a sweeping motion, spraying the surrounding area with lead in an effort to keep the VC on the run so they couldn't shoot back. Rick dropped the M16; as quickly and carefully as he could, he slipped the man into the harness. The sailor tried not to, but he cried out in pain. Given the extent of his injuries, Rick was astonished the man wasn't constantly screaming in agony; his legs were all but shredded.

The cable was now dangling above him, but too far; Rick had to motion for more slack. Because the man couldn't stand, Rick needed the cable all the way to the ground so he could latch it onto the harness.

The moment he attached the cable to the harness a black clad figure burst into the clearing; the sun glistened off the long bayonet attached to the end of his AK47. He charged. At the last possible moment Rick jumped aside and lunged for the soldier's weapon. He managed to grab onto the rifle's barrel and because he was considerably larger and heavier than the North Vietnamese soldier, Rick was able to hold his ground.

Due to his momentum the attacking warrior, still clinging to his weapon, swung in an arc and came to a stop facing Rick. The bayonet had slashed the underside of his forearms, but Rick didn't feel it, he was too terrified seeing the enemy's rifle pointed at his belly.

Jerking wildly, Rick pulled the off-balance soldier toward him and stepping to one side, grabbing the middle of the AK47 with his right hand while keeping his left on the barrel. He fell backwards, pulling the surprised warrior with him. As his back hit the ground he lifted his legs and thrust his boots into his opponent's stomach, knocking the wind out of him and tossing him into the air. The Viet Cong soldier lost his grip, flew over Rick and landed on his back with a heavy thud.

They both got to their feet. Rick swung the rifle toward the man in black and pulled the trigger. Nothing happened. The gun was either jammed or out of ammunition, which explained the bayonet charge. His opponent grinned, reached behind his back and produced a surprisingly large knife.

Having never been trained in the use of a bayonet, Rick quickly flipped the rifle around, grasping it by the barrel with both hands. As his opponent charged, Rick swung the weapon at the soldier's head with all his might. Teeth and blood flew out of the VC's mouth as he crumbled to the ground.

Dropping the gun, Rick frantically motioned for the chopper to take off; the pilot wasted no time in complying with the request. As the wounded SEAL was lifted into the air, Rick grabbed on to the harness' straps with a death-grip for what was to turn out to be the longest five minutes of his life. Dangling thirty feet underneath the helicopter and three hundred feet off the ground, Rick hung on for dear life until the pilot could locate a safe area to land and bring them aboard; the winch didn't have enough power to hoist them both up at the same time.

Rick visited Paul Haydon several times while he was in the hospital recovering from his wounds. The Navy SEAL couldn't thank Rick enough for risking his life to save him. Though he was close to losing consciousness by the time he was strapped into the harness, he remembered seeing Rick put up a fight he said was worthy of a Navy SEAL.

The two quickly became friends. Paul explained that this was his second tour and he'd had enough of the war. His enlistment was up in a few months and he wanted out. He'd always had an interest in law enforcement and once home planned on going back to school and eventually becoming a cop or private eye. And although he hailed from Arizona, he'd taken a liking to the Bay Area and planned on living in San Francisco, Alameda or Oakland.

The last time Rick saw him in the hospital, Paul jokingly said he'd never forgive Rick if he found himself in the Bay Area and didn't look him up. Then, a few moments later his expression changed drastically, and with a look of honest sincerity Rick would never forget, Haydon insisted that if Rick ever needed help, any kind of help, to call him.

But that was thirty years ago—1972. How could he ever find Paul Haydon? And if he did, would he remember him? Rick dismissed the ridiculous question—of course he'd remember him. But was he in the right line of work? Did he actually become a cop or P.I.? And if he had, would he remember his promise to Rick those many years ago? Or was it a rhetorical promise; made at the time as a friendly gesture with the understanding that it was never expected to be kept? Rick couldn't remember—it was just too long ago.

"So…why did you visit Ms. Kostreva the other night?" It wasn't the question, it was the voice; that cold, heartless voice. She tightened her grip on the receiver, momentarily speechless. She knew it was foolish to see Alexis, but she had to. She had to talk with her or she'd burst. The guilt, the tension and pressure had built up to an explosive level. She had to talk with someone she cared about.

"You…you, you never said I couldn't see any one," Cynthia Klash managed to stammer out in a meek, almost childish voice.

"No, I didn't. But I *did* warn you about telling any one else about our little arrangement, didn't I?" Nick Ragosta's voice never sounded more menacing.

"I didn't tell her anything…I, I swear!"

"You're lying!"

"No! No I'm not!" Klash's voice betrayed her panic.

"You told her everything, didn't you, you stupid *bitch!*" His tone was building in harshness consummate with its volume. "You told your little dike friend all about your little problem! What you were being forced to do and how devastated you are about it!"

"No...no I didn't," she was trembling now, her clammy hand had trouble holding on to the telephone. *"I swear to God!"*

"You stupid, stupid cunt! You've killed her, *Cynthia.* You've killed your lesbian lover!"

"Oh *God* no!" Cynthia Klash cried into the phone. "Oh please...please don't harm her! I **beg** you!" She was now weeping uncontrollably.

"Keep your fucking mouth shut and do as you're told...**or the next time it will be your little Bridget!**" Ragosta slammed the phone down.

Alexis Kostreva didn't show up for work the next day. Or the next. She was found on the side of the Massachusetts Turnpike, between Springfield and Worchester, with a broken neck.

Paul Haydon was easier to locate than Rick had anticipated. He never really appreciated what a wonderful tool the Internet was. On a whim he did a *Google* search of the San Francisco area's listings of private investigation agencies and found Haydon's Investigations. He glanced at his watch—ten fifteen. Not too early to call the west coast. He bit his lower lip and dialed the number. After three rings he heard the click of the receiver being picked up.

"Haydon Investigations," a deep, rich voice declared. To his surprise, Rick recognized it.

As most servicemen do, Rick and Paul promised to stay in touch, and they did for the first few years after Vietnam. But as the years went by the phone calls turned into occasional letters and the letters turned into Christmas cards as their lives became busier. Fifteen years ago even the Christmas cards fell by the wayside. Rick felt a strange awkwardness as he began to speak.

"Paul? Paul Haydon?" he asked hesitantly.

"Speaking."

"Paul Haydon, former Navy SEAL?"

Hesitation at the other end of the line confirmed he'd found his old friend, Paul Haydon. The question about his past clearly took him by surprise. It was several moments before Rick heard a cautious, *"Yes—?* Who is this?"

"Paul, this is a voice from the past. Rick—"

"*Rick Miller!*" Haydon exclaimed excitedly, suddenly recognizing the voice. "Well...I'll be dipped in shit! How the hell are ya buddy?"

"I'm fine, Paul, just fine. How about yourself?"

"Outstanding! Would you believe I just became a grandfather?"

"No shit!" Rick replied, mildly surprised and suddenly feeling old. "Well, congratulations!"

The two quickly updated each other on their lives, attempting to cover twenty years in twenty minutes. Rick was shocked to hear that Paul's wife died of an aneurysm shortly after giving birth to their only child, Amy, and he mildly rebuked his old friend for never telling him about her death. Rick had never met Vicky; silently, he wished he had. She must have been some woman—Paul never remarried.

"Just never found another woman who measured up, I guess," Paul said light-heartedly, yet with a touch of melancholy. "Came close with a wonderful lady in '92, but in the end it didn't work out." Haydon paused for a moment, cleared his throat and said, "So, Rickie...something tells me that because I haven't heard from you since what...1982, that your call isn't just for catching up. Am I mistaken?"

Rick chuckled. "You really are a detective! But hey, don't make me the heavy. You've got a finger too; you could have called me!"

"You've got a valid point."

Rick hesitated a moment then said, "You're right though, Paul; I didn't call just to bullshit." Then, remorsefully he added, "And...I'd like to add that I feel kinda bad about having a motive to call you...after all these years."

"Rick, don't be ridiculous," Haydon replied dismissively. "We both have lives. Hell, I've gotta apologize for not looking *you* up." There was a long pause. When Rick didn't pick up the conversation, the private investigator suspected his friend was still feeling self-conscious about the call, so he prompted, "Come on, Rickie. What's up?"

In an unmistakably serious voice Rick said, "Paul...I have a favor to ask you."

"A favor? Christ, Rick...anything. God knows I owe you a few."

"Paul, it's...it's a *big* favor—not trivial by any means."

Haydon softened his voice; reassuringly he said, "Rick, like I said, I owe you one. Shit...I'll *never* be able to repay you. You saved my life, man. Because of you I'm a father—and now a grandfather. How do you repay someone for something like that?"

"Paul...that was a long time ago, and I was just doing my job."

"Bullshit!" Haydon snapped with a touch of anger. "In '71, two guys from my unit died because their Search and Rescue team didn't have the balls to drop in a hot area. Ask your favor, Rick."

Rick let out a defeated sigh. "Alright. I need your professional services, Paul. And I can't afford to pay you a lot."

"You'll pay me nothing," Haydon shot back. His tone was adamant, leaving no room for debate. Surreptitiously, Rick was relieved; he had little in the way of disposable income. But his friend's blind generosity made him feel even worst. Until he'd actually asked Paul for his services, Rick hadn't really considered what an imposition his request might be.

"Paul...I appreciate that; I *really* do. But I think you should hear me out before offering me your assistance...gratis. You don't have an appreciation yet of how *big* this favor is."

This time Haydon let out a weary sigh. "You let me worry about that, alright?" he said placidly and paused for a moment. "Don't you remember what I told you back in Nam? That if you ever needed any help—to call me." Rick was taken aback; amazed that Paul remembered the thirty-year-old conversation as he did. "I'm grateful, Rick," he continued with dignified sincerity. "I know it happened a long time ago, but to me it still seems like yesterday. I grateful you're calling and giving me a chance to repay you for my life."

The avowal was said with such earnestness that conferring any further opposition to his offer would be an insult. "Okay, Paul—you win."

"That's more like it," Haydon said triumphantly.

"When can you spend a day or so in Minnawaka, Wisconsin? What I have is a complicated matter. I can't...don't want to really, explain it over it on the phone."

"Where the *hell* is Minnawaka?" the investigator asked with a chuckle.

"About forty miles outside of Milwaukee."

"Well, I'm finishing up a case now, Rick. I just have to get a few documents into the hands of my attorney-client. And as luck would have it, I have nothing else on the books that can't wait. Can you meet me at the airport next Tuesday?"

"You bet," Rick answered excitedly. "E-mail me your flight information when you know it and I'll see you then!"

"Okay. Until then, Rick."

CHAPTER 9

▼

"Jesus Christ, Sandra! This is getting out of hand!" Wendell Finley whispered raucously to the young woman sitting across from him. Between bites of Prime Rib he nervously glanced around. Just because this was one of Washington D.C.'s most posh restaurants didn't render it free of eavesdroppers. Most likely just the opposite, Finley thought.

Sandra Beach studied her lover for a moment, trying to gauge his actual state-of-mind. She'd worry if he was starting to panic, but she didn't think he was at that point yet; he was just apprehensive. Regardless, she had to somehow calm him down; dispel his concerns before dinner was over and reassure him everything was under control.

She looked down at her untouched Beef Wellington and considered what to say. Then, after quickly glanced around herself, she leaned in a little towards Finley and said in a hushed voice, "Rago—" she caught herself. Although she shared much about P3 with Wendell, she still kept Nick Ragosta's name a secret. It was the wine—it almost caused her to let the name slip. "—Our man assured us her death was absolutely necessary. He had to make a point. If necessary, that's part of the plan, Wendell."

Finley leaned in as well. Quietly, but forcefully he said, "Well, I don't like it!" He frowned; his eyes darted around again and then fixed on Sandra. "Indirectly, I've got the blood of two people on my hands!"

"Don't be ridiculous," she scoffed. "You, as the client, can't hold yourself responsible for how the plan is executed."

He stared at her, an arcane look came across his rotund face. Incredulously he said, "And you, as an employee of Noble Consultants, don't feel any responsibility for these…decisions?"

His retort caught her off guard. The two deaths didn't really bother her in the least, but she didn't want her lover to think her heartless. She decided she'd better change the tone of their conversation. She shifted uncomfortably in her chair, smiled meekly at him and said, "Wendell, sweetheart…I suggest you forget about the details and keep your eye on the big picture. We're starting to see results; our man *is* producing. Soon you, Saxton and Kennelly won't have to worry about the prospect of fuel cells cutting into your profits and destroying your industry."

Finely grimaced; slightly turned off by his mistress' cold logic. He took a sip of his wine then said cantankerously, "Well, I hope so. I just wish your man wasn't so goddamned trigger happy!"

She let out a theatrical sigh, "Honey, he does what he has to do. This guy is a professional; we're giving him wide latitude and it's paying off—we're seeing results."

Wanting to put finality to this conversation she looked at the fat but incredibly wealthy man before her, licked her lips and gave him her best sultry glance. Under the table she kicked off her shoe and began to rub her foot up and down his leg. Giving him a wink she said, "C'mon, let's forget all this and go to our room."

The CEO of ENDICORP remained silent for what Sandra felt was an uncomfortably long period of time. After wiping his mouth with a napkin, folding it and placing it on his plate he said, "Not tonight I think."

"*What?*" Sandra Beach replied in stunned surprise, dropping her foot from his leg.

Wendell Finley sighed. "I'm really not in the mood right now. And besides, I promised my wife I'd accompany her to a cocktail party tonight, so I need to fly home."

Sandra was miffed. With one exception he hadn't been "in the mood" for a long time. Genuinely frustrated she said, "Why didn't you tell me about this *party* yesterday when we made arrangements? I wouldn't have bothered to book a room."

He shrugged. "She just mentioned it to me this morning, before I got on the Lear to fly out here."

She was mad, but knew it was best to curb her anger. Teasingly, but with a touch of sarcasm she said, "So…your wife is taking precedence over me now?" She immediately regretted saying that; he was becoming visibly irritated.

"Occasionally my dear, I have to at least *act* like a husband!" he snapped.

Sandra wanted nothing more than to tell him to go to hell, but she reminded herself to keep *her* eye on the big picture. But she was becoming concerned. Their last few encounters had been strained, and it had been over a month since they'd last slept together. Although he'd shown no outward signs of disenchantment with her, she was worried that her plan might be starting to come apart.

"Of course you do," she conceded congenially. She gave him a hopeful smile and added sweetly, "When can we meet again, Wendell? I…I, miss you." She started running her foot up and down his leg again.

Finley finished off the rest of his wine then said flatly, "I don't know. I'll call you." With that, he got up and without so much as a kiss on the cheek, left the table.

Sandra Beach watched him walk out of the restaurant with narrowing eyes. Within her, along with a mixture of anger and anxiety, she could feel a growing contempt.

As much as he hated to admit it, Paul Haydon had his reservations. After meeting with Rick and listening to his plight, the investigator warned his friend that in taking on this case, he might be biting off more than he could chew. Haydon Investigations, he explained, typically concentrated on fraud and embezzlement cases for small to mid-sized companies. He'd never investigated a blackmail case before—if that's what it was. For Rick, however, he'd of course try.

Rick explained that the peculiarities he was encountering were happening at both Global Fuel Cell Technologies and Unlimited Energy Systems. Not wanting to endanger Cynthia Klash in anyway, Rick asked his friend to concentrate his investigation only on UES. Because of the similarity and timing of the incidences between the two companies, there had to be a connection. Rick reasoned that if Paul ferreted out who or what was behind the problems at UES, they'd most likely have answers for the situation GFCT.

He'd of course do what Rick asked, but Haydon wasn't keen on the idea of just investigating Unlimited Energy Systems, and told Rick as much. As it stood now, Cynthia Klash offered him his only concrete lead—a starting point. Without the information he'd be able to wean out of her, his investigation would be much more difficult and take more time—he'd be starting from scratch.

The fact that Paul Haydon was financing this venture out of his own pocket made Rick feel all the worse for handicapping him by insisting that he only focus on UES. But Rick had to balance that against his conscience and the personal torment he'd have to endure should some harm befall the woman on account of him. He hoped that Paul would understand.

Gaining access to Unlimited Energy Systems was a simple matter. Like most companies, UES used a janitorial service and the owner of Troy Custodial Services was delighted to finally find and hire someone whose primary language was English. But Todd Neumann, owner of the service was initially suspicious; he wondered why this seemly educated, responsible and reliable looking white man was willing to take this kind of job—and for minimum wage no less. But when Haydon explained that he was a homeless Vietnam Vet, no more questions were asked about his motives.

Neumann was a little perturbed by Paul Haydon's one request—insistence really. He would only work for his service if he was guaranteed the offices of one particular customer—Unlimited Energy Systems. It was close to his apartment and he could save money by not having to drive to and from work. Not wanting to risk losing one of the most promising potential employees he'd interviewed in years, Neumann agreed to Haydon's terms for employment. Besides, Carlos Rodrigues, who was currently assigned to clean UES, would be happy to work another building. He'd often complained that UES was too big for only one janitor.

Progress had been excruciatingly slow. He'd been with the cleaning service for over two months now and had yet to learn anything of significance. Haydon would arrive at UES at about four o'clock—two hours sooner than he was required to—using the excuse that he need more time to properly clean the big complex. However, he used the time to mingle with the employees. Being the gregarious person he was the people at UES warmed to him quickly and gladly took time from their normally monotonous routine to chat with him.

But this form of information gathering had proved disappointing. About the only thing he'd learned so far was that everyone seemed to be frustrated with the company's setbacks. Most of their problems seemed to be self-inflicted from above, and they couldn't understand that. He'd also heard a few comments about the CEO Daniel Stallinger; most of the employees liked him, but said he didn't seem himself lately.

His lack of progress compelled him to do something he'd rather have not done. A month ago, back in July, he'd planted a bug in Stallinger's office. He would have preferred to tap his phone, but he was a detective of limited technical resources. The listening device was voice activated and turned on a recording machine in the one bedroom efficiency he rented by the month. The device switched itself off after one minute of silence. It was a low-tech solution, but it did the job.

To Haydon's consternation, Stallinger's conversations both on the phone and with employees in his office had yet to provide any type of lead. He'd never been on a case where he'd gone so long without obtaining some kind of useful clue. And for more than just professional reasons the investigator was almost desperate for concrete progress; the novelty of being a janitor was beginning to lose its luster.

As he knew it would, the price increases Rick was forced to give Unlimited Energy Systems and Global Fuel Cell Technologies raised a chorus of protest from the various buyers and engineers he worked with. Typically, shortly after implementing an increase in price, a customer's upper management becomes involved. There'd be all sorts of posturing and threats of how they were going to pull their business. Statements of how the offending company was going to be de-sourced and would never do business with them again—or any of their subsidiaries. There would be earthquakes, floods and locust—a full gamut of disasters on a Biblical scale—unless the decision was reversed and the price increase rescinded. Rick had been through it many times with different companies; reaction to a price increase was predictable.

Except in this case. His managers couldn't understand it, but Rick didn't find it strange when the fuel cell company executives didn't follow this time-honored pattern. It only strengthened his belief that something was afoul, and made him feel better about his decision to involve Paul Haydon.

For a brief time Rick was hopeful that he wouldn't have to give GFCT and UES the price increase. Donald Kampnel, seeing the sales dollars from these companies starting to roll in questioned the necessity of the action. He even came into Rick's office to discuss the matter. Rick jumped at the chance to plead with the company's owner not to take this step. The margin report must be wrong— no one on the floor was complaining about the jobs. And if they go through with the price increase, they could count on losing GFCT and UES as customers. But in the end it was David Greene and his bogus report that Kampnel believed. Of course he'd believe Greene over a salesman, Rick fumed; after all, he was *just* a salesman.

The price increases imposed by the two companies Donald Kampnel owned were bad enough, but combined with those of Drextal Industries and Rayonicx, UES had no choice but to raise the price of their residential units. Daniel Stallinger tried to block the price adjustment, but was overruled by the board of directors. The increase, along with the better than expected sales of the US1 residential units helped to mitigate the effect UES felt from their vendor's higher component cost.

At GFCT there was talk by lower level engineers of finding new suppliers for the hoses, anode and cathode plates and the power conditioning modules. But Rick, and the other veteran salespeople knew that for the short term, it was just that—talk. But the seasoned representatives also knew that if they wanted their companies to be players in this business for the long term, they would have to persuade their employers to lower prices. And pricing would have to be reduced without a change in process, something the quality and engineering departments of the fuel cell companies (most manufacturing companies for that matter) would not allow. The age-old adage for salespeople still rang true: selling to a customer was easy; selling an idea to their own company was the hardest sell of all.

Inwardly, Rick was becoming discouraged by his friend's lack of progress. Worse, he felt terrible that the costs—all the costs—were coming out of Paul's pocket. He constantly offered to chip in knowing full well that if Paul ever accepted, he'd probably soon be broke. But thankfully for Rick, his detective friend remained adamant that he'd shoulder the entire financial burden.

Paul Haydon knew that Rick was uncomfortable with their exploit's funding arrangement, so to ease his friend's conscience he explained that the investigation business had been very good to him. Compensation for several of his larger cases involved a percentage of this client's winnings, and his clients were normally lawyers. Consequently, those settlements had been quite substantial so he could easily afford to bankroll this investigation. Although there was some truth to that, this investigation was starting to take a toll. But that didn't matter; Paul Haydon was determined to repay Rick Miller.

To his trepidation, in one week Laurence Haggerty had received a call from Congressman Radakovich, Senator Plecha and Congresswoman Zwart. In the course of the conversation all three eluded that their decision to withdrawal support for the zero emissions bill was wavering. Up to this point, Haggerty had considered Curly accomplished; by the time he was on the phone with the third lawmaker he realized that he had been premature in declaring that strategy of P3 successfully completed.

Frustrated, he struggled to maintain his composure as he again reiterated the information he'd presented to them during their initial meeting; the many negative aspects fuel cells presented to their constituents and the future of their political careers. He understood and appreciated the pressure they were under to support the technology, but the risks were too great. For the good of both their constituency and themselves, they simply had to withdraw their support for the bill.

To his relief, after the lecture all three politicians once again seemed convinced of the need to not support the bill. However, they might delay their veto and debate the bill some more; they couldn't appear too eager to drop their support for the technology. After all, several fuel cell companies—including GFCT and UES—had members on their board of directors who were major campaign contributors.

It was sickening the amount of hand-holding these elected officials needed. They had no backbone. Haggerty was disgusted by politicians and the games they played.

CHAPTER 10

▼

Nick Ragosta watched in amusement as the owner of Noble Consultants bit his nails. He'd never seen him bite them before, and bite probably wasn't the right word; he was gnawing at them.

Dropping his hand from his mouth, Laurence Haggerty, completely deflated, looked dolefully at the contract killer. "That makes three problems then, doesn't it?" Ragosta solemnly nodded his head. "How'd you learn of it, Nick?"

"To be truthful, by accident," Ragosta answered, then took a sip of coffee. "By chance I first saw them together at the Dulles Airport Sheraton—at the bar. I had a lot of coffee that afternoon and I couldn't hold it any longer. So I stopped at the hotel to take a piss before parking my car at the ramp. I happened to look in the bar on my way to the men's room, and there they were."

"I take it they didn't see you?" Haggerty inquired.

Ragosta shook his head. "No. They were too preoccupied with each other. Or, should I say...she was preoccupied with *him*." He took another sip of coffee. "Anyway, I followed them for a few months. There's no doubt in my mind that they're sleeping together." He paused then added solemnly, "I, ah...I know how you feel about her Laurence, so I wanted to be sure before I said anything to you."

"Fuck!" Haggerty roared, slamming his fist down on the desktop. Then, shaking his head he muttered, "Sandra, Sandra, Sandra. This isn't good." He sighed and folded his arms over his chest. After sulking for a minute he said, "I'll ah...I'll talk with her. I know she'll level with me. I refuse to believe she'd say anything to him that would compromise The Committee or P3." Ragosta grimaced and gave him a disbelieving glance.

"Goddamn politicians were wavering too," Haggerty mumbled, rubbing his face with his hands. After dropping them he added, "Based on my last conversation with the spineless bastards I'm not really sure anymore how much influence they actually have over their colleagues. But I'm not too worried; I doubt Hanson's zero emissions bill will get up for a vote this session—it's an election year." Haggerty paused, looking thoughtful for a moment then added, "It could well pass in 2005, however." He sighed, got up from behind his desk and walked towards the coffee pot. While pouring himself a cup of coffee he said, "In any case, I don't think the bill is an immediate threat to our client." The hit man said nothing; he just nodded his head.

The owner of Noble Consultants sat back down behind his desk. After taking a small sip of coffee he gave Ragosta a hard stare and said, "And lastly…Moe has been ineffective so far. Correct?"

The assassin put his cup of coffee on the table and tightly folded his arms over his chest. Looking discouraged he answered, "That's right. The price increases are having little effect. Unlimited Energy Systems is passing its increased costs on with no repercussions; numerous utilities are still buying them. Global Fuel Cell Technologies' parent company, Global Technologies Corporation, is simply absorbing the increase. My guess would be that it's pocket change to them."

"Turn up the heat!" Haggerty snapped angrily while jumping to his feet. Feeling indifferent, Ragosta watched him walk over to the window and absently look outside. Presently, Haggerty turned and faced the assassin. "Shit! UES goes into production with their new US3 in less than a year! The supply chain infrastructure of these companies *must* start to crumble before then!" Ragosta again calmly nodded his agreement.

Haggerty started nibbling at one of his fingers again, lost in thought. The hit man noticed he had a determined yet worried look on his face. After about a minute of deep reflection he looked at his finger, broke into a disgusted expression then dropped it. He raised his eyes to Ragosta.

"What are you going to do, Nick? I don't want any more fatalities if possible."

Ragosta let out a long sigh and stood up himself. He shoved his hands in his pockets and said, "I don't know yet, Laurence. But I'll send a message to all my friends clearly stating my impatience with their lack of progress. I admit that up to this point I've been easy on them; I didn't think it necessary to be firmer. But I guess it's time I kick Moe into high gear."

Haggerty raised his hand to his mouth, looked at it, grimaced, and then dropped it. "Good. By Saturday, let me know what you're going to do. I have to fly to London on Sunday to update The Committee." Ragosta pursed his lips and bobbed his head in acknowledgement.

"*LAURA!*" the office door opened a moment later. His young administrative assistant quickly, but calmly entered her boss' office; she had grown accustomed to his occasional outbursts. "Laura, find Ms. Beach and tell her I want to see her immediately!"

"Yes, Mr. Haggerty."

Finally, Paul Haydon got a break. Lumbering into his tiny apartment at two-thirty in the morning he threw his keys and a bag of burgers on the table and when straight to the small refrigerator to grab a beer. As he pulled off the bottle's cap he glanced jadedly at the Wendy's bag he'd brought home after another dreary day of sweeping floors, empting wastepaper baskets and cleaning toilets. With a grunt, he plopped down on the couch and realized he didn't have much of an appetite, at least not for burgers again.

Over the last seven months he'd gained a genuine respect for people in the sanitation industry. The work was mind-numbing, but essential. It didn't seem right that so many people took it for granted. There was a boss' day, secretary's day, teacher's day, a day for almost every occupation, except sanitation. Taking a sip of beer he thought how there should be.

Seven months! Haydon thought despondently while shaking his head in disbelief. Not for the first time, he questioned the magnitude of the debt he owed his friend Rick Miller. His investigation was going nowhere and if something didn't break soon, he might be forced to throw in the towel. Not from a financial standpoint. Much to his amusement the owner of Troy Custodial Services was so pleased with his work that be doubled his salary. Living simply, the private investigator could actually make ends meet and still have a few bucks left over to enjoy the finer things in life—the bottle of beer in his hand was testimony to this. No, he'd have to fold from lack of progress. He feared that Rick might interpret his leaving the case as a tacit accusation of him dreaming the whole thing up. As much has he loathed the thought, at some point you had to call it quits, and he was concerned that that point was rapidly being reached.

What made the situation so frustrating was that Rick was still suffering setbacks. Haydon had learned enough at UES to confirm that something was going on, and it hurt his professional pride that he couldn't flush it out. Taking a long swallow of beer he began to feel petulant, and thought how things might be different if Rick would have let him talk to Cynthia Klash.

His thoughts went back to Rick, and how he complained that every other week it seemed as if another competent engineer was let go by either UES or GFCT. Haydon could confirm this. Some of the brightest young engineers were being let go at UES while they kept the less capable ones. He wasn't a business-man, but even he knew this was no way to make a company prosper.

From the start, his friend was certain that Cynthia Klash was being black-mailed, and suspected Daniel Stallinger was suffering the same fate—*if only I could confirm this!* Now, Rick told him he thought his boss, David Greene, was in on it too. Unlike Klash, Rick wasn't sure if Greene was being pressured by out-side forces. After all, the man was never a fan of the fuel cell industry. But Rick said he'd given it a lot of thought and said he found it difficult to believe Greene would deliberately ruin an opportunity that would eventually generate tremen-dous revenue for the company. It couldn't possibly be in Greene's interest to do so.

With effort, Haydon reached over and pushed the rewind button on his recording device. While it was rewinding he apathetically unwrapped his double bacon cheeseburger. As he did every morning after coming home from work, he munched his food, had a few beers and listened to the numerous conversations of UES' chief executive officer. Listening to what the man went through everyday, if given a choice, Haydon decided he'd rather be a janitor. He took a bite of his cheeseburger, looked at it disdainfully and tossed it back on the table.

After listening for forty five minutes—five phone conversations and two brief meetings—he began to tune out. It was then that he heard what he'd been des-perately hoping to hear for so long. A lead. Or at least what he believed to be a lead. He put his beer down, rewound the tape for a few seconds, pushed play, and sat attentively with his ear turned to the recorder.

It wasn't what was initially said, but rather how Stallinger said it. There was no question the man was terrified by whoever was at the other end of the line. And as he listened to the conversation a second time, it was evident to the detec-tive that the CEO was struggling to put up a brave front.

"Not long enough, Mr. R," was said with uncharacteristic scorn. There was a pause. "No, there's no one else in my office." A pause, longer this time. "No, I'm certain no one suspects yet; certainly not any member of my staff and none of the board members. Though, I must say I raised a few eyebrows when I objected to the price increase. It's understandable." Pause. "*What?*" Pause. "What the *hell* do you mean not fast enough?" A long pause; so long in fact that Haydon was wor-ried the machine might automatically shut down. If it did, he might lose precious clues as it cycled and turned back on when Stallinger did speak again. Finally, "I...I had to! I had no choice." The detective let out a sigh of relief.

At this point Haydon bitterly regretted that he didn't tap the phone. He cursed himself for not taking the time and money to obtain the equipment. Pushing the thought aside he continued to listen to Daniel Stallinger on the tape. "I *had* to agree to the price increase; the board was all over me." Pause. "I told you, *I tried goddamit!* Don't you understand? I would have aroused suspicion if I'd pushed too hard. I had to give in and agree." Long pause. "*You* were the one who told me to take it slow, to be cautious!" There was another very long pause causing Haydon to worry about the machine again. But fortunately, the pause was only about forty seconds.

When Stallinger spoke again the private investigator could tell he was clearly panicked. "*No! No!* That won't be necessary! I'll think of something." Pause. Now Stallinger's voice began to tremble. "Please, *please* don't harm him. You'll have your results, I promise you that." A very short pause. "Soon."

Haydon heard Stallinger hang up the phone. The sound of the handset falling into its cradle was soon followed by, "Jesus Christ," in a shaken voice. The CEO of Unlimited Energy Systems began to mumble to himself. Despite his best attempts, Haydon could only make out a few words, but "Brett" was clearly one of them.

The detective listened to the conversation several more times; there was no question in his mind now that the man was being blackmailed. This "Mr. R" was definitely pressuring him. Ricky's suspicions were right—thankfully.

Sipping his beer again his mind began to race; so much so that he didn't even notice the beer was now warm. Who was this Mr. R and what was his motive for pushing Stallinger to destroy the company? How could he use this precious tidbit of information? Where the hell should he go from here? What was the connection between Stallinger's company and GFCT? There had to be some connection. Who would stand to benefit from the collapse of these two companies?

Haydon set his beer down and began to rub his temples. He was tired but knew he'd never sleep now. Before he could attempt to go to bed he'd have to agree with himself on a course of action, and it didn't take long for him to decide what to do. He promised Rick he wouldn't approach Cynthia Klash, but not Daniel Stallinger. He really saw no other choice but to confront him. If he'd interpreted the one sided conversation he'd just listened to correctly, there was no one else at UES who knew, or even suspected what Stallinger was up to. Daniel Stallinger was his best—his only lead.

Although it was extremely difficult for him, Haggerty maintained his composure until Sandra Beach was comfortably seated in the plush chair in front of his desk. By her manner and mood it was clear she had no idea why he'd summoned her; she appeared quite relaxed. As she crossed her legs Haggerty thought again how much he wasn't looking forward to this confrontation.

Over the years he'd come to admire and respect the young woman; often wishing Julie, his own daughter, was more like her. And he considered her like a daughter too, which made this situation all the more painful. He struggled to understand how she could have used such poor judgment to carry on an affair that could put P3, him and Noble Consultants at risk.

His sudden crestfallen expression erased the smile from her face and prompted her to ask, "Laurence is everything alright?"

He looked at her for the first time and swallowed hard, but found he couldn't continue looking at her. Turning his face from her he sternly asked, "Sandra…what do you think you're doing?"

His grave tone as well as his odd and unexpected question caught her off guard. Her head jerked back slightly and her face took on a perplexed expression. "What are you talking about, Laurence? I'm doing…what?"

"You're doing Finley!" he snapped angrily. This was the first time in their long relationship he'd ever taken a hostile tone with her and she was completely taken aback; as much by his temperament as by the realization that her affair with the CEO of ENDICORP had been unearthed.

For several seconds her mouth moved but nothing came out; her face was blank with shock. She finally managed to utter, "Laurence, I…I—"

His fist slamming down on the desktop cut her off and caused her to recoil. ***"Dammit Sandra!"*** he bellowed while leaping to his feet. "What the *hell* are you thinking? Do you realize what you could be doing? How you could be compromising P3 and placing one of our clients in harm's way?" He stormed around the desk and planted himself directly in front of her. Looking down at her he shook his head and added, "The thought ever occur to you?"

She was shaken but quickly pulled herself together. Looking up at him she said mellifluously and with sincere conviction, "I'd never do *anything* to jeopardize you or this firm, Laurence. My god…I'd hope you'd know that by now!"

All at once Haggerty's entire body went limp. He moaned despairingly, fell back and sat on the edge of his desk. Gazing at his feet he softly said, "P3 is not going well, Sandra. And you of all people complicating matters—" he threw his hands in the air and looked at her, "—is more than I can fathom."

With a touch of defiance her boss considered arrogant given the situation she replied, "Do you really think I'd tell him anything that would compromise P3, or compromise him for that matter?" She thought she sounded so convincing she almost believed her own lie. "C'mon Laurence, do you really think I'm that stupid?" With a gasp that expressed her wounded feelings, she tightly crossed her arms over her chest and kept her expectant eyes locked on her boss, waiting for him to respond.

It took him far longer to reply than she would have liked, but when he did his answer was reassuring. "No. Of course not," he said calmly. "But it could happen, Sandra. A slip of the tongue when your mind isn't fully engaged…or while drinking." He paused a moment then asked, "How long has this been going on anyway?"

She shrugged. "A little over a year and a half now."

Haggerty's eyes widened in disbelief. "*A year and a half!*" he exclaimed. "Eighteen fucking months and you don't think you've said anything in all that time that could be damaging?"

She gave him a censorious look. "It's not like we're living together. We see each other occasionally—when it's convenient for him. I can assure you, Laurence, I've said nothing. We've never even discussed P3!" Haggerty noticed she now had trouble keeping her eyes on him—she had to be lying. They couldn't have spent all their time together in bed; Finley was his age for Christ's sake, not twenty-five. And what could they possibly have in common to talk about other than their professional relationship?

He looked down at her with a dubious expression, then his face turned sour. Shaking his head he asked, "What…exactly do you see in him anyway? I mean…he's over twice your age and not exactly what I'm sure most women would consider, ah…handsome."

Men, Sandra thought to herself. *It's always about sex with them!*

"You're a fine looking woman, Sandra," Haggerty continued in a reassuring, fatherly voice. "I'm sure if you put your mind to it, you could find a man your age."

"No, he's certainly not youthful or the best looking guy I've ever, ah…" she paused for a moment, looking for the right words. "…ever been with. But he's got something most men—particularly men my age—don't."

"And what's that?"

Fire flared in her eyes as she answered, "A fortune!"

Her reply shouldn't have shocked him—he knew she was a determined woman, sometimes to the point of being pushy—but it did. "Ohhhh Sandra," he moaned. "I know you're ambitious, it's one of the traits I admire about you. But I never figured you for a…a, gold-digger." A hurt look quickly flashed across her face, but Haggerty didn't regret what he'd said. He continued. "You're not so naïve as to think he'd leave his wife for you?"

The young woman stiffened and put on an assertive air. "Yes. Frankly I do," she declared confidently. "He'll leave her." She paused, turned away from Haggerty and pulled her arms tighter to her chest. A moment later her head snapped back and an aura of unbridled greed began to radiate from her. With narrow, austere eyes she said, "It's not just the money I want, Laurence." A small, devilish smile came across her face. "It's the power and position that come along with it!

He couldn't hide the disgust and disappointment he'd suddenly felt toward her; but he had to maintain his composure. He took a deep breath and pushed aside the emotions that were contorting every muscle in his face. Evenly he said, "I had no idea that was so important to you."

"Perhaps you don't know me as well as you think you do," she replied scornfully. Sandra jumped to her feet and stood inches from her boss. Hands flailing she shouted, *"Goddamit, I want to be somebody!"* Angrily she spun and stepped away from him. She folded her arms across her chest again and let out a long, despondent sigh. Keeping her back to him she said more calmly, "I don't want to spend the rest of my life being somebody else's lackey." She slowly turned to him. "No offense." Haggerty said nothing; he continued to look at her sullenly. Insolently she added, "If I have to sleep my way to prominence, so be it. It's the one advantage I have as a woman!"

Neither said anything for over a minute; they just stared at each other; Sandra defiantly, the president of Noble Consultants morosely. Haggerty broke the impasse; he grimaced, and with the sincere concern of a parent said, "He's just using you, Sandra. Can't you see that? Once he's tired of you he'll toss you aside like he's undoubtedly done with so many others. What makes you think you'll be the exception?"

Before she could answer he blurted out, "You'll have to stop seeing him!"

"What? Why?" she shouted insolently, then was suddenly embarrassed by her own stupidity; she knew the answer to that question all too well. She looked away from her boss and asked solemnly, "And if I refuse?"

Despondent, Haggerty dropped his chin to his chest and walked around the desk. Plopping down heavily in his black leather chair he looked up at the young woman before him and softly pleaded, "Please don't put me in that situation, Sandra."

But she pushed. "What if I do, Laurence? What will you do?" When he remained silent she took a deep breath, leaned her head back and looked at the ceiling. After a moment's contemplation she looked back down at him and said in humble sincerity, "I'll never get another chance like this, Laurence. Never." Her boss remained unmoved. He continued to study her, not saying a word. "Can I have a few days to…to, think this through?" she added.

His expression turned hard; until now she never would have believed she could feel uncomfortable in his presences. "You've got until the end of the week," he answered harshly. "Should I learn that you're still seeing him after that time, I'll…" He paused. Sandra could clearly see that he was having difficulty completing the statement. "I'll have no choice but to terminate you." Her alarmed expression caused him to quickly add, "I mean terminate your employment with Noble Consultants, of course." Had it not been for the hiring of Nick Ragosta, she wouldn't have thought twice about Haggerty's use of the word "terminate." But the fact that he quickly amended the sentence gave her cause for concern. "You *know* I don't want to do that."

She gave a slight nod of her head. "I know," she replied, then tried vainly to give him a warm smile.

When in the office, Laurence Haggerty's morning routine seldom varied; it was a schedule Sandra Beach knew well and was counting on this morning. As he headed to the men's room for his morning constitution, Sandra slipped into his office. She knew his password and quickly typed it to gain access to the files on his hard drive. She glanced at her watch. Like most men, Laurence would be on the throne far longer than was necessary to complete the job. In his case, a minimum of ten minutes—the time it usually took him to scan the *Washington Post*.

From the pocket of her trousers she quickly produced a floppy disc; to her surprise she saw that her hand was slightly trembling. She nervously glanced at the door to the office then slid the floppy into Haggerty's computer. As she listened to the jagged hum of the A drive burning a copy of P3 she allowed herself to relaxed a little. The document was long and detailed, but she should have it copied before Laurence got to the paperwork portion of his current task.

She breathed a sigh of relief as she punched the floppy disc out and put it back in her pocked. The day may come when she'd need an ace up her sleeve.

CHAPTER 11

▼

Bob Curran, material's manager for Global Fuel Cell technologies, stared at his computer's monitor with a mouth slightly askew. He was completely perplexed by the email he had just received from Drextal Industries' sales manager.

Although welcome, the action the company was taking came with no explanation. Drextal's recent price increase came with no justification and the letter he was now reading, reversing that increase, didn't come with one either. Damned curious, he thought.

Perhaps most intriguing to Curran was the reaction of GFCT's executives to Drextal's price increase, and the price increase imposed on them by several other of their strategic suppliers. There *was* no reaction from them. It was an anomalous situation. Upper management was completely oblivious to that which normally caused all hell to break lose.

Typically, when Cindy Klash even caught wind of a possible price increase by a vendor, she would be all over her staff to take whatever actions were necessary to prevent it from actually being implemented. In all his twenty-two years in purchasing—twenty of them at three other large companies—he'd never seen a situation quite like this. Understandably bewildered, his buyers were coming up to him asking what the hell was going on. All he could do was shrug his shoulders and tell them the truth—he had no idea.

In addition to lowering their prices on the Anode and Cathode plates they supplied to GFCT (5% below the initial price), the letter went on to state that Drextal Industries would make a renewed effort to assist GFCT in their research and development efforts. They valued GFCT as a customer, wanted to increase their business with them, blab blab blab, so on and so forth. With a few clicks of his mouse he forwarded the message to Cindy Klash and the rest of the staff with a plea that if anybody knew what was going on, he'd appreciate it if they'd bring him into the loop.

At hearing the news Nick Ragosta was absolutely livid. He actually lost his cool—something he rarely did. When Maltese—one of the men hired by Haggerty to electronically monitor GFCT's compliance to Ragosta's terms and conditions—informed him of Drextal's price decrease, Ragosta picked up a chair and threw it across his hotel suite.

"You're sure Drextal reversed the price increase?" Ragosta growled into his cell phone after his rage subsided a bit.

"Positive," Maltese replied. "Our..." he hesitated, not wanting to use the word 'tap' over the phone. "...equipment we've placed on, ah...the lady's and others, ah...you know, have been working flawlessly. I've even got two of the executives talking about it. Care to hear it?"

Ragosta ran a hand through his short, black hair. "No. That won't be necessary." He let out a long sigh. "Goddamit! Looks like I need to schedule a trip to Lawrence, Kansas. I fuckin' hate Lawrence, Kansas!"

As his flight landed at Albany International Airport, Rick Miller noticed that the leaves were finally starting to change color. It was the end of September, rather late for the leaves to just begin turning. But despite the delay it was shaping up to be a beautiful fall; his favorite time of year.

Perhaps this gorgeous afternoon was a good omen. Maybe tomorrow he'd get some encouraging news for a change. It took three months, but he finally got an appointment with Greg Goulman, Unlimited Energy Systems' vice president of engineering. Greg wasn't apposed to meeting with Rick; it was just that he was so busy they could never find a time to get together that was convenient for both of them. Last week, Rick tried again to schedule a meeting with Greg and the man finally had an open hour during lunch. The salesman wasted no time inviting him out for a bite.

Rick felt it crucial to meet with Goulman. Over the years he had learned that an actual meeting provided far more information—accurate information—than a telephone conversation or an email exchange. In this era of instant electronic communications there was still no substitute for an old fashion face to face talk. It added a touch of humanity to a business world that, through technology, was rapidly eliminating actual human interaction.

"It's hard to believe," Goulman said after he'd ordered a club sandwich and handed his menu back to the waitress. "But despite it all, we are making progress." He paused, grimaced and added, "As you well know, Rick, we've been our own worst enemy."

Rick nodded his head. "I'd be less than truthful if I said I wasn't a little frustrated by some of the decisions coming out of your company lately."

"Frustrated? Shit, I'd be pissed as hell if I were you!" the engineer animatedly responded. Pleased with his retort, he smiled and then turned serious. "Flexible Tubing Technologies and Flexible Sealing Solutions have put a lot of work into us; it's understandable they'd want to see some progress, some return on investment." He paused a moment. Then, flashing Rick an admonished look said, "Your recent price increase isn't helping matters."

Discomfiture contorted Rick's face and he glanced down, watching his hands smooth out the napkin on his lap. "I know," he replied softly. Then, looking back at Goulman he added with conviction, "Believe me, Greg, I fought the increase tooth and nail—to the point where if I kept pushing the issue, they'd broom me. But," he shrugged, "at the end of the day, I'm just a peddler."

"A damn good one though," Goulman said sincerely. "You've been invaluable to me and my engineers and I appreciate it. If it wasn't for you're past efforts, we wouldn't be having lunch together right now."

Rick smiled self-consciously. "Thank you…that means a lot." He was truly touched by Goulman's complement. It was exceptionally rare for a customer to complement the efforts of a vendor's representative. But wanting off the subject of his company's price increase, Rick quickly asked, "So tell me, what progress are you making?"

"In spite of Stallinger," Goulman said sourly, "we'll start production on the US3 by July of 04. We also expect to announce at that time that we're going to begin development on a new residential unit. One that will not only supply power to a house, but will also have the added capability of providing fuel— hydrogen pure enough for use in a fuel cell powered vehicle. The consumer will be able to fill up his car at home. It will be a hell of a convenience."

The concept was intriguing and Rick said so. But hearing Goulman mention Stallinger made him curious about the CEO; in particular, how he was perceived by the employees at UES. As a condition for conducting the investigation for free, Paul Haydon, much to Rick's dismay, refused to provide him any detail on the investigation. Haydon justified this policy by explaining to Rick he might inadvertently let slip something to somebody at UES that might tip them off to the clandestine investigation. Rick had no choice but to accept his friend's terms, and knew that Paul would tell him what was going on when he felt the time was right. Rick just had to be patient. But curiosity was getting the better of him.

The waitress arrived with their food and Rick began nibbling on a French fry. Casually he asked the engineer, "I've heard a lot of talk around UES about Stallinger; how he's changed and made some questionable decisions. What's up with him? I mean, is he having some kind of problem…or under a lot of pressure from the board of directors?"

Greg Goulman shrugged. "I don't know. I don't think so. Of course, I don't know what's going on in his personal life; but if there are problems at home I would hope they wouldn't effect his business decisions. I'm as baffled by him as everybody else."

The engineer took several bites of his club sandwich. As he was chewing Rick took the opportunity to ask, "From what I've heard he's kind of wishy-washy. He doesn't sound like a very methodical guy. You're around him a lot; is that true?"

Goulman raised a finger indicating he'd answer as soon as he was done chewing. Several moments later he said, "It's strange. He'll go weeks acting normal—like his old self. Then boom! It's like he's on some kind of drug. He acts…I don't know…like…well, just plain irrational." He shook his head. "What I can't understand is how members of the board don't see this and take some kind of action. Shit, if I were one of them, I'd be asking him some pretty tough questions. He could easily cause the company irreparable damage."

The engineer put his sandwich down; he looked uncomfortable. "I really shouldn't be telling you this, Rick. I consider Dan a friend. But you've been involved with UES for so long and helped us so much, I don't mind sharing this with you. You…will of course keep this to yourself?"

"Of course I will," Rick assured him. "Like you said, I've got a lot invested in UES—not only my company's time and money, but also my reputation at FSS and FTT. I've pushed harder for United Energy Systems than I've pushed for any other customer in my career. I've pushed our engineers, chemists and management to the point of being obnoxious because I really believe in both your company and its product. I don't want to see it fail."

Goulman nodded his understanding. Rick continued. "Has the board had *any* reaction to his strange behavior and…" he searched for the right word, but it didn't come to mind. "And, well…poor decisions?"

Goulman took a sip of soda and pondered the question for a moment. He put the glass down and said, "To the best of my knowledge none of the board members have actually *seen* his bizarre behavior. With regard to his judgment, I can only guess that as they haven't taken any action against him yet they still see his decisions as best for the company…strange as that may be."

Rick decided he'd pushed the subject far enough and moved on to more mundane matters. He left the lunch meeting feeling thwarted. He was glad to hear that UES was moving forward, but disappointed that he didn't learn anything new about the CEO that could be useful. He hoped Paul Haydon was having better luck.

Sending a signal to the CEO of Drextal Industries would be a little tricky; Patricia Pennington's husband was a "kept man." He didn't have a job and they had no children. As a consequent, Mr. Pennington didn't have an established routine—something that made planning and executing a hit so much easier.

Three days of observation confirmed that Pennington's husband had no pattern to his day. One day he golfed, the next he spent around the house—undoubtedly annoying their housekeeper—and the third day he spent at the track with several older gentlemen who appeared legitimately retired. To top it off, his wife wasn't a bad looking woman. In fact, she was gorgeous. If he weren't rich himself, Nick Ragosta would be jealous.

Finding a suitable location to kill her husband would be next to impossible. Reluctantly, the assassin decided he would have to make a snap decision when a relatively good combination of area, surroundings and time of day presented itself. And that would have to happen soon; he had other pressing matters to attend to.

To his relief that opportunity came the next evening.

About two in the afternoon Jeff Pennington started bar hopping. Ragosta had followed him to no less than five different establishments when he'd finally entered one that showed promise for the necessary combination of elements. A little after eight he walked into The Exotic Kingdom—a sleazy little titty bar on the outskirts of the city.

The assassin hid in the shadows of an alley near to where Pennington had parked his BMW. If no one was around when he left the bar, the hit would take place here. A very light rain was starting to fall and Ragosta lifted the collar of his coat to ward off the chill. He lit a cigarette, something that until recently he didn't do very often, and leaned against the cold, damp brick wall.

Blowing out a cloud of blue smoke he thought how he'd much rather kill Patricia Pennington; Christ, the bitch actually had the balls to defy him. But if he killed her, who would reinstate the price increase? He'd have to start the whole goddamn process over again with whoever replaced her. No, regrettably, her husband had to be the one to go.

Two hours and four cigarettes later, Jeff Pennington stumbled out of The Exotic Kingdom; he was clearly inebriated. His condition made Ragosta smile; assassinating him would be that much easier. The CEO's husband appeared to be disorientated; he walked a short distance and stopped under a streetlight. Ragosta watched him look up and down the dark, misty street, obviously trying to remember where he'd left his car. Ragosta glanced around himself; the street was empty—the conditions were ideal. Under his breath Ragosta cursed when he saw Pennington begin to walk the wrong way. The assassin shook his head in disbelief. How the hell did the dumb son-of-a-bitch expected to drive in his condition? Being married to the daughter of the founder of Drextal Industries most likely had its advantages, Ragosta thought. If charged with drunk driving, he could probably buy his way out of the charge. Well, Mr. Pennington wouldn't have to worry about that tonight.

The kept man only walked about fifty feet before he realized he was going the wrong way. As Pennington approached the alley, Ragosta scanned the area and peeked around the corner again to make sure it was still deserted. The assassin cursed again; two men were now walking about a hundred yards behind his quarry. But his trepidation was short lived—they turned into The Exotic Kingdom.

Pennington was now close; Ragosta heard him mumbling to himself. He couldn't make out what he was saying—not that it mattered. As soon as he came into sight Ragosta quickly stepped out of the alley, threw a rabbit punch to the man's Rectus Abdominis—knocking the wind out of him, then slapped a hand over Pennington's mouth and dragged him into the alley.

"Complements of your wife," the assassin snarled sadistically, then rammed a long, thin knife below Pennington's ribcage straight up into his heart. The husband of Patricia Pennington gasped, and then crumpled into a pile of twitching flesh.

After using his victim's coat to wipe off his knife, Ragosta pulled Pennington's wallet from his back pocket. He withdrew all the bills; they appeared to add up to about three hundred dollars. After putting the bills in his pocket he threw the wallet next to the corpse to make the murder look like the result of a simple robbery.

Just minutes before it closed, Nick Ragosta pulled into McDonald's for a cup of coffee. The young girl at the drive thru window was clearly not thrilled to see him; and she was even more perturbed when he ordered a cup of coffee. With forced politeness she explained that the restaurant was about to close and they had no brewed coffee; would he perhaps care for a Coke? With a big smile,

Ragosta said no, he really wanted coffee and didn't mind waiting while they brewed it up. Making no effort to conceal her anger, the girl left the window to make the coffee.

Arms crossed over her chest, she impatiently waited by the coffee machine as it slowly brewed up a pot. Occasionally, she would glance contemptuous at him as he patiently waited in his car. He'd smile brightly at her through the window in turn, as if absolutely oblivious to her annoyance, further infuriating her.

Finally, she approached the window with his coffee. "One sixteen," she sneered before handing him the large Styrofoam cup.

The young girl's eyes lit up and her brace-filled mouth fell open as he handed her all of Pennington's money saying, "Keep the change, darlin." He winked and drove away.

The CEO of United Energy Systems was sitting at his desk, hunched over his keyboard, unenthusiastically pecking away. He'd occasionally stop, stare at the keyboard and after some moments passed, begin typing again. His mind seemed to be elsewhere. His tie was loosened and his hair—normally perfectly combed— was disheveled. He looked very tired. It was approaching six-thirty in the evening; he and the janitor were the only ones left in the building. Paul Haydon stood in the doorway, unnoticed, and observed the executive for several minutes. He then decided the time was right.

Haydon spent several days considering the best way to approach Daniel Stallinger; he finally decided on a mixture of truth and lies. If the executive didn't cooperate—which Haydon fully expected—then perhaps he could pressure him by making up a plausible story. He really didn't want to do that; the last thing the poor bastard needed was more pressure in his life. Haydon took a deep breath and knocked on the door.

"Good evening Mr. Stallinger. Working pretty late tonight, huh?" The investigator said in his friendliest timbre.

Stallinger slowly lifted his head. "Oh, hello Paul," he replied wearily, then went back to his typing.

After empting the wastepaper basket Haydon asked, "Mr. Stallinger, could I speak with you for a moment? It's rather important." The executive stopped typing again and gave Haydon a quizzical look that asked: *what could a janitor possibly have to say that's important?*

Stallinger let out a tired sigh. "I'm really rather busy, Paul. I'd like to get this done and go home. Is it really important?"

Haydon stared hard at Stallinger for a moment and then asked pointedly, "Is your son's life important to you?"

Stallinger was so shocked by the question he threw himself back against his chair. Any fatigue he was feeling disappeared from his face. Wide-eyed and with a trembling voice he asked, "How do you...? How could you possibly know about that?"

"How I know isn't important," Haydon replied while stepping up close to Stallinger's desk. "What's important is that you're being blackmailed; forced to destroy this company—I assume—for reasons that are unknown to you. I want to know who's doing this to you and why."

Stallinger slumped in his chair, his blank eyes returned to the keyboard. Quietly he said, "I don't even know that." Then his head shot up; he looked coldly at Haydon for a moment, and then narrowed his eyes. "You're no janitor! Who the hell are you?"

"Actually, over the last few months I think I've become a damn good janitor," Haydon replied in an attempt to add a little levity to the situation. The attempt was wasted on Stallinger. The CEO's serious eyes continued to probe him. Haydon cleared his throat and continued. "I'm a private investigator; I was hired by your chairman."

"*Dick?*" Stallinger said, sounding surprised. "Dick Alfonse hired you? Why?"

"He and several other board members have...*concerns* about some of your recent decisions and the direction those decisions are taking the company. They don't see the logic in them. They want to know what's behind your line of reasoning, or, as one board member put it, lack of it."

Daniel Stallinger gave him a suspicious look. "BULLSHIT!" he blurted out. "If they had *concerns*, as you so charitably put it, they'd just confront me. It's that simple. The board isn't a timid group, I assure you. They'd fire me in a New York minute if they thought I was dropping the ball."

Paul Haydon cringed inwardly; he was afraid Stallinger would say something like that. He'd thought long and hard about how to respond to that kind of statement and could think of no good answer. All he could do was fain ignorance and hope for the best. "I can't answer to that, Mr. Stallinger. I may not know their true motives. However, that's not why I approached you. By speaking with you I've just ended my contract with the board of directors."

"Why *are* you speaking with me then?"

"Because I know they—whoever *they* are—are threatening your son's life. I'm a parent too, Mr. Stallinger. I can't imagine what you're going through. But I believe I can help you...if you'll let me."

Stallinger sat stiffly in his chair, solicitously scrutinizing the man before him. Slowly, his expression turned morose. "You can't help me," he said glumly. "I'm not admitting to anything, Paul, or whatever your name is. I appreciate your concern and offer to help but…I'm doing as I'm told. And I would thank you to stay out of this matter. Now, if you'll excuse me…"

"Mr. Stallinger, I'm good at what I do."

The CEO's looked at Haydon with alarm, a chill shooting through him like he was shocked by electricity. *"I'm good at what I do." The same words used by Mr. R.,* he thought.

"I'm confident I can—"

"NO!" the executive shouted, cutting the investigator off. He rose to his feet. "Being *confident* doesn't do it! A guarantee wouldn't do it! I don't think you understand or appreciate what I'm dealing with." Haydon didn't respond; he only looked at Stallinger mournfully as the man sat back down and buried his face in his hands.

A few moments passed, then Stallinger lifted his head and with moistened eyes said, "You can do one thing for me, Paul. Is it Paul?"

"Yes. My name is Paul, Paul Haydon. What is it I can do for you?"

"Don't tell the board of directors we talked. Tell them that you can't find any irregularities in my character; that my day-to-day dealings with the employees of UES appear normal and that my decisions seem sound—always in the best interest of the company and based on current information. Do this for me, Mr. Haydon. Do it and you'll save my son's life."

The private investigator looked into the pleading eyes of United Energy System's Chief Executive Officer. The man once again looked tired, beaten and defeated. Haydon realized he was asking that he be left alone so he could complete the task of destroying his company. *If it was my daughter,* Haydon thought, *would I do anything different?* Being honest with himself he knew he probably wouldn't.

Haydon suddenly became depressed. He realized the investigation was over. Months of clandestine observation and analysis down the toilet he was now so adept at cleaning. He couldn't go any further without endangering the life of Stallinger's son. Staring at the defeated man before him, Haydon thought about how his friend was right—there was a conspiracy at UES. He also thought about how Rick will be disappointed that his friend, the so-called detective, was unable to ferret out those behind it. But when Rick learned that a young man's life was at stake, he'd understand because it was essentially the same situation they faced with Cynthia Klash.

The bogus janitor sighed. Dolefully he said, "Yeah…I'll do it."

"*OH MY GOD! I…I DIDN'T THINK YOU WERE SERIOUS!*" Patricia Pennington shrieked over the phone. "Oh dear God, you've…you've killed my husband!"

"*You stupid bitch!* Ragosta snarled. "What did you think I'd do? You were warned! You think I was kidding? Huh? You think this is some kinda game? You think I do this to get my fuckin' kicks?"

"I…I…" was all the CEO of Drextal Industries could manage to say in reply.

"Now you know I'm not playing games, Pennington. Raise your goddamn prices! Raise them tomorrow and keep them there. Fail, and you're next! Understood?"

"Ye…ye…yes," she stammered.

"*DO YOU UNDERSTAND?*" the assassin sneered again loudly for emphasis.

"Yes! Yes! I understand!"

Nick Ragosta slammed down the phone and smiled. The "Moe" strategy of P3 was, back on track. After he receives verification from Maltese that Pennington indeed complied, he'd inform Haggerty. Maybe he'll stop biting his nails, Ragosta thought.

Slowly putting the phone back in its cradle, Patricia Pennington broke into a smile of her own. She'd been convincing enough, she thought. She took a sip of her Vodka Tonic, leaned back in her recliner and crossed her legs. She wondered why she hadn't thought of this in the first place. It was so incredibly simple; and she could have spared both her employees and her customer a lot of unnecessary paperwork. Unfortunately, she'd have to put them through the drill one more time. Oh well, that's life!

It worked out perfectly; Mr. R came in rather handy. Unwittingly, he saved her a tremendous amount of money and trouble—she almost wished she could thank him.

With immense satisfaction she thought about how it wasn't just the money, though she would have lost plenty of that. Divorcing Jeff would've been ugly, and in the settlement she undoubtedly would have lost either the lake home in northern Minnesota or the condo in Hawaii, both of which she adored. Mr. R graciously eliminated her bum of a husband quickly and efficiently, saving her from what would have been months, if not years of prolonged legal agony. Comfortably buzzed, she raised her glass in a mock salute the killer and took another long sip.

Her eyes turned to an old picture on the fireplace mantle, taken on their honeymoon, of her and Jeff in a smiling embrace. She sighed and recalled that she did love him once—and thought he loved her. But it became painfully clear shortly after the honeymoon that he had married her for daddy's money. He had threatened many times that if she ever tried to leave him, he'd take her to the cleaners. As luck would have it, Jeff's best friend happened to be a crack divorce attorney—the best in the state. There was no question he would have milked her—and her family—for everything he could. The Pennington family would have lost millions, possibly even the company her father had labored so long and so hard to build.

She was a fool; she should have listened to her father and had Jeff sign a pre-nuptial agreement before they got married; it would have saved her years of agony. But she was young and in love—and so sure nothing would ever come between them. *God almighty, I was stupid,* she thought. *Oh well, I forgive myself.*

She'd put up with his shit for twenty years and freedom from connubial bondage might be at the cost of losing Global Fuel Cell Technologies as a customer—but it was a small price to pay. A very, very small price.

"Jesus Christ!" Bob Curran exclaimed the next day as he read the email from Drextal's sales manager. "I wish they'd make up their mind!"

CHAPTER 12

▼

She decided she needed a drink. She put the document down and headed for the kitchen cabinet. She stirred her rum and coke and solemnly watched the ice cubes twirl around inside the glass; wishing the cocktail in her hand could return her wounded pride as well as calm her tattered nerves.

Lifting the glass, Sandra Beach thought about how she'd been drinking too much lately. At first the alcohol helped, but she found she progressively needed more of it to numb the pain. 2003 ended terribly for her, and 2004 wasn't starting out much better. But she was determined that she wouldn't go down quietly—no way in hell! She'd destroy; just as she was being destroyed.

For the sake of appearance she waited for a few days; she wanted it to look like she was dwelling on the matter. Then she told Laurence Haggerty that after much deliberation she'd decided that she wasn't going to stop seeing Wendell Finley. She loved her job and she loved Laurence like a father, but the CEO of ENDICORP presented her with an opportunity that she'd never have again—she just couldn't pass up.

For several weeks her boss agonized over the decision—or so he said—but shortly before Christmas he asked Sandra to leave. He provided a generous severance package and offered to write her a glowing letter of recommendation, claming it was the least he could do. He insisted that it pained him to let her go; he considered her much more than just an employee. But she left him no choice. He had to put his client's interests and those of his firm first.

Although she knew Laurence would eventually fire her, when it actually happened it hurt, and she fell into a depressed state. To obtain her severance pay, she had to pledge that she'd keep any and all information she knew about Noble

Consultants to herself. It was a promise that was easy to make and she had every intention of keeping. If the time ever came where she had to explain her actions, she could point to the fact that technically, she never compromised the firm itself.

It was that bastard Finley she'd get even with.

Their relationship had actually taken a turn for the better prior to the New Year; his interest in her returned with a vengeance. Between Thanksgiving and the end of January, 2004, they had spent almost every weekend together—a good portion of that time in bed.

By April she felt it was time to make her move; she had played "lady-in-waiting" long enough. They'd been seeing each other for almost three years now and it was time for her lover to make a commitment. It should be no big deal for him, he'd gone though it before—twice in fact—what was one more divorce?

On Saturday, April 24th, over pre-dinner drinks at an exclusive Georgetown restaurant she told Wendell Finley about her departure from Noble Consultants. She would have preferred not to tell him of course, but he would have eventually found out. She wanted him to hear her version of why it happened first.

Oddly, he didn't seem to be surprised or concerned about her parting with Laurence Haggerty's firm, and only asked if she'd like a position within ENDI-CORP. She was half-tempted to tell him then and there the title she wanted, but decided the time wasn't quite right. She'd wait just a little bit longer.

After a wonderful meal she suggested they go for a walk; it was a lovely evening, much warmer than normal, and she wanted to work off that decadent dessert she just couldn't say no to. She knew being in the presence of college kids somehow put Wendell in a good mood. Maybe it was because his youngest daughter, Patricia, was attending the University of Connecticut. Whatever the reason, Sandra discreetly aimed for the area where college kids hung out as they left the restaurant and began walking hand-in-hand. Putting him in a better mood could only increase his receptivity, she reasoned. There would be no better time to confront him.

They strolled in comfortable silence for about fifteen minutes and she noticed the smile on Wendell's face as he watched the young people hop in and out of bars and go about their business on the busy sidewalks. The time was right. "Let's sit down for a minute, hon," she said, gesturing to a bench at the entrance of a small park. He nodded his agreement and sat down next to her. He reached in his coat pocket and produced a huge cigar, a Cuban of course; she detested them, but never made that feeling known. She'd long ago reconciled with herself that to achieve her aim, she'd have to take the good with the bad.

After he lit the expensive cigar she asked, "Wendell…how long have we been together now, three years?"

"Yeah, something like that," he replied indifferently, watching a small group of students pass by.

She was not pleased with the tone of his answer, but she steeled herself and turned to face him. She began to feel the butterflies in her stomach. This was the defining moment; the accumulation of everything she'd strived for over these last years. Either she'd win him or she wouldn't.

"In all that time I've grown to love you," she said as tenderly as she could. Although she'd rehearsed this speech for months, to her surprise she still found the words hard to say. With profound sadness, she wondered how many times she'd wished there was a man in her life, one she could say those words to with complete sincerity. "I need to know," she continued, "if you feel the same about me?" She paused a moment for effect. "Well…do you Wendell? Do you love me?"

When he didn't look at her, but only puffed on his cigar and stared out at the street, she became worried. Then, in a matter of seconds, she watched his facial expression change and realized with growing despondency that he was struggling with how to answer the question.

Finally, he turned to face her, a glint of suspicion in his eyes. He pulled the cigar from his clamped teeth, blew out a thick cloud of smoke from the corner of his mouth and asked, "What are you getting at, Sandra?"

She frowned; he was throwing it back at her. Guardedly she said, "I think you know what I'm driving at."

Wendell Finley turned away from her and stared glumly at nothing in particular; the cheerful mood he was in just moments ago had vanished. She could clearly see that compunction was beginning to wrinkle his round, hefty face. He let out a long, weary sigh; not bothering to look at her he replied emphatically, "I'm not leaving Mindy, if that's what you're getting at." He put the cigar back in his mouth.

His blunt statement had a definiteness to it that struck her like a slap on the face. Instantly she was overcome with anger. She tried to control her temper but couldn't. *"Why not?"* she demanded to know in a voice filled with hostility. "I *thought* we had something…something special between us!"

Stunned, Finley turned to face her with an astonished expression. He plucked the cigar from his mouth and let out a terse, contemptuous laugh. *"Something special?"* he began incredulously. "Something special?" He waved his hand in a dismissive gesture. *"Shhhit* woman, you're my mistress—nothing more! I've had *something special* with many like you before and they'll be plenty of women in the years ahead I'll have *something special* with." Sandra Beach couldn't believe her ears; she was completely taken aback. She'd thought she was prepared for rejection, but never fathomed he'd respond like this—in such a cruel, heartless manner. Mouth agape in disbelieve, all she could manage to do was stare at the man who—after all these years—was announcing his true feelings; malicious feeling she had absolutely no idea he harbored.

"Do you know how many of my former mistresses have wanted me to leave my wife and marry them?" he continued, but much calmer. "Huh?" Still completely dumbstruck, Sandra didn't respond. "Damn near every one! That's how many." He spun away from her and watching a young woman cross the street said, "You score no points for originality my dear."

Still speechless, Sandra gazed at his profile for a moment as he continued to stare straight ahead. Although he was trying to put on the appearance of insouciance, he was clearly agitated and took quick little puffs on his cigar. Anger was starting to overcome her shock; her face hardened and her body stiffened. She took in a deep breath and said, "Wendell, I—"

But the CEO of ENDICORP cut her off. "You think I'm stupid, Sandra?" he asked rhetorically, giving her a side-glance. "You don't love me! None of them ever loved me. *Christ*...I'm getting old, I'm fat and not at all good-looking. What's to love except my pocketbook?" He paused a moment to take a puff on his cigar then added, "It's my money you and the rest love." He shook his head sadly and softly said, "Don't deny it."

She jumped to her feet. "***You bastard!***" she shouted; several people nearby turned to look in their direction. From her scarlet face, fiery eyes stared at him with murderous intent. "You just *used* me!" she sneered. "You consider me nothing more than a...a plaything. Your personal whore!"

Finley sighed; thinking how many times he'd been down this road before. He looked at his cigar, frowned, then threw it on the ground and crushed it out with his foot. He looked up at Sandra Beach serenely and calmly asked, "*Really?* And how does that differ from what you had up your sleeve, my dear?"

The truth of his query only served to anger her further. "***Shut up!***" she snapped viciously. With a huff she picked her purse up off the bench and threw its strap over her shoulder. Still staring at him with hateful eyes she growled, "Nobody fucks with me, Finley. *Nobody!* You haven't heard the last of me, you son-of-a-bitch!" She abruptly turned and stormed off.

Wendell Finley watched her until she rounded a corner and disappeared behind a building. He then pulled out another cigar and clamped it between his teeth. Lighting it, he wondered what she meant by her last statement.

She sipped at her rum and coke while looking at the document. Laurence had made some significant additions to the plan since she'd first read it. Names, dates, actions taken, expected outcomes and obstacles encountered up to the present. She smiled spitefully. This will be the story of the decade, she thought. When it breaks, Finley will go down hard and fast. She savored the mental picture of her former lover penniless and in prison garb. He'd get a minimum of thirty years— maybe life if they can connect him to the deaths.

She carefully slipped a copy of the document into a large FedEx envelope, took another sip of her drink, and then sealed it shut. She debated whether or not to add more to the cover letter, but she decided she'd said enough. Besides, the document was self explanatory—any idiot could understand the significance of it. She wrote the name of Joey Howells on the airbill and to remain anonymous, put down a fictitious return address. She finished her rum and coke, then got in her car and drove to the nearest FedEx drop box. A copy of P3—and her vengeance—deserved nothing less than overnight delivery!

Sandra Beach loved Newport Rhode Island and vacationed there every chance she could. During their affair she even convinced Wendell Finley to spend some time with her in the fashionable little resort town. And when in Newport, she always made a point of reading the *Providence Gazette*, mainly because of one reporter—Joey Howells. He was a journalist with the newspaper and Sandra admired his reporting. She particularly enjoyed reading the *Providence Gazette* when he contributed commentary on a current topic. If anybody could break the P3 conspiracy with the fanfare she desired, Sandra reasoned it was Joey Howells.

After depositing the package in the FedEx drop box, she decided to take a leisurely drive to Newport. It would be lonely without a companion, but maybe she'd get lucky and meet a guy at the Rusty Pelican, her favorite bar. She'd stay until she read Howells' article—then she'd have some serious decisions to make.

Laurence Haggerty hadn't briefed The Committee for some time, and had no intention of doing so until he received a call from World Energy's CEO Kenneth Saxton, hinting—none too subtly—that a briefing was long overdue. Without Sandra Beach to assist him, preparing for a meeting with the three men was a substantial amount of work. There was no one else within Noble Consultants to whom he could delegate some of the tasks; none of his employees knew anything about the conspiracy.

Ever efficient, Laura informed the assistants of Wendell Finley and Theodore Kennelly of the date, time and location of the meeting and made all of her boss's travel arrangements. She was a sharp and perceptive girl, and never inquired as to what these meetings were about, or why they were now held in London. Her prudence had always impressed Haggerty and more than once he'd considered approaching her to see if she'd be interested in replacing Sandra Beach; but he always decided against it. Despite the fact that she lacked a four-year degree she was the perfect candidate: smart, efficient, aggressive and single so she'd have no pressing relationship commitments to interfere with the demands he'd place upon her. But the information she'd become privy to had the potential of placing her in danger, both legal and bodily. Although he desperately needed a new lieutenant, he just couldn't bring himself to put Laura Olsen in that position.

Typically, The Committee sat quietly and listened attentively to his report, saving their questions until he finished a topic. That wasn't the case this afternoon. Had he not known about Sandra's affair with the CEO of ENDICORP, Haggerty would have been terrified by Finley's knowledge of the murders. Undoubtedly, he shared this information with PETROCOMP's CEO Theodore Kennelly and World Energy's CEO Kenneth Saxton.

After conformation that the boardroom had been swept for surveillance devices and brief opening pleasantries, Haggerty began his update. He had barely gotten out his first sentence when they pounced.

"Laurence," Saxton began in the thick, aristocratic English accent Haggerty was beginning to find annoying, "I believe I speak for Ted and Wendell when I say we're more than a bit concerned by the state of P3." Faces grave, Kennelly and Finley bobbed there heads in agreement. "I dare say it appears to us that you've lost control."

The president of Noble Consultants began to redden. "I know it appears that—"

"I'm completely appalled that blood has been shed in the execution of this plan," Kennelly said sharply, cutting him off. "I *never,*" he emphases the word by slamming his fist on the table, "would have agreed to the scheme had I known murdered was involved."

"Mr. Kennelly, to be—"

"If this plot of yours is discovered and we're," Finley gestured to his two colleagues, "implicated in any fashion, we're *fucked!* You *do* realize that, don't you, Mr. Haggerty?"

Haggerty took in a deep breath and did his best to remain calm. Evenly he said, "The plot is not going to be discovered, Mr. Finley, I can assure you."

Briefly, Haggerty wondered if Finley resented the fact that he asked Sandra to leave his firm. As far as he knew, they were still seeing each other.

"*Really?*" the CEO of ENDICORP shot back brassily. "You don't think the murders are going to spark investigations? Investigations that could lead to our doorstep!"

Losing patience, Haggerty began pinching the bridge of his nose. "That's *not* going to happen," he replied irritably. "I've hired the best in the business. He doesn't leave a trail of breadcrumbs."

"No one's infallible, Laurence," Kenneth Saxton offered in an uncharacteristically sardonic tone. "The more he kills, the better the odds are he *will* leave a crumb or two."

"I don't understand why anybody had to die!" Kennelly exclaimed, tossing his hands into the air. "Jesus Christ! How much are we paying this guy anyway? If he's such a goddamned professional—as you claim—why can't he get the job done without resorting to lethal measures?" That said, Kennelly crossed his arms tightly over his chest and slouched back in his chair. His face furrowed with such displeasure that if Haggerty didn't know better, he'd have though Kennelly was pouting.

Of the three men, the president of Noble Consultants was beginning to develop a profound dislike for Theodore Kennelly. There was no pleasing the old bastard and Haggerty was fed up with his belligerent attitude. Perhaps it was because Kennelly reminded him so much of his own father—who he was none to fond of—both in physical appearance and temperament. The only discernable difference between the two Haggerty thought, was that unfortunately, Kennelly was alive.

"Perhaps most disturbing, Laurence," Haggerty's head swung in the direction of Kenneth Saxton, "is that there doesn't appear to be *any* progress. I haven't hear or read anything since we commissioned this little escapade that would indicate the fuel cell industry is suffering any setbacks. On the contrary, if anything, they seem to be making better than expected progress. I've seen nothing but glowing reports about the advances being made by Global Fuel Cell Technologies in *Automotive News.*"

"And there doesn't seem to be any foot dragging in Washington either," Finley offered resentfully.

"*Gentlemen, if I may—*" Haggerty pleaded in a vain attempt to regain control.

"I think we should pull the plug on this whole sorry mess!" Kennelly blurted out, still sitting in his chair, radiating childish discontentment. He turned to face Haggerty. "You've really fuc—"

"ENOUGH GODDAMNIT!" Haggerty roared, slamming his fist on the table with such force coffee cups bounced in their saucers. Simultaneously, the heads of all three members of The Committee snapped back and they glared at him in utter shock; they weren't accustomed to being preempted in such a manner; particularly by someone who was essentially just an employee. Haggerty continued, leaning aggressively forward in his chair, arms resting on the table with clenched fists. He made no effort to mask his anger and exasperation. *"WHAT THE HELL IS IT YOU THINK WE'RE TRYING TO DO HERE? ASK SOMEONE TO RECONSIDER THEIR POSITION ON THE ENVIROMENTAL IMPACT OF HOG FARMING?"* Haggerty threw himself back in his chair and let out an angry sigh, running both hands over his balding head. Then, having composed himself he straightened in his chair and looked at his three clients who were still gawking at him in silent astonishment.

Haggerty clasped his hands together, took a deep breath and slightly dropping his head said contritely, "I'm sorry. That was unprofessional of me." He looked back up. "I assure you, gentlemen, everything is on track. I won't deny we've had a few setbacks, but those were dealt with quickly. I believe my associate when he said the eliminations were necessary. As I've pointed out numerous times, he's the best in the business. He's..." Haggerty paused for a moment, searching for the right words, "...resorted to eradication many times in his career. There have been seven extremely prominent people whose deaths were investigated by their country's best investigators—no one has ever come close to him. I assure you, gentlemen, you have nothing to be concerned about."

The three men relaxed a little; their faces slowly turning placid.

"Now, let me address the issue of progress if I may," Haggerty continued with restored confidence. "As I explained at the start of this operation, we are striving to bring about the demise of the fuel cell industry—by imposing insurmountable obstacles, among other things—without drawing undo attention. To perform this clandestine operation successfully, it must be done gradually.

"Progress *is* being made, I assure you. The increased costs Unlimited Energy Systems and Global Fuel Cell Technologies are experiencing through the price increases we've coerced through their strategic suppliers will have a devastating impact. But I don't expect much of a reaction until they publish their annual report.

"Now..." Haggerty paused long enough to take a sip of coffee; he felt he was back in control. "UES did raise the price of their product to compensate for their increased component cost, but it won't be enough to off-set the damage."

"Why did you allow UES to increase their price at all?"

Haggerty smiled for the first time. "I'm glad you asked that, Mr. Saxton. This is where hiring a professional is paying dividends. Daniel Stallinger, CEO of UES is being most cooperative—thanks to the persuasive skills of our operative in the field. Had he not taken that action, UES' board of directors would most certainly have become suspicious. More than likely Mr. Stallinger's ouster would have been the result; forcing us to start all over again with a new chief executive."

"If that was such a brilliant move, why didn't GFCT increase their price also?" Theodore Kennelly asked with unbridled pomposity.

"Because it wasn't possible, and really wasn't necessary, Mr. Kennelly," Haggerty answered evenly. Then, with the slightest of patronizing grins he added with a hint of condescension, "You seem to have forgotten that GFCT doesn't have a product on the market yet; so there's really no one to pass an increase on to." He saw the old executive flush with embarrassment. *You should be embarrassed,* Haggerty thought. *That was the question of a freshman business major. That should shut the old fuck up!* He then continued to speak as he normally did, like a college professor lecturing a hall full of students. "But even if they did have customers, Mr. Kennelly, it would be unlikely that they would increase their price. GFCT's parent company is huge, and has deep pockets. They would most likely absorb the increase until such time that they have a good foothold in their market. But when they do start selling their product, it *will* erode their profit margins—and quickly.

"Ultimately gentlemen, the price increases will erode investor confidence. The questionable market for this product, the eventual failure of the zero emissions bill to pass and the weak bottom line will cause investors to flee from the technology. The stock price of the fuel cell companies will collapse."

The Committee remained quiet for several moment; all three men looked at each other. Saxton broke the silence. With a trace of irritation he asked, "How long must we wait before we begin to see tangible results?"

Haggerty poured himself another cup of coffee then answered the question. "Unlimited Energy Systems is just starting production of their new US3 units and is scheduled to go to market with it soon. Because of the situation in Iraq and the threat by OPEC to limit production to raise prices, I suspect the sale of the unit to be brisk—particularly in the North East where the majority of home heating oil is used; many consumers will opt to convert to electrical heat. But by July their first financial analysis will be complete and the true impact of their increased costs will be realized.

"In August they will have their semi-annual shareholders meeting; the numbers will be made public…and they'll be dismal. The investor exodus will begin."

Laurence Haggerty outlined his dealing with select members of Congress and gave more detail on specific measures being taken with the fuel cell companies and their strategic vendors. By the time he'd left the corporate headquarters of World Energy for Heathrow two hours later, he was certain he'd convinced The Committee concrete progress was being made and P3 was on track. They should be off his back for a little while anyway. He only wished the progress *was* as substantial and he'd lead them to believe.

In truth, he wasn't the least bit satisfied with the progression of P3. It wasn't until he'd prepared for this meeting, putting all the pieces together for the first time in months, that he could appreciate what little progress there had actually been. He'd put on a good show for his clients of course; what choice did he have? But unless there was significant movement in the next few months, he'd be forced to take more aggressive action. What that action would be, he didn't know yet. But it was certain to be unpleasant for all involved.

The loud thud of a briefcase slamming on top of a desk caused Joey Howells' co-workers to stop what they were doing and look to see what was going on. When they saw it was Joey, most smiled, shook their heads and went back to work. Joey's current spat with his on-again, off-again girlfriend was the talk of the office; providing particularly juicy gossip for the single women at the *Providence Gazette*.

He wasn't in the mood to work and hadn't been for sometime. He'd left the office early yesterday because his girlfriend called to tell him the faucet he'd fixed over the weekend was gushing water. It was working fine until she used it. Despite his incessant pleas to be gentle, every time she shut the water off she slammed down on the handle so hard he was amazed the fixture was still attached to the sink!

He and Heather shared an old Victorian house and the plumbing—amongst other things—wasn't updated. There were no shut-off valves under the sinks and when he fixed them he had to shut off water to the whole house. That made him nervous; if he screwed up the repair, there'd be no water anywhere. He just couldn't stomach the idea of paying out the big bucks for a plumber.

After he repaired the faucet they got into another all-night argument which bounced from one grievance to another. As they usually did, this fight led to him sleeping on the couch, again.

Joey sighed heavily as he sat down and looked at yesterday's mail. It was more than usual and formed a small piled on his desk. Most were from his "fans" who tended to be older and apparently unaware of the existence of the Internet. They wrote via snail-mail to tell him how much they loved his reporting and offering to give him the scoop on some "crucial story." Most were from lonely old women whose sole ambition in life was to see their name in his column before it appeared in the obituaries. Maybe one in a hundred of the letters he received merited further research.

Because of the problems with his girlfriend his mind wasn't on work; and he had a column to write that needed to be in his editor's hands by Thursday afternoon. He was working on several good stories that had depth and complexity, but would also require a significant amount of research. These stories had the potential of providing him with enough material to take him through the end of the year; but his personal problems were preventing him from finding time to do the necessary research. This would have to change, and soon, before his editor started to suspect.

He started to sort through the thirty or so letters sitting on his desk and immediately eliminated eleven simply by looking at the return address. They were from his regulars; people who wrote to him repeatedly and never had anything interesting to say. He began to open and read the others. After reading five submissions that would be of absolutely no help to him this week he began to scan the others. Then, sticking out from under his copy of yesterday's *New York Times* he noticed the corner of what appeared to be a FedEx envelope. He pulled the newspaper aside and confirmed that it was. Whoever delivered his copy of the *Times* covered it up, otherwise he would have noticed it immediately.

His first thought was that the envelope was put on his desk by mistake; he rarely received anything FedEx. Picking it up he saw that it was addressed to him and from Washington DC. Occasionally, he'd receive a letter from Boston or Hartford, but he couldn't remember ever receiving anything from as far away as DC. His curiosity peeked, he opened the envelope.

He pulled out a bounded document that was about a quarter of an inch thick; on top was a letter attached to it with a paperclip. After quickly thumbing through the document he pulled off the letter and began to read it:

Dear Mr. Howells,

Occasionally, I have the opportunity to spend time in Newport, and when I do I make a point of reading your column. I travel extensively and read many newspapers; I find your reporting to be thorough and accurate. Interesting, Howells thought. The letter isn't gushing with adoration like most them. *Because of this, I'm going to pro-*

vide you with a story that will define your career. "Yeah, that's what they all say," he mumbled to himself skeptically.

Enclosed you will find a document call "P3." It outlines—in detail—a conspiracy underway involving the three largest oil companies in the world. Their goal is to destroy the commercial potential of fuel cells. What the hell is a fuel cell?

This document is self-explanatory. Break this story and you'll soon be receiving offers from CNN and Fox News. Having read your work, I believe you can do better than the Providence Gazette. "So do I!"

The enclosed document is not a hoax; this will be proven with a minimal amount of investigation on your part. I choose to remain anonymous. I was part of this conspiracy and after your story sparks a federal investigation, I'll try to avoid prosecution. I look forward with great anticipation to reading your story.

Good luck!

He put the letter down and picked up the P3 document. Briefly scanning it, he saw it was filled with names of companies and individuals, dates and timelines. It looked authentic enough; but he wasn't sure what he was looking at. Seeing the names of several congressmen and a senator was promising. *Shit, could this be real?* he thought with mounting excitement.

He leaned back in his chair and hailed Peggy Scotch, the reporter in the cubical next to him. He was secretly enamored with her. But like all truly desirable women she was married, and to a man who didn't appreciate her.

"Peg, what the hell is a fuel cell?"

She leaned back to look at him; lips pursed and brow furrowed. "I dunno. I think it's some kind device that makes electricity. I think I read somewhere that they're used on spaceships. Why?"

"Ah…just curious, never mind. Thanks." She shrugged and went back to work.

Howells studied the document some more. It seemed interesting enough, but at first glance it hardly appeared to be a career builder. But, he wasn't in a position to be choosey; it was already Tuesday and this was better than anything else he had. He could hurriedly write a story around it to fill a column. He wouldn't have time to verify any of the information so he'd have to write the story as breaking news based on unnamed sources—a developing story. This should be good enough to pacify his editor. Brushing aside the rest of his mail he got on his computer and began to throw the story together.

"Joey, this is crap!" his editor bellowed, throwing the draft article back at its author who was standing in front of his boss' desk. It skidded to a stop in front of Howells who looked down at it forlornly. He said nothing, he agreed with his editor. "Ever since you and Heather started going at it you haven't put out anything worthy of your talents—and you know it!"

Looking contrite the reporter replied, "I can't argue with you, Ed. But I've got a couple of excellent stories in the works. I just need to get through this week. Come on, work with me. It's not *that* bad!"

The gruff old man shook his head. "You gotta patch things up with that woman of yours, Joey. I want your mind back on your work. I haven't heard anything yet from the folks upstairs about the lemons you've written these past couple of weeks, but I will if you keep this shit up; it's just a matter of time."

"I know, I know," Howells said, frowning.

The editor's eyes shifted to the draft he'd thrown back at his reporter. Motioning to it with a sharp nod of his head he said, "Based on reports from unnamed sources? A developing story?" He grimaced and slowly shook his head, "Son, I'd take a chance putting something like this out without any real evidence—not a shred for that matter—to back it up. It's pretty damn dangerous to be throwing accusations around; particularly against prominent lawmakers. They could litigate a little pee-on newspaper like us out of existence in a heartbeat!

"All you've really got here, Joey, is a document that could have been dreamed up by some bored person with too much time on their hands. If the sender had identified himself, that would be different; I'd be willing to work with that. Did you trace the return address?"

Howells nodded. Glumly he replied, "Turned out to be the address of a Washington D.C. area grocery store."

The editor sat in silent deliberation for a moment then flatly announced, "I'm not going to run it. Come up with something else."

"*Ahhhh Christ*...come on, Ed!" the reporter whined and flapped his arms. "I don't *have* anything else! Give me a break."

"What the hell do you think I've been doin' these last few weeks, Joey?"

"I promise you'll love what I have for next week, Ed. This will be the last piece of shit I put out. I'm gonna fix things with Heather—I'll get back in the game."

The editor stared at his reporter, frowned and let out a sigh. His eyes then dropped to the draft. He leaned forward, picked up the article, then sat back in his chair and read it again. Joey Howells watched him with hopeful anticipation.

"He threw the rough copy back at the reporter and said, "Alright. But condense it. And get rid of all names—the politicians, the companies, everything. I'll throw it in as a filler on 8A."

"Come here, Ed. Let me kiss you," Howells said playfully.

"Get outta here! And next week better be good."

CHAPTER 13

▼

Hoping this would be the day, Sandra Beach woke early, quickly showering and dressing. She was filled with anticipation as she drove to the mini-mart to purchase Friday's edition of the *Providence Gazette,* then to her favorite little café in Newport to have coffee and read the newspaper. She was disappointed when she didn't see the article on the first few pages; then concluded that the story didn't make the day's addition. She reminded herself that she'd just have to be patient; most likely Joey Howells needed more time to verify some of the information. If she were him, she thought, she wouldn't rush into this story either.

Having given up on seeing her revenge in today's addition she sipped at her coffee and leisurely looked through the rest of the newspaper. When she got to page 8 she perfunctorily glanced at it and was preparing to turn to the next page when something stopped her. She went back and purposefully scanned the page. There, at the bottom left-hand corner were the words that caught her eye "Fuel Cells." She looked at the short article, thinking it couldn't possibly be the instrument by which she had hoped to destroy Wendell Finley. This had to be just a coincidence—another article concerning fuel cells. But when she read the title and saw Joey Howells name at the end of the article her heart sank.

FUEL CELLS CAUSING CONCERN AT OIL COMPANIES

An unnamed source is causing speculation that a conspiracy exists to destroy the potential benefits of fuel cell technology. Fuel cells are an electrochemical energy conversion device that combines hydrogen and oxygen to produce electrical power without combustion.

Details are still sketchy and all information, as well as accusations, have yet to be verified. However, enough evidence exists to lend credibility to the charge that three major oil companies and several prominent congressmen are behind the plot to destroy this potentially advantageous technology.

This informant contends that advances in fuel cells have caused concerns amongst the major oil producers that this technology will soon dramatically reduce the need for oil. Allegedly, the top management of three oil companies and a Washington D.C. based consulting firm have devised a strategy to stop the development of these devices.

The *Providence Gazette* will continue to follow this developing story and work to verify its authenticity. Joey Howells

After reading the article her first emotion was shock, and then disappointment that quickly grew into rage. *The idiot!* she thought to herself. *I give him the biggest story since Watergate and he treats it like it's nothing more than a sports scandal!*

Speculation! Details sketchy! My ass! I gave him everything! Why didn't he use the names, mention Larry, Moe and Curly and discuss the timelines? She dropped the newspaper on her lap in disgust. This pitiful story wasn't going to destroy anybody—except maybe her.

Shortly after mailing P3 to Joey Howells she began to question the wisdom of doing so. Incensed with Finley, she hadn't considered the possible repercussions of going public with the document. She was well aware of the criminal consequences she faced if she was linked to the plot by the FBI or any other law enforcement agency; but she hadn't given any thought to her personal safety.

She tried to convince herself that Laurence Haggerty would never physically harm her—no matter what damage she caused. He'd be furious with her, of course, but he could never bring himself to hurt her. But the line of reasoning didn't work. She knew better than most that money can, and usually does evaporate love and loyalty. She herself was a prime example; she'd left Noble Consultants in her quest for wealth.

Would her former employer forgive the fact that she was trying to deprive him of seventy-five million dollars; not to mention fingering him and his clients for criminal prosecution? Not very likely. And there'd be no denying she leaked the document. She was the only person besides Haggerty himself who had access to his computer. The moment he saw this article, and she was sure he would, she'd be a marked woman.

She'd given it a lot of thought but decided to put off the actual decision until after she'd seen the story in print. Now that she had, pathetic as it was, she couldn't put if off any longer—she'd have to go into hiding. As soon as he learned of the article, or more accurately, the betrayal, Laurence Haggerty would send someone after her—he'd want answers. And for a moment she found herself paralyzed with fear, realizing that that someone would probably be Nick Ragosta.

She took the newspaper off her lap, lethargically folded it back up and put it on the table. Taking a sip of coffee she looked through the café's window at the gentling bobbing boats tied up to the docks. She wanted to savor this last peaceful moment; she knew she wouldn't see Newport's harbor again for a very long time. The shitty little story Howell wrote may blow over quickly in the press, but it wouldn't in the mind of Laurence Haggerty.

Maybe she should go public with the story? Notoriety might lend her some measure of protection. Maybe she could plea-bargain with the Feds to obtain a lighter sentence. She immediately dismissed the idea. People were dead; prison was a certainty. Turning state's evidence she could negotiate to avoid a life sentence, but that was probably the best she could do. Even if she turned herself in and cooperated fully, she was still looking at a substantial amount of time behind bars.

Finishing her coffee she decided that the only question now was: where to go?

Rick Miller was pleasantly surprised to see the email from Tom Clarkston; he hadn't heard from Tom in over six months. Seeing that the message had an attachment, Rick briefly hoped Tom was sending him a request for quote. Rick hadn't seen an RFQ from anybody for quite some time.

He and Tom hit it off from the first sales call. They were both the same age, hailed from Indiana, had kids the same age and both served in Vietnam. Tom Clarkston was the materials manager for Duplex Products, a small manufacturing company just outside of Providence, Rhode Island. Unfortunately, there wasn't much Rick could sell him. But they had a great rapport and Rick considered him more of a friend than a potential customer. When his schedule permitted, Rick always stopped by to visit with him when he called on Global Fuel Cell Technologies, which was relatively close to Duplex Products.

Rick clicked open the message. He knew he shouldn't be, but he couldn't help but be slightly disappointed when he saw it wasn't a request for quote. Instead, Tom's message explained that he recalled Rick's interest in fuel cell companies, and when he saw this article in the *Providence Gazette,* he assumed Rick would want to see it. He concluded by reminding Rick to stop by the next time he was in the area; lunch would be courtesy of Duplex Products.

Rick opened the attachment. His eyes widened with each sentence of Joey Howells' article. "I knew it, goddamit!" he shouted to himself, slapping the desktop. He read the article three more times, and then sat motionless in his chair, staring at the story on his monitor.

Rick hadn't abandoned his efforts to try and find out what was going on at the fuel cell companies, but Paul Haydon had. At the time, Rick understood and agreed with his friend's decision—pursuing this wasn't worth endangering a boy's life. But now there was new information, with no connection to Daniel Stallinger and his son. But even so, Rick couldn't bring himself to ask Paul to reopen the case, even though he desperately wanted to. He knew that his friend must have spent a fortune on his behalf—and had little to show for it. If only this article would have appeared earlier; Paul would have had the substantial lead he so badly wanted.

Rick snapped out of his reverie and typed out a reply. He thanked Tom Clarkston for thinking of him and sending the extremely interesting story. Should any more articles on fuel cells appear in the *Providence Gazette*, Rick asked him to forward them immediately. He ended his message by promising to take Tom up on his lunch offer the next time he visited GFCT.

Immediately after sending his message to Clarkston, Rick impulsively wanted to forward the story to Paul Haydon. With effort, he resisted the temptation. He'd decided not to send it over his concern that Paul may get the wrong idea— that he was sending the story to subtly ask him to reopen the investigation. Rick printed a copy of the article, closed Clarkston's email and went back to work.

But he couldn't concentrate; Joey Howells' report kept coming to mind. Rick again began to debate with himself whether he should share the article with Paul Haydon. After fifteen minutes of wasted deliberation he realized he was being ridiculous. Why deny it? He wanted Paul back on the case. But even though he had a solid lead in the reporter Joey Howells, Rick was still hesitant to actually ask his friend. Finally, he decided there was no sense in worrying how Paul would react—he'd read into it whatever the hell he wanted to. Rick forwarded the article simply saying: *Paul, I thought you might find this interesting.*

Twenty minutes later his phone rang.

"Flexible Sealing Solutions, Rick Miller."

"Ricky—Paul." An uncertain smile swept across the salesman's face, and he bit his lip to force himself to think before blabbering away. The last thing Rick wanted to do was to say something that might guilt his friend into going back to work on his behalf.

"Hey Paul, how ya doing? I, ah, suppose you're calling about the story I sent you? What do ya think?"

"What do I think?" Haydon replied in an intonation Rick couldn't delineate between exhilaration or exasperation. He breathed easier when he hear Haydon add, "Hell, I gotta talk to this reporter! See if I can sweet-talk him into showing me this evidence."

Although elated, Rick tried his best to sound dissuading. "*Oh Paul,* there's no need to do that. Christ, you've done enough already! Look…we both know there's a conspiracy, and that there's not a damn thing we can do about it." He let out a dramatic sigh. "I've accepted the fact that my *years* of work with GFCT and UES are down the shitter!"

"You give up too easily," Haydon replied flatly.

Rick couldn't have been happier with his friend's response, but wanted to make sure he put up a convincing front. Although he did have genuine concerns about the amount of money Haydon had put into this venture he replied evenly, and with mixed feelings, "It's not a matter of giving up, Paul. You spent months and God knows how much money playing janitor at Unlimited Energy Systems—all on my account. I…I just don't want to see you bleed any more cash."

"How about you let me worry about that!" Haydon snapped, almost tersely.

Rick said noting for several moments, and then asked guardedly, "Are you serious? You're going to jump back in?"

"You're damned right I'm serious," the detective said sternly, then paused. Rick could tell he wasn't done talking yet, only stopping momentarily to garner his thoughts. Though pleased his friend was taking up the case again, Rick was a little surprised by the intensity of emotion he was sensing from Paul.

"It's been gnawing at me, Rick—I didn't crack the case; didn't solve it. Hell, truth be told about all I did was verify your suspicions. It was the most dismal performance of my career. I can't live with that; I don't accept failure easily. I'm a profess—"

"*Paul…*" Rick cut in, wanting to stop his friend's self-disparagement. It suddenly dawned on him that *he* really was the cause of Paul's anguish. He cringed then continued, "Give yourself a break. There's no doubt in my mind that you would've solved the case, given more time. You quit the investigation—had to—for all the right reasons."

"Yeah, that sounds good, but I'm not going to hide behind it. The conspiracy is still going on. If I can stop it, perhaps protect Stallinger's son and God knows who else, I'm going to!"

Rick closed his eyes, dropped his head and let out a sigh of relief.

"I just can't believe she did it," Laurence Haggerty said despondently, head down and hands clasped around his third glass of Johnny Walker Blue Label. "After all I've done for her. I treated her like a daughter," he snarled softly. Then, looking up at Nick Ragosta snapped, *"like a fucking daughter and she betrayed me!"* He threw back the rest of his drink and staggered to his office's liquor cabinet for another.

"I never much cared for the bitch," the assassin said in way of empathy. Haggerty let the comment pass. "So, Laurence, the question now is what do *you* want to do about it?"

The owner of Noble Consultants poured himself a generous drink. By way of gesture he offered one to the assassin who declined. Haggerty sat back down and allowed his body to slump in the chair. He took a long sip, but said nothing. He just looked at the drink he was twisting in his hand with a blank expression.

Nick Ragosta was not a man with an overabundance of compassion, but he could see that the man was hurting. And not from the prospect of P3 failing. He had been betrayed at a personal level, by someone he genuinely loved. But the time for compassion was over. He had to snap Haggerty out of his despondency, and quickly.

"Laurence...pull yourself together! You've got to do something—we're too far along. We've got to stop any further spread of this story and find out who else she's shot her mouth off to! Damage control, Laurence. Damage control." Ragosta felt a little uncomfortable with the role reversal—it was Haggerty who should be giving direction. But at the moment he wasn't mentally capable of doing it.

Ragosta surprised himself by how much P3 now mattered to him. If the plan failed it was no skin off his nose; he didn't need the money—he wanted it, but he didn't need it. He'd never admit it to Haggerty, but he wanted to kill Sandra Beach; despite the fact that she was a woman. If there was one thing he detested it was a turncoat. Especially one who could finger him. The woman had to go.

"What I want to know is *why!*" Haggerty said almost pleadingly.

The assassin thought he sounded pathetic. He impatiently rolled his eyes to the ceiling, sighed, then said, "For Christ's sake, Laurence, snap out of it! She fucked you—accept it and move on. We'll eventually uncover her motive. Right now we've got to act before this story spreads and the whole goddamn house of cards falls in!"

"You're right of course," Haggerty said pensively. "It's just that...you can't imagine how I feel. It's—" he grimaced, not finishing the thought. He then looked hard at Ragosta. "Go to Providence; find this reporter and make sure there's no follow-up story. It will soon be forgotten."

Ragosta nodded; a small smile of satisfaction on his face. "And Beach?"

"Find her. Don't harm her. Bring her to me."

2004 was an election year. Senator Plecha, Congressman Radakovich and Congresswoman Zwart still intended to try and prevent passage of the zero emissions bill, but didn't push for a vote. None of their colleagues on either side of the aisle—with the exception of Congressman Hanson—would either. There wouldn't be a vote on any bill of significance until after the election. Why risk it? Whether a bill passed or not, how any given politician voted would be on record for all their constituents to see. Inevitably, a sizeable group of their electorate would be pissed-off by how their representative voted, possibly affecting how their constituents would cast their ballots in the fall.

The fate of the zero emissions bill had no influence on the Department of Energy or the State of California. On the same day in June when the incriminating article appeared in the *Providence Gazette*, the Governor of California—in the thick accent critics and comics alike enjoyed poking fun at—proudly announced a joint program between his state and the DOE to place two hundred hydrogen fueling stations throughout California. The popular governor explained the program was a two-fold effort. The stations would support the fleet of fuel cell vehicles the state intended to purchase and would also act as an incentive for the residents of the state to buy hydrogen-powered cars.

These initial two hundred stations would be located at the state's Department of Transportation maintenance garages. Any state resident who purchases a fuel cell vehicle within three years after they become commercially available would be eligible to obtain hydrogen fuel from these state owned locations at minimum cost. California's goal, the governor announced, was to be the first state in the nation with a minimum of twenty five percent registered "Green Machines" on the road.

If Joey Howells had any doubts about the authenticity of the document entitled P3 sent to him by his anonymous fan, he didn't by the end of the day of June 11th. He and much of the staff of the *Providence Gazette* were watching live coverage of President Ronald Reagan's funeral on CNN when the receptionist called to tell him he had a visitor in the lobby. An admirer of the great president, the disruption annoyed him.

"I'm not expecting anybody," he growled. "Who is it?"

"Some guy named Paul Haydon."

Howells thought for a moment but didn't recognize the name. "I don't know him. What does he want?"

"Look, Joey, I'm not your personal assistant! Get your ass down here and find out for yourself." The phone went dead. Joey Howells looked incredulously at the receiver and wondered how the paper could've hired such a brusque woman as their receptionist? What a first impression she must make on visitors!

"Crap," he growled under his breath. He glanced at the large television hung in the corner of the news room and watched for a moment as the motorcade entered Andrews Air Force Base. He then headed for the lobby.

"Joey Howells," the reporter identified himself, approaching Paul Haydon with an extended hand.

The private investigator shook his hand firmly. "Paul Haydon. And thanks for seeing me without an appointment."

The reporter flashed him a weak smile then said, "You caught me at a bad time, I'm rather busy right now. What is it I can do for you, Mr. Haydon?"

"I need to speak with you about your recent story on fuel cells."

Howells seemed to redden a little. "Oh, *that* article!" He shrugged. "It wasn't my, uh, my best piece of reporting," he said contritely.

"Well, as far as I'm concerned your story was priceless," Haydon replied. "How'd you come upon it?"

"Actually…I didn't. It was sent to me," the reporter replied, slightly embarrassed.

Haydon raised his eyebrows in mild astonishment. "May I ask by whom?"

Howells scrutinized him for a moment then said, "I'm sorry Mr. Haydon, but I can't reveal my sources. But even if I could, I couldn't help you. It was mailed to me—anonymously. I wasn't lying when I said it was an unnamed source. I haven't a clue who sent it." He could see that the detective was crestfallen, so he added, "All I can tell you is that it came from D.C., and for what it's worth, I don't intend to follow-up on the story." Howells paused a moment then asked, "Why are you so interested in it anyway?"

"I'm a private detective and I'm working on a case that involves a fuel cell company possibly affected by the plot you mentioned." Howells suddenly became interested in the article. If a detective is on the trail of this story, it must be credible. Perhaps he had been a tad too hasty in dismissing it so quickly. It never hurts to have a story tucked away for those times when news is slow.

Haydon let out a defeated sigh. "Damn. Your story was one of the best leads I had on this case. If I could find out who sent you that information I could easily uncover the culprits." The detective grimaced then added, "Well, I'm disappointed I've reached a dead end here, but I thank you for your time Mr. Ho—"

"Wait a minute!" Howells blurred out. Haydon's eyes widened; the sound of the exclamation filling him with a twinge of hope. Howells put a fist to his mouth and reflexively bit the side of his index finder. It appeared to Haydon that the reporter was debating with himself.

A few seconds later Joey Howells asked tentatively, "*If*...I gave you a copy of the document, would that help you?"

Haydon was pleasantly shocked by the potential offer. He had wanted to ask Howells for a copy, but didn't bother assuming he'd never part with it because of journalistic prudence. Smiling, the detective said, "Yes, I'm certain it would be helpful. I'd be very grateful to you if you did."

"I don't know how much of a help it will be to you, Mr. Haydon. There's a lot of information, but it doesn't mention any real names. It appears to be written with coded names for the actual conspirators. But...okay, here's the deal Mr. Haydon. I didn't plan on pursuing this story because frankly, I just don't have the time. I've made other commitments to my editor. But it's clearly a story that merits further investigation. If I give you the document and it's helpful, I get an exclusive on anything you find out. Deal?"

"Sure, why not?" Haydon replied without giving the terms any real thought. They shook hands. Ten minutes later the detective left with a copy of P3.

After giving Paul Haydon a copy of the document, Joey Howells returned to his desk; pleased with himself for thinking up the deal. Undoubtedly, the detective would uncover specifics that would provide for a great story. And the beauty of the deal was that a minimum amount of work would be required on his part. When finished, Howells looked forward to rubbing his editor's nose in the story.

Many of his co-workers were still watching coverage of the funeral. He decided to join them again but was stopped by his ringing phone.

Exasperated, he picked up the phone. "Joey Howells."

"You have another visitor, Joey."

"*What?*" he replied in surprise.

"You heard me. Nice looking guy too. Find out if he's single," she asked half-jokingly. Knowing he stood no chance of talking the receptionist into getting rid of him he told her he'd be down in a moment. Sighing in dismay, he again headed for the stairs.

Entering the lobby he wasn't surprised to see the receptionist talking—probably flirting—with his visitor. It was well known around the office that Karen was desperate for a man. She'd probably land one if she wasn't so bitchy all the time,

Howells thought sourly. By the expression on his visitor's face Howells could tell he wasn't exactly enjoying the one-sided conversation.

They both looked at him as he approached; Karen looked disappointed, his visitor relieved. "Joey Howells," he said, offering his hand.

"How do you do?" Nick Ragosta replied. He glanced at the receptionist. "Could we talk outside, Mr. Howells?" Karen frowned and went back to her desk.

If it wasn't for Karen, the reporter would have thought it a strange request. "Sure, I guess so. It'll give me a chance to have a cigarette."

It was a cloudy day and a little cooler than normal for early June. Howells recalled that early on in Reagan's funeral it had been raining; he wondered if Providence would see rain today. He reached in his pocket and pulled out a pack of Newport Lights. He offered one to his visitor, who declined.

Howells lit his cigarette and blew out a large cloud of smoke. Then, looking at the well built middle-aged man said, "I didn't catch your name."

"I didn't give it to you," his visitor said coldly while scanning the area around him. Howells gave him a perplexed look. Ragosta turned and faced the journalist; an arduous expression came across his face. "Mr. Howells, I'm going to cut to the chase. I'm not a man you want to fuck with." Howells' face furrowed in shock. Considering he'd never met this person before, he found the blunt statement rather audacious. But the man had his attention.

Ragosta stepped a little closer to the reporter. "I'm going to talk and you're going to listen. Understood?"

Howells was becoming annoyed. *Who the hell does this guy think he is?* "Listen, Mister, whoever you are; I don't have to—aaagggghhhh" The powerful punch Ragosta threw into his stomach prevented Howells from finishing the statement. The cigarette flew out of his mouth and he buckled over, fighting to catch his breath. A young woman who was approaching them on the sidewalk stopped. Horrified, she gawked at the scene before her. Ragosta glared menacingly at her; she quickly turned around and walked in the other direction.

He looked back at the journalist. "You don't listen too well, do you Mr. Howells? I said I'm going to talk and you're going to listen. Have you got that now?" The reporter nodded his head as he attempted to straighten up. Ragosta bent down, picked up the cigarette and gently placed it between the reporter's lips. "Listening?"

"Yeah…I'm all ears," Howells uttered hoarsely. He pulled the cigarette from his mouth and locked his eyes on the menacing looking stranger.

"Good. The document you referred to in Friday's article on fuel cells, I want it; and every copy you may have made. If you gave a copy to anybody, I want their name and their copy back. Then, I want you to forget you ever saw that document or wrote that article. There'll be no follow-up stories."

Howells gave him a profoundly startled look. *The fuel cell article? What the hell was going on?* After writing it he hadn't given the story a second thought. Then, out of the blue, a private investigator inquired about it and now he was getting roughed up by some thug over it. Howells thought about the detective who had just left the lobby no more than ten minutes ago. He was the only person besides himself who had a copy of it. The paper's editor had absolutely no interest in seeing it.

With a trembling hand he took a puff on the cigarette while glancing nervously at his tormentor. He was about to tell the brute the truth. Why not? He initially never intended to follow up on the story anyway—was it worth getting the shit kicked out of him? But his aching stomach made him remember who and what he was. What kind of man would he be if he crumbled so quickly at the first sign of trouble? Was he that afraid of getting slapped around a little? Many of his contemporaries had suffered far worse for the sake of keeping their sources secret; he became defiant. How could this son-of-a-bitch possibly know if he'd given a copy to anybody?

Howells stiffened. "Look, don't hit me again, okay? But I'd like to know why. I mean, the story is of no importance to me—I had no intention of following it up."

Ragosta smirked and then asked contemptuously, "If it wasn't important, why'd you write it?"

"It was a filler, that's all. Something to take up space until I got what my editor considered a *real* story. Shit…why the hell do you think it was on page eight? If we took it seriously it would have been front page news." He took a quick drag on his cigarette and glanced around anxiously.

Ragosta said nothing for a moment; he just looked coldly at the reporter who continued to puff away uneasily. With lightning speed he slugged Howells again in the stomach—the exact same spot as before. The journalist dropped to his knees; his cigarette first sticking to his bottom lip, then falling to the pavement with him as he curled up in a fetal position.

"*Agggghhhhh…Christ…God!*" Howells mutter, wrapping his arms around his stomach and trying to catch his breath. His chest began to burn as he fought for air; the pain was excruciating.

The assassin watched him wither on the ground for a moment. He though of kicking him in the teeth, but decided against it. "You're wasting my time," Ragosta snarled. "I want that document and any copies now!" He paused a moment and then asked, "Are there any copies?" Getting to his knees, Howells shook his head. "Good. Then all you have to do is retrieve the document."

The reporter slowly got to his feet. He remained a little bent over so Ragosta pushed against his chest, forcing him to stand up straight. Howells groaned in agony. The hit man then smiled satirically, as if nothing had happened, and parentally brushed his hand over the journalist's shirt. "I'll wait in the lobby and chat cordially with your charming receptionist for four minutes—not one second longer. If you're not back in the lobby with the document by that time, you won't live to see tomorrow." He turned Joey Howells toward the lobby door. As the reporter started to walk off Ragosta threatened one more time, "If you don't see me in the lobby when you return, that means you took too long and you're a dead man."

Through experience, Nick Ragosta had learned that five minutes was typically the fastest the police could respond when called in an emergency. If Howells got cute and called them, there would be time to slip away. Not that he'd need to worry about that in this instance; he judged the *Providence Gazette* reporter a spineless worm.

In less than two minutes the perspiring journalist returned to the lobby with the P3 document in hand. Karen, the receptionist, was so engrossed with trying to be engaging to the handsome stranger that she didn't even look at Howells. Had she, she couldn't have failed to notice his distraught look.

After flashing the woman an enchanting smile, the hit man turned to the approaching reporter and said, "Ah, Mr. Howells. Please join me outside."

Once out of the lobby he snatched the papers from Howells' hand and quickly thumbed through them. He looked ominously at Howells, "You're absolutely sure there are no other copies?"

The reporter shook his head. "No," he replied in a shaken voice. "That's the original I got anonymously in the mail; I swear." He wiped his pale forehead with the back of his hand and licked his parched lips.

Ragosta eyed him suspiciously for a moment and then said forebodingly, "You'd better not be lying to me, young man. Should I learn that there are other copies—and believe me, I'll find out—I'll kill you." Howells swallowed hard; for a moment he had second thoughts about remaining silent concerning the copy he'd given the P.I. But he said nothing.

"And one last thing, Mr. Howells. This really goes without saying, but I'll say it anyway. No more articles concerning the topic of fuel cells in your paper."

"No...don't worry about that," the journalist replied. "But who's to say this nameless person didn't send a copy to some other reporter. I doubt I'm the only one he sent it to."

"If so, you were the only one stupid enough to use it." Ragosta turned and quickly walked away.

After the bastard was out of sight, Joey Howells lit another cigarette and leaned against the building, immensely proud of himself. Under pressure he didn't crack; didn't reveal the fact that he'd given away a copy. While the son-of-a-bitch was grilling him he quickly reasoned that private detectives don't publish stories, so it was very unlikely that the copy he gave away would pop up again. He hoped so. There was no question in his mind that the thug would make good on his threat.

For the first time in God knows how long, he was proud to be a reporter. He'd lost the follow-up story, true, but he'd defied someone who'd threatened his life; and that felt good. He'd never entirely put behind him the disappointment he felt in himself after turning down a recent job offer. *USA Today* offered him a position; but his first assignment would've been as an on-site reporter in Iraq. Though it would have been an important career move and paid over three times what he was making at the *Gazette,* he turned it down out of concern for his safety. But now he'd redeemed himself.

He crushed out his cigarette and decided to take the rest of the day off.

CHAPTER 14

▼

Cynthia Klash sat motionless in her darkened office, staring vacantly at the slow moving star-field screen saver on her computer's monitor. She had tried—God knew she had tried—but the momentum was too great. Too many technical advances had been made, too much money had been invested, too many people: the board of directors, shareholders, proud employees, particularly Global Fuel Cell Technologies' sale force, had been pushing for the launch of its first product. Despite her best efforts, GFCT was ready to go to market with their fuel cell powertrain for sedans and light trucks. Tomorrow she'd hold a press conference where she'd announce her company's intentions. Thinking they were rewarding her for all her effort, the board of directors insisted she make the announcement personally. The irony; if they only knew!

It was eleven o'clock in the evening. She had come to her office to make the phone call to Mr. R. A phone call she didn't want to run the risk of her husband or children overhearing. She had no choice but to tell him that she'd been unsuccessful; that tomorrow it would be official. She'd done all he had asked and more, but it wasn't enough. She was going to plead for the life of her son. If necessary, offer hers in place of his. After all, she was the one who failed, not him.

She'd try and reason with him—if that was possible. Many factors leading to GFCT's success were completely beyond her control: The U.S. invasion of Iraq causing instability and speculation in the world's oil market—gasoline prices approaching record levels. Prices at the pump spurring the sudden popularity and demand for hybrid cars along with renewed interest in the marketplace for alternative forms of energy. The cumulative result being GFCT's soaring stock price.

Any reasonable person would understand that she had no control over these events. But, was Mr. R reasonable? She doubted it.

She could do no more; both her actions and attitude were arousing suspicion amongst several of the more influential board members and some on the engineering staff. She suspected that the Board's "suggestion" that she make the press announcement was nothing more than a ruse to test for loyalty. It sounded far fetched, even to her. But had she been a white male, she would have been fired long ago. Many of her decisions and actions over the last three years were nothing less than a display of blatant incompetence. Of course, any show of ineptitude was forced on her by Mr. R, but nobody knew that except her and her tormentor.

Fortunately for her, GFCT's parent company, Global Technologies Corporation, had recently been hit with several sexual discrimination class action lawsuits. Having a female CEO in one of their divisions had been extremely helpful in mitigating the damage. Sadly, she recognized that she was nothing more than a token—a figurehead. It was a dreadful end for what was once a promising career.

With a trembling hand she reached for the phone.

Daniel Stallinger *was* being replaced; he had gone too far. The board of United Energy Systems had voted unanimously to oust him. But they did so in an unconventional manner. Instead of letting him go immediately they agreed to keep him on until a suitable replacement could be found.

The final nail in the coffin of his career with UES was his opposition to a proposed joint venture with GFCT. The suggestion was made directly to the board of directors by Shelia Scotch, their director of marketing,. To speed up development and reduce costs of their HEVF (Home Energy Vehicle Fueling) unit—a product that would not only supply electrical energy to a home, but also provide pure hydrogen for fuel cell powered vehicles—she suggested that they join forces with GFCT prior to going public with news of the new unit. The thought was that if the leading manufacturer of automotive fuel cells was behind their program, there would be no question in the public's mind about the legitimacy of the product. Perhaps it would also serve to squelch any remaining skepticism about fuel cell technology in general.

Stallinger was furious that Scotch went around him, but he understood why. Taking into consideration his leadership of late, he'd have done the same thing if he were in her shoes. It was an adroit move on her part; she obviously knew that if she had gone through the proper channels her idea would have never made it to the board. And it was a good idea—one that would propel her career at UES.

Stallinger's outright dismissal of Shelia Scotch's proposal prompted an unscheduled meeting of the board of directors and a swift vote of no confidence in him. However, in recognition of all his earlier efforts and successes, his firing would be made to look—as much as possible—like the decision to leave Unlimited Energy Systems was his. Of course, no one would be fooled. After the vote the board agreed that the first task of the new CEO—when he or she was found—would be to approach Global Fuel Cell Technologies about the joint venture.

The dismissal pushed Daniel Stallinger to the verge of a nervous breakdown. Impeding the progress of his company's product slowly took an emotional toll on him, and despite all his efforts, he knew he wasn't making satisfactory progress. Because of this he was surprised that he didn't hear from Mr. R more often; but he'd certainly be hearing from him now.

When he thought of the potential repercussions of the board's action, the anxiety caused his chest to tighten and for a few moments he had to fight for air. After the sensation passed, he wondered how on earth it came to this. Was there any way to protect his loved ones now? What could he possibly do to get out of this unbelievable nightmare? In the privacy of this beloved E class he threw his hands to his face and wept uncontrollably.

"You're failing, Haggerty…miserably!" Wendell Finley all but shouted. The announcement by Cynthia Klash that Global Fuel Cell Technologies was now ready to supply the automotive industry with reliable and affordable fuel cell powertrains prompted an emergency meeting of The Committee. Due to Finley's enraged state of mind, no one dared ask him if the room had been swept for surveillance devices.

Because of its urgency, Finley insisted the meeting be held at ENDICORP headquarters in Houston, Texas; only Kenneth Saxton would have to travel a significant distance. But if it took him too long to get there, Finley was prepared to start without him.

"You haven't achieved a *goddamn* thing and now *THIS!*" Irate, Finley hurled a newspaper in front of Haggerty. "Have you seen the press we've gotten in the *Providence Gazette?* For Christ's sake…!" He turned his scarlet face away from the head of Noble Consultants in disgust.

"I'm afraid I'm forced to agree with him," Kenneth Saxton said with uncharacteristic vehemence. "Almost three years have passed since we've hired you and instead of being on the decline, it would appear that the fuel cell industry is thriving! And now," he gestured toward the newspaper, "the public accusation that the oil industry is trying to obstruct the development of fuel cells. This is bloody awful!" To drive home his utter discontent, Saxton looked down and shook his head.

"Already, no less than four automotive manufacturers have offers on the table for GFCT," Theodore Kennelly offered disconcertedly. "One domestic and three foreign. I don't have to remind you, do I, that if fuel cell cars start rolling off the assembly line, we're *fucked,* to put it mildly." He paused a moment, ran a hand over his head, then continued in a voice brimming with antipathy, "If we're not already fucked by the article in that New England newspaper. Absolute incompetence!" He stared menacingly at Haggerty and added, "As far as I'm concerned, we should fire you here and now...and you're out seventy-five million!"

Laurence Haggerty sat silently; he desperately tried again, but couldn't think of a response that would reassure his clients. Knowing full well what was in store for him, he thought about what to say during the entire flight to Houston. The fact that Finley sent his private jet to collect him was a clear signal that he and the rest of The Committee were panicking. At this moment the only thing Haggerty knew for certain was that he needed more time.

Recent events supported his clients' allegations and nothing he could think of would immediately reverse the gains made by the industry. But somehow he had to convince these three men, here and now, that everything was under control; that recent events were expected and shouldn't be worried about. He had to reassure them that P3 would soon reach critical mass and spell the end of fuel cell technology. But, he thought sourly, it was hard to convince others when he couldn't convince himself.

It was absolutely critical—critical to Noble Consultants and to himself—that P3 succeed. Funds from the initial installment of twenty-five million were almost exhausted. Because of the complexity of the plan—both the development and execution—he had made a conscious decision not to pursue new clients or opportunities. These oil conglomerates would generate more than enough revenue, but they would also stretch his company's resources to the limit. The consequences of that flawed decision were becoming painfully clear—Noble Consultants had no cash flow it could count on to stay afloat.

Laurence Haggerty was uncomfortably seated in his chair and sweating profusely. He hated the south. It didn't matter how good the air conditioning was, it was always too humid for him—especially this time of year. Sticking to his cloths and seeing the hostile faces glaring at him made it all the more difficult to concentrate.

Nick Ragosta had recently told him of the setbacks at GFCT and UES. Both CEO's claimed to have done everything they possibly could to comply with the demands placed on them; but despite their best efforts the goal was not achieved. Haggerty believed their claims. Ragosta kept the pressure up and Stallinger lost his job because of it. The fact that they survived in their positions as long as they did proved—in his mind—that they had done a competent job of trying to sabotage their company's development efforts.

Competent as they were, they did not succeed. Due to their failure, Ragosta inquired whether he should make good on his threats and eliminate the family members. The owner of Noble Consultants said definitely not; doing so would serve no purpose. Ragosta seemed relieved by the decision, but Haggerty realized that the assassin himself would soon be a problem if he wasn't paid the balance due for his services. Given all his other problems the last thing Haggerty needed now was the best hired gun in the business pissed off at him.

Donning his poker face and doing his best to keep calm, Haggerty said evenly, "Recent events were not unexpected, gentlemen. I know it appears that the industry is moving forward, but it's noth—"

"Appears, my ass!" Finley cut in.

Haggerty ignored the comment and remained composed. "Nothing more than statements to calm nervous investors. The steps we've taken are having a devastating effect on both companies. Neither will go to market profitably. Soon they'll be audited, and given the recent accounting scandals, I sincerely doubt any books will be cooked. The auditors will bring to light the fact that these companies are operating at a tremendous loss. Once that information is made public, investors will scurry for cover like cockroaches caught in a spotlight. The companies *will* crumble."

"Well…you'll pardon me if I don't believe a bloody word you're saying," Saxton blurted out with such abrasiveness that even Kennelly gave him a double glance. "Your firm started this little venture in November of 2001. It's now August of 2004. I've turned three companies around from the brink of bankruptcy in less time than it's taken you to try and take down two!"

The head of Noble Consultants tugged at his collar; he regretted wearing a tie. Looking at the three angry men he knew this was the moment. He had to say something; and what came out of his mouth next would make or break both him and his company. The upcoming fuel cell convention was the only thing that came to mind. He hadn't been to Las Vegas in years and was looking forward to it. He'd have to work with that—there was nothing else.

"Gentlemen," Haggerty began boldly. "I guarantee you that by the end of January, 2005, that for all practical purposes, the industry will cease to exist." The Committee didn't appear impressed. They didn't bother to ask how he could promise the technologies' demise by that time; rather, their peering eyes made it explicitly clear they expected details from him. And details were something he had in rather short supply.

Haggerty swallowed hard and then continued; formulating his response as he went along. "The last week in January there will be an international fuel cell convention held in Las Vegas. GFCT and UES will have exhibits there, of course, along with a number of smaller fuel cell manufacturers.

"I understand your skepticism, gentlemen. I know it *appears* that there's been no tangible results, but there have been."

"Yes," Theodore Kennelly cut in, his voice coarse with sarcasm. "Of course there's been tangible results—people have been murdered!"

Haggerty grimaced, but otherwise ignored the comment. "As you know—as I hope you know—we've achieved the goal of making the manufacture of fuel cells unprofitable; now, and far into the foreseeable future. There's *no way* these two companies can bridge the increases given to them by their strategic vendors."

"Get to the point, Haggerty," Kennelly quipped. "You're wasting our time." Then, as a second thought he quickly added, "Along with our money. Don't be disappointed if we," he spread his arms, gesturing to his colleagues, "don't embrace your assurances with the ardor you're hoping for."

Haggerty silently fumed. Kennelly seemed particularly eager to humiliate him and no doubt was secretly hoping with unbridled passion that P3 would fail. He hated the old bastard.

The Consultants sighed wearily. "If you'll be so kind as to indulge me for—"

"*Indulge you!*" Finley blurted out. "Shit! We've paid twenty-five million to have our illicit plans published in a fuckin' newspaper!"

Lifting both hands as if physically holding them off, Haggerty shook his head and said contritely, "I fully admit that was an error."

"An error!" Kennelly sniggered softly. "Come come, Laurence, let's not mince words. You fucked up!"

In exasperation the owner of Noble Consultants replied, "The situation has been handled, gentlemen. There'll be no further mention of the plan in the news media."

"I certainly hope so," Saxton said firmly.

It came to him then; an idea. An idea that would not only sound credible, but would work—he was instantly sure of it. Haggerty's face contorted in a peculiar expression of delight and he stared off in the distance, quickly thinking how best to present the scheme. The look on his face didn't escape the attention of The Committee, who glanced at each other questioningly.

"If you'll allow me to finish," Haggerty implored, vaguely smirking.

"Please," Saxton replied sarcastically with a nod of his head.

"There will be," the consultant began slowly, turning to face Kennelly, "an…*incident*, at the international fuel cell expo. A technical glitch that will cause one of GFCT's demonstration vehicles to malfunction…badly."

Saxton, Finley and Kennelly turned to each other again, then back to Haggerty. The consultant looked intensely at each man in turn, trying to gauge the impact of his declaration. After a few moments of awkward silence Saxton cleared his throat and asked, "Define *badly*…Laurence," a strange mixture of skepticism and concern in his voice.

Suddenly feeling at ease for the first time since being ordered to attend this meeting, Haggerty sat back in his chair. He took a moment to take a sip of coffee then said, "My associates and I haven't worked out all the details yet, but—"

"Of course not," Kennelly blurted out contemptuously; he couldn't help himself.

Haggerty gave him a withering stare; it was the first time he'd ever shown any overt form of animosity towards one of his most valued clients. But he couldn't hold back any longer; he found the man nauseating. To his delight, Saxton and Finley joined him in visually rebuking the CEO of PETROCOMP. Apparently they were also tiring of his verbal malice. Kennelly's eyes darted between the three men. He got the message and settled into his chair, clearly belittled.

Haggerty continued. "The malfunction will serve two purposes. One, the viability of fuel cells will, again, be questioned in the mind of the public. And two, most importantly, the incident will be the catalyst for bringing all our earlier efforts together. Given the aforementioned price increases, the fact that there is no hope of manufacturing this product profitably and now a questionable market caused by this incident, the bean-counters at UES and GFCT will raise enough of a stink to force their boards to act. Under pressure from apprehensive investors, they'll drop their efforts in order to cut their losses. They'll have no choice."

The three members of The Committee sat silently, contemplating Haggerty's proposal. A minute later Finley asked, "How can you be so sure it will work as you've just laid it out? It almost seems, I don't know," he shrugged, "too simplistic." Haggerty was pleased, for the first time in the meeting Finely was composed.

The head of Noble Consultants let loose a patronizing sigh. He felt more confident now than he had in a very long time. Almost condescendingly he asked,

"What drives…what motivates businesses and investors alike? You know full well, Mr. Finley. Profit! Plain and simple. There will be no hope for profit. Even Global Fuel Cell Technologies, with its deep pockets will question the wisdom of proceeding with the program. There will be no way to justify continuation of the programs and no one with any influence to champion them. No," he shook his head, "the proper business decision will be made. Fuel cells will cease to be a threat to oil interests for decades to come."

Another period of silence ensued, after which Kenneth Saxton asked, "This…*malfunction*, no one will be hurt, will they? I, and I believe I speak for Ted and Wendell, don't want any more blood on our hands." The other two CEO's nodded in agreement.

Haggerty hesitated. He had no idea yet what the malfunction would be. But he had to say the only thing that would guarantee his seventy-five million dollar payday. "Of course not."

The three men considered this for a moment then the CEO of World Energy looked sternly at the consultant and said. "I want to be very clear on this point, Laurence, very clear." Saxton's eyes narrowed and his face became as hard as Haggerty had ever seen it. "No more screw-ups! Put this endeavor to bed once and for all! By the start of fiscal 2006 I don't ever want to worry about fuel cells again."

Saxton's appearance softened a little and he continued. "I appreciate the complexities you face in this endeavor, but mistakes such as the *Providence Gazette* could have ruined us. We were lucky your disgruntled employee chose a little-read newspaper and wasn't bright enough to shot-gun it to other news outlets. Also that your agent was able to intercept the document." At the reference to Sandra Beach, Wendell Finley averted his eyes from Haggerty; but only momentarily. "Bottom line, Mr. Haggerty…Finish the bloody job!"

The secretary looked up from the file she was reading when she noticed the door to her boss' office begin to open. "Laura, call our private investigator, Mike Swenson. Tell him I want to see him immediately."

"Yes, Mr. Haggerty."

The head of Noble Consultants shut the door then walked over to his office's wet bar to pour himself a drink. "Want anything?" he asked Nick Ragosta.

The assassin looked at his watch and replied sarcastically, "Nah, never before nine thirty in the morning."

Haggerty shrugged indifferently. "Suit yourself!" He poured himself a scotch. After placing himself behind his desk he said, "When Swenson gets here I'm going to have him run a background check on all the GFCT engineers who will be attending the expo in Las Vegas. One of them is sure to have a problem or weakness we can exploit."

"What's the plan?" Ragosta asked, pouring himself a cup of coffee. He then sat down on the couch and noticed for the first time how haggard his employer looked. The stress of P3 appeared to have caused him to age considerably over the last few months.

Haggerty had had plenty of time to formulate a plan on the trip back to Washington D.C. He contacted Ragosta immediately upon returning to the capital; he didn't want to waste any time in planning the operation. It was bottom of the ninth, the bases were loaded and he had three balls and two strikes against him. This had to work; and it had to work right. But he didn't want to share with Ragosta how desperate the situation with The Committee had become for fear that the assassin might decide to back out.

After taking a sip of his drink he serenely looked at Ragosta and said, "Sabotage. We're going to the heart of the matter, Nick. I want one of GFCT's demonstration vehicles to fail during the exhibition. Fail in a big way. The failure must be catastrophic; something that can't be fixed easily or cheaply."

"An explosion would do the job nicely," Ragosta offered.

Haggerty nodded. "I'm afraid it's going to come to that. The Committee made it clear that they don't want any more fatalities." He took another sip of his straight scotch, his face then turned hard. *"But fuck-em!* I'm not letting seventy-five million slip through my fingers." Ragosta smiled, but was a little taken aback by the man's sudden disregard for life. An explosion during a demonstration could kill dozens of people and probably wound two dozen more. "Besides," Haggerty continued, "if we achieve the desired outcome, they won't give a damn if anybody is killed. Oh, they'll piss and moan—make a show of it, but after that we won't hear another word about it."

"So, we're going to find an engineer to do the job?" Ragosta asked.

Haggerty nodded. "Yep, that's the plan. We'll persuade one to rig the system so that it goes up in front of everybody; preferably with the press present. The safety of fuel cells has always been an issue on the fringe; always on everybody's mind but seldom voiced. Well..." he took another sip of his Scotch, "I'm going to make damn sure it's no longer a peripheral issue. It's going to be front page news. P3 will be accomplished and the operation will be completed. We collect our money. End of story."

"You're sure it will work?"

"Positive."

"Good. To be honest with you, Laurence, I'm tiring of the whole thing."

"As am I, and The Committee."

"Do you want me to use the usual method of persuasion on this engineer?"

Haggerty shook his head. "No. I've given that a lot of thought. I'd prefer to use the carrot rather than the stick. I want willing cooperation to make sure it works."

An hour later Mike Swenson arrived and Haggerty put him to work.

CHAPTER 15

▼

Paul Haydon had no intention of honoring his commitment to Joey Howells. This character flaw didn't exactly fill him with pride, but he felt he really had no choice. The *Providence Gazette* reporter would be furious that he didn't get his exclusive, but if Howells wouldn't investigate the story, he'd have to find somebody who would.

Swallowing his pride, the private investigator conceded to himself that a prominent investigative reporter could do the one thing he couldn't—force those behind the plot to come out of the woodwork. They had a tool he lacked; the power of the press.

Haydon was determined to solve this case and break up the conspiracy. He would redeem himself in his own eyes and the eyes of his friend, whom he suspected thought him a failure for giving up. The question he now faced was which media and which reporter should he approach.

His first inclination was to contact Frank Tirpitz of *USA Today.* Tirpitz was a good reporter and often featured; Haydon liked his work; and *USA Today* probably had the widest circulation of any newspaper. But when reporting a story, newspapers tended to be too comprehensive, too thorough. Not that this was a bad thing, but it wasn't what this story needed—what *he* needed. What was required was sensationalism. A story that was short, to the point, and presented in a provocative manner.

Of course, there was no shortage of TV news magazines that presented stories in a melodramatic or outlandish fashion; the problem was they all lacked credibility and no one who had at least a high school education took them seriously.

There was one exception: *Hour Report.*

In Haydon's opinion, there was no news magazine that was better at blowing up a story to make it more than it was than *Hour Report*. And it was exactly for that reason he didn't like the show and seldom watched it. But its hosts presented their stories in a fairly intelligent manner that didn't assume the audience was a bunch of idiots, giving it an air of credibility. And occasionally they hit upon a truly provocative story. Their report on the abuse of prisoners in Iraq opened a can of worms that went all the way to the President. If any news organization could find and bring the conspirators to light, *Hour Report's* inflammatory method of reporting could. If it couldn't, Haydon thought, all would be lost; he'd swallow his pride and give up the investigation for good. With minimal conviction the private investigator decided this particular new magazine would serve his purpose better than any other newspaper or magazine.

Mary Hildahl would be the reporter he'd approach and try to convince to take the story. She wasn't featured often on the program; therefore she wasn't as popular as the other so-called reporters. He figured he stood a better chance of actually meeting her and presenting her with the opportunity. Another advantage of Ms. Hildahl, Haydon thought with a twinge of guilt, was that she was absolutely beautiful. He wouldn't mind taking her to dinner!

Paul Haydon knew the process of making contact with the reporter would be very difficult. Considered a celebrity, albeit a minor one, undoubtedly there would be numerous barriers to overcome before he could actually speak with her. But he'd faced that problem many times before and it didn't discourage him. The only real problem in his mind was that *Hour Report* was produced in New York. He'd only been to New York three times; two of which were really just a drive through the city on the way to Interstate 95. The other was a short afternoon excursion to bring a report to a client that had to be hand-delivered. But navigating the massive city, even for that short period of time, left a bad taste in his mouth. With a profound lack of enthusiasm he logged onto Orbitz to make his travel arrangements to the Big Apple.

"What've ya got?" Haggerty asked Mike Swenson the moment the private investigator stepped into his office. The owner of Noble Consultants didn't bother to greet Swenson or even look up from what he was working on, but rather cut right to the chase.

Haggerty didn't like Swenson. He respected him and was satisfied with the work he did for his firm, but he didn't care for the man. If Haggerty could find another P.I. who did as good a job for the money, he'd hire him. But such a person didn't exist in the D.C. area; heaven knows he'd searched.

The reason he disliked Swenson, other than that last bit of bad advise that resulted in the death of Bob Hobbs, was because he wasted his talents, and that bothered Haggerty. One thing the consultant detested was a person with God-given abilities they let go to waste. Mike Swenson was an extremely intelligent man and had the faculties to be an outstanding professional: attorney, doctor, something like that. Instead, he chose to spend his life following unfaithful spouses and searching for missing persons, and do so for peanuts. It was a terrible waste.

"The best bet we have is a man named Terrance McChaffee," Swenson replied, tossing a file onto Haggerty's desk. Haggerty picked it up and began to thumb through it while Swenson continued to talk. "He'll be in Las Vegas for the entire expo. He's got the soft spots we're looking for."

"Such as...?"

"For one thing he's a disgruntled employee. Considers himself one of the most knowledgeable fuel cell engineers at GFCT and is pissed he was passed over to replace his boss, a guy by the name of Bob Hobbs, after his death.

"Another thing is he's in debt—serious debt. Maxed out on his credit cards, falling behind on his mortgage and car payments, and has nothing in the way of assets; no mutual funds, CD's, bonds, so forth."

"Kids?"

"Yeah, one. Two-year-old daughter; his ex has custody. Also, he's barely making his child support payments. Has fifty bucks in the bank. Creditors are starting to call and most likely his car will be repossessed."

"How'd he get into such a bad state?" Haggerty asked, his nose still buried in the file.

"Don't know. He's recently divorced; I suspect the settlement set him back. He's clearly not fiscally savvy"

Haggerty closed the file and looked at Swenson for the first time. "Any other candidates?"

The private investigator shook his head. "None that I'd risk approaching."

"Do you think this McChaffee is approachable?"

Swenson pursed his lips and half shrugged. "If the price was right, I'm pretty sure he'd listen."

Haggerty leaned back in his chair and folded his hands over his stomach. "And what would that be, in your estimation?"

Swenson considered the question for several moments then said, "He needs at least twenty thousand to get him out of the hole. But I don't think he'd do it for just that. He owes two-fifteen on the house his wife got, eighteen on his car and has yet to set up a college fund for his daughter, which was part of the settlement. I think five hundred thousand would do it."

Haggerty looked out the window and thought about the figure. Half a million to conclude P3 and collect seventy-five million. There was the added bonus of never having to deal with Theodore Kennelly again. Sounded like a sweet deal.

He turned to face Swenson again. "Thank you, Mike. Good work. He'll be the one we approach. However, I want you to dig deeper into the other employees, just in case this McChaffee doesn't work out."

"You bet," the detective said with a nod of his head, then walked out of Haggerty's office.

As he figured, Paul Haydon got nowhere trying to contact Mary Hildahl through regular channels. The best he could do was leave a message with the program's executive assistant asking that Ms. Hildahl call him as soon as possible—he had a breaking story. The assistant dutifully took the message; but by her facial expression it was clear she heard that line twenty times a day.

When he pushed her, emphasizing that this really *was* a big story, that it was imperative he speak with Hildahl as soon as possible, the old woman gave him a sardonic look and said with the satirical snide of a typical New Yorker, "Honey, you know how many *really big* stories Hildahl and the rest of them get a day?"

Haydon sighed and kindly thanked the cantankerous old woman. He assumed the reporter probably wouldn't even get the message. If she did, she'd probably be influenced by the ancient executive assistant who undoubtedly thought him a nut, and she wouldn't bother to call him. The detective decided he'd have to go back to basic surveillance. He'd observe her, and when the time was right, approach her.

He spent the next day leaning against a building across the street from *Hour Report's* studios. He initially tried to wait in the lobby but was soon approached by a knuckle-crushing security guard who asked if he had business there. Hoping he could sweet talk his way into remaining in the lobby he tried his best to be charming. Eyeing the name-tag pinned to the big man's generic uniform he even addressed him by his first name; but all to no avail. Huge arms folded over his massive chest the guard listened attentively to Haydon's line of bull, but was clearly not impressed. Eventually forced to admit that he didn't have any legitimate business in *Hour Report's* studio, Clarence, the security guard, promptly showed Haydon to the door.

To pass the time he read various newspapers and magazines while periodically glancing at the studio's front doors. He also took up his old habit of chewing tobacco—something he hadn't done since Vietnam. Surveillance was one part of his job he detested and tried hard to avoid—it was so damned boring. Unfortunately, this situation called for surveillance; there was no way around it.

But it paid off. After watching the door to the lobby for three days he learned that Mary Hildahl arrived at the studio—in a chauffeur-driven limousine—at approximately nine-thirty in the morning and departed at three-forty-five. He never saw her leave for lunch. Overall, not bad hours. On the morning of his fourth day in New York he made his move.

Standing outside adjacent to the studio's lobby door, he was struck by how nervous he was; and for good reason. If he botched his initial approach to her he probably wouldn't get a second chance—Clarence most likely would see to that.

At nine-fifteen he spit the Copenhagen chewing tobacco out of his mouth and straightened his tie. He was wearing a suit in the hope it would make him look more professional and less like some crazy fan stalking her. Ten minutes later he saw the limo approach the curb. The back door opened and Mary Hildahl hopped gingerly out of the car while conveying thanks to the driver.

Paul Haydon swallowed hard and quickly took several steps towards the reporter. "Ms. Hildahl, may I take just two minutes of your time? It's very important."

Being hailed by someone from the street, the woman instinctively stiffened. She turned around with an alarmed expression and for a moment Haydon feared she would make a dash for the lobby door and the security of Clarence. But after her eyes ran him up and down, she could sense he wasn't a threat and her face softened.

She quickly glanced at her watch. "I'm running late."

"I'm very sorry to approach you like this, but I promise to be brief. After you listen for a moment, if you don't like what I have to say just say so and I'll walk away." She appeared to be wavering and took a step toward the door. Without thinking, Haydon wailed, "*Pleaseeeee!!!*"

Sounding like a little boy begging for ice cream she gave in. She stared at him for a moment, sighed and said, "Alright mister—?"

He walked up to her and extended his hand. "Haydon, Paul Haydon. I'm a private investigator and I need your help."

She accepted his hand and said, "I'll give you two minutes. More if what you have to say sounds good."

"Thank you, Ms. Hildahl."

The reporter set her briefcase down and crossed her arms over her chest. Her eyes narrowed and she leaned back a little, clearly indicating though body language that she was waiting to be impressed. "What have you got?" she asked tersely.

"Conspiracy."

She shrugged indifferently. "Nothing juicy there; common everyday stuff."

"Not like this, Ms. Hildahl. I've got proof that several of the largest oil companies have joined forces to eliminate an emerging technology. The conspiracy also involves several prominent members of Congress."

The reporter's eyebrows shot up. Anything involving politicians was newsworthy. And if the lawmakers are well-known, the feature would be that much better. *Hour Reports'* producers loved nothing more than trashing politicians; perhaps there *was* some potential here. "And what exactly is this emerging technology?" she asked.

"Fuel cells. Are you familiar with them?" The reporter nodded her head.

Haydon saw that he'd caught her attention. He quickly added, "I don't know yet how far up the conspiracy runs, but...we have an oil man in the oval office."

Mary Hildahl picked up her briefcase. "Come with me." As he passed the burly security guard and the old receptionist on the way to Hildahl's office, the detective couldn't resist flashing them a brusque smile.

"Please, have a seat," the reporter said when they'd entered her office. Haydon complied and took a quick look around. She was on the nineteenth floor and had a view of the adjacent building. The glass and concrete structure was very close to her window; so close in fact that he thought if he leaned out the window he could probably touch it. Not what he'd consider a very impressive vista. And her office was smaller than he would have thought for a TV personality; it had almost nothing in the way of personal curios.

When he turned to look at her, she was taking off her jacket and hanging it on a hook on the back of her office door. He was struck by her beauty. She was much more attractive in person than on television, with a stunning body, long, shapely legs, shoulder-length auburn hair and sultry green eyes. Her nose was surrounded by freckles; they were cute, he thought, but they must cover them up with make-up before she gets in front of the camera. He was disappointed to see a wedding ring on her finger. But of course she'd be married; a woman this beautiful would be snatched up quickly. Lucky guy!

"Would you like some coffee?" she asked as she settled down behind her desk.

Engrossed by her attractiveness it took a moment for the question to sink in. "Ah...yeah, yes, that would be nice."

Mary Hildahl picked up the phone and asked her assistant to bring them some coffee. After she hung up she folded her hands and asked, "So, Mr. Haydon, you mentioned that you needed my help. What is it I can do for you?"

"I've been investigating this case for some time now and I've sort of run into a dead end. But I now have a document that outlines—in detail—the specifics of the plot, however..." he hesitated for a moment. He feared that what he was about to say might put a damper on her willingness to report on P3.

"However what, Mr. Haydon?"

The assistant appeared with two large mugs of coffee. Handing him his cup she asked, "Cream and sugar?"

"Thank you, no," he replied, giving her a smile. She returned the smile and left the office. He turned back at Hildahl and continued. "The document—incidentally, the plan is called P3—names the fuel cell companies, their strategic vendors and executives within those companies to be targeted along with the politicians they are trying to influence. But, it doesn't name the oil companies or the people who are behind it."

To his relief, Hildahl didn't look as disappointed as he thought she would. After taking a sip of coffee she said, "So in other words, there's no one to point the finger at."

"Yeah, I guess you could say that. But there's no question oil companies are the culprit here. My job is to find out who the benefactors of P3 are and put an end to their plans."

"Who hired you?"

The private investigator hesitated; he didn't want to involve Rick Miller and his family. If *Hour Report* took on the story and knew he was the client, they would certainly involve him to some degree.

"I'd, ah...I'd rather not say. And it's really not important anyway. Hildahl seemed a little disappointed but accepted the response.

"What is it you want me—*Hour Report*—to do?" Hildahl asked.

"Investigate the story and put it on the air. Like I said, I've hit a brick wall in my efforts to find out who's behind this plot. I'm betting that whoever is sponsoring P3 will quickly make a concerted effort to deny any link to the scheme. That will put my investigation back on track. Your doing this story would be a win-win for both of us."

Mary Hildahl sat back in her chair and stared off into the distance, pondering what she'd just heard. Haydon interrupted her train of thought. "There's something else you should know, Ms. Hildahl, you're n—"

"Please, call me Mary."

A huge grin formed on the detective's face. Then it's Paul."

"Alright, Paul, you were saying?"

"If you air this story, you won't be the first to do so."

"Oh? Who else is reporting on it?"

"Well, to my knowledge, on one else is actively pursuing it. The *Providence Gazette* first broke the story, but it wasn't much of an effort. I talked with the reporter and he said he wrote up the article solely because he had a deadline to meet and he needed something to write about. He had no interest in following it up. The idiot didn't know what he had."

The reporter pressed her lips together tightly; she looked as if she was debating whether or not to say something. She decided to. "I've got to be honest with you, Paul. I'm really more of an anchor person than a reporter." Haydon opened his mouth to say something, but Hildahl quickly added, "That doesn't mean I've *never* done any investigative reporting. It's just been a while."

"I've got the utmost confidence in you, Mary."

Hildahl smiled at the remark, then nodded thoughtfully and said, "Okay, Paul. I'll talk with the producers and see if I can get it approved. May I see a copy of this P3 document?"

"Of course. I'll have a copy sent to your office this afternoon."

"May I call on you for assistance should I require help?"

"I'd be crushed if you didn't!"

"Alright then," Mary Hildahl said while rising and offering her hand. "We'll be in touch."

Terrance McChaffee opened his wallet only to find a single dollar bill. He'd only had three tap beers and he wanted a few more. But a buck wouldn't cut it. His state of destitution made him feel like crying.

"Like another one, buddy?" the bartender asked as he picked up McChaffee's empty glass.

The engineer looked into his wallet again, grimaced, and shook his head. "Yeah, I'd love another one; but I'm broke." The bartender shrugged indifferently and began to walk away.

"This one's on me," the man one stool over from McChaffee said, throwing a twenty onto the bar.

The engineer looked at him suspiciously for a moment. "Uh…thanks, buddy." He paused and then added somewhat sheepishly, "I'm, ahhh…I'm straight."

This made the man chuckle. "That's good to know. So am I."

The bartender placed another glass of beer in front of McChaffee who raised it in salute to the man who bought it for him. Nick Ragosta acknowledged the salutation with a nod of his head, then lit a cigarette.

After blowing out the first cloud of smoke Ragosta said, "I am interested in talking with you, however. If you can give me a few minutes of your time." He paused, then after giving the engineer a quick side-glance added, "I'll make it worth your while."

Terrence McChaffee gave the stranger a perplexed look. He didn't know this guy; what could he possible want with him? He considered the request for a few seconds more then grimaced and said, "Why the hell not? Maybe you'll buy me another beer, huh?"

"Be happy to," Ragosta replied, flashing him a reassuring smile. "Let's go sit at a table. Bartender! Set us up with another round, will ya?"

Ragosta led McChaffee to a table in the back of the bar. A dark and quiet spot where they wouldn't be overheard. The bar, *Bob's*, was located just about a mile away from Global Fuel Cell Technologies and chances were good that other employees of the company frequented the establishment.

After they sat down the engineer asked, "And who do I have to thank for the beer?"

Ragosta extended his hand. "Just call me Nick."

"Okay, Nick; thanks again," McChaffee said, shaking his hand. After taking another sip of beer he asked, "Do I know you?"

Ragosta shook his head. "No, you don't. But I know you. I know a lot about you." McChaffee stared at him distrustfully and didn't bother to hide it. Ragosta waved a dismissive hand in front of him and said, "Don't worry, it's nothing like that. I'm here to offer you help. Help I know you need. In return, you can do something for me."

The young man took a long sip of his beer, keeping his eyes locked on the mysterious stranger sitting across from him. After slowly putting the glass down he asked warily, "What kind of help? And how do you know I need any?"

Ragosta, looking completely at ease, gave him another little smile and said, "Everybody needs help, Terrance. You just need it more than most right now—financial help, that is."

McChaffee was shocked. "How do you know my name? And that I'm a little pressed for money?"

The assassin tried not to sound patronizing, but he did. "Like I said, I know much about you. *How* isn't important. And…I'd say you're a tad more than just a little pressed for money. You're in debt up to your ass."

Brusquely, the engineer responded, "Are you one of those guys from a collection agency? Because if you are, I've got nothing to say to you. Thanks for the beer. Goodbye!" McChaffee started to stand up.

"Whoa, hold on young man!" Ragosta said, reaching for McChaffee's arm and lightly gripping it. "Please sit down and let me buy you another beer. I'm *not* one of those guys. Like I said, I'm gonna make this worth your while."

McChaffee stared indecisively at Ragosta for a moment, then slowly sat back down. "Alright, I'm listening."

"Good." Ragosta raised his hand to hail the bartender. "Barkeep, two more please." After receiving the bartender's acknowledgement he looked back at the engineer, his face becoming serious for the first time. "What I'm about to both tell you and ask you must remain between us. I have no way of preventing you from disclosing this to anyone other than your word as a man. Do I have that?"

Taking a glass of beer from the bartender McChaffee simply said yes.

"That's good enough for me," Ragosta said sincerely. He sighed heavily, leaned into the table while placing one hand on top of the other and said, "I represent some people who don't want to see fuel cell technology gain a foothold in the market. They're quite concerned about the progress your company, and several others, have made over the last few years. They want not only to stop it, but reverse it."

The engineer said nothing; he only looked at Ragosta, waiting for him to finish what he had to say. The fact that he showed no emotion—no surprise, no aversion—to the initial statement concerned the assassin, but he continued. "I want *you* to accomplish that for them. I want you to ensure fuel cells never make it to market." To signal that he was ready for a response, Ragosta stared back at McChaffee and took a sip of beer.

Now the engineer's face showed what he was feeling—bewilderment. There was no mistaking it. McChaffee sucked in his lower lip then said, "*Why* would I want to do that? And…and if I did, *how* the hell would I do it?"

"You want to do it because there's a substantial amount of money in it for you. A lot! So much money in fact, that all your problems will be solved. How you do it, that I'm afraid I'm going to have to rely on you to figure out—I'm not an engineer."

Using his name for the first time, McChaffee was beginning to sound intrigued. "Nick…I'm an *engineer*…not a marketing executive. I have no idea how to keep this, or any product for that matter, off the market."

"I didn't make myself clear," Ragosta replied patiently. "I can tell you how to keep it off the market; I need you to arrange the incident that will make that happen."

"*Incident?*" the young man asked questioningly through squinted eyes.

"Yes. At the end of January there's a fuel cell exposition in Las Vegas you'll be attending as a technician. When—"

"How do you know all this about me?" McChaffee protested, shaking his head in disbelief.

"Let's just say it's my job to know, and leave it at that, shall we?" The engineer was clearly not satisfied with the answer but accepted it. Ragosta continued. "As I was saying, when the time comes for Global Fuel Cell Technologies to demonstrate its fuel cell powertrain to all the spectators and media, you're going to ensure it doesn't work—that it fails."

"And exactly how do I accomplish that?" the young engineer asked.

"Sabotage," Ragosta responded impassively, "plain and simple." Having said that, it was time to test the waters; see if McChaffee was warming to the proposal. "You know fuel cells, you have the technical expertise. How would you go about sabotaging one for failure; keeping in mind that the malfunction must look like an accident—a technical glitch?"

McChaffee thought for a moment, shrugged and said languidly, "A short across the membrane could cause a fire."

Trying to lead the young engineer on, the assassin shook his head. "No…not big enough, not spectacular enough. We'll need so—"

"Wait a minute," McChaffee cut in; his voice bordering on irritability. "What's the point? I mean, one fuel cell that doesn't work is hardly going to keep them off the market. People understand that mechanical glitches happen. They happen all the time! And as I'm sure you know, we're not going to be the only ones exhibiting at this show. They will be plenty of fuel cells there that function as intended."

A sadistic smile formed on Ragosta's face; so evil that McChaffee couldn't suppress the shiver that involuntarily erupted from what seemed like his very soul. With penetrating black eyes the assassin stared coldly at the young engineer for a long moment. Then slowly, with deliberation he asked, "How would you, Terrence…how would *you* go about sabotaging a fuel cell for…*catastrophic* failure?"

McChaffee's eyes narrowed and his jaw tightened. Keeping his eyes locked on Ragosta he slowly brought his glass of beer up to his mouth. The assassin noticed the young man's hand was slightly trembling. After taking a long sip McChaffee guardedly asked, "Define catastrophic."

Ragosta studied the engineer for a moment, leaned back in his chair and answered with a question. "Are there any concerns about the safety of fuel cells?"

McChaffee shook his head. "Fuel cells, no. But hydrogen...well...well yeah. Most people still believe the Hindenburg was brought down by a hydrogen explosion when in fact it was the coating covering the blimp's fabric that went up in flames."

"Yessssssssss," Ragosta drawled the word out while narrowing his eyes. "Perception is everything, isn't it? What do you think the response from the buying public would be if a fuel cell vehicle, such as the one your company will demonstrate at an upcoming trade show, blew up?"

McChaffee pursed his lips and shook his head. Assuredly he said, "Can't happen. A fuel cell can't explode. At least I've never heard of one exploding, or read of any kind of incident like that in any industry-related papers or published articles."

Keeping his intense gaze on McChaffee, Ragosta asked, "How could you make it look like the fuel cell exploded?"

"You can't!" McChaffee stressed. "You could make its fuel source explode, the hydrogen storage system, but not the fuel cell itself."

"How? How could you make the hydrogen fuel source explode?"

"Simple...the introduction of oxygen to the hydrogen and a spark. But everybody will know it's the compressed hydrogen that went up, not the fuel cell itself."

"Will they?" Ragosta asked rhetorically. "If there's an explosion, and I mean a *big* explosion, do you really think the general public will differentiate between the two components, or even care which one of them actually went up? Hell no! The only thing they'll recognize is that the damn thing blew up. It would be the Hindenburg of the automotive industry."

"A hydrogen explosion would be huge, Nick, dangerously big. People could get hurt...even killed."

"What's your point?" Ragosta asked nonchalantly, then immediately regretted the comment; McChaffee was visibly horrified. Quickly he added, "I mean, our goal is to sour the public on this technology; question its feasibility and safety. If we can do that, they'll never be successful in the market and the devices, along with the industry, will die."

"Stop using pronouns!" the engineer snapped. "*I* haven't agreed to do anything for you!"

Ragosta's forehead deeply furrowed as his eyes widened in conviction. "Oh, but you will my young friend," he replied confidently and with a smirk. "How much would it take to get you to agree to work for us?"

McChaffee said nothing; he chugged his beer and indicated that he wanted another one. "And throw in a double shot of Wild Turkey while you're at it," he shouted to the bartender.

They sat in silence while waiting for the bartender to bring the drinks. It wasn't awkward because McChaffee was clearly lost in thought; chewing on his thumb nail, his eyes remained locked on a distant object somewhere on the floor. As he mused, Ragosta studied the young man, wondering how little he could pay him to do his bidding.

"*Well?*" Ragosta pushed after the engineer poured the liquor down his throat, following it with half a glass of beer. "Throw out your figure."

But Terrence McChaffee was far more shrewd than Ragosta had anticipated. Smirking he asked, "What are you willing to pay...upfront?"

Ragosta dawned a knowing smile then said, "One hundred thousand; followed by another hundred if you're successful."

McChaffee let out a contemptuous snort. "Forget it. I'm not going to risk spending the rest of my life in prison for attempted murder for a measly two hundred thousand. You'll have to do better than that. A lot better."

Ragosta sat back and folded his arms over his chest. He looked hard at McChaffee for several moments then asked, "Let's cut to the chase, shall we? What's it going to take for your cooperation?"

The engineer looked down at his empty shot glass, then back up at the assassin. Ragosta could tell by the young man's eyes that the Wild Turkey was hitting him; but McChaffee retained his composure. "Like you said yourself, Nick, I'm in debt up to my ass. Since you seem to know so fucking much about me, I'm sure you know how far in debt I am. You obviously represent people who don't work for minimum wage. I'd want enough to not only get out of debt, but to live comfortably for the rest of my life." He paused to down the rest of his beer and hail the bartender for another. He then looked Ragosta square in the eye and said, "Two million ought to do it! One now, one after the explosion."

After reading the document Mary Hildahl became even more excited about the story. It had the potential to be the biggest feature of her career so far. Only one obstacle stood in the way—her producer.

Her relationship with Buddy Worther had been icy for the last few years. He hit on her shortly after she joined the cast of *Hour Report*. Married himself, Mary was disgusted by the advance. But this was nothing new to her; she'd been hit on many times before in her broadcasting career. She was experienced enough to know that how she handled the advances would determine how successful she'd be at the network. She'd rebuffed him, but did so in a savvy manner that didn't cause him to lose face.

Mary Hildahl was deeply in love with her husband and would never consider being unfaithful to him. Unfortunately, being in the entertainment business meant balancing fidelity with impiety. Every time she interacted with Buddy Worther—which thankfully wasn't too often—she braced herself for another attempt.

She arrived outside his office for her 3:30 appointment, ran her hands over her short skirt, took a deep breath and knocked. She'd deliberately dressed provocatively in a sexy, low-cut dress and high-heals because she knew it would help her sell the story to Worther. Sometimes she hated the business.

"Mary! Good to see you…" his eyes widened and he took a prolonged look at her. "Very good to see you!" he added in a low, desirous voice. He then waived his hand to dismiss his comment as if it were a joke. "Seriously, I was surprised, but delighted to see you on my appointment calendar. Please, have a seat." She sat down and could feel his eyes undressing her. She crossed her legs showing a pair of the shapeliest in the business, and Worther had difficulty taking his eyes off them. After he did he sat down, grinned and asked, "So, to what do I owe this pleasure?"

Mary Hildahl didn't waste any time. She told him about Paul Haydon and his request, the circumstances surrounding the story and the potential she believed it had. The producer looked skeptical until she mentioned that the conspiracy may go all the way to the White House.

After she'd finished she asked, "So, Buddy, what do you think?" She then leaned forward in her chair just enough to give him an excellent view of her ample cleavage.

The producer smirked; he knew exactly what she was doing. Shamelessly glancing at her breasts he asked unabashedly, "How badly do you want to do the story, Mary?" She sat back, reversed her crossed legs and playfully said, "Not that badly, Buddy…at least not yet."

Her response caused the man to chuckle. Then he was all business. "Alright Ms. Hildahl, have at it. As usual I'll want a progress report every other week." He looked at a calendar. "I'll want your preliminary story ready for editing before Christmas and we'll shoot to have it air the last week of January. Schedule the necessary resources as you see fit but stay within budget."

Hildahl was taken aback; not only by his approval, but by the atmosphere of the meeting itself. It was actually cordial and—by his standards—professional. If he hadn't mentioned the budget it would have been perfect. But perhaps that was asking too much.

"Thanks Buddy, you'll be pleased with the end product." The producer said nothing, he only gave her a quick nod of his head. But she could feel his eyes on her ass as she left his office.

"Two million dollars!" Haggerty cried, running a hand over his smooth head. Since the start of P3, Nick Ragosta had noticed that what little color the man had in his hair was now gone. He was completely gray; and the little hair left on the sides of his head was thinning. Musing over Haggerty's head rather then what he was saying, Ragosta toyed with the idea of suggesting he just shave his head bald and be done with it.

The assassin tuned back into the conversation. Flatly he said, "And the first million has to be upfront."

Haggerty frowned. "I thought you could handle him! Keep the costs down around the half-million mark. *Fuck!* I don't have a million!"

Ragosta sat down on the couch, crossed his legs and lit a cigarette. He was smoking way too much now; he regretted starting again. While studying the burning cigarette between his fingers he said calmly, "Laurence, you were the one who told me to use the carrot, not the stick. I'm much better with the stick." He paused; a dubiously expression came across his face. He looked at the owner of Noble Consultants and in a voice pitched a couple of octaves higher asked, "You don't have a million?"

"No. I'm tapped," Haggerty replied, averting his eyes from Ragosta in embarrassment." He let out a defeated sigh. "But I'll come up with it somehow. When you give it to McChaffee, threaten a little stick to make sure he doesn't fuck-up, or do something stupid like fly to Mexico."

"I will."

Haggerty sat grimacing for a moment then said, "Change of subject. Have you found Sandra?"

"No, but I know where she is. I asked Swenson to keep tabs on her until I had time to deal with her. She's next on my agenda."

"Where is she?" Haggerty inquired half-heartedly.

"Cody, Wyoming."

Haggerty's head jerked back and he gave Ragosta a surprised look. "Cody…Wyoming? What the hell is she doing there?"

"Besides hiding?" the hit man took a long drag on his cigarette. "She took a job cleaning rooms at some hotel."

"I wonder why she'd do that?" Haggerty said under his breath but still loud enough for Ragosta to hear.

The assassin offered, "She doesn't need the money but she's probably bored out of her mind waiting for this thing to blow over. It gives her something to do. I assume she took a job as a maid because it's an occupation where she doesn't have to interact with a lot of people."

"I suppose you're right. But like I said before, bring her back to me unharmed."

"And if she refuses to cooperate?"

Laurence Haggerty had pondered this question ever since Sandra Beach stabbed him in the back. His affection for her began to wane as P3 started to unravel. Though probably not fair, he blamed Sandra for all of P3's misfortune up to this point. She had caused him a tremendous amount of extra work and God knows how much money. He still didn't want to harm her if possible, but he would if necessary. After all, this was business.

The consultant turned his back to Ragosta and said solemnly, "Then get what you can out of her…and eliminate her."

Ragosta said nothing. He crushed out his cigarette and walked out of the office.

CHAPTER 16

▼

Even though the bill would not reach the floor this session, Senator Plecha had talked with Congresswoman Zwart and Congressman Radakovich several times in the last three months, gauging their commitment to abandon support for fuel cell technology. The lawmakers assured him they had no intention of supporting the zero emissions bill when it did come up for a vote after the election.

Not completely trusting the information provided him by the owner of Noble Consultants, shortly after Laurence Haggerty had again persuaded him to drop his support for the bill the senator had set up his own fact-finding commission. He set two of his brightest aides to the task of assessing both the progress of this technology and its impact on the automotive infrastructure. He was terrified when they reported that the information Haggerty had provided was essentially accurate. If anything, the assessment provided by Noble Consultants failed to underscore the full impact of fuel cells on the automotive industry; it would be catastrophic to all internal combustion-related industries. And the demise would be quick—a matter of a few short years. Even though this new industry would create jobs, it would only create a fraction of what would be needed to absorb the millions of people put out of work by the disappearance of the traditional automotive engine.

Plecha trusted the information provided by his assists because his study went one step further than Noble Consultants' analysis. He had his aids take a poll within his constituency and found that over 80% of the general public would gladly purchase a fuel cell vehicle if it was comparable to conventionally powered cars in price and performance—which, his study confirmed, they would be. The skyrocketing of oil prices and the growing belief within the country that America's young men and women were being sacrificed in Iraq for the sake of oil most certainly had an influence on how people felt. Be that as it may, he couldn't ignore the results.

This afternoon he would meet Radakovich and Zwart to pass along this information. He would ask that they contact other lawmakers and share his study with them—stopping fuel cells was clearly in the interest of everybody on the hill.

But he'd have to be careful how he handled this. He'd stress that this suppression would need to be done quietly; that no one politician grandstand the issue—use it for his or her political advantage. Plecha suspected most would cooperate; but of course there would inevitably be a few who just couldn't pass up an opportunity to look good.

After his meeting with the other two congressmen, he would then begin the painful process of calling the individual board members of Global Technologies Corporation, Unlimited Energy Systems and several other smaller but significant fuel cell manufacturers to notify them of his withdrawal of support. This wouldn't be easy; passing along news that had the potential of inflicting severe political damage never was.

Senator Plecha was still debating with himself whether he should tell the board members the truth—how he really felt. Perhaps if he did, he wouldn't lose the generous financial support he'd received from the majority of them over the years. Deep down he still believed in the technology and truly wanted to see it come about. But his commission had convinced him that for the good of the country the change had to happen slowly, gradually. The economy would need time to adjust to the dramatic changes the introduction of the fuel cell automobile would bring about. Many investors would instantly profit by the successful entry of fuel cells to the market, but far more people would be ruined by it.

He'd struggled for days about just how to break the news to the board members; what he could say or advise to lessen the impact. He now believed he had a persuasive argument. He'd soon find out. A clammy hand picked up the telephone.

"Office of Nigel Tennis," a mature, sexy female voice declared at the other end of the line.

"Yes, good afternoon. This is Senator Plecha. May I speak with Mr. Tennis please?"

"One moment, Senator." Plecha gnawed on his bottom lip as he waited for Global Technologies Corporation's chairman to answer the phone.

"Landon! Always a pleasure. How've you been?" The voice was strong; and sounded as if he was genuinely glad to hear from Plecha.

"Hello Nigel. Not bad. And you?"

"Great. Got my game down to 97. Not too bad I think…for an old man."

The lawmaker let out an obligatory chuckle. "And how's Beth?"

"Doing well, overall. Her arthritis gets the better of her occasionally. What's on your mind, Landon?"

The senator took a deep, silent breath; he closed his eyes and tightened his grip on the receiver. "Nigel, I'm afraid I've got some news that I'm pretty sure you and the board will find disturbing. But I feel obligated to inform you of it, along with several other prominent members."

"Oh…? What is it?" Tennis' voice quickly changed tones, taking on an almost intimidating quality.

"I've decided to pull my support for the zero emissions' legislation. I'm not going to vote for it, and I'm asking other members of congress to do the same." There was silence on the other end of the line. When Plecha couldn't stand it any longer he cautiously said, *"Nigel?"*

"That's, ummm…that's disappointing indeed, senator." All cordiality in his voice vanished; Plecha feared he'd taken the news harder than expected. Naturally he'd be upset. He, the rest of GTC's board and all the other shareholders were relying on this bill to not only boost sales for their company, but also accelerate the growth of the fuel cell industry as a whole.

"May I inquire, senator, as to the reason for your reversal?"

"Of course, Nigel. And when I'm through explaining I hope you'll agree with my decision and continue to support me." He paused, hoping he'd receive some kind of response from the influential businessman, but all he got was continued silence. He continued: "It's a matter of conscience, really. I've done a significant amount of research into the fuel cell industry as it relates to the automotive industry. Until I saw the results I never appreciated just how damaging…devastating, really, fuel cells will be to all the industries that revolve around the support and manufacture of gasoline-driven engines."

"I was unaware you've been probing into our industry, senator. That makes me a little nervous."

"It's nothing like that, Nigel, I assure you. You know I was an ardent supporter of fuel cells. Still am. But some time back I was visited by a gentleman named Laurence Haggerty. He owns a consulting firm here in D.C. He opened my eyes to the damage the introduction of your company's product will have on the economy. Not wan—"

"Bullshit! If anything, this new industry will help the economy grow—create jobs!" Tennis protested.

"Yes, eventually it will," the senator responded evenly. "But not for a long time. In the meantime thousands, if not millions of jobs will be lost."

"How can that be?" the chairman asked skeptically.

"All you have to do, Nigel, is give it a little thought. Think about how many businesses revolve directly around the internal combustion engine, let alone support them: Steel, plastic, rubber, electronics, machining. Then there are the support services: repair shops, auto parts stores, service centers for mufflers and oil changes, and so forth. I could go on and on." He paused a moment then added for effect, "You and most of your board members own a substantial amount of stock in many of the companies that will be affected."

Nigel Tennis said nothing for a long period of time as he considered what the senator had just told him. Finally he said, "I uh, I see your point. But...it's not as if fuel cell vehicles are going to instantly replace what's on the road now!"

"That's what I thought, Nigel. But my study doesn't support that. I'll admit I didn't take what would be called a good, statistical survey, but the results were conclusive. People are worried about the cost of gas continuing to rise. And many are far more concerned with the environment than we care to believe. If priced comparably to a conventional car, and if it performs like a car on the road today, they'll buy it. Granted, it'll take decades before conventional powered automobiles disappear. But it'll have an immediate effect on new car sales. By the way, I'll send you a copy of my findings."

"I'll look forward to it," Tennis said unenthusiastically.

"Nigel...along with telling you this, I also called to make a request of you."

"Your timing could be better. What is it?"

"I need you to..." Plecha's mouth suddenly went dry. He quickly took a sip of water and continued in a weak voice. "I need the introduction of GFCT's product to the market...delayed."

"*What*...? I don't believe I heard you correctly. You want *what?*"

A little stronger this time, the senator said, "I need you to arrange a delay in GFCT's production. Actually...I need you to prevent it."

"*Are you out of your mind, Plecha?*"

"And you're going to have to persuade the rest of your board to go along with it," The senator added, ignoring Tennis' last comment.

There was a long pause, after which the chairman of the board said, "Senator, assuming I even *did* agree with you on the matter, we're in the process of negotiating contracts, we've made commitments. Hell, we'll be exhibiting at the International Fuel Cell Exposition in Vegas in a few weeks..."

"Nigel, I think that once you've absorbed my study, understand the magnitude of what's unfolding here, you'll decide to cooperate with me—and have no trouble convincing the rest of GTC's board to follow suit. You'll be compelled to react, if not from a sense of civic responsibility, then from the fact that soon you and everybody else who owns shares of affected companies will be left with nothing but valueless slips of paper, so to speak."

The director let out a sigh. "What about *our* employees? If we delay the start-up, we'll be forced to reduce costs, people will lose their jobs. Not to mention how Wall Street will react to the news; our stock's value will plummet. How long are we talking here, senator…three, four months?"

This time the senator was slow in responding. "More like…years, Nigel. A minimum of ten."

"*TEN?*"

"In about ten years we'll slowly introduce fuel cells into the market. There's no other way, Nigel. No other way that won't throw our economy into complete and utter chaos.

"But don't say anything to anybody; don't change any plans until you've read and grasped all the data. Follow through with the exposition, business as usual. In the meantime, I'll also be relaying this same message to your counterpart at Unlimited Energy Systems and several other fuel cell manufacturers."

"Christ, Plecha, this is…just…."

"I know, Nigel. I know. I wish I could say I'll make it up to you, but I don't think I can. This is one of the most difficult phone calls I've ever made. I wish that I could share this with the electorate; show them that there *are* politicians with a conscience."

"Goodbye, Senator Plecha," Nigel Tennis said abruptly. After he hung up the phone he leaned back in his chair and ran his hands over his face. *"Shit!"*

She never would have imagined that she'd enjoy a blue-collar job. Working as a maid in a small, privately owned hotel was far from mentally challenging, but unlike her job at Noble Consultants—and most jobs in the corporate world she figured—it was completely stress-free.

Snapping a sheet in the air to spread it out over the queen-sized bed, Sandra Beach turned her head to look out the window. She'd been in Wyoming ten months now and hadn't yet tired of the state's natural beauty. And speaking of natural beauty; she had recently started dating a man who had the cutest ass she'd ever laid her hands on. Like so many of the gorgeous guys around here, he was a cowboy who performed in the local rodeo. Thinking of him widened the smile already on her face and made her all the more anxious for six o'clock when she'd meet him for a beer.

As she began to tuck the sheet under the mattress her thoughts turned to the room she was cleaning. It was supposedly haunted. The hotel had been built in 1909 and legend had it that the daughter of the original owner was murdered in this room. Several of the employees who had worked at the Tumbleweed Inn for many years swore they had seen her in this room. Sandra humored them; she didn't believe in ghosts.

Bent over and working her way around the bed she had only a few more tucks to complete when she sensed someone—or something—was watching her. A chill ran down her spine. She stuffed the rest of the excess sheet under the mattress and slowly straightened. She just stood there, her back to the pair of eyes she was sure were watching her. She was dismayed with herself—she had to work up the courage to turn around. If it was the ghost of Samantha McFarland, she'd piss her pants; she was sure of it.

Sandra Beach gritted her teeth and quickly spun around. She gasped and stiffened at the sight. There, standing in the doorway was something far worse than the apparition of a young woman—it was Nick Ragosta.

"*Ragosta!* Ho…how in the hell did you find me?"

Ragosta dropped his sinister smirk and replied, "Come now, Sandra; you were easier to find than a remote lost in a couch. *What*, no big kiss and hug for a friend you haven't seen in almost a year?"

Completely in shock from the unexpected surprise, Sandra mouthed a few words but nothing came out. With a startled expression she took a step back and cursed as she stumbled into the bed. Nervously she said, "If I was so easy to find, why'd it take you this long?"

Offhandedly, the assassin replied, "I had more important matters to attend to." He then started to slowly approach her.

"Take one more step and I'll scream!" she threatened.

"Scream and I'll kill you where you stand," he replied with terrifying sincerity. He pulled a pistol with a silencer from his sport coat. Slowly putting the gun back in his shoulder holster he said, "You'll accompany me back to Washington. Laurence is dying to see you."

She pulled her eyes from the pistol and stared at Ragosta. "I suppose he is. But I'm afraid I won't be able to join you; I have a date tonight," she said nervously in jest.

"Oh, well. Far be it from me to impede upon young love," he replied mockingly. His tone then became serious. "Let's go! I've got a chartered plane waiting and the meter's running. Don't even think about trying to run away or calling for help. It will be the last thing you ever do. Now move!"

It was a little past nine o'clock in the evening when Sandra Beach walked into Laurence Haggerty's office with Nick Ragosta close behind. Still dressed in her maid's uniform she was tired, but surprisingly she wasn't worried. She just couldn't bring herself to believe her old boss would harm her. She was sure he'd want to know why she betrayed him; then she'd receive a lecture and he'd send her on her way.

But as soon as she saw the expression on his face she realized she'd badly misjudged his intent. Never during their relationship had she seen him with such a look on his face; a blend of abhorrence and disillusionment—and it was directed at her. He didn't offer her a chair; instead Ragosta prodded her forward until she stood within inches of her former employer's desk.

Haggerty sat silently in his chair, hands pressed together in front of his tight-lipped mouth as if in prayer. Maintaining that terrible expression he studied her for a long time. Sandra became extremely uncomfortable and found she couldn't bear looking at him; she dropped her eyes to the floor. Her stomach suddenly began to cramp from the fear that was beginning to envelope her.

After what seemed like an eternity Haggerty dropped his hands and said calmly, "Do you have any idea how much money your little stunt has cost me?" Sandra said nothing; she only looked at him placidly. Obtaining no response from his former employee, Haggerty slammed his fist on the desk with such force she flinched and reflexively jumped backwards. The assassin immediately pushed her back in front of Haggerty's desk. ***"WELL, DO YOU?"*** he screamed, leaping up from his chair.

Sandra noticed that Ragosta was no longer standing behind her. He was taking a seat on the couch. Looking very relaxed, he lit a cigarette and settled down to enjoy the spectacle. She turned back to Haggerty and saw his face twisted in rage. Suddenly, she was terrified.

"Laurence, I…I, di—" she stammered, but Haggerty cut her off.

"Don't call me Laurence! It implies that we're on friendly terms and I assure you we're not." He walked over to the bar and poured himself a straight Scotch. As he did so, she glanced again at Ragosta. The bastard was enjoying himself. When he noticed her looking at him he flashed her a patronizing little smirk.

After taking a sizable sip of his drink, Haggerty leaned back against the bar, resting the glass on its surface from his outstretched arm. Contemptuously he said, "I don't know what upsets me more, Ms. Beach. The fact that you've cost me millions and nearly destroyed any chance of P3 being successful, or that you betrayed my trust."

Drink in hand he walked over to the window behind his desk. While looking out at the lights of Washington D.C. he asked, "Who else did you give the P3 document to?"

"No one," Sandra Beach replied nervously. "I only sent it to that one reporter from the *Providence Gazette.*"

Haggerty turned around to face her. "Well young lady, that was one too many. What am I to do with you? Huh?" He gestured toward the assassin. "Nick here is of the opinion that we should kill you." The statement shocked Sandra so badly that for a moment she struggled to control her bladder. "But I said no," Haggerty continued. "I wanted to see you first; try and understand why you'd do this to me."

She started to walk around the desk, her hands spreading apart in an imploring manner. "I never meant to hurt you, Laur...ah, Mr. Haggerty," she began pleadingly. "It was Wendell Finley I wanted to punish—to get even with." She paused. Then timorously she added, "It was a stupid thing I did...I know that now. But at the time I wasn't thinking straight. I was so furious with him."

Haggerty shook his head and sat back down behind his desk. "Bullshit, Ms. Beach! That's a bunch of crap! You're far too intelligent to not have known the consequences of publishing that document." The owner of Noble Consultants took another long sip of his Scotch, then put the glass down on the desk. He leaned back in his chair, let out a long sigh then said coldly, "I'm afraid I'm inclined to agree with Mr. Ragosta." A chill shot though Sandra and her knees became weak; she couldn't believe what she was hearing. "Unfortunately, I can't afford to have you loose, running around and telling others of my plan."

Panicked and beginning to sweat, the woman pleaded, "I...I won't say *anything*, Laurence, I swear! I've...I've had almost a year to tell anybody else, but I haven't. That should prove it to you!"

Haggerty's face showed no emotion; he just stared at her with a barren expression. Mournfully he said, "I trusted you, Sandra. Hell...I loved you like a daughter. And what did you give me in return? Betrayal. You couldn't have cared less if I went to prison for the rest of my life, or received a death sentence. And all because your greedy little scheme didn't work and you were scorned." He looked away from her and derisively said, "*Christ almighty!* I really thought you were better than that, Sandra." He turned to look at Ragosta. "Be quick. I don't want her to suffer."

"Gladly," the assassin said, crushing out his cigarette and leaping to his feet. He pulled the pistol from his jacket.

Sandra Beach gaped at him open-mouthed. What was happening was inconceivably surreal. She couldn't believe what he'd just said; that he'd actually have her killed. But his detached expression made her realize that he was going to go though with it. She began to weep as the hit man moved behind her. "*Pleaseeee*, Laurence! Oh *God* please don't—"

Looking at the gun in Ragosta's hand, Haggerty imperceptibly shook his head. The assassin put the pistol back in its holster. Sandra let out an audible sigh of relief. Wiping tears from her cheek, she gave Haggerty a look of sincere gratitude. "*God*…thank you, Laurence, I've—" she never finished the sentence. The room filled with the sound of a startlingly loud snap. Swiftly, Ragosta took her head in his hands and violently twisted it almost one hundred eighty degrees. Her neck snapped, Sandra Beach fell into a flaccid pile of twitching flesh at his feet.

Haggerty showed no emotion as he stared at the dead woman. He turned away and with tears welling in his eyes said, "Make sure the body is never found." After Ragosta had left with Sandra's body Laurence Haggerty wept shamelessly.

Terrance McChaffee had his best Christmas ever and was now having the time of his life in Las Vegas. Flush with money, he'd hired a beautiful escort to continually be at his side as he bopped from one casino to another. He was enjoying himself so much he'd almost forgotten that he had a job to do; both for Global Fuel Cell Technologies and for the enigmatic man who bestowed upon him his new-found wealth.

A few days after accepting his down payment of a million dollars, McChaffee began to discuss with Nick how he intended to trigger the explosion of GFCT's demonstration vehicle. Mistakenly, he was under the impression that he'd have a free reign as to how to accomplish the task.

To ensure the intensity of the blast could be controlled and happened at the right time, the engineer wanted to use small explosive devices he'd attach to the SUV's hydrogen storage system. Use of a radio signal to trigger the detonators would take care of the timing issue. A little C4 plastic explosive would easily puncture the storage tank allowing time for a small amount of compressed hydrogen to escape and mix with the surrounding air. The second charge would be set off a few seconds later and bring about the main explosion.

But his benefactor instantly shot down that idea. Nick Ragosta pointed out that pieces of the triggering device would easily be found by investigators, not to

mention chemical traces of the C4 explosive itself. Investigators would conclude—-correctly—that the vehicle was sabotaged.

"But doing it any other way," McChaffee objected, "we won't be able to control the size of the explosion. Shit, the blast could be huge! A lot of people could
die." He looked away from Nick, shook his head and quietly added, "I…I don't
want that on my conscience."

"You're missing the point," Ragosta countered. "My clients *want* this to look
like a malfunction. Anything less, and the potential exists that the incident will be
dismissed as nothing more than a glitch. I agree with Finley that we nee—"
Ragosta froze, realizing he'd just made a catastrophic mistake. He let slip Wendell
Finley's name. He was so comfortable talking with the engineer he became complacent and without thinking was going to share with him something Haggerty
told him Finley suggested during one of The Committee meetings. Becoming
complacent—it was the mistake of an amateur, and he cursed himself. He immediately tried to cover it up.

"I, ah, I mean Flinch—Flinch. Ever hear of William Flinch?"

McChaffee shook his head. But he suspiciously eyed the man across the table.
Why would he look so startled just because he used a wrong name? "No.
Enlighten me," the engineer casually asked. "Who's this Flinch guy?"

Ragosta was clearly struggling to look relaxed, awkwardly he answered,
"Flinch was an, ah…an old Scottish philosopher who believed that if you want to
make people believe something, show it to them." The assassin cringed inwardly;
that sounded like the bullshit it was. He tried to make his explanation sound
more erudite. "He theorized that people only believed physical proof. Essentially,
the only way to fully convince someone is to show them tangible proof of something." Ragosta desperately hoped McChaffee would buy the line of crap he was
feeding him. "That's why I want a malfunction," he continued, more relaxed
now. "I want it instantly cemented in the mind of the public that hydrogen-powered *anything* is unsafe—a deathtrap."

The engineer frowned. "I can appreciate that, Nick, but I see no other way to
do it without using a small amount of explosives."

Up to this point, Ragosta had tried hard to adhere to the carrot approach as
Laurence Haggerty had suggested. Doing so, he would receive willing cooperation; something that would not only make his job easier, but increase the chances
of a successful conclusion and hopefully bring this seemingly endless operation to
an end.

Haggerty probably wouldn't agree, Ragosta thought, but there are times when
the stick is needed. Observing the young man's body language in connection

with his sudden pacifistic attitude, Ragosta concluded that Terrance McChaffee required a little motivation to awaken his creative juices. For the first time in their short relationship, the assassin expressed malevolence.

Fixing cold, emotionless black eyes on the young engineer he said dully, "I want it to look like a malfunction *without* the use of explosives. You're the goddamn engineer—figure it out!" McChaffee's brow furrowed and he became visibly nervous. The engineer's reaction convinced Ragosta he'd used too much stick too soon for this particular individual. He tried to lighten his tone. "Look Terrance, you've been paid well, haven't you?" McChaffee grimaced in response. "For a small amount of effort your troubles are over—you're set for life. Take some time to figure out another way; another method that won't leave any evidence of tampering. We'll meet again in a week. I'm sure you'll have come up with something by then."

Mollycoddling McChaffee this way was killing him. Ragosta wanted nothing more than to beat him within an inch of his life—that would motivate the sniveling little bastard. Instead, he gave the engineer a fatherly smile and got up to leave.

"There...is another way," McChaffee said meekly.

The assassin stopped and slowly sat back down. "I'm listening," he said, staring intensively at the young man.

"It will leave no evidence and look like a malfunction. But the explosion could be...well, nothing less than catastrophic."

Nick Ragosta smiled. *That's my boy!* he thought. "Well? Don't keep me in suspense. What is it?"

The engineer sighed. "I didn't suggest it earlier because of the amount of time it'll take to rig. I questioned its feasibility." He hesitated until he saw Ragosta's expression, clearly demanding him to continue. "During the exhibition I'll have unlimited access to the vehicle, but so will the others engineers in our group. If one of them looks at the powertrain long enough, they'll spot the set-up. I'll need to do this right before the curtain goes up."

Ragosta said nothing; he just continued to look intently at McChaffee, waiting for him to explain. The engineer continued. "By loosening the fuel line just enough to create a leak path I can vent hydrogen from the system. I'll have to rig the hydrogen pressure sensor so that it continues to read normal—that's the part that will take a long time. I can run a wire from the ignition switch to the leaking fitting that will spark when the key is turned. That will trigger the explosion."

Ragosta slowly nodded his head, seemingly pleased. But he asked, "If you do it right before the demonstration, how do you know the blast will be big?"

"You have to remember that the hydrogen is under very high pressure. Once I loosen the fuel line from the intake manifold, hydrogen is going to gush out. Like I said, I don't know how long it will take me to fuck with the pressure gauge. But I know it will be long enough to vent a large amount of hydrogen and time for it to mix sufficiently with the surrounding atmosphere." The engineer paused a moment, then underscored, "I wouldn't want to be around when Klash turns the key."

Ragosta's forehead furrowed. *"Klash?"* he asked in surprise.

McChaffee just assumed he didn't know who she was. "Yeah, she's the CEO of the company; she'll have the so called *honor* of being the first to show off our handiwork to the public."

Ragosta grinned. Although he had no further designs on the woman, her elimination would purge one more person who could someday talk. Dropping his smirk the assassin asked, "I just thought of something: won't she smell the gas?"

McChaffee shook his head. "No. The hydrogen fuel has no odor—yet. Eventually, legislation will come about that will require hydrogen suppliers to add a rotten egg smell, or some kind of very noticeable scent to the hydrogen—similar to what's done with natural gas. But for now it can't be detected by smell."

"Excellent, Terrence, excellent!" the assassin said, slapping him hard on the back. "I guess you know what to do. Once the deed is done, I'll meet you in the lobby of the Hilton with the balance owed."

After that conversation, McChaffee fell into a state of depression. He struggled with whether he should go through with it. Cynthia Klash would surely die, along with any others in the vicinity. More than once he had picked up the phone and started to call Nick—to call it off; he'd return the money—but he never pushed the last number. He remained in despair until he received a call from his ex-wife's attorney, threatening legal action if he continued to disregard the terms of their divorce settlement. Opening up a 529 plan for his daughter with an initial installment of $25,000 quickly improved his spirits.

With a cynical eye Mary Hildahl studied the P3 document for the better part of a day and concluded that there was no question as to its authenticity. She was amazed at the seemingly outward simplicity of the strategy, but appreciated how difficult actual implementation would prove to be. Using several different search engines, she spent the next day on the web researching fuel cells and the companies listed in the document Paul Haydon had provided her. She was puzzled at how the reporter from the *Providence Gazette*—or any reporter for that matter—could fail to realize the significance of what was written on these pages.

Determining the best way to attack this story was proving a little more diffi-cult than she had anticipated. On those rare occasions when she'd come to an impasse on how best to develop a feature, she would normally consult with one or two of the other cast members of *Hour Report*. Typically they proved helpful; but she didn't want to do that with this story.

For the past few months the show's ratings had been dropping and competi-tion among the talent for spectacular stories was beginning to develop. Everyone wanted to be the one who *saved* the show. Because this story had the potential to skyrocket a career, it wouldn't surprise her if one of the other anchors approached Buddy Worther and tried to steal it from her. She had seen it happen once before, when she was with another network: *the story was too big for such a junior member of the troupe; ratings would be much higher if one of the more popular anchors did the reporting.* And knowing Worther, he would probably fall for this kind of bullshit logic.

Why risk it? She was going to keep her mouth shut about this story for as long as possible.

Other than the names of the beneficiaries, the private detective failed to men-tion that the document lacked one other tidbit of information—the person or persons who created it. If she could find out who they were and get one of those people on camera, ferreting out who hired them—or, at a minimum, useful information that could eventually lead her to the conspirators—should prove easy. Unless they'd been through the ordeal many times before, it was amazing how intimidated most people were by on-camera interviews. It was her experi-ence that when she was armed with the right facts, potentially culpable parties were quick to pass the buck when challenged in front of a camera.

But where best to begin? She didn't have a lot of time, and a limited budget. Some of the smaller companies mentioned in the P3 document may be able to provide her—unwittingly, most likely—with some of the information she'd need to nail those ultimately responsible. But given her deadline and meager financial resources, would they be the best place to start? She was a realist and knew that even if she was able to squeeze useful information out of the people she inter-viewed, finding those ultimately responsible for the plot would prove time con-suming and difficult at best. So she didn't hesitate to accept Paul Haydon's offer of assistance.

When she saw the private detective the next day, she explained her quandary. "I'd certainly get easier access to, and better cooperation from, employees of the companies listed in P3. But obviously, I'd make much faster progress if I could get hold of one of the people who drafted this damn thing." Showing mild disgust, she threw the document on her desk. "But I've no clue how to even begin to track them down. I'm sure they're guarding their identity as closely as they're guarding that of their clients."

Haydon nodded his head empathetically. "I've given it a lot of thought. As prominent politicians are involved, it only stands to reason that some, if not all, of those who dreamed up this scheme are probably located in the Washington D.C. area."

"What makes you think that?" Hildahl asked.

"It's been my observation, Mary, that large corporations rarely trust the advice or suggestions of their own employees. Why? I've no idea. But because of this they rely heavily on consultants. American industry spends billions each year to get advice from these so-called experts who have absolutely no interest or stake in the welfare of the companies that hire them."

The reporter looked at him strangely. "That doesn't make a lot of sense!"

Haydon gave her a sour look and shrugged. "No. It doesn't, does it? Anyway, using the suggestions of the consultants, along with the services of well-paid lobbyists, large corporations attempt to influence policies that affect their business. If you want to cut to the chase on this matter, I'd suggest you start looking around the D.C. area for consulting firms that have ties to the oil industry. If you get nowhere talking with these people, then start talking with the fuel cell companies and their suppliers."

The ringing phone startled him out of a fitful sleep. Cursing, Nick Ragosta fumbled for his cell phone on the nightstand. He was exhausted and felt like he hadn't slept for months. All the problems associated with P3 had him running around—putting out fires—like never before. By no means did he ever expect the plot to unfold flawlessly, but he certainly didn't anticipate this level of complication, either. The late Sandra Beach could be blamed for much of it, and he told Laurence Haggerty that he suspected they hadn't heard the last of the problems resulting from her little stunt. He was right.

"*WHAT?*" he barked into the little device irritably, still half-asleep. He squinted at the clock on the nightstand, it was a little after nine in the morning. The woman he'd hired to keep him company last night rolled over and let out a soft moan. He glanced at her contemptuously, realizing he fell asleep before he even got this money's worth out of her.

"Guess who I just got a call from?" the owner of Noble Consultants asked in a panic.

Ragosta ran a hand through his disheveled hair and frowned. "Haggerty, I'm not in the mood for twenty fucking questions."

Haggerty continued, completely oblivious to the assassin's reply. "Mary Hildahl! Do you know who she is?"

"Name sounds familiar, but no, I don't."

"She's one of the reporters on *Hour Report*," Haggerty replied. His voice was high-pitched; it usually was when he was under duress. "She's got the P3 document and said she's investigating a huge conspiracy story."

Ragosta covered his eyes with his free hand and moaned loudly. He then realized with surprise that Haggerty mentioned the plan over the phone. Of course, the way things were going the man probably thought he had nothing to lose. But Ragosta thought he'd better remind him. Worked up as he was, chances were Haggerty probably wasn't thinking straight.

Fully awake now and sitting on the edge of the bed, the assassin said, "Laurence, are you sure you want to talk about this over the phone?"

"No! But we have no choice; time is short. Besides, the odds that we're being tapped are pretty fuckin' remote!"

"Wait a minute," Ragosta said. He put the phone down then turned around. Using one of his feet, he shoved the sleeping woman off the bed and onto the floor.

"Hey! What the fuck!" she protested, rising to her knees, long black hair covering her face.

"Get out!" he snapped. He pulled two hundred dollars from his wallet and threw the bills on the bed. She flipped her hair over her shoulders and gave him a scornful look. She was a high-class call-girl and not used to being treated like a common whore. She then picked up the money and started to put her cloths on. Before she could even zip up her dress, he pushed her out the door of his hotel room and threw her shoes out after her.

"Asshole!" she spat out scathingly.

"Yeah, I love you too," he replied mockingly and shut the door.

He walked back to the nightstand and picked up the phone. "I *knew* Beach was holding out on us—the bitch! I told you what she did would come back to haunt us. *Christ!* How did this reporter link Noble to the document? Your firm isn't mentioned by name in the thing. Hell, you don't even advertise in the Yellow Pages!"

"She hasn't made the connection yet; at least I don't think she has. She said she was calling lobbyists and consulting firms in the D.C. area."

"That'll take her a while. What'd you tell her?"

"Nothing of course. I claimed ignorance. Denied I knew anything about it; that I hadn't a clue what she was talking about."

Ragosta sighed. "Well…what do you want to do? Want me to go after her, too?" he asked in weary frustration.

Haggerty mused then said, "Maybe." He paused for a moment then asked, "How's it coming along with McChaffee? The exposition is next week."

"Good. He's devised a way to do it clean. But it's a certainty there'll be casualties. The CEO of Global Fuel Cell Technologies will be one of them."

"Cynthia Klash?"

"Yeah. She's the one who's going to drive the vehicle around the convention center."

"That's not altogether bad," Haggerty said thoughtfully.

"I didn't think so either."

"Nick…this has to work! *Everything* is riding on it. It can't fail!"

Ragosta didn't want to ask, but he had to. "What if it does?"

It took Haggerty a while to respond. "If it fails…go after Hildahl. You'll have to go after her and anybody else who may have the document."

The assassin frowned deeply. "Laurence, this…this—"

"This what?"

Ragosta wanted to tell Haggerty that this whole thing was getting out of hand. That he couldn't go around killing every person who may now have a copy of the document and every reporter that might be working on a story about it. Doing so would garner more scrutiny and almost certainly cause the FBI to become involved. It wouldn't take them long to figure out the common denominator of the murders.

But he didn't tell Haggerty that—yet. If the sabotage of GFCT's vehicle didn't work, then he would dutifully go after the reporter. But he would soon come to a line in the sand that he wouldn't cross, and his involvement in P3 would come to an end, regardless of the end result. "Nothing," the assassin replied. "It's not that important."

Haggerty didn't press the issue. "Stress to McChaffee that his plan had better work!"

"I already have."

"Do it again, Nick. Do it again."

"Right."

Arriving back in Las Vegas three days before the show, Terrence McChaffee volunteered to stay late and "fine tune" GFCT's fuel cell powered demonstration vehicle. He urged his two fellow engineers to go out on the town and have a good time. They tried to convince Terrence to come along; he'd have plenty of time to work on the car in the next few days. But he argued that he'd been in Vegas not all that long ago, and besides, he wasn't in the mood to go out. They accepted his excuse and headed for the strip. McChaffee relaxed a little now that he'd gotten rid of them. He could work without worrying about them looking over his shoulder.

There was very little he could do beforehand to try and minimize the time he'd need to prepare the vehicle for destruction. He studied the fuel system to verify where best to create a leak and where to place the ignition wire. Fortunately the hydrogen pressure gauge wasn't digital. He wondered whether Klash would even bother to look at the gauges before she turned the key.

Lying under the dash he loosened the two set-screws holding the clock-like device to the instrument panel. Doing this wasn't much in the way of preparation, but it would save him some amount of time. When the time came he would cut the power wire to the hydrogen pressure gauge, pull it out, pop off the bezel and manually turn the hand to indicate normal pressure. The part he worried about was putting the bezel back on and placing the gauge back in the instrument panel. This would take some time due to the limited amount of space he had to tighten the set-screws. He had worked with this pressure gauge several times over the last two years. Taking it out was always easy; but putting it back in was a bitch.

He connected the wire that would produce the spark to the ignition switch; then rigged the switch to allow power to flow into the wire from the vehicle's small auxiliary battery when the key was turned. After replacing the ignition switch's plastic cowling, he coiled up the spark wire and taped it to the back of the power brake booster. Shortly before Klash began her demonstration, he'd string the other end of the spark wire to an area just short of the leaking connector. When the CEO turned the key a short would be created causing a spark that would detonate the leaked hydrogen.

After completing all the preliminary work, McChaffee decided he needed a drink. As he left the convention center for the nearest bar, he again became distraught over what he'd agreed to do. But when he looked at the numerous hundred dollar bills in his wallet his spirits took a turn for the better. It was a wonderful feeling knowing he was rich. No more on-the-job ass kissing, no more worries about paying bills, no more hassles from his ex, no worries whatsoever. And why should he be concerned about Cynthia Klash? She certainly didn't care about him or anyone else for that matter. Hell, she didn't even bother to attend

Hobb's funeral. As far as he was concerned, he owed her and Global Fuel Cell Technologies nothing.

After pounding the beer he decided to find some female companionship—for the rest of his stay. That wouldn't be hard to do in Las Vegas, and he smiled knowing he could easily afford it.

Rick Miller tried to persuade his company to cover his expenses to the International Fuel Cell Exposition. Over the years he'd had a good deal of success obtaining leads on potential new customers at these shows and acquiring useful intelligence by networking with the various people who represented a wide variety of industries. His argument had been persuasive; had the show been anywhere other than Las Vegas he might have succeeded. It's an unfortunate fact that the management of most companies believe tradeshows are nothing more than one big party—at company expense. This show, being held in Las Vegas, served to add legitimacy to that bogus perception.

Rick had no way of getting around it; if he wanted to expense the trip, he had to tell his boss the event's location. And because it was a fuel cell exhibition, Dave Greene took pleasure in telling Rick that "jaunts to Sin City" wouldn't be covered by either Flexible Sealing Solutions or Flexible Tubing Technologies. The denial didn't surprise Rick; each passing year the company seemed to be getting tighter and tighter on covered expenses. But it was worth a shot.

So Rick decided it was time to take Terri on a vacation. His wife had never been to Las Vegas, and he hadn't been there himself since '84. Wisconsin winters being what they were, January was the perfect time to escape. Besides, next month he'd have to spend a week at Flexible Tubing Technologies in Lake Rapids. As far as Rick was concerned, Michigan had the worst winters in the country—they were so gray and gloomy. Might as well soak up as much sun as possible while he can.

But Rick wanted to go to Las Vegas and attend the convention for another reason. Paul Haydon would be there. Rick's friend told him he intended to mingle with people from fuel cell companies other than UES and GFCT. He wanted to try and find out if they were involved in the conspiracy and if so, to what extent. He'd also use the opportunity to bring Rick up-to-date on the investigation. Rick was excited; he thought it would be intriguing to accompany his detective friend as he made the rounds.

Rick and his wife met up with Haydon for dinner the evening before the show. Terri Miller was looking forward to it. She had heard much about Paul

Haydon from her husband, but had never met him. She found him every bit as captivating as Rick had boasted, handsome and quite charming.

Over dinner the investigator told the couple about his new strategy and latest activities. Rick and Terri were astounded, and impressed, that Haydon was able to convince Mary Hildahl of *Hour Report* to work with him and run the story.

"Maybe you're the one who should be in sales," Rick jokingly said to his friend. "Convincing a celebrity to join forces with you—that couldn't have been easy to do."

Haydon smiled at the complement then announced, "As a matter of fact, she's going to attend the show. Would you like to meet her?"

The couple glanced at each other in surprised delight. "Why, sure!" Rick responded excitedly. "I've never met anyone famous before."

"How'd you manage to even meet her, let alone get her to agree to do a story?" Terri asked.

The private investigator donned a prideful smile. "How I met her, Terri, is a trade secret. Pure charm did the rest."

"You never tire of bullshitting, do you, Paul?" Rick asked in jest. "No, seriously, how'd ya do it?"

Haydon shrugged. "I had to case her for a few days to learn her routine. Then, during a small window of opportunity I approached her and gave her my well-rehearsed spiel. I apparently convinced her; she wanted to hear more."

"What time does the show start tomorrow?" Terri asked. "I'd like to get a little shopping in if I could beforehand."

Her husband looked at her with a startled expression. "*You* want to go to the show? I didn't know that. *Why?*"

"I've been listening to you whine about these companies for years," she replied flatly. "I want to see what all the fuss is about. Besides, I understand they're going to drive around one of those fuel cell powered cars. I'd like to see that."

Rick looked at his detective friend who shrugged and said, "Opens at two. I'll meet you guys outside the main doors around one forty-five, alright?"

The two nodded in agreement.

CHAPTER 17

▼

Terrance McChaffee had set the alarm for six AM, but he didn't need it. Tossing and tuning all night, at four forty-five he decided to just get up. Last evening he'd toyed with the idea of having Brandi, his five-hundred-dollar-a-day escort, spend the night with him. He was glad he didn't; it would've been a waste of money.

From the day he met Nick, the engineer had struggled with the moral implications of the actions he'd agreed to undertake. He didn't give a damn about GFCT, but he was no murderer, either. At first he thought killing the company's CEO wouldn't bother him. But now it did. His anxiety grew with each passing hour. Soon, he'd have to fulfill his obligation.

Sleep eluded him because he spent his nights trying to think of a way to walk away from his commitment. Giving back the money wasn't an option any longer—he'd spent too much of his initial million. In anticipation of success and his second installment—all of which he intended to squirrel away—he'd been spending money like a drunken sailor. His best guess was that he'd already spent over $450,000. He congratulated himself for at least having the sense to take care of his family obligations first.

Try as he might, no brilliant idea came to mind and he came to the painful conclusion that it was too late to back out now. Much of the problem was that he couldn't figure out Nick. And he didn't trust him either. With one minor exception, Nick had never shown the slightest bit of belligerence toward him. But McChaffee somehow knew Nick wasn't a man to be toyed with—certainly not one to disappoint. He admitted to himself that the man scared the hell out of him.

In his sleepless agitation he also called on all his considerable engineering talents to devise a way of limiting the size of the explosion. Too small, and it wouldn't have the dramatic effect Nick and his customers, whoever they were, demanded. Too large, and he could literally blow the roof off the convention center. But like his attempt to think of a way out of this nightmare, trying to determine a method to regulate the blast was futile. No matter how small he made the leak, if Cynthia Klash decided to make a long-winded speech prior to turning the key, an ample amount of pure hydrogen would have time to adequately mix with the air around the vehicle. The longer she delayed, the more time the explosive mixture would have to diffuse into the surrounding area.

McChaffee left his room a little after six. He went to the hotel's restaurant and walked up to the buffet. At the sight of the scrambled eggs he decided that anything he ate would find its way out the way it went in. Nervous, tired and beginning to sweat, he decided to walk to the convention center.

"Rick, honey, I'm having a wonderful time here," Terri Miller said, hanging onto her husband's arm as they strolled down the street. "I can't believe we've never considered vacationing here." She paused for a moment, looked around her then added, "I'm so glad you decided to come—and take me along with you!"

The salesman looked lovingly at his wife. "When you see all the wonderful applications for fuel cells, I think you'll understand why I'm so captivated by them."

The couple ascended the steps to the main doors of the Las Vegas Convention Center. Rick was pleased to see so many people waiting for the doors to open; it was a good omen. "Christ, I wish we had this kind of attendance at some of the shows *I* do," he commented enviously. Looking around, he was surprised to see so many media trucks scattered throughout the enormous parking lot; it rivaled what he'd seen at major sporting events or political conventions. He scanned the area again to see if he could spot *Hour Report*'s Mary Hildahl. He wasn't disappointed when he couldn't; after all, Paul had promised to introduce her to them. Rick was really looking forward to meeting her and wondered if she was as pretty in real life as on television.

"There you guys are!" Paul Haydon shouted as he pushed his way through the tight crowd. "Wow, can you believe this? All these people!"

"It's something, isn't it?" Rick replied. "I'll bet a fair number of people are here because they lost their asses gambling."

"Just like us!" his wife retorted sourly. Her husband reddened slightly with embarrassment.

The trio was fascinated by every booth they passed. Displayed were applications for the technology they'd never considered: power supplies for lap-top computers, high intensity spotlights, wheelchairs, various types of communications equipment, security systems and even an electric razor.

"I had no idea that there were so many fuel cell companies," Paul Haydon commented with a touch of astonishment.

"And not all the companies are exhibiting," Rick replied. "Ever been to a trade show before?" Haydon shook his head. "Well, you can tell which companies are 'Mom and Pop' operations by their booth's lack of opulence."

"Microsoft lacked opulence at one time," Terri Miller pointed out.

"You're absolutely right, honey." Turning to his friend Rick asked with eager anticipation, "So…when do we get to meet Mary Hildahl?" His wife gave him a withering look.

"We're meeting her at four-thirty in front of Global Fuel Cell Technologies' booth. We wanted to meet at the main stage, where GFCT is displaying their car, but we figure there'll be too many people crowded around there. She wants to find a good vantage point to film Klash driving the vehicle off the stage and down the ramp. After the demonstration Mary arranged an interview with Klash. She told me she'd be happy to meet you after that."

"OH BOY!" Terri Miller blurted out sardonically.

Both men looked at her, amused. Haydon then glanced at his watch. "Wow, fifteen minutes from now. Where the hell has the time gone?"

"Have you seen him today?" Laurence Haggerty asked with a noticeable slur. Anxiety was getting the better of him and he'd begun drinking earlier than normal. It was six-thirty in Washington D.C. when his contract killer called him, and it came as no surprise to Nick Ragosta that Haggerty was inebriated.

"Yeah, I saw him earlier this afternoon."

"He's gone!"

Dismayed, the assassin shook his head. He hated talking to Haggerty when he'd been drinking. "No, no, no, Laurence. He's off doing his job."

He could clearly hear the owner of Noble Consultants let out a sigh of relief. "Oh."

"For Christ's sake, Laurence, relax. In an hour all your problems will be over." Even over the phone Ragosta could hear the tinkling of ice cubes hitting the insides of a glass.

"How the hell can I relax, Nick?" Haggerty replied in a trembling voice. "Everything is riding on this, this…whatshisname? Oh yeah, his McChaffee guy!"

"There's, ah…there's another thing you should know," Ragosta said hesitantly. Given his employer's current state of mind, he wasn't sure if telling him was a good idea; but he decided he would.

"What?"

"David Greene, that executive from Flexible Tubing Technologies, he got a call from that Hildahl woman." There was silence at the other end of the line and Ragosta concluded that the news was too much for Haggerty to absorb at the moment. He decided to quickly change the subject. The assassin glanced at his watch and said, "Showtime is in about half an hour. Why don't you have a drink and relax."

"I am drinking."

"I know," Ragosta said dryly.

"Call—"

"I'll call you the moment the *event* is over, Laurence," Ragosta cut in, sounding a little annoyed. "Talk to you soon." He quickly snapped his cell phone shut.

Haggerty looked at the receiver in his hand, grimaced, and then hung up himself. After pouring himself another Scotch he sat back down, sighed, and fixed his eyes on the top drawer of his desk. Slowly, he pulled it open, reached in and picked up an envelope. With a sense of deep foreboding he studied the one-way ticket to Rio de Janeiro, Brazil.

Twisting the ticket in front of his face he thought about the countless ways the engineer from Global Fuel Cell Technologies could fall short. Most likely would be if the vehicle failed to explode and the tampering was discovered; or evidence was found after the blast pointing to sabotage. Regardless of how it happened, the engineer's inability to successfully compete his mission would lead to only one conclusion: the failure of P3. And should that happen, Haggerty had no intention of sticking around. He'd flee the country.

The Committee would be out for blood, but Ragosta—not having been paid—would extract it. Now that he'd worked with Ragosta for some time, he concluded that the assassin had his talents, but investigating wasn't one of them. Were it not for Mike Swenson, there was no question that P3 would have taken much longer and Sandra would have never been found. Haggerty was literally betting his life that Ragosta would never find him in South America.

"Are you alright?" Tim Larson asked with genuine concern. "Shit, Terrance, you look like death warmed over!" The three engineers from GFCT were having coffee at a dilapidated, food-stained table in the exhibitor's lounge. McChaffee was uncharacteristically quiet, and it didn't escape the notice of his two co-workers that he was constantly checking the time.

McChaffee looked up from his watch and gave them a nervous smile. "Huh? Oh, I'm, ah, I'm fine. Just a little worried, I guess."

"Worried? Worried about what?" Larson inquired, a touch of surprise in his voice.

The question caught McChaffee off guard; saying he was 'worried' was a stupid mistake. After a moment of quick thinking he said, "Ahhh…I don't know. Just that something might go wrong with the demonstration." He glanced at his watch again. It was time; the curtain would open in twenty minutes. His stomach began to spasm.

"What could go wrong?" Nancy Ranger, the third member of the trio asked. "We've gone over every inch of that vehicle. It'll run flawlessly."

"Yeah, I suppose you're right," McChaffee said. He waited a moment then added, "Ah…but just the same, I'm going to take one more peek at the ignition system." He got up from his chair and stumbled, clutching Larson's shoulder to steady himself.

"I'll go with you," Nancy Ranger announced. "I've got nothing better to do." She began to push herself away from the table.

Terrance McChaffee froze in fear. It never occurred to him that someone might offer to come along with him. He tried to remain calm but could feel himself begin to perspire. He cursed under his breath for agreeing to join Tim and Nancy for coffee; he should have remained alone. But as they were the only people who could uncover what he was doing he thought it best to keep an eye on them. He'd know exactly where they were when he took the final steps to prepare the vehicle to explode.

McChaffee tried desperately to look nonchalant. "That's okay, Nanc. You finish your coffee with Tim. It'll just take me a minute to look it over."

Giving him a dismissive wave of her hand she stood up. "I'll come anyway. Hell, I don't even like this coffee—too harsh."

"*NO!*" McChaffee blurted out in panic, causing the other two engineers to give him a startled look.

Quickly he softly added, "Please, Nanc. You've done most of the work. I insist…you relax."

The woman looked at him with suspicious, narrow eyes and opened her mouth to protest when her cell phone rang. "Oh, hi honey," a smile swept over her face. She looked at McChaffee; then waved her hand for him to go ahead without her and sat back down. Breathing a sigh of relief, he thanked the gods that Nancy had insecure kids who felt it necessary to frequently call her. This was the third call of the day. He gave the other two engineers a wave and quickly walked out of the lounge.

Approaching GFCT's demonstration vehicle, a converted 2004 Nissan Pathfinder, McChaffee took a quick look around the stage area. There were two guys talking in the wings. They would probably take no notice of him. He looked at the huge curtain hiding his company's pride and joy from the boisterous spectators he could hear on the other side. When the time came, Klash was supposed to drive down a specially built ramp connecting the stage with the floor. After slowly driving through the audience that was expected to part like Moses parting the Red Sea, she would drive once around the convention center and then back up on stage. The idiots in advertising thought film of people oohing and aahing as the vehicle slowly drove by would make a great commercial when they started mass marketing. McChaffee thought the idea was stupid. GFCT's customers were the car manufacturers or what's called the OEM's, the original equipment manufacturers. They were wasting money advertising to the general public. But the department insisted commercials would create greater demand for fuel cell powered vehicles. Who knew? Maybe they were right.

When he reached the Pathfinder the engineer saw that the two men were security guards. They would certainly notice him working on the car; but they would most likely figure he was conducting a last minute check. Oddly, the guards didn't concern him. It was Larson and Ranger he was worried about. But provided they stayed in the lounge, he should be able to complete his work without any problems.

Reaching through the open window, he pulled the lever to pop open the hood. As he suspected, the two security guards halted their conversation and looked in his direction. McChaffee gave them a smile and a nod. They nodded back and continued chatting, completely uninterested in what he might be doing. Some security. But what can you expect from rent-a-cops paid $6.50 an hour?

With shaking hands, McChaffee pulled the coiled wire he had hidden earlier out from behind the power brake booster. For some reason his mind flashed back to all the debate they had about the booster, whether to keep it or not. How could they have power brakes without it? With no vacuum from an engine how could they make it work? The problem was solved by connecting the booster to a vacuum pump used for the climate control system. His idea, of course.

After threading the spark wire through the fuel cell compartment he crawled under the Pathfinder to finish stringing it. It was a tight squeeze under the vehicle, but fortunately he was skinny and the small SUV had just enough ground clearance.

A steel frame member was located next to the fitting that connected the hydrogen storage tank to the fuel line. When the key was turned, the result would be a spark between the wire, its end stripped of insulation, and the steel frame. He wedged the end of the spark wire into a tight crevasse between two frame members so that it was hanging in between the nut connecting the fuel line to the hydrogen storage tank and next to the steel frame member. He then tucked the excess spark wire into a tiny gap between two stainless steel hoses. That completed, he pulled a crescent wrench out from his back pocket and began to loosen the nut connecting the fuel line to the tank.

Someone lightly kicked his foot. "Hey buddy, how's it going?" The nudge startled McChaffee and he slammed his forehead against the hydrogen storage tank. He let out a quiet curse and waited a moment to allow the initial sting to subside a bit before answering. "Good! Good. Just givin' it the once over before the curtain rises."

"Yeah. I suppose you know that everybody is really excited about seeing this car," the voice said. "It seems to be the only thing people are talking about."

McChaffee filled with annoyance; who was this clown? He simply didn't have time to shoot the shit. After glancing at his watch he said, "I gotta get this done. So, if you don't mind..."

"Oh, sure," the voice replied. "Good luck!"

McChaffee listened to the departing man's fading footsteps. "*Fuck!*" he muttered to himself.

Placing the crescent wrench back on the nut, he twisted left, but the nut didn't move. He pushed harder but still it didn't budge. Frustrated, worried about time, and now terrified that the nut might be too tight for him to loosen, he pushed on the wrench with all the force his confined body could muster. Suddenly the nut came lose, and the abrupt lack of resistance along with the momentum of his thrust caused his hand to surge forward and slam against a sharp corner of the frame. He howled in pain as the crescent wrench went flying out of his hand, making pinging sounds as it bounced on the concrete floor. He cursed when he saw it was out of his reach.

An explosive hissing sound filled the stage; the nut had twisted much too far. *"Shit!"* he cried loud enough for the security guards to hear him. He cursed under his breath again as he heard their approaching footsteps. Using his fingers he tightened the nut until he could only hear the hushed whisper of leaking hydrogen fuel.

"Everything alright under there, sir?" one of the guards asked, bending over trying to see the man under the vehicle.

McChaffee rolled his eyes. *"Yes!"* he snapped curtly. "I'm fine;" *Goddamit.* "I just need to be left alone!" The two security guards looked at each other, then disdainfully at the pair of legs protruding from underneath the vehicle. They shook their heads and walked away.

"Yeah, get the fuck outta here!" McChaffee whispered to himself. After squirming out from under the Pathfinder, the young engineer stood up, brushed his clothes off with his hands and began to walk off the stage.

"Shit!" he cried out to himself. He was so focused on the first two steps he'd completely forgotten to freeze the hydrogen pressure gauge. He turned around to go back to the vehicle and stiffened at the sight of Cynthia Klash strolling towards him.

She was dressed to kill; and for the first time McChaffee thought her very attractive. He'd never seen her in a dress before; she always seemed to be wearing a business suit. It was amazing what a pair of high-heel shoes could do for a woman's legs.

Admiring her, he realized he could do nothing about the hydrogen pressure gauge. It was too late.

Seeing him she smiled; then stopped and bent over to pick up the crescent wrench lying on the stage floor. He'd forgotten he'd left it there.

"Is this yours?" she asked, offering the wrench to McChaffee.

"Ahhh...yeah. I forgot about it—it fell out of my pocket. Thanks." Looking embarrassed, he took the tool from her.

Affably she said, "I'm sorry, but I don't remember your name."

McChaffee was stunned; he couldn't believe the CEO of his company would even acknowledge his existence, let alone talk to him. She seemed almost human.

"My name? Oh...I'm McChaffee. Terrance McChaffee."

"Well, it's nice to meet you, Terrance," she offered her hand. "I'm sorry I haven't made more of an effort to get together with you and the other two engineers here from our company. It's just that I've been so busy."

The engineer gave her a nervous smile. He didn't want to shake her hand; his palms were terribly sweaty. "Oh, that's alright, Ms. Klash." Quickly, he rubbed his hand on his pants and took her extended hand. "We know you're a busy woman."

"Well, that's really no excuse." She smiled at him again, then turned to look at GFCT's demonstration vehicle and frowned. "Well…I guess it's show-time, huh?"

"Ah, yeah. I guess it is."

Jokingly she asked, "Your creation isn't going to blow up on me or anything, is it?"

He visibly shuddered at the spurious question and turned white; his knees became weak and he buckled. What were the odds she'd say something like that? Klash turned from the vehicle and looked at him. Her eyes narrowed slightly at his timorous appearance.

"Ahhh, no. No! Of course not," McChaffee replied, struggling to maintain his composure. "Enjoy your ride."

As she approached the vehicle, he was overcome with an unbelievable sense of guilt; he'd never before felt such overwhelming remorse. She wasn't the cold-hearted bitch he pictured her to be. *Oh my God, my God. Dear God, what am I doing?*

A large part of him desperately hoped she would see the pressure gauge dropping and call off the presentation. But a smaller, more powerful part of him wanted to see the car explode—he wanted the money. Shaking, McChaffee turned and quickly walked away.

"MAY I HAVE YOUR ATTENTION PLEASE," a deep, rich voice bellowed through the loud speakers. "Momentarily, Global Fuel Cell Technologies will be presenting its fuel cell powered Sports Utility Vehicle. Anyone interested in seeing this demonstration should proceed immediately to the main stage area."

The noise from the audience was almost deafening; Cynthia Klash looked at the stagehand and nodded. Slowly, the curtain began to part.

"LADIES AND GENTELMAN, IT IS MY PRIVLAGE TO PRESENT TO YOU MS. CYNTHIA KLASH, CHIEF EXECUTIVE OFFICER OF GLOBAL FUEL CELL TECHNOLOGIES."

The boisterous, applauding audience brought a superficial smile to the CEO's face. Looking out over the sea of people, she sadly thought about how much sweeter this moment would be if that son-of-a-bitch *Mister R* hadn't come into her life. As a result of the destructive actions she'd been forced to take, GFCT would be out of business now were it not for the deep pockets of the parent company. What must the board think of her abilities? She'd never be offered a top spot again—by any company. And of course there was Alexis Kostreva; her lover, dead.

Retaining her smile, Cynthia Klash raised her hands in an effort to quiet the audience. Several attempts were required before the noise slowly began to subside. She was filled with a strange sensation of sorrow mixed with nervous jitters. How she would've liked to savor this moment, but instead she only wanted to get it over with.

"Ladies and gentlemen," she began. The wireless microphone attached to her lapel carried her voice clearly throughout the entire convention center. "Oba the years—" at the verbal stumble she threw her hands over her face in embarrassment. Dropping them she bent at the knees and did a quick dip. She giggled and said, "God, I'm *so* nervous!" The audience warmed to her honest declaration and scattered laughs could be heard emanating from the huge crowd. Normally, she would never have excused herself for starting out a speech so poorly. But this wasn't a formal presentation and would most likely be the last one she'd ever give as a chief executive officer—she might as well have fun with it.

Cynthia Klash composed herself and continued. "Sorry about that," she said with polite insincerely. "Years of grueling research, testing, and a tremendous amount of investment have accumulated into the converted vehicle you see behind me." She turned and gestured to the SUV. "This, ladies and gentlemen, is the *future* of transportation!" The spotlight moved from Cynthia Klash to the Nissan Pathfinder behind her.

The crowd applauded enthusiastically. Rick Miller wanted to get closer but couldn't; there were just too many people packed around the stage. He, his wife and Paul Haydon were stuck. The throng was so dense they couldn't even move backwards.

Rick thought the rapid clicking of cameras almost sounded like machine gun fire; their flashes brightened the dimmed auditorium with a strobe like effect. Terri Miller commented to Haydon about the feeling of anticipation and excitement in the air—the atmosphere around them felt electrically charged.

Klash continued. "Although fuel cell powered cars are nothing new, up until now they were all experimental, and in my opinion, never taken seriously by the automotive industry.

"The vehicle you see before you has changed all that." More applause. "The FC-seven powertrain system is the first ever to match the performance and reliability of conventionally powered cars. And now—" she paused to let the clapping subside. "And now we can mass-produce this system at roughly the same cost as gasoline powered engines and their transmissions.

"We chose to convert a Nissan Pathfinder, a current production model, to show the feasibility, the ease of exchanging power plants without costly redesign to the platform. Most vehicles on the road today could accept an FC-seven powertrain with little or no alteration to their engine and transmission compartments."

Another round of applause broke out accompanied by several loud whistles. Cynthia Klash bowed her head slightly in recognition of the spectator's approval.

"Now, so you all can have a good look, I have the distinct honor and pleasure of taking her for a spin around the building. Slowly!" Light-hearted laughter could be heard as the CEO of Global Fuel Cell Technologies stepped up to the vehicle and got in.

As she reached for the key already in the ignition switch, she noticed the hydrogen pressure gauge. She squinted, dropped her hand from the key and tapped on the instrument's clear plastic bezel. "This can't be right," she mumbled to herself. The gauge read low; so low in fact that she had doubts the car would even start. *Wouldn't that go over well?* she thought mordantly. Because her engineers had gone over the SUV with a fine tooth comb over the last few days, she concluded that the gauge must have just stopped working minutes ago; but it felt strangely loose in the dashboard when she tapped it.

She didn't want to delay any longer. Her hand went back to the key. She looked up at the audience, smiled and turned the key.

For the sake of convenience, Laurence Haggerty put the bottle of Scotch and a bucket of ice on the table next to the sofa; he didn't want to be bothered with leaving the couch for a refill. With a trembling hand he aimed the remote at the television sitting on the bookshelf and tuned in CNN. The network would probably be the first to break any news from Las Vegas.

Except for the flickering light of the television, his office was dark; he hadn't bothered to turn on any lights. The darkness mirrored his mood. The hand holding the remote fell limply to his lap; he dropped his head back against the top of the couch and stared blankly at the ceiling. His despondency increased with each glass of Scotch.

It wasn't supposed to be like this, he thought. Where the hell did it all go wrong? He never intended that anyone be killed. Roughed up a little, perhaps—that couldn't be avoided. But killed? No. And now he was waiting for news of God knows how many more murders—murders he sanctioned. *Christ, what have I turned into?*

Haggerty took a sip of his drink and his mind went back to the question that had been nagging him all night: Where did it all go wrong?

He knew the answer, of course; and it still pained him terribly to think about it. But Sandra Beach wasn't the true reason; she was just one of its victims. Just as Wendell Finley, Kenneth Saxton, Theodore Kennelly, Nick Ragosta and he himself were victims. For that matter, damn near everyone were casualties of it. He admired that minority of people who had the strength of character, the moral conviction to fight it; to not let it control their lives the way it now controlled his.

Greed.

Even the sound of the word was evil. This one human failing was the cause of all the world's problems. If one really looked, really scrutinized every problem mankind faced, greed would be found at its core. Why the hell would God—who in theory loves his children—instill such a trait in them? He laughed at himself; he wasn't sure if he even believed in God. He thought about the words of Michael Douglas in his favorite movie *Wall Street*. His character, making a speech to investors started out by saying: "Greed is good." Greed is good…bullshit!

Haggerty refilled his glass; he was surprised at how much effort it took. After dropping in a couple of ice cubes he again allowed his body to become a lump of jell on the couch.

When did greed become the driving force in his life? He didn't start out that way. He studied law and became a lawyer with the intention of helping people; that was what motivated him to work two jobs during college and law school. Unlike so many of his classmates, his family wasn't rich. But he believed that working his way through school gave him the moral character his counterparts lacked. Well, any ethical ascendancy he once had over his well-to-do classmates was now certainly gone.

He let his head drop back down and locked his eyes to the television. Excruciating as it was, there was noting to do but wait.

In an effort to compose himself, Terrance McChaffee sat in a stall in the men's room for several minutes before rejoining Nancy Ranger and Tim Larson in the exhibitor's lounge. He tried to appear normal but he couldn't. The unmitigated guilt he was feeling was overwhelming, suffocating. He was trembling slightly and his forehead was covered with beads of perspiration. His eyes darted nervously between his two co-workers as he pulled out a chair to sit down.

She had talked to him, acknowledged his existence. Having actually carried on a brief, but pleasant conversation with him she now had a human face, and that face wasn't the high and mighty CEO of Global Fuel Cell Technologies. She was a person, a woman, who had hopes and dreams and people who loved her, and he was about to end her life.

"There's definitely something wrong with you, Terr," Nancy Ranger said with concern as he clumsily sat down. "Are you feeling alright?"

"Yeah, you look like shit," Larson added.

Nancy Ranger had provided him an opening for an excuse about his appearance and he jumped on it. "No, as a matter of fact I'm not."

"Yeah, you *really* look like shit," Larson accentuated.

Ranger frowned at Larson, then turned to McChaffee and asked, "What's wrong?"

"I don't know, Nanc. All of a sudden I feel sick to my stomach."

"Probably those Nachos you ate last night," Larson offered. "didn't I tell you not to eat so many?"

"Maybe you should go to your room and lie down," Ranger suggested.

"I'll be alright," McChaffee replied. Looking pale, he had his arms wrapped around his stomach and was bending slightly forward in his chair. "I think I just need to rest for a minute," he added.

"Well…if you're sure," she responded. She waited a moment then said, "While you're resting here, I think I'll go watch the demonstration." She quickly rose from her chair. "What to tag along, Tim?"

McChaffee's head immediately snapped up and he gave her a sharp look. *"NO!"* he roared; so forcefully that it startled the other two engineers.

Appearing confused, both Ranger and Larson stared at him. "*Why not?*" she asked, visibly perplexed.

McChaffee looked vacantly at his co-workers who continued to glare at him dubiously. If he didn't come up with a good, credible reason, and quickly, he'd just given himself away. The way he'd been acting he figured he probably already had. "Uh…I don't want you to go…there's something I want to discuss with you. A, ah…a rather delicate subject I've been meaning to talk to you guys about for some time now."

Ranger pursed her lips and narrowed her eyes. "And what might that be?"

"Ummm…my, uh, situation with the divorce. I mean, you've both been there. Is there any way I can obtain full custody of my daughter?" It worked. A sympathetic look came across Ranger's face and she sat back down.

Larson shrugged and leaned back in his chair. "For what it's worth, I'll give you my two cents," he said.

Internally, McChaffee breathed a massive sigh of relief.

"Well, that's a rath—" Suddenly, the entire building shook with incredible violence. It was followed by a tremendous rumble that sounded as if they were in the middle of an enormous thundering cloud. At the food kiosk fruit stacked on the counter was flung to the floor, coffee cups bounced on the tables and dust, shaken from the rafters, began to drift down on everyone in the exhibitor's lounge. *"WHAT IN GOD'S NAME WAS THAT????"* Nancy Ranger cried in terror.

The convention center was filled by a flash of blinding light, followed by a deafening roar that seemed to reverberate endlessly off the walls of the huge auditorium. At the back of the building, Nick Ragosta threw his hands up to shield his eyes; he heard a piece of shrapnel whiz by his head and imbed itself in the concrete pillar next to him. When he lowered his hands, he saw a huge fireball rising to the ceiling. His eyes dropped from the whirling ball of flames to where GFCT's Nissan Pathfinder had once been; a small pile of something unrecognizable was burning intensely. His tightly pressed lips bent into a tiny smile of satisfaction.

The convention center was deathly quiet for several moments after the blast. One loud, shrieking scream broke the silence; the lone cry was quickly joined by a chorus of others. Soon, the building was filled with chaotic shouting, screaming, and cries for help.

It took a moment for Rick Miller to realize he was lying on top of the person who had been directly behind him; the attractive woman who had been in front of him was now lying face down across his legs. She was twitching, and his left leg began to feel warm and wet.

Suddenly filled with fear, he sat up and frantically looked around for his wife. She was nowhere to be seen. Rick struggled to get up; when he moved he felt a burning sensation in his right leg. He pushed at the woman who was pinning him down and after several attempts she rolled lifelessly off his legs and onto her back. Rick jerked back in revulsion and let out a weak cry. Frozen, dead eyes met his; the once beautiful woman had a massive gash across her throat; dark red blood was everywhere.

Rick heard a groan through his still ringing ears. He looked down to his right at Paul Haydon who was struggling to sit up. He shook his head. "My God...what happened?" the detective mumbled. He turned to Rick. "You alright?"

Clearly panicked, Rick replied, "I can't see Terri!" Painfully, he got to his feet and extended his hand to help his friend up off the floor. They both began to scan the area. A minute later Haydon nudged his friend and pointed; a wave of relief swept over Rick. In the distance he saw his wife slowly getting to her feet. She was about twenty yards away from him and like everybody else, she looked dazed. He was so elated to see her that he didn't even notice that the blast had shredded her shirt, leaving her in just her bra. But he did notice that her skin was blackened in several places, as was her short, blonde hair.

She began to slowly spin around in place. *"RICK!"* she shouted, her face contorted with fear.

"TERRI!" her husband shouted in reply. She didn't hear his cry but saw him madly waving one arm. Her face melted in relief and she rushed to his arms, thoughtlessly stepping over several bodies along the way. When they embraced, Rick felt a searing pain in his left shoulder. From its intensity he suspected his shoulder was dislocated.

"OH, RICK!" she cried, her face buried in his chest. They held each other tight for a long time. When they separated, Terri Miller reached out to Paul Haydon and squeezed his arm. "Paul, are you—"

"I'm fine, Terri, thank you. Thank God you're alright. Here—" he took off his shirt and offered it to her.

For the first time she noticed she was only wearing a bra; she gladly accepted it with a nod of gratitude and quickly put it on. *"My God!"* she whispered in disbelief as the three began to take in the horrific scene around them.

Everyone in the auditorium was shocked, stunned and confused. Those who were knocked down by the blast were slothfully getting to their feet; but many remained sprawled on the floor, motionless. Terri saw a man blackened and wearing only half a shirt, his hair disheveled and smoking. Next to him a young woman was on her knees, blood spilling from her head. She wobbled and then fell forward on her face. Acrid smoke was rising to the ceiling with nowhere to dissipate. She turned her head toward the stage and saw that nothing was left of the demonstration vehicle but a small heap of burning, twisted metal. Only small segments of the heavy curtain were left hanging; what remained was shredded, singed and smoldering. Then she looked down and screamed; noticing for the first time the severed leg at her feet, a red high-heeled shoe still on the foot. Terri Miller turned and buried her face in her husband's chest.

"A bomb...a terrorist attack!" Rick declared, tightly holding his weeping wife and continuing to scan the area.

"So it would seem," Haydon replied. "Come on, Rick, Terri. Let's see what we can do to help."

"That was an explosion!" Tim Larson exclaimed, appearing bewildered. Neither he or the others noticed that he was soaked in coffee.

"An explosion?" Ranger cried in disbelief. "An explosion…what could, how cou—"

"I have no idea," Larson retorted, cutting her off.

Ranger spun in her seat and looked at him in shock. "You don't think?"

"That's, ah…that's impossible," McChaffee offered feebly. He couldn't face them so he looked toward the door of the lounge.

Larson and Ranger jumped to their feet and dashed toward the door. McChaffee slowly followed.

Bedlam breaking out all around him, Nick Ragosta serenely studied the piece of shrapnel that narrowly missed his head and lodged in the concrete pillar he was leaning against. It was a rather large, thick piece of jagged metal; if he were to guess, it probably came from some area of the vehicle's frame. He took one final look at the carnage around him, grinned, and then strolled out of the auditorium.

The sound of numerous sirens filled the air; their wailing intensifying as they approached the convention center. The assassin lit a cigarette, flipped open his cell phone and pushed the speed-dial button for Noble Consultants. This was a call he looked forward to making. Laurence Haggerty would be relieved. However, by now he'd more than likely be hammered; but despite his drunken haze Ragosta was certain the high-priced, so-called consultant would understand *this* message with absolute clarity.

Just one more thing to do and it would be the end of this bungled plot—at least as far as he was concerned. After completing this final task, he'd pay Mr. Haggerty one last visit, collect what was owed him and retire in style and comfort. He couldn't wait.

Mary Hildahl wiped blood from her eyes; she had a small gash in her forehead. But she wasn't too concerned about the amount of blood because she knew that head wounds bleed profusely. David Johnson, her cameraman, was sitting with his head in his hands. The reporter knelt beside him and gently took hold of his arm. "Dave, you alright?"

The cameraman responded with a groan then slowly stood up. "Yeah. Except for my ears; they're ringing like hell."

"Mine too." She saw his camera on the floor. Pointing to it she asked, "That thing still work?"

Johnson shrugged, picked it up and quickly studied it. After pressing a few buttons, checking the connection to the battery and looking into the eyepiece he said, "There's a little damage, but I think it will still tape."

"Then for God's sake, Dave, let's start recording!" She searched the area for her microphone and found it next to a young man holding his stomach and moaning in pain. She felt slightly guilty just ignoring him and picking up her microphone; but she had a job to do. She glanced behind her and positioned herself so that the camera would record the burning debris on the stage just to her left. Johnson finished adjusting the large camera on his shoulder and gave her a little nod; a moment later she was illuminated by the camera's bright light.

For effect, she began her report by wiping more blood off her forehead. "As you can see," she turned and gestured to the twisted, burning metal behind her, "a terrible accident has occurred here at the Las Vegas Convention Center—just minutes ago." She sounded as traumatized as she looked. "It appears Global Fuel Cell Technologies' demonstration car just...just exploded!" She looked at the stage again; when she turned back to face the camera her expression was the epitome of concern. "I...I don't know if there have been any fatalities—but." She took a few moments to glance from side to side, her eyes narrowing at what she considered points of interest. "I see bodies all over. With an explosion of this magnitude I would think there'd...there'd have to be!

"My cameraman and I were standing well over fifty yards away from the stage and we were both flattened by the blast. Dave, scan the area please." He made a slow, sweeping arc around the convention center. He took the time to shoot close-ups of strewn bodies, crying people, and the remains of GFCT's demonstration vehicle burning on the stage. Anything the editors thought too disturbing could be edited out.

He focused in on Mary Hildahl again. "Because the explosion happened just moments ago, I have no factual reports to pass along at this time. We don't know what caused the blast—whether it was an accident, a terrorist attack, or something else. However, there certainly will be more on this terrible tragedy soon. For *Hour Report*, I'm Mary Hildahl."

The camera's bright light went out. She dropped the microphone from her face, stared at her cameraman and began to cry.

Nancy Ranger stopped dead in her tracks, panting. Tim Larson ran up beside her and froze at the sight. Several moments later they were joined by an extremely timid Terrance McChaffee who kept averting his eyes from those of his co-workers.

"Oh my God!" Nancy Ranger whispered in complete disbelief. They were the only words spoken by any of them for well over a minute.

Standing a couple of feet behind the two stifled engineers, McChaffee reluctantly forced himself to look out over the panorama of destruction. Cynically, his first thought was that he'd earned his money. The explosion was far more potent than his most pessimistic estimate, and certainly more powerful than he'd intended. Sprawled out everywhere near the stage was debris and bodies—and not all the bodies were whole. The caustic odor left by the blast was quickly being replaced by the metallic stench of blood.

The sight seemed surreal; McChaffee was mesmerized by it. He found it difficult, if not impossible, to accept reality—that he was responsible for the devastation before his eyes. Something in his mind kept the thought at bay as he continued to gaze in amazement at the disjointed scene.

But then he saw them. He tried to tear his eyes away from the sight, but couldn't. What he saw and heard shattered the invisible shield in his head, driving home for the first time the magnitude of the atrocity he'd committed.

Kneeling beside the broken body of her little boy, a mother wailed in the most soul-shattering sound of grief McChaffee had ever heard. She rocked back and forth, sporadically burying her face in her hands, then dropping them to caress her lifeless son.

McChaffee completely fell apart. He turned and ran to the nearest exit with all the speed he could muster. So gripped by the incomprehensible horror of what they were viewing, neither Larson nor Ranger had even noticed McChaffee was behind them.

McChaffee tripped on something and stumbled out the door. Not waiting to regain his balance, he turned and continued running along the side of the building until he found himself near the main doors of the convention center. He stopped and leaned against a glass wall, his chest rapidly heaving up and down as he tried to catch his breath and calm down.

The sight of the anguished mother and her dead child kept flashing through his mind. The boy couldn't have been more than twelve-years-old. *God help me, I murdered a child! How many more children were in the audience? How many children lost a parent today? How many wives are now without a husband?* These tormenting questions and the uncertainty of their answers made it impossible for him to divert his attention to anything else. Falling to his knees, Terrance McChaffee buried his face in his hands and began to sob uncontrollably.

The engineer slowly dropped his hands at the deafening sound of numerous fire trucks, ambulances and police cars charging into the huge parking lot. He was stunned at the sight of so many emergency vehicles. Uninjured people were flooding out of the convention center while firemen and paramedics rushed in. The outside of the building was a sea of mass confusion as hundreds of people, many of them hysterical, were desperately searching the area for friends or family. No one took notice of the crying man kneeling next to the building.

Transfixed by the spectacle before him, McChaffee didn't think of fleeing the area until he saw two paramedics hurrying out of the building carrying a woman on a stretcher. The victim was ghostly white and moaning softly. A stiff breeze caught the sheet covering her body, momentarily lifting it to reveal yellow entrails hanging from a huge gash in her side. McChaffee stood up to leave, but then bent over and vomited violently.

"Talk to me!" Laurence Haggerty all but shouted. Despite his condition, he had the phone to his ear before it had a chance to complete its first ring. Nick Ragosta was amused; that was damn quick for a hammered man. Funny how a life-changing event can quickly sober even the most ardent of drinkers. He inhaled deeply on his cigarette, blew the smoke out of the side of his mouth, smirked, but said nothing.

"Goddamnit, Nick!" Haggerty threw his other hand over his eyes and rubbed them, taking a moment to regain his composure. His head was pounding and his mouth had the texture of cotton. He'd been drinking for so long he was developing a hangover—and he still had a half-finished drink sitting on the table. Now running the hand over his balding head he said, "Stop fuckin' with me, Nick! Did it work?"

The assassin quickly scanned the area around him. Satisfied no one was within earshot he let out a grunt and said, "Did it work? *Oooh yeah*, it worked! It worked real good. I told you that there was nothing to worry about, didn't I?" The owner of Noble Consultants closed his eyes, hung his head and let out a long sigh. He then walked over and sat down on the couch.

With renewed concern that someone might be tapping his telephone, Haggerty didn't ask for too much detail, or use words that could carry incriminating connotations. The two had discussed it earlier and Nick knew just to allude to the facts.

"Will my clients be pleased?" Haggerty asked, referring to The Committee.

"Most definitely. I don't think they'll have to worry about any drop in sales; certainly not during the balance of their tenure, or that of their successors for that matter. This will ensure the loyalty of their customers for *years* to come; I doubt they'll ever trust the reliability of the new product again."

Haggerty clearly understood. "Any waste?" he asked, referring to fatalities. He desperately hoped there wouldn't be.

"I didn't stick around long enough to take a count, but given the size of the event there has to be. And I'd guess quite a bit."

The consultant closed his eyes and rubbed the bridge of his nose. He truly felt remorse that more people had to be killed. He remained silent for a moment then whispered, "Damn. That's unfortunate."

Ragosta, sensing Haggerty's despondency said, "Laurence, I warned you of the possibility. The size of the event was all but impossible to control." When Haggerty didn't respond the assassin added, "Look…you got the result you wanted. Hell, the result you needed!"

"Yes. Yes I did. But Nick, I thou—" Haggerty stopped talking; the television caught his attention. "Hold on Nick. Looks like CNN is interrupting their programming for something." He put the phone down, picked up the remote and turned up the volume; the anchorman was already reading from a sheet of paper. It had to be breaking news if they didn't take the time to put it on the teleprompter.

"—kind of explosion at the Las Vegas convention center. Details are sketchy, but many people are injured and there appears to be a large number of fatalities." Haggerty cringed. Someone handed the anchorman another piece of paper. He quickly read it then said, "The explosion was massive. There are confirmed fatalities but we don't know how many yet. Emergency crews from three counties are responding and we'll have a reporter on the scene very soon. The explosion happened at approximately—"

Haggerty turned off the television, then slowly picked the phone back up. He looked at it bitterly, grimaced, then put it to his ear. "It's on the news. Looks like our work is done."

"I still have one more thing to do," Ragosta replied.

"Yeah, I know." Haggerty hung up.

With effort he got up off the couch, picked up his drink and sat down at his desk. He turned around to face the window and stared expressionlessly at the lights of Washington D.C. He was overwhelmed by a feeling of immense sadness, the likes of which he'd never felt before. He wanted to blame the intensity of his sorrow on the booze, but knew he couldn't. He began to think of the people he'd killed, in particular Sandra Beach.

She had parents and others who loved her, nurtured her. She grew up; like everybody she had good times and bad, fell in and out of love, knew joys and sorrows, had hopes and dreams. She laughed, cried, enjoyed doing certain things, and didn't like doing others. It took years to educate her and just as many experiencing the raw lessons of life for her to develop into the unique person she was. Then, in the blink of an eye that life was over—stolen from her. Tears began to streak down Laurence Haggerty's cheeks. Who but God has the right to end another's life? Who? And now he had stolen many lives. Unique souls—human beings who, like Sandra, enjoyed life and had so much more to experience. But he'd selfishly taken their precious existence away from them. Murdered them. All because of his greed.

He dropped the drink and buried his face in his hands. *"God forgive me,"* he whispered, then sobbed uncontrollably.

Several hours after the blast, Nick Ragosta called Terrence McChaffee on his cell phone. But he didn't answer. He tried again an hour later, but still nothing. Becoming a little concerned he left a message on his third attempt, stating that he wanted to make arrangements to get together; he'd earned the rest of his share. "Mr. Nick is nothing if not honest, Terrance," Ragosta said lightheartedly in closing. "I want to pay up."

CHAPTER 18

▼

Terrorism was initially blamed for the tragedy in which forty-seven people died and one-hundred and nineteen were wounded. Seven victims remained in critical condition, four of whom were not expected to survive. But three days after the blast it was determined that no foul play was involved; the car had a catastrophic defect and exploded; the exact cause was still under investigation.

As they do with all disasters, the media went overboard. Fuel Cells were the topic of the week and all kinds of so-called experts were thrown in front of a camera and interviewed on fuel cells and the industry. All the major networks were reporting on the tragedy as were the various news programs of all the significant networks. Articles were written in major newspapers and magazines about the dangers of hydrogen and fuel cells, and it didn't take long for the incident to be compared with the other famous disaster blamed falsely on hydrogen. One headline in an automotive trade magazine read the same words uttered by Nick Ragosta: *"Hindenburg of the automotive industry."* Because of the scale of the catastrophe in Las Vegas, few fuel cell advocates spoke up in defense of the technology. Those that did couldn't understand how the explosion occurred.

For the first time in over two years there was an aura of contentment amongst the three members of The Committee. Although in a dour mood himself, Laurence Haggerty felt no malice toward anyone, even Theodore Kennelly, the CEO of PETROCOMP.

Kenneth Saxton, CEO of World Energy and host of this meeting, was all smiles when the owner of Noble Consultants arrived. Wendell Finley of ENDI-CORP was distant, but not altogether unfriendly. He even offered Haggerty one of his cigars, which the consultant politely declined. The four men settled down in the boardroom. An attractive secretary place coffee and doughnuts on the table and left the room, closing the door behind her.

"Room's been swept?" Kennelly asked.

Kenneth Saxton nodded then said, "Laurence, allow me to be the first to congratulate you on the success of your recent venture. It appears there will be no adverse repercussions. The authorities seem to be satisfied that the cause of the explosion was a malfunction in the vehicle. Well done, sir!" A huge smile came across Saxton's face.

Haggerty was stunned that none of the three men said anything about the number of people murdered by the explosion—given how adamant they were that no blood be shed. He'd broken into another crying fit when he'd heard the final tally and the deaths were still weighing heavily on him. They were *so* concerned about the first couple of people Ragosta eliminated; now, they didn't even bother to give this mass killing lip-service. It filled him with contempt for his three powerful clients. Laurence Haggerty pursed his lips, imperceptibly bobbed his head and replied, "Thank you, Mr. Saxton."

The sullenness of the consultant's reply did not go unnoticed. But the CEO of World Energy continued in his pompous English accent, "I daresay we can consider P3 a complete success! The stock price of Global Fuel Cell Technologies—all fuel cell manufacturers for that matter—continues to plummet and rumor has it that the OEMs are going to cancel all contracts for GFCT's fuel cell powertrain; all this only two weeks after the event in Las Vegas!" Saxton looked at the other two members of The Committee. "I don't foresee any loss of market share to this technology for years to come…if not decades." The other two men agreed.

Haggerty cleared his throat. He kept his eyes on his folded hands resting before him on the highly polished table. "If that's the consensus, gentlemen, then I'd greatly appreciate Noble Consultants being paid the balance owed, and that we bring this business transaction to a conclusion."

No one said anything. Theodore Kennelly broke the silence by saying, "Mr. Haggerty, I would like to ask one final question, and I'd appreciate a straight answer." Haggerty said nothing, but braced himself. He looked at the executive, nodded, and thought about how much he hated the CEO of PETROCOMP.

Kennelly's eyes narrowed and he asked menacingly, "*Is* this really over? Are all the loose ends tied up? Is there any—and I mean *any*—chance our companies could be implicated in the future?"

The answer was no, it wasn't over. There was one person who could possibly bring down the house of cards—and he was missing. But Laurence Haggerty wanted his seventy-five million. More accurately, he needed it. The Committee didn't need to know this one small detail. The problem would soon be resolved.

"Yes," he replied curtly. "No chance at all." Kennelly eyed Haggerty suspiciously for several moments, then leaned back in his chair. It was blatantly obvious he didn't believe the consultant, but he prudently kept his mouth shut.

"Have you anything to add, Wendell?" Kenneth Saxton inquired after he was certain Kennelly wasn't going to say anything else. Finley, cigar smoldering in his mouth, shook his head. "Well then, Laurence. I believe our relationship has come to an end. A draft for the balance we owe you will be deposited in your account by the end of the week. Will that be satisfactory?" Haggerty simply nodded.

"Goddamit Nick, you waited too long!" the owner of Noble Consultants bellowed in frustration when he met with Ragosta for an update. "You should've dealt with him immediately after the car went up!"

The assassin was somewhat disturbed by the hostility in Haggerty's voice; but he was more surprised by the fact that the consultant wasn't drunk. Perhaps because he was sober, Ragosta began to take offense at his tone of voice. This was the first time Haggerty appeared to be criticizing his job performance. The assassin didn't like the insinuation Haggerty seemed to be conveying—that he was less than professional.

Calmly, Ragosta said, "That would have been impossible, Laurence. The son-of-a-bitch disappeared before the debris hit the floor." Gritting his teeth behind sealed lips, the muscles in his jaw tightened and jutted out from the sides of his face. His eyes narrowed threateningly and he took a step toward the older man. "I don't much care for your tone of voice, *Laurence*. And I hope you're not…questioning my ability."

Haggerty stiffened in fright; he knew Ragosta wouldn't hesitate for a minute to kill him. He took a step back and quickly erased any hostility residing within him. Composing himself as best he could he said, "Take it easy, Nick. Okay? I'm not implying anything. I just want to point out that if he's not calling you to pick up the rest of his money, that can mean only one thing. Can't it?"

To Haggerty's relief he saw the tension in Ragosta's body ease. The assassin frowned and said. "It means that he's having second thoughts."

"Exactly," the consultant replied.

Ragosta remained silent for a moment; a small look of embarrassed came across his face. "Look Laurence, I know I fucked up when I let slip Finley's name. I really didn't think McChaffee caught it…but I have to assume he did. Not to worry, I'll set the situation right. I'll have Swenson help me track him down."

Haggerty let out a sigh and replied evenly, "You'd best do it quick, Nick. The Committee's check hasn't cleared the bank yet. If they catch wind of this, there'll be hell to pay. Keep me advised."

Terrance McChaffee checked into a budget motel on the outskirts of Las Vegas. He thought the room's furniture dated back to the '50's, and for some reason that depressed him all the more. He spent two days—a good majority of it curled up on the bed in the fetal position—agonizing over what he'd done. He didn't leave the room even to eat, and snapped at the Mexican maid to go away when she came to clean his room. His conscience couldn't bear the weight of his guilt any longer and he had to do something to ease the pain. But what? He considered suicide, but knew he wouldn't have the will to kill himself. But if he died right now, he wouldn't care. He considered confessing, but didn't want to spend the rest of his life in prison.

He impassively listened to several of Nick's messages and erased them. He didn't want the rest of his blood money, and something told him that he shouldn't meet with the man again. McChaffee had never experienced a premonition before and wasn't really sure that was what he was feeling now, but he decided it was best not to ignore it.

On the third day of his self-imposed exile, haggard, hungry and consumed in a fog of self-pity, he remembered Nancy Ranger mentioning that there was a reporter from *Hour Report* at the show. He typically tuned Nancy out when she went on one of her talking sprees, telling anybody within earshot what wonderful kids she had, how she wanted to quit working and become a soccer mom, or about some show she watched the night before; anything to hear herself talk. But her mention of *Hour Report* caught his attention. He occasionally watched the program because it was one of the few that didn't rely on sensationalism to acquire its viewers, but rather good investigative reporting. He recalled briefly wondering at the time what reporter from *Hour Report* Ranger was referring to.

Hugging his knees to his chest and slowly rocking back and forth on the floor, McChaffee began to wonder if perhaps telling this reporter—who must have been present during the blast—what he knew would in some small way start to make up for the evil he'd committed. If, of course, he or she was still alive. But even if this person wasn't, there'd be others with *Hour Report* who'd be interested in picking up the story—there'd have to be. Maybe telling what he knew would begin to ease his tormented conscience.

He then stopped rocking and frowned, realizing his dilemma. He was yet again dragged into another internal debate. There was no way he could tell what he knew; it would be tantamount to a confession. And given the magnitude of the crime he'd committed, most likely anybody with half a conscience would run to the police. He'd end up on death row, or worse, spend the rest of his life as someone's bitch. *Think, Terrance, think! There's got to be some way around this quandary.*

But what did he really know? He'd been hired by a mysterious man who offered him a tremendous amount of money to sabotage GFCT's demonstration vehicle at the International Fuel Cell Exhibition. He knew nothing of the man himself other than he went by the name of Nick, and he'd been hired by some unknown clients to discredit fuel cell technology. It'd be different if he knew who Nick's employers were; then perhaps he could establish a motive—ascertain why these people were so determined to destroy the technology.

Hugging his knees tighter to his chest and beginning to rock again, McChaffee let his mind go blank for a short period of time. Then it came to him. That strange face Nick made before telling him some stupid story about some unknown philosopher. He'd mentioned a name, suddenly appeared scared, and then quickly mentioned a different one. Why would he, or anyone for that matter, react so strangely to throwing out a wrong name—and for an insignificant story at that?

The engineer racked his brain for a moment; the only reasonable explanation was that Nick let slip a name he shouldn't have. Perhaps it was the name of somebody else who was connected with the scheme to discredit fuel cells. Nick refused to say who his clients were.

McChaffee stopped rocking and began to bite his fingernails. What *was* that name Nick mentioned before changing it to that philosopher, Finch? He remembered it sounded a lot like Finch; kind of an Irish-sounding name. He racked his brain; but as is so common when trying to remember a name, his mind went blank.

He got up off the floor to urinate. Watching the golden stream cascade into the toilet, it struck him. *Finley!* That was the name, Finley! As soon as he left the tiny bathroom he wrote it down in case it slipped his mind again. At least now he had something to tell the news magazine. Maybe the name would mean something to the reporter he ended up talking to—if indeed he was able to speak to one.

Remembering the name Finley and having decided on a course of action, he felt a little better and could no longer ignore his intense hunger. As he sat in a booth at McDonald's, munching on a super-sized order of fries, he listened to several more of Ragosta's messages. Overall, he'd left fourteen that ramped from friendly requests to call him back to desperate pleas to contact him immediately. With each appeal the engineer felt more certain that the man meant him ill. Why else would he be so eager to part with a million dollars? He'd wait a few more days and then call Nick to tell him to take the money and shove it.

A week went by and still no word from McChaffee—despite the numerous messages he'd left in his voice mailbox. Ragosta was worried that McChaffee had deduced his true intentions; though how, he had no idea. He had to find that goddamned engineer, he couldn't wait any longer. If only he hadn't let Finley's name slip out! He shook his head, disappointed in himself. Although he was certain that McChaffee would never recall the incident and remember the name, Ragosta had felt it necessary to tell Haggerty about the slip. He was glad his employer wasn't too upset, but even if he was, to hell with him—he was nobody special. *No one* questions his talent for this line of work! Others he'd worked for over the years had tried to cheat him, and regretted it. But Haggerty hadn't; he'd been a square shooter so far. So Ragosta let the insult go and was determined to correct his mistake.

He was about to call Mike Swenson to solicit his help in tracking McChaffee down when his cell phone rang. Seeing the engineer's number in his cell phone's view screen, he became excited and fumbled while trying to open it—almost dropping the phone. They made these things so goddamn small!

"*Terrance!*" he bellowed, trying hard to subdue the rage he felt. "Where the *hell* you been? I've been trying to get hold of you for a week!"

"I know." McChaffee's reply was flat, hollow, inanimate.

Eyes narrowing, Ragosta asked, "What's going on, Terrance? Don't you want the rest of your money?"

"No!"

The assassin's forehead furrowed; he pressed his cell phone so tight to his head it almost snapped in two. "What do you *mean* you don't want it, McChaffee? Are you trying to tell me something?" Ragosta's voice was suddenly so threatening that a few drops of urine escaped from the engineer's penis. He tightened his stomach muscles to prevent the entire contents of his bladder from pouring out.

McChaffee took a deep breath and said, "I…I can't stand it any longer, Nick—or whoever you are. I can't live with myself. I…I, I *murdered* innocent people. I've never killed anything before in my life! And now I'm one of the largest mass murderers in this country's history. *God*, man…doesn't that bother you?"

"No, not at all," Ragosta replied coldly. "And you should've thought of that before you agreed to take my money."

McChaffee stared blankly at the tree before him; he was sitting in its shade on a park bench. Despite the cool spot, he was sweating—but not from the heat. "I don't dispute that," he replied wryly. "I should've. But there's nothing I can do about that now. All I can do is try and make up for my horrendous mistake—if that's possible."

"What are you saying, McChaffee? What the hell do you mean by making it up?"

"I'm..." the engineer began to tremble. He glanced at a young mother joyfully pushing her little girl on a swing, then looked down at his feet. "I'm...going to the press. I'm going to tell them everything I know."

To McChaffee, the silence at the other end of the line seemed to last an eternity. Finally, Ragosta replied ominously, "That would be the biggest mistake of your life." Then in an even darker tone he added, "If you do that, you're a dead man."

The young engineer steeled himself. "I don't care! If you find me, if you kill me, I don't care. I can't live with myself the way it is now."

"Then enjoy the day, Mr. McChaffee. Because it's your last!" Ragosta slammed his cell phone shut. Furious, he immediately called Mike Swenson and told him to get on the next flight to Vegas; he'd meet him at the airport.

Terrance McChaffee stared at his phone for a moment, then closed it and put it in his pocket. He watched the mother and daughter and yearned to have what they had, a normal, mundane life. Her and her husband's only worries were probably making mortgage, paying off some credit card debt and what to have for dinner tonight. Slowly, he got up off the bench and left the park.

Under pressure from Buddy Worther, her producer, Mary Hildahl was forced to change her story from strictly a conspiracy theory to the dangers of fuel cells. She vigorously protested the decision and after a heated argument, Worther finally agreed to let her keep the conspiracy segment as part of the report. But he warned her that it better be a small part of the story.

Paul Haydon's face fell when Mary Hildahl told him about her producer's decision, and his first thought was concern that this change would impede her efforts at helping him flush those behind the plot out of the sewer. He was temporarily at a loss for words and could only manage to sit and look at her despondently.

"I'm pissed off about it too, Paul," the reporter said irritably, finding it hard to look at the detective. "But my goddamned producer was adamant about it. Frankly, I'm lucky to be able to investigate the conspiracy theory at all!" Haydon's continued silence and forlorn expression tugged at her. She had become quite fond of him and didn't want to disappoint him.

"Tell ya what," she said softly while getting up from behind her desk to pour them both a cup of coffee. "I'll concentrate on the scheme first. Buddy Worther will never know."

Her pronouncement brought a smile to the investigator's face. The tragedy at the convention center made him more determined than ever to find those responsible for the plot. He was convinced that the explosion was not just a malfunction. He'd picked up enough knowledge about the technology while working undercover at Unlimited Energy Systems to know how difficult it would be for a fuel cell system to explode. The vehicle had been tampered with. He didn't have any proof of that, but he was sure of it.

"Mary, that would be great! What do yo—"

"Paul, don't get too excited," she interrupted him with a raised hand. "Don't forget, I'm under a deadline. As much as I don't want to, I'll have to focus on the dangers of fuel cells if I see I'm running out of time. I, uh…I want to keep my job ya know."

Haydon grimaced and nodded. "I understand," he replied after taking a sip of coffee.

Hildahl sat back down in her chair. She held her coffee cup in both hands and looked at Haydon over the rim. "What do you think?"

"It had to be an inside job, Mary. Had to be," he said passionately. "Somehow that car was sabotaged, I'm certain of it. And only someone who had access to the vehicle, was familiar with its systems and knowledgeable about fuel cells could have done it."

"You'd think that would substantially narrow down the list of suspects," the reporter replied. "But do you trust the findings of the Las Vegas Police? Are you sure it wasn't a bomb. If it was, that would open up the list of suspects to damn near anyone."

"They're right," Haydon replied. "There was no trace of explosives; I read the report myself. That means that the car was rigged to trigger its volatile fuel. There were only a handful of people there that day who both had access to Global Fuel Cell Technologies' vehicle and who had the knowledge to rig it to blow up. Of those, I've learned that one is missing. An engineer by the name of Terrance McChaffee. I suggest we start with him. I got his cell phone number from a woman named Nancy Ranger, his co-worker. The FBI is working on the same assumption we are; we need to get to McChaffee before they do."

Through his mole at National Credit Associates, Mike Swenson learned that McChaffee had purchased a one-way ticket to New York. Unfortunately, his flight left Las Vegas thirty-five minutes before Swenson got the information. On the way to the airport, Nick Ragosta called Haggerty for the fifth time in less than three days.

"Laurence, we found out he's on his way to New York."

"New York? Why New York?"

"I'm fairly certain that he's going to follow through with his threat. He's going straight to the press. Wh—"

"Jesus Christ! You've got to stop him, Nick. Got to!" Haggerty cried. He wailed so loudly Ragosta had to pull the phone away from his ear.

The assassin grimaced; Haggerty was drunk again. Though drinking, he, unlike many people, had the ability to effectively use his brain. The assassin rather admired that quality. "What I need to figure out now, Laurence, is who is he going to squeal to? Any ideas?" He could hear the ice tinkling as Haggerty lifted the glass to his mouth.

Presently he replied, "Yeah, I've got a pretty good idea. Shortly after the blast, CNN ran a tape with…with…*fuck!* I can't remember her name. She even called me!" Ragosta waited patiently, listening to the ice clink inside the consultant's glass. "*Hildahl!* That was it; Mary Hildahl of *Hour Report*. Produced someplace in New York. You should have no trouble finding it."

"What makes you think he's running to her? I mean, Christ, every major network is in New York."

"Because she was the first reporter on the scene," Haggerty shot back confidently. "She did a follow-up report for CNN a couple hours after the blast where she subtly alluded to foul play. I'm betting he saw the report."

That makes sense, Ragosta thought. "I hope you're right, Laurence. If not, we'll waste precious time." Ragosta hung up.

"So do I," Haggerty said dryly to himself as he placed the phone back in its cradle. He thought about his ticket to Brazil and prayed he wouldn't have to use it. He'd know soon. If indeed McChaffee does connect with anybody in the press and they believe him, Haggerty assumed he wouldn't have much time to get on the plane. If they found the engineer credible, they'd air what they had learned from him immediately. Wendell Finley's name was sure to be mentioned. He poured himself another drink.

McChaffee had to remain in hiding until he made contact with one of *Hour Report's* correspondents. He didn't consider it wise to stay in Las Vegas any longer than he already had, and he certainly couldn't go back home to Massachusetts. It only made sense to go to New York, where *Hour Report* was produced. Low on cash, he had to use his credit card to purchase his one-way ticket to JFK.

When his plane landed and the flight attendant announced that cell phones could be turned on, he wasn't surprised to see he had messages. He'd already received three today from Nick meant to unnerve him—and they did. He was hesitant to listen to any more messages. But yesterday Nancy Ranger had left one, and he even received one from his ex-wife. He was compelled to listen to them.

You have…four new messages. To listen to your messages, press one, the most well-known female voice in history stated. Sighing, he pressed one and listened.

"Mr. McChaffee, this is Captain Stevens of the Las Vegas Police. I'd like to ask you a few questions. Call me as soon as possible." The engineer didn't bother to write down the detective's telephone number.

"Terr, Nancy. Thought I'd try you again. Please call me. I'm worried about you. Why did you disappear? There are some…some nasty rumors about you flying around the office—at least among those of us left. Did you hear about the lay-offs? They're massive. Call me…please!"

McChaffee frowned and erased that message too.

"Hey McChaffee," the engineer's stomach immediately cramped. *"You can run, but you can't hide, as they say. I think I'll visit New York…what do ya think? Been a long time since I've been in the Big Apple."* As a matter of fact, I'm on the flight right after yours! Isn't that exciting? See ya soon—very soon."*

How the hell did he find out I was going to New York? McChaffee thought to himself. He looked out the window. *Christ, the goddamn plane has been taxiing forever! When will it get to the gate?* He deleted that message and listen to his last one.

"Mr. McChaffee, this is Mary Hildahl of Hour Report. McChaffee sat straight up in his seat; his eyes widened in surprise. For an instant he wondered if he'd heard right. *I very much would like to talk with you about Global Fuel Cell Technologies and the events in Las Vegas last week—off the record, if you'd prefer. Would you please call me at your earliest convenience? If you get my voice mail, please have me paged. I'll be in the office all day today."* The question of who from *Hour Report* was at the show appeared to be answered—and she'd survived the explosion. She was clearly very eager to talk with him; she not only gave him her direct number,

but also her cell phone and email address. He'd call her as soon as he got off the plane.

"Thank you, Mr. McChaffee. I look forward to speaking with you."

He listened to the message three times to ensure he'd written the numbers down correctly, and then saved it. With Nick on his heels, as soon as he made the call he'd look for a place to hide. He'd never been to New York before and he had no idea where to hide. But he'd find someplace; it was a big city.

After what seemed like hours, the plane finally reached the gate. McChaffee watched out the window as the skyway ramp approached the forward fuselage door. Minutes later he began to fume; the operator of the walkway must have thought she was docking with the space shuttle the way she was adjusting it back and forth, side to side, making sure it was positioned just so. With Nick on his heels, McChaffee felt like strangling the woman; her quest for perfection burnt up more of his precious time.

As usual, the line in front of him to exit the aircraft moved at a snail's pace; and he was stuck in seat 23B. The amount of time it took small women and little old ladies to pull their oversized luggage from the overhead bin made him want to scream. Minutes were feeling like hours.

When he finally got to the skyway ramp he dashed through it, brushing past other passengers in an effort to make up time. After running through the gate area he stopped and looked for a place in the airport that would afford him a little quiet and privacy. The only place he could immediately see was a deserted Starbucks. He sat at a table and dialed the number Mary Hildahl left him. A moment later he got her voice mail.

"Shit," he cursed under his breath and pushed 0 for the operator.

"Hour Report," the receptionist said sweetly. "How may I direct your call?"

McChaffee tried to moisten his dry lips by quickly running his tongue over them. It didn't help. "Yes, would you please page Mary Hildahl for me?"

"I'm sorry, but I'm not allowed to page anyone. Would you like her voice mail?"

The engineer was momentarily stunned. "But…but, uh, she asked me to page her!" he replied in a panic.

"Your name please?"

He breathed a sigh of relief. "McChaffee. Terrance McChaffee."

"One moment please, Mister McChaffee."

A moment later he was listening to classical music; even though it was playing softly he found it terribly annoying. He glanced at his watch, two-thirty-seven. He began to look at the people passing by the coffee stand, scrutinizing every man with dark hair who appeared to be forty or older. He couldn't keep up—there were too many of them walking too fast. He looked at his watch again—two-thirty-nine. *Come on, lady!* Using his cell phone, he worried about abruptly losing his connection. It wouldn't be the first time.

Gazing back out into the corridor he froze in terror when he saw a dark-haired man staring at him. The young engineer almost dropped his phone. A moment later he realized it wasn't Nick. The man was just looking into the Starbucks, probably trying to decide if he should get a cup of coffee. McChaffee briefly wondered if it wouldn't have been smarter to make this call from a taxi. But he was so anxious to contact Hildahl the thought never occurred to him.

His eyes again began to dart nervously around the wide passageway. *Christ, where is she?* Everything he did today seemed to take forever! All he wanted to do was get the hell out of the airport and find a place to hide until he could finish his business with *Hour Report.* After that, he'd decide what to do next.

Finally, with a click the music went dead. *"Mr. McChaffee!"* it was the sultry but breathless voice of Mary Hildahl. "Thank you for returning my call. I'm sorry to have kept you waiting." She must have run some distance to the phone, McChaffee thought.

Had he not been fearing for his life, talking with Mary Hildahl would've been a momentous event and he'd probably be as giddy as a teenage girl meeting her favorite rock star. But circumstances weighed heavily on him and his demeanor was quite subdued.

"Well, uh…Ms. Hildahl, truth be told, I was hoping to contact you."

She was mildly stunned by the comment and after a moment's hesitation she replied, *"Really?"*

"Yes. It's my understating that you, or someone from *Hour Report,* were at the Las Vegas convention center when Global Fuel Cell Technologies' demonstration vehicle exploded."

"Ahhh, yes. As a matter of fact it *was* me. How did you—"

"Excuse me, Ms. Hildahl," he cut in abruptly. "I don't mean to be rude, but I'm in a lot of danger. I need to get out of the airport immediately. I wanted to return your call as soon as possible to let you know I'd like to tell you what *I* know about the…" he paused, summoning the strength to use the right word and nearly choking on it, "…*tragedy*…in Las Vegas. But I must call you later."

"Airport? Where are you? What kind of danger are you in?"

McChaffee fearfully scanned the area around him and then said, "New York. JFK. Someone is trying to kill me because of what I know. He's on his way here as we speak."

"*Kill you!* Oh my God." The reporter's mind began to fill with questions, but she pushed them aside; the tone of his voice left no doubt as to the seriousness of his situation. She wanted to help—had to help! She was tantalized by the potential gold mine of information he had and didn't want to lose him. Paul Haydon popped into her mind. Maybe he could help? Perhaps he could protect Terrance McChaffee? It was worth a try.

"Mr. McChaffee, why don't you come to my office? You'll be safe here until we can figure out what to do. I'll also listen to what you have to say."

The engineer breathed a sigh of relief, as if she'd answered his prayers. But at the same time he was hesitant to actually meet her. After all, she could implicate him once he told his story. He had to be certain she wouldn't betray him.

"I'd like that very much, Ms. Hildahl. But, uh…" His voice trailed off.

"But *what*, Mr. McChaffee?"

It took several moments for the engineer to answer, and Hildahl could sense the man's tenseness even over the phone. When he spoke next his voice left no doubt as to the seriousness of his demand; negotiation would not be an option. "You must give me your word, Ms. Hildahl, your word that you will not identify me after I tell you what I know. I *must* be, and remain, a confidential source that you cannot identify—to anyone, under any circumstances!" He wasn't exactly sure yet what he'd tell her, but he certainly had no intention of incriminating himself. But just in case he should inadvertently implicate himself—let something slip he shouldn't have—he wanted this insurance.

"That, Mr. McChaffee, goes without saying. You have my word. It would be unethical for me, for *any* journalist to reveal their sources if they asked for anonymity."

He was quickly becoming even more uncomfortable than he already was. He was starting to sweat and his clothes were beginning to stick to him; it was terribly annoying. Apprehensively, his eyes continued to dart around the concourse. He gripped his cell phone tighter, pushing it harder to his ear. "Alright," he replied uneasily. McChaffee bit his lip then asked, "I don't have a car, can you pick me up?"

"Very few people who work in Manhattan have a car. You'll have to take a cab." After she finished giving him the address of *Hour Report's* studios she said, "When you get here, have security call me. I'll be right down to get you."

"Yeah," was the engineer's only response. He snapped his cell phone shut and got up to leave.

Immediately after hanging up with McChaffee she called Paul Haydon and asked him to come to her office right away. She gave him a brief summary of her conversation with Terrance McChaffee and told Haydon she'd explain what she wanted him to do as soon as he arrived. She was relieved when he said he could be there in less than an hour.

When she had a minute to catch her breath the seriousness of the situation hit her like a slap on the face. In all her years of reporting, she'd never come across a story like this. The man said someone was trying to kill him. *Actually kill him!* And he clearly wasn't joking. She knew she was working on a big story, possibly the biggest of her career; but now she was struck by the realization that she may well be dragging herself into something more than just a story—she could be committing herself, and Paul Haydon, to something dangerous.

But could she really believe McChaffee? Why would someone want to kill him? He must know something about the explosion. What other plausible explanation could there be to explain why he was missing? He'd obviously gone into hiding. Could there be a link between the oil companies and politicians Haydon claims are behind this conspiracy and the disaster in Vegas? The police are convinced the blast was caused by a malfunction, and to date the FBI has yet to find any evidence to the contrary. If indeed McChaffee supplies information that proves a plot was conceived and carried out by oil conglomerates and their political cronies, even stubborn Buddy Worther would agree that she should concentrate all her efforts on developing the conspiracy story. *Hour Report* would have the scoop of the decade!

Mary Hildahl looked at the clock and prayed traffic would be light.

CHAPTER 19

▼

It was getting dark by the time McChaffee's cab pulled in front of *Hour Report's* studios. Once he left JFK he quickly understood why Mary Hildahl said nobody drives in New York—and he had thought Boston was bad. After paying the driver he stepped out of the cab and quickly dashed to the studios' main entrance. Once in the studio his personal safety wasn't foremost on his mind and he realized how hungry and tired he was. But food and rest would have to wait.

He walked up to the reception desk occupied by a burly security guard. The man was young, couldn't have been more than twenty-five years old. He dropped his magazine and with a stone-face, gazed at McChaffee, who didn't have a lot of respect for "Rent-A-Cops." The guard appeared annoyed by the interruption.

"Would you please call Mary Hildahl and tell her I'm here," McChaffee asked wearily.

"And who are you?" the guard countered in a low, nasally-sounding voice.

"Terrance McChaffee."

The young man looked at him suspiciously; not that McChaffee could blame him. He knew he looked like hell, and probably smelled worse. In the hotel he'd only worked up the ambition to shower once, and his clothes looked like he'd slept in them for the last two days—which, he actually had.

The guard glanced at his watch. "It's kinda late. You got an appointment?"

What is this, twenty fucking question? McChaffee let out a sigh. He was becoming irritated himself. "*Yes,*" he replied with a touch of rancor.

The guard quickly scrutinized the man before him then reached for the phone. "Ms. Hildahl, Ted. There's a man in the lobby by the name of…" he put his hand over the receiver and looked at McChaffee, who had stepped away from the reception window to look at the plaques hanging on the wall. "Dude, what was your name again?"

The engineer spun around and glared at him; he made no effort to hide his annoyance. "McChaffee! Terrance McChaffee," he snarled.

"Ummm, Terrance McChaffee waiting in the...hello? Ms. Hildahl? You there?" He looked at the receiver, shrugged and hung up the phone. Appearing completely indifferent he picked up his magazine and began to page through it.

McChaffee stared at him incredulously for several seconds, and then asked, "Well... *Ted*, is she coming down?"

From behind the magazine he shrugged and said, "I don't know."

McChaffee stormed up to the counter. All the stress, guilt and frustration he'd experienced over the last week came to a head, and he snapped. He slapped the magazine out of the young man's hands and it went flying over the counter. It landed with a thud and slid several feet under one of the lobby's chairs.

The startled guard looked at McChaffee in disbelief, then his eyes narrowed and he jumped to his feet. He was a foot taller than the engineer and easily had more than a hundred pounds on him. But once the expression on the visitor's face registered, he froze. Something in the man's eyes made him uneasy, almost frightened.

"Page her! Or get off your ass and find her! I don't give a damn how you do it, *just do it!* Get her down here! *NOW!*" he screamed, slamming his fist on the counter. He leaned toward the big security guard, his hands now clutching the edge of the countertop so tightly they were turning white. "THIS IS FUCKING URGENT!" he bellowed.

The young man took a step back and threw up his hands, "Okay, okay, man, take it easy!" McChaffee continued to glare at him; his face remaining saturated with hostility. "I can't leave the desk unless it's an emergency...but give me a few minutes, I'll find her...geez!" he spit the last word out while reaching for the phone. He continued to give McChaffee a guarded look, as if ensuring he wasn't going to leap over the counter and strangle him.

Seeing action, McChaffee turned and began to pace the lobby. A few moments later he saw the magazine he'd slapped out of the guard's hands, and walked over to retrieve it. As he picked it up he heard the ding of the elevator stopping at the floor. A man and woman emerged; he recognized Mary Hildahl, but not the man. The engineer assumed he was just riding the elevator down to the main floor. But when they both approached him he became visibly alarmed.

"Mr. McChaffee, Mary Hildahl," the reporter said, giving him a beautiful smile while extending her hand.

McChaffee took it while suspiciously eyeing the man next to her. "And this is Mr. Paul Haydon," she said, turning and gesturing to him. "You can trust him. He's a private investigator. We're working together."

The tension in the engineer's face remained a moment longer then melted away. He took the hand Haydon offered him.

"Let's go up to my office," Hildahl said, and they entered the elevator. In the elevator they said nothing; like most people, they only watched the flash of the ascending floor numbers. The closed quarters accentuated McChaffee's lack of personal hygiene and Hildahl, despite herself, crinkled her nose.

"Please have a seat," Hildahl said as they entered her office. All three sat down; Hildahl seating herself behind her desk. "Can I offer you some coffee, a soft drink perhaps?" McChaffee shook his head.

She noticed McChaffee glance at Haydon, clearly questioning his role. "Mr. Haydon here," Hildahl began, slightly tilting her head toward the private detective, "has been investigating an alleged conspiracy to destroy fuel cell technology. He's made some progress, but recently ran into a wall. He's asked me to see if I can flush those responsible out in the open by use of *Hour Report*—make damaging insinuations that should scare them into vehemently denying any involvement. Naturally, everyone will deny it, but I've been interviewing people for a long time; I'm certain I can tell who's lying. Once fingered, we'll begin a thorough investigation of their company."

"The conspiracy exists," McChaffee declared flatly. The reporter and detective exchanged grave looks.

"How do you know?" Haydon asked.

McChaffee crossed his legs and tried his best to look relaxed. "Because I was approached by someone who asked me to sabotage Global Fuel Cell Technologies' demonstration vehicle; he offered me a substantial sum of money." The look of reproach that formed on Haydon's and Hildahl's face made him quickly add, "I refused, of course."

"Do you think this person found somebody to do it?" Haydon asked.

"I know he did," the engineer replied confidently.

"When you refused, didn't this person worry that you'd go to the authorities and report him?" Hildahl asked.

The question made the engineer uneasy; he shifted in his chair and avoided eye contact for some moments. Then, locking piercing eyes on Hildahl he replied assuredly, "You only had to look at him to know you'd better not do that." He paused a moment then added, "Although he seemed friendly enough—at least initially." He seemed to reflect for a moment and it was apparent to Hildahl and

Haydon that he had more to say. Not wanting to cut him short on anything he might have to offer, they remained silent. A sickened look came across McChaffee's face. "You could tell he was one of those people who'd kill you just as soon as look at you. He's one scary son-of-a-bitch—and he's the one after me. He knows I'm talking to the press."

How does he know that?" Hildahl asked. Then abruptly she added, "Surely you didn't tell him you were coming to us."

Christ, why did I tell him? the engineer asked himself. It was a stupid thing to do, but he wasn't going to admit that to these two people. "I don't know," was all he said.

"What did you mean by 'initially?'" Haydon asked. "After refusing you had further contact with him?"

McChaffee realized he shouldn't have told them that, but he easily recovered. "No, I didn't. But I knew the person who did."

"The guy who's threatening you; what's his name?" Hildahl asked.

The engineer shrugged. "I don't know his full name. He told me to call him Nick; he didn't tell me his last name, and I didn't ask."

"And who was the person he persuaded to sabotage the vehicle?" the reporter asked as a follow up.

McChaffee looked forward to answering this question and was ready with the perfect answer. "Cynthia Klash, the Chief Executive Officer of Global Fuel Cell Technologies."

Both the reporter and private investigator were clearly stunned. Taken aback, they glanced blankly at each other for several seconds. Hildahl then turned to McChaffee in total disbelief. Shaking her head the reporter asked, "But why would she commit suicide?"

"And take so many others with her." Haydon added with a touch of abhorrence.

His statement caused McChaffee to wince, but he quickly recovered. "I don't know, she must have had her reasons. Most likely this Nick either had something terrible on her or threatened her in such a way that she decided killing herself was the only way out."

Paul Haydon gave McChaffee a doubtful look and asked, "How do you know she willfully did it?"

The engineer let out a mournful sigh. "She confided in me. She knew Nick had approached me. She knew I wouldn't talk. Maybe she just needed someone to talk to. But I know she wasn't happy about what she was being forced to do."

"What did she tell you?" Hildahl asked.

"Not much, really. Only that she was being forced by Nick to cooperate in the ruin of fuel cell technology, and, of course, that she didn't want to be part of it. She said I should consider myself lucky that I could refuse....I suppose I was."

The private Investigator studied the young engineer for a moment then asked, "Did she tell you how she was going to accomplish the downfall of fuel cells?"

McChaffee shook his head. "No. I had no idea how she was going to go about it. The blast came as a surprise to me, too. But..." he hesitated.

"But what, Mr. McChaffee?" Hildahl prompted.

"I don't think she meant for the Pathfinder to blow up. I think she just wanted the fuel cell's stack to catch fire." He shrugged. "That's my feeling anyway."

"She was the company's CEO—an executive. How did she know how to rig the vehicle?" Haydon asked.

"She was a degreed engineer," McChaffee replied impassively. Then, as an afterthought added, "Actually, quite a remarkable woman."

The room fell silent while Haydon and Hildahl considered what they'd heard. Presently, the detective asked, "So, why *are* you telling us this? Putting your life in danger?"

McChaffee didn't reply for a long time; distraught, he just gazed down at his shoes. Finally he said, "I just couldn't live with myself knowing what I know and not telling anybody. Especially when so many people have been killed. I know the Las Vegas police want to question me and I'm sure the FBI does too—they probably consider me a suspect. I wanted to come to you with the truth first."

"That's very admirable of you, Mr. McChaffee," Haydon said sincerely.

"And very brave," Mary Hildahl added, looking at the engineer with veneration. McChaffee blushed slightly, and smiled for the first time in weeks.

"Mr. McChaffee..." the private detective said then stopped. The other two looked at him and waited for him to continue. Haydon seemed to be struggling with what he wanted to say. He scratched the back of his head then said, "I'm, ah...I'm going to believe what you've told us here tonight. I have no reason not to. But, I'm afraid to say, what you've told us really isn't going to do us a lot of good. It's really all speculation unless it can be proven in court. Do you have any hard evidence you can give us, any type of documentation, something like that?"

McChaffee shook his head. "No. I'm afraid not."

Haydon continued. "Is there anything else, anything you can tell us that may give us a clue as to who this Nick is, or who he might be working with—or for? Anything, anything at all?" It sounded to Mary Hildahl like he was pleading.

"Yes," McChaffee replied with a grin. But the smile quickly faded when he added, "At least I think I do. I wasn't going to leave here without mentioning it."

"Please go on," the detective prompted. "I assure you, you have our undivided attention."

"One time, when I was speaking with Nick, I—"

Hildahl's eyebrows shot up. "One time?" she cut in. "You spoke to him more than once? I thought you said you only met him once?"

McChaffee cursed himself again. *What the hell am I thinking?* He decided to clarify the issue and put it to bed. He hoped it wouldn't hurt his credibility. "Uhhh, yeah. Perhaps I didn't make myself understood earlier. He approached me several times and I refused to talk with him. The last time he approached me we talked—a little. I guess I didn't consider it a significant conversation. But again I refused his offer and he left me alone after that."

"Oh, I see. Sorry. Please continue," she said.

McChaffee reversed his crossed legs and shifted a little in his chair. "When we spoke, he let a name slip. He made a clumsy effort to cover it up, but I'm fairly certain it's the name of someone he's dealing with. The name was Finley."

"Finley?" Haydon repeated, looking at Hildahl. The reporter wrote the name down. "Mean anything to you, Mary?"

Mary Hildahl shook her head. "No. But I'll do some research tonight. See if I can come up with anything." She leaned forward over her desk and looked hard at McChaffee. "Would you agree to talk with me on camera? Of course, we won't use your real name and we'll either blur out your face or film you in a shadow."

McChaffee nodded. "Yeah, I'll do that."

The reporter glanced at her watch. "Well, it's getting late and you look exhausted, Mr. McChaffee. Could we meet here first thing tomorrow morning and get started on the interview?" The engineer nodded.

Paul Haydon stood up. "You'll come back with me to my hotel room. We'll get you cleaned up—some fresh clothes and something to eat. Until this thing blows over you'll be under my protection. I'll talk with the Vegas police and the Feds; maybe we can get you into the Witness Protection Program."

"That would be great," McChaffee replied with a noticeable lack of enthusiasm.

Nick Ragosta threw his cigarette on the sidewalk then crushed it out with his foot. "Bingo," he said softly, smoke still wafting out of his mouth. His eyes were locked on the building across the street.

Standing next to Ragosta, Swenson trained his eyes on the building they were casing and saw Terrance McChaffee following another man through the building's main doors. "Your hunch proved to be right," he said. "Who's that with him?"

The assassin, keeping his eyes locked on the engineer, shook his head, "I don't know. But I don't give a fuck about him." They saw the man with McChaffee trying to hail a cab. "Come on, let's go!"

Ragosta and Swenson moved to the edge of the street and looked at the on-coming traffic. It was much heavier than they thought it would be. Suddenly, the assassin jumped out into the street; a cab came to a screeching halt inches from him. The taxi was almost rear-ended by the car behind him; the drivers blew their horns fiercely.

"What da fock you think you doing?" the cab driver, leaning out of the window, shouted angrily at Ragosta in a thick Indian accent.

The line of cars stuck behind the cab continued to honk furiously, Ragosta ignored them. He pulled out a thick wad of cash and waved it in front of the driver's face. "See this? It's yours if you do what I say."

Staring transfixed at the money, the taxi driver's eyes were almost as big as the turban he was wearing. "Get in, man!" he said excitedly without a moment's hesitation.

Swenson and Ragosta quickly jumped in; the assassin sat in front. He pointed across the street. "See those two trying to hail a cab?" The driver nodded. "When they get one, I want you to follow it, but not too close. Understand?"

"Yes," was all the man said. He threw the car in gear and quickly worked his way to the left lane. He caused another chorus of angry honking when he made an illegal U-turn and parked on the side of the street about a hundred yards from McChaffee and Haydon. Ragosta was impressed.

Not being native New Yorkers it took Haydon and McChaffee several minutes to get a cab. As soon as their taxi turned into traffic, Ragosta's driver was in pursuit. "Don't lose them, Hadji!" the assassin snarled. The driver gave him a quick annoyed look, but said nothing.

They followed McChaffee's taxi for about fifteen minutes when it pulled in front of a rather old looking hotel with a neon light hung over the sidewalk proclaiming it *The W nds r*. The "i" and "o" were intermittently flashing. Ragosta's driver pulled over to the side of the street about a block behind them.

They watched McChaffee and the other man leave the taxi and walk into the hotel. Ragosta pulled out his wad of cash and gave half of it to the driver. "Wait here," he ordered.

"Sure," the taxi driver replied, gleefully thumbing through the bills he quickly estimated as over five-hundred dollars.

Mike Swenson was the first to enter the hotel's lobby. Seeing it empty, he signaled for Ragosta to come in. The place, though clean, had certainly seen better days. It was clearly built in the 1920's and was last remodeled in the '50's. The lobby smelled stale, and other than an old vinyl-upholstered couch with several tears in it, the vestibule was devoid of any furnishing that might have spruced the place up. The area's one redeeming quality was that it was brightly lit.

The two men approached the counter. Sitting behind it was a fat, ugly woman who looked to be in her late forties. She was wearing a dirty, faded blue dress adorned with what appeared to be a variety of small flowers. Even though she was a large woman, the dress looked like a tent draped over her. She was watching a small television and eating potato chips. The woman turned her head to see who was at the counter; apathy radiating from her unsightly face.

"Want room?" she asked in a thick Russian accent. Slowly, she lumbered to her feet and wiped her greasy hands on the soiled dress.

"No," Ragosta replied. "Information. The two men who just came in here, who were they?"

The fat woman's eyes darted from Ragosta to Swenson and back again. "I no give dat out." she said irritably, upset that she'd gotten to her feet for no reason. She started to turn back to her chair. She stopped when from the corner of her eye she saw Ragosta slip a fifty dollar bill on to the counter. She eyed the bill, then Ragosta, but remained silent.

Ragosta flashed her a wan smile, then pulled out another fifty and stared at her callously. Swenson crossed his arms over his chest, clearly looking annoyed.

The woman stepped up to the counter and slowly pocketed the bills. "I no know who smaller one is. Other is Haydon. He be here for week. How long he stay," she shrugged her fleshly shoulders, "no know."

"What's his first name?" Swenson asked. "And where does he come from?" The prodigious woman shook her head, then bent over and pulled a book out from under the counter. "You use a register?" Swenson asked in amazement. "You don't have a computer?"

As she opened the book she replied flatly, "No computer. Is too much money." She began to thumb through the pages. She stopped, lowered her head a little and squinted. "Paul. Is Paul. Home…Oakand, Calieforniea."

"Do you have an address?" Ragosta asked.

The woman shook her head. "No. No address—just Oakand."

Without saying another word the two men turned and walked out the door. Once on the sidewalk Ragosta turned to Swenson and said, "Check him out. See what you can find out about this Paul Haydon. We'll make our move tomorrow."

"I'll get it," Terri Miller said, getting up off the couch. She and Rick were watching a *Frasier* rerun; it was about the only TV show they watched. She walked to the kitchen and picked up the ringing phone. "Hello?"

"Hey Terr, Paul."

She broke into a smile. "Hi Paul, how are you?"

"Not bad for someone forced to temporarily live in New York. How are you kids?"

"I'm fine," she replied. "But Rick is...well, he's kinda depressed."

"What's wrong with him? Is he still shaken by what happened in Las Vegas?"

She let out a weary sigh. "No, not at all. I'll let him explain." She put her hand over the receiver. "*Rrriiiccckkk*, it's Paul."

Several moments later Rick walked into the kitchen. He grimaced and took the phone from his wife. "Paul, how's it goin'?" he asked perfunctorily

The detective noticed Rick's rather uncharacteristic lackluster greeting. "Good. I hear you're not doin' too well though. What's wrong?"

The salesman frowned and glanced at his wife, who was walking back into the living room. "Terri tell you that?"

"She just said you're feeling a little low, that's all."

"Well...I am, Paul. Years of work down the fuckin' shitter! Christ, everything has dried up—orders, projects, even people. Hell, damn near every time I call somebody at Global Fuel Cell Technologies or Unlimited Energy Systems, I hear the same thing, 'he's no longer with the company.'"

"I'm, uh, sorry to hear that, Rick. But I'm sure you must've expected that to happen."

Rick didn't immediately respond. Several moments later Haydon heard his friend let out a defeated sign and say, "yeah...I did. But, ya know, you always hold out a little hope that it won't." His voice became harsh. "What makes it so bad, Paul, so unbearable really, is that Greene, my boss, is rubbing it in. He was never a fan of fuel cells to begin with, and now he's gloating. The asshole!" He paused a moment then added glumly, "I guess I can't really blame him. I'd do the same thing if I were in his shoes."

Haydon was glad he was talking to Rick on the phone; despite himself he smiled. It was amusing to hear Rick so cantankerous.

"Well, Rick, I've got some news that might cheer you up."

"I doubt it," the salesman retorted.

The private investigator ignored his friend's doleful response and said, "I think we're going to crack the case, Rick. I really do."

The salesman's eyes widened, his aberrant self-pity vanished. "No shit? What's happening?" he asked eagerly.

"Are you familiar with an engineer from GFCT named Terrance McChaffee?"

Rick thought for a minute then replied, "Uh, yeah. Kinda. I've heard his name mentioned a few times, but I didn't have any contact with him because I think he was a systems engineer. He didn't deal with component design. Wasn't he the guy who was working with Bob Hobbs when he was electrocuted?"

"Yeah. Anyway, Mary tracked him down. She got a tip from someone in the Vegas police department that he was missing."

"*Mary?*" Rick said teasingly. "Sounds like you two are gettin' awfully cozy."

"I wish," the detective replied ruefully. "If she wasn't married…Anyway, she got hold of him and surprisingly he said he had been trying to contact her—go figure! Anyhow, when we met, McChaffee confirmed that the incident in Las Vegas was no accident; that someone, or some group was behind it. The man's given us something to go on."

Rick pulled a chair out from the kitchen table and sat down. "Well, don't keep me in suspense. What'd he tell you?"

Haydon hesitated a moment then said, "I'm uh…I'm not going to tell you, Rick. Not yet anyway."

"Why the hell not?"

"It turns out we're dealing with some nasty people here, my friend. McChaffee told us his life is in danger. He's been directly threatened by what I believe is a hired hit man—a professional. Until Mary breaks the story, the fewer people who know his information, the better. If I told you, I'd fear for you and Terri and should anything happen, well, I wouldn't want that on my conscience."

"Paul! Come on! You can't tease me like this! Besides, who the hell is going to know I know anything?"

"Ricky, if my suspicion is correct that an assassin is after McChaffee, that means he's been hired. Hired by someone or some group. They have money—they'd have to. Employing a hired gun doesn't come cheap. That means whoever he's working for has bucks, lots of them, and resources. Who knows what they're capable of finding out—or doing?"

The salesman sighed. "Alright, I understand. But I hope you crack this thing. *God* how I'd love to rub Greene's nose in it!"

Haydon chuckled. "I'm pretty sure you'll have a chance to do that. I'll be in touch, Rick. Take it easy."

"Paul…be careful," Rick said sincerely. He then added jokingly, "This time I won't be there to pull your ass out of the fire."

Haydon smiled. "I will."

"His name is Paul Haydon. He's a private dick. Has an agency in Oakland California," Mike Swenson told Nick Ragosta the next morning over coffee.

Ragosta mused. "What does he specialize in?"

"According to his website, pretty much what I do when I'm not working for Noble. Missing persons, tracking unfaithful spouses and so on."

The assassin looked blankly off toward the little café's kitchen. "Did you find out anything about *him*—his background?" he asked impatiently.

Swenson yawned then replied, "Took me most of the fuckin' night, but yes." He took a sip of coffee but said nothing more; he just stared at the coffee cup in his hand.

Not hearing a summation forthcoming, Ragosta stopped looking off toward the kitchen and fixed a stare on Swenson that actually scared him. Wearing a cold smile, the assassin shook his head slightly and said, "Don't be holding out on me, Swenson. Tell me everything you know about Haydon, and tell me now!" His face then filled with a hideous intensity. "Don't make me pry it out of you," he added in a voice that shot a chill through the private investigator.

Ragosta could see his callous demand had the desired effect, though Swenson tried to appear unaffected. "I'm not holding out on you, Nick. Give me a fuckin' break, I'm tired. I've been up all night researching this shit for you. I could use some sleep."

"You'll have time to sleep after we're through here. Spit it out."

Swenson grimaced then said, "He's fifty-three years old. He grew up in Tempe, Arizona. He's not married; his wife died in seventy-two giving birth to his only child, a daughter, her name is Amy. He was a cop with the Oakland police from seventy-three to eighty-eight when he started up his agency. From what I can tell, he's been a successful P.I. He's not what I'd consider rich, but he's got a few bucks tucked away. Has over six hundred fifty thousand in his personal savings account—which seems to have been drained substantially over about the last year."

Ragosta smiled. He was always impressed with Swenson's ability to quickly obtain information on anybody. He never revealed how he obtained someone's personal information; he'd only confess to having many friends in diverse lines of business.

Before Swenson could continue Ragosta asked, "Know anything about his daughter? Does she work, is she married, have kids and so on?"

The private investigator shook his head. "I tried to, but…"

"But what?" Ragosta queried.

"I, ah, I fell asleep," Swenson replied, flushing in embarrassment. The assassin frowned but otherwise showed no disappointment, "Well, find out what you can. I may need her for leverage."

Swenson looked down at his coffee cup and said, "There's something else you should know about Haydon."

"Yeah, what?"

"He's a Vietnam vet—a former Navy Seal." The hit man's face filled with concern. It was the first time Swenson ever saw that happen.

Before he'd erased his existence from public record, Ragosta had been a first lieutenant in the Marines. He had command of a reconnaissance platoon and worked closely with UDT's on several occasions. He had great respect for their skills and capabilities.

Although this acronym stood for Underwater Demolition Team, demolitions were only part of their job. The Navy referred to them as "Seals," an elite, highly trained group of sailors who conducted clandestine operations behind enemy lines or, during peace time, within countries hostile to the United States in which intelligence was required that could only be obtained via infiltration. They did it all: reconnaissance, sabotage, assassination; and they did it exceptionally well.

As a young Marine Lieutenant, Ragosta, who considered himself one of the toughest men to ever walk the face of the earth, made the mistake of picking a fight with a Navy Seal who appeared to be no match for him. It was the only time in his life he'd had the shit thoroughly kicked out of him. His opponent walked away without a scratch.

Ragosta pulled himself together and looked at his watch. "Let's go, we need to get into position."

Mike Swenson suddenly looked frightened. "I can't believe you're going to do it! I mean…in broad daylight! And how do you know they'll be going there?"

Rising from his chair and throwing a ten dollar bill on the table Ragosta replied, "Where the hell else would they go?" He placed a cigarette between his lips and added, "We may not get another chance before he does too much damage. Come on, let's go."

CHAPTER 20

▼

Paul Haydon and Terrance McChaffee stepped out of the taxi. Because of the heavier than normal traffic this morning along with the cars and delivery trucks parked along the side of the street, the driver, despite his best attempts, had to drop them off about a block from *Hour Reports'* building. The young man apologized profusely, saying New York City cab drivers were better than this and seldom dropped their fares so far from their destination. Haydon tried vainly to assure him it was no big deal, but the driver kept apologizing.

"Stay close to me," Haydon said to McChaffee before leaning into the taxi's passenger side window to pay the contrite cabbie.

While Haydon was busy doing this, McChaffee took the time to look at the astonishing bustle surrounding him. The young engineer was amazed how people could actually live in New York City. The sidewalks were crowded with hurried pedestrians and the streets jammed with cars, trucks and cabs, many honking, as if their blaring horns would make a difference and unsnarl the jumbled traffic. Looking down the street McChaffee could see for many blocks. Fascinated, he watched as great masses of people crossed the street concurrently when the light changed, block after block, as far as he could see. He was startled when Haydon grabbed him by the elbow. After one last look around, he began to dodge the oncoming waves of humanity as he and his companion made their way to Mary Hildahl's office.

He saw them coming and was relieved. For the last hour and a half he'd been intensely scanning the area around him, quickly glancing at the faces of countless oncoming people and was starting to develop a headache from the effort. Without a doubt this was the most challenging stakeout Ragosta had been forced to undertake because there was no adequate place from which he could conduct his surveillance. The buildings in the area were attached to each other so there were no alleys to hide in, and even if there were, they wouldn't have afforded him a view with the distance he required. And every doorway he tried had an obstructed view. The assassin's main concern was being spotted by McChaffee before he saw him; and standing by a parked car, the odds of that happening were in his quarry's favor. If McChaffee did see him, he'd alert Paul Haydon and either run like a scared rabbit or hide behind the former Navy Seal who was undoubtedly armed. Without complete surprise, the assassin's plan would fail.

Eyes locked on his prey, Ragosta quickly blew the smoke out of his mouth and flicked the cigarette into a puddle on the sidewalk while forcefully slapping the roof of the car he'd stolen late last night, startling Mike Swenson who was dozing behind the wheel. Never taking his eyes off the two oncoming men, he quickly crossed the sidewalk, ignoring the dirty looks and vulgar comments he received from the people he collided with.

Haydon and McChaffee were now no more than fifty yards away. Swenson started the car and then opened the backseat door facing the sidewalk. He closed it again but not fully, so the door remained unlatched. Now standing against the building adjoining *Hour Report's*, people hurriedly walked past him occasionally forcing him to stand tiptoe to keep his eyes on his victims. This was one of the few times the assassin wished he was taller.

Luck was with Ragosta and his accomplice this morning. Haydon and McChaffee were approaching the main entrance to *Hour Report's* studios from the east, and because Ragosta and Swenson started their stakeout so early, they were able to obtain a parking spot just a few yards east of the entrance. This would make the abduction of Terrance McChaffee quick and easy.

Twenty yards away; it was time to make his move. Ragosta lifted the collar of his coat and began to quickly walk toward Haydon, gracefully moving around people in his path. When he was about thirty feet from the two men he dropped his head to hide as much of his face as possible behind his raised collar. Simultaneously, he tighten his fist around the heavy brass knuckles hidden in his right pocket. He seldom needed to use this aid, but it would greatly increase the power behind his punch. Because Haydon was an ex-Navy Seal, Ragosta wanted to be damn sure one blow did the job. He had considered shooting the private detective outright, but ruled it out fearing that a gunshot would cause panic in the people around them, hindering his escape.

Haydon was now five feet away on his left; he took one more step. "*HAY-DON!*" Ragosta cried out. With a startled expression the private investigator instinctively stopped and turned toward the sound of his name.

The assassin swung with every ounce of strength he could muster. The brass knuckles did their job; his fist smashed into the side of Haydon's face with tremendous force and Ragosta could feel the man's jaw shift out of place, knocking him out cold. McChaffee's bodyguard crumbled to the sidewalk, his world going black before he could even see his assailant's face.

A young woman let out a high-pitched scream. People in the area stopped to see what was happening. The assault on Haydon took place so fast McChaffee didn't immediately comprehend what was going on. Gape-mouthed, he looked from Haydon's body sprawled on the sidewalk to the man standing over him. Because he was still in shock by what he'd just seen, the engineer didn't immediately recognize the assailant.

Ragosta swiftly kicked Haydon hard in the ribs to ensure he was down. Satisfied that the private investigator posed no immediate threat, he turned his attention to McChaffee. It was when they locked eyes that the young engineer realized who was standing before him, and a wave of terror swept through him with an intensity he'd never before experienced. Blood drained from his petrified face and he wet himself.

"*NICK!*" McChaffee managed to say before Ragosta, with lighting speed, grabbed his lapel and pulled the engineer toward him, jamming his knee into the man's groin. McChaffee bellowed out in pain and doubled over. The assassin hurriedly dragged the young man across the sidewalk, flung open the back door of the stolen sedan and threw McChaffee, head first, into the car.

Ragosta instantly followed him in, slammed the door shut and screamed, "*FUCKING GO!!!!*"

Mike Swenson shot out into the street, darting right in front of a semi-truck which slammed on its brakes and barely missed hitting them. The trucker cursed and honked furiously.

The assassin pulled out his pistol and thrust it into McChaffee's side. "Move and you're dead! Understand?" The young engineer was too terrified to speak. Deathly pale and wide-eyed, he could only manage to stare blankly at Ragosta and nod his head.

Providence remained with the kidnappers; the traffic had thinned and only a few cars were between them and the first stoplight. Pushing the pedal to the floor, Swenson cursed at the Ford Taurus' incredible lack of pick-up. *Of all the cars he could have stolen,* he thought, *Ragosta picked a Taurus!*

Because the first stoplight was only about half a block from where Haydon lay, they risked it. Swerving around the vehicles ahead of them, they ran the red light; violently turning to evade several taxis but unable to avoid getting hit in the right rear quarter panel by a delivery truck. The collision's impact was enough to swing the back of the Taurus a couple of feet, but it didn't slow them down. Swenson kept going and once through the intersection they had a block of clear sailing before they hit the next wall of traffic. Their plan helped alleviate Ragosta and Swenson from concern about the congestion. Because they didn't have far to go, as long as the traffic kept moving they'd be okay.

The next stoplight turned green and the cars ahead of them began to move before they had to slow down. At the intersection Swenson took a sharp right, drove about a block then pulled into a parking garage. Parking is always at a premium in New York, but with a few bucks to an amenable parking lot attendant, two stalls could be had for a short period of time.

The car's tires squealed, their shrill sound reverberating off the concrete walls of the garage as they swiftly circled their way up the floors. On the sixth level they ran over the orange highway cone the attendant had placed in front of an empty stall and skidded to an abrupt stop. Swenson and Ragosta then scanned the area to ensure no one was around before they transferred themselves and McChaffee into the dark blue utility van parked next to them.

"Remember, not a word," Ragosta said ominously as he grasped McChaffee by the collar and dragged him out of the car. The terrified engineer was yanked so forcefully that when he left the backseat he stumbled and fell to his knees; Ragosta quickly jerked him to his feet.

"Get in the fucking van and sit down!" the assassin snapped angrily. Swenson opened the rear doors and the young engineer saw that there were no seats or windows. Because he hesitated he was brutally pushed inside.

McChaffee sat on the floor and leaned against the side of the cold, dark vehicle. He pulled his knees to his chest, hugged them tightly and began to cry shamelessly.

Ragosta followed him in, closing the doors behind him. "*Ohhhh for Christ's sake, shut up!*" he howled and sat down across from the weeping man. Arms resting on his elevated knees, he had a lose grip on the pistol hanging from his hand. He stared at the petrified engineer with a little satisfied smile and it was clear to McChaffee that the bastard was enjoying this.

Swenson got behind the wheel and leisurely drove to the exit. He pulled up to the booth and rolled down his window. "Hey, buddy, thanks again for the two spots," he said cheerfully and gave the young man a hundred dollar bill. "Here, a little something extra for your help—something to remind you to keep your mouth shut if anybody starts asking questions."

The parking lot attendant smiled and quickly pocketed the bill. "Count on it. Hey man, come back here anytime!" He pushed a button raising the gate. Swenson winked at him and pulled out into the street. It was a sunny day and he was forced to squint until his eyes adjusted to the bright light.

He drove cautiously, careful not to break any traffic laws. The two occupants in the back bounced up and down as the van drove over numerous potholes; the condition of the streets was deplorable. Ragosta remained silent; he continued to stare and smile arrogantly at McChaffee, who kept his head down and occasionally sniffled.

"How long before we get there?" Ragosta shouted up to Swenson, never taking his eyes off his captive.

The detective shrugged. "In this traffic…maybe an hour."

McChaffee slowly raised his head exposing swollen, blood-shot eyes. Meekly he asked, "Where are you taking me?"

The assassin's smile broadened and his face brightened. With sadistic pleasure he replied, "To a place where you and I can have a nice little chat. A place where we won't be disturbed—where no one will be around to hear us."

A wave of terror so intense swept though McChaffee that for a moment he thought he was going to faint. From the moment Nick had abducted him he knew, but didn't want to accept it. This was going to be the last day of his life. He lowered his head and began to tremble.

A group of people formed around Paul Haydon. A woman knelt beside him; having been a battered woman herself, she felt an odd sympathy for the man. She reached out and gently touched his cheek, then looked up at the crowd gathered around them. Her eyes focused on a smartly dressed young woman with a computer bag hanging from her shoulder and a bottle of Aquafina in her hand. "Let me have that," she said to her, gesturing to the bottle.

The young lady hesitated for a moment, looked around at the people staring at her, and then handed the kneeing woman her water. The woman twisted off the cap, carefully lifted the unconscious man's head then splashed a little water on Haydon's face. "Sir…sir, wake up," she said softly while gently slapping his cheeks. Haydon shuddered, his eyes blinked rapidly and he unconsciously pushed the woman's hand away from his face.

He let out a moan and with difficulty, sat up. His jaw throbbed mercilessly and his head felt like it was in a fog. Rubbing his chin he turned to look at the woman kneeling next to him. She was a compassionate looking woman about his age. She smiled at him and got to her feet. It was then that Haydon noticed all the people surrounding them.

"What the hell happened?" he asked.

The woman took hold of his hand and helped him stagger to his feet. "How do you feel?"

Haydon slowly shook his head. "Like I ran into a train."

"Well, you took quite a blow. I'm surprised you regained consciousness so quickly."

Realizing the show was over, one by one the crowd began to disperse. The private investigator looked hard at the woman holding his hand; his expression told her he expected an answer to his question.

She let go of his hand. "Some man just came up and, and…hit you. Hard. He then hauled off the guy you were with."

"*McChaffee!*" Haydon quietly declared in shock, he'd momentarily forgotten about him. He stared at the woman with piercing eyes. "Did you see what he looked like?"

She shook her head. "I'm afraid not, it all happened so fast."

"I got his car's license plate number," a man interrupted, stepping up to Haydon and handing him a small piece of paper.

"Thank you," the detective said gratefully. He quickly glanced at the slip of paper then put it in his pocket. He'd give the information to the police, but suspected it probably wouldn't do him much good. He then turned back to the woman who'd helped him. "And thank you, Ms…?"

"Touton, Liz Touton. You need to go to the hospital," she said with concern. "You could have a concussion."

Haydon shook his head, then wished he hadn't—it hurt. "No. I can't. But thank you for your concern. I've got to find the man who was with me." He gently squeezed her shoulder and headed for the doors of *Hour Report's* offices.

"You've got the bastard? Good!" Laurence Haggerty exclaimed with relief into his cell phone. As usual, he was stuck in traffic on the 495 loop around Washington D.C. "I'll get to Baltimore-Washington International as soon as I can; catch the shuttle to New York and meet you at the warehouse. I want to question him myself."

"Right," Ragosta replied.

"Loosen him up a little—but not too much, got it? I want him completely coherent when I question him."

"Understood." Ragosta snapped his cell phone shut and placed it back in his coat pocket. "How much fuckin' longer?" he yelled out to Swenson in frustration, his cold eyes remaining glued to the vanquished young man sitting across from him.

"We're almost there," Swenson shouted over his shoulder. "Keep your fuckin' shirt on!"

"It had to be that Nick guy McChaffee told us about," Paul Haydon said to Mary Hildahl. His jaw was throbbing terribly and he found it difficult to speak. Gently rubbing his chin and wincing he added, "Christ…I've *never* been hit this hard!"

"You're lucky he didn't kill you!" she replied, her back to him as she wrapped ice in a borrowed handkerchief. She had asked her assistant to go to the lounge and get every ice cube in the freezer. While she was doing that, Hildahl walked around the office until she found a guy with a clean handkerchief she could borrow. She gave the makeshift compress to Haydon. "Here, put this on your jaw."

He took it from her and eyed the handkerchief. "I, ah, I trust this is unused?"

Slightly annoyed, Hildahl placed her hands on her hips and looked at him as if he were an errant child. "Don't be so friggin' picky, Paul!" she scolded. "You're lucky you got that." She paused a moment then added, "You really *should* go to the hospital, you know."

The private investigator dismissed her suggestion with a wave of his hand, then tried to smile and winced from the attempt. Reluctantly, he put the cold compress against his jaw. As she turned and walked behind her desk he thought again what a lucky guy her husband was. Although he had no intentions of ever marrying again, a woman like her just might change his mind.

Mary Hildahl sat down and rubbed her face; she dropped her hands to expose a tense and worried expression. "Do you think they'll kill him, Paul? Do you really think they will?"

Haydon dropped the ice pack to his lap and stared at it solemnly. "Yes," he replied ruefully. He looked back up at the reporter, "But I don't think they'll do it right away. They'll want to question him first; otherwise he would've been killed on the spot. That gives us a little time. A guy who witnessed the attack on me gave me the license plate number of their get-away car; before I came up here I called it into the police." He let out a defeated sigh. "But it won't do any good."

"Why not?"

Because they changed cars shortly after they abducted McChaffee—I'm sure of it. They're professionals and wouldn't do anything stupid like remain with a vehicle that was most likely stolen." He lifted the cold compress back up to his chin.

Hildahl grimaced and shook her head. "The poor guy." She paused a moment then added in a somber, guilt-ridden voice, "God, I feel responsible."

"Well, don't!" Haydon said firmly. "He knew what he was doing. If anybody's at fault here it's me. I was supposed to protect him."

"There was no way you could've prevented what happened, Paul. He—whoever he is—obviously had this well planned out." Finding it hard to sit still, she got back to her feet. "Do you think you can find him?"

The detective turned away from her, embarrassed by the admission he was about to make. "Truthfully...no. Not in the amount of time I suspect he has left. I'm afraid..." he dropped the ice pack to his lap again and looked up at her sadly. "I'm afraid he's finished."

There was a long silence. Mary Hildahl crossed her arms over her chest, walked over to the window and stared blankly out at the building next to hers. Haydon could sense that she wanted to be left alone with her thoughts so he sat quietly, pressing the quickly melting compress against his jaw. He began to ponder how best to try and track McChaffee but soon gave up. He was certain it would be a futile effort.

The ice pack was beginning to drip on his pants. He was about to get up and go to the men's room when Hildahl said, "Well, Paul...I guess that's it. No interview, no evidence, no story." She turned away from the window and looked at him despondently. "I'm sorry; I wasn't much help to you."

Surprised, Haydon looked at her incredulously. "What do you mean it's over? Aren't you forgetting something?" She gave him a confused look. "*Finley*. The name Finley. What'd you find out about him?"

Her face lit up. This morning's chaos and the loss of McChaffee had caused her to completely forget about the research she did yesterday. How could she forget? Of course, learning of the day's events when she arrived home last night didn't help either. She was beginning to wonder if she'd reached the point where she had to make a choice—career or motherhood. Juggling both was just getting to be too much. She wasn't Super Woman—no woman was. And last night was total bedlam.

Home later than usual because of all the work involved in trying to link the name Finley to someone who could possibly be relevant to the conspiracy, she found her husband in a pissy mood. Normally wonderful with the kids, last night had tried his patience.

Her oldest son, Markie, had hurt himself in hockey practice again. Six-years-old and already he'd had a total of twenty two stitches in five different locations on his small body. Undoubtedly the emergency room staff were beginning to question what kind of parents they were, and she cringed at the thought that they might suspect she and Kevin were beating their children. She didn't like hockey, thought it was far too violent; especially for such a young boy. But her husband, Kevin, having grown up in Minnesota, was absolutely crazy about the game and insisted their boys play. She arrived home at the same time her husband and son returned from the emergency room.

While Kevin was at the hospital with Markie his mother-in-law, who was watching their other son, Blake, called Kevin in a panic—the boy had taken a nasty tumble down the steps and she didn't know what to do. After speaking with Blake over the phone, he'd determined that the boy was fine; it was his mother-in-law who was traumatized. It took him over fifteen minutes to calm her down.

Mary's husband—though thankful for his mother-in-law's help in babysitting—often complained that the woman was getting too old to watch a spunky four-year-old *and* their one-year-old daughter, Lauren. He didn't come right out and say it, but he was essentially accusing his wife of neglecting her duties as a mother. And she couldn't blame him; he had a job too. He didn't want to take on the majority of the parenting responsibilities, it just worked out that way.

Gently striking her head with the palm of her hand she said, "Finley, yes, of course!" She opened a drawer and pulled out a manila file; it appeared to be rather thick. Hildahl walked around to the front of her desk and sat on top of it. Parked right in front of him, Haydon was thankful she was wearing a pants-suit. With no shapely legs to distract him, it was easier to concentrate on her eyes as she sifted through the open file.

"As I'm sure you already know, Paul, *Finley* is a rather common name." He nodded. "Thank God for the Internet! I did a Google search and came up with over seventy names of prominent Finleys. After reading each one—which I might add took a considerable amount of time—I believe I've narrowed it down to three possible suspects.

"The first person is Daniel Finely. He's a multi-millionaire who's founded an alternative energy business. His company, Turbo-Source, is developing mini-turbojet engines that generate electricity. According to their website, their units can cost-effectively supply electrical power to any building as small as a house to as large as a hospital. They also claim that these mini-turbines are environmentally friendly."

Paul Haydon mused for a moment. "Did the site mention anything about the potential use of these turbojet engines for the automotive industry?" Hildahl shook her head. The detective frowned. "If that's the case, I don't see any connection between the sabotage of Global Fuel Cell Technologies' vehicle and his company."

Mary Hildahl pursed her lips and nodded in agreement. "The second person is a Canadian woman by the name of Linda Finley. She's a board member of Quebec Power Corporation. From what I could find out about her, she's a real advocate of converting coal to oil; much like the Germans did toward the end of World War Two when the Russians overran the Romanian oil fields, cutting off the Nazi's main source of petroleum."

Haydon was impressed by her knowledge of history. He thought for a moment then asked, "And the third person?"

It took some time for Mary Hildahl to thumb through the file. Apparently, she'd collected quite a bit of information. The brief interlude caused Haydon to again feel the full intensity of his throbbing jaw; he pushed the melting ice pack harder against his chin.

After about a minute she finally stopped shuffling through the pages. "Ah, here we go. A guy by the name of…Wendell Finley. He's the CEO and owner of ENDICORP, the largest privately-owned oil company in the world."

When he heard the name "ENDICORP," Paul Haydon suddenly froze; his eyes shifted back and forth furiously. Slowly, he dropped the dripping compress from his face and stared at Mary Hildahl. "Wendell Finley, you say?" The beautiful reporter nodded. Very gradually Haydon's face took on an expression of comprehension. "*Oil!*" he exclaimed softly. "Oil…as everybody knows, is made into gasoline, right?" He knew the answer of course; his revelation forced him to think the rhetorical question out loud.

Hildahl nodded, her face now expressing realization of the obvious. "Fuel cell powered automobiles would…" she looked off into nowhere. "Fuel cells would…spell the death of cars as we know them today, wouldn't they?"

Solemnly, the private investigator smiled. "They would—"

"They would eliminate the need for gasoline!" Hildahl cut in, finishing Haydon's sentence for him.

The detective deliberated for a moment then said thoughtfully, "It's…it's so simple. Almost *too* simple."

The two looked at each other as if they'd just found the missing link. But the smile faded quickly from Haydon's face. "ENDICORP is owned by this William Finley guy?"

"Wendell Finley," she corrected him.

"Right, Wendell Finley." He looked hard at her. "How big is ENDICORP? I mean, what's their market share?"

The reporter thumbed through more papers. "According to this, as of 1999 ENDICORP had nineteen percent market share."

"Nineteen percent?"

"Yes."

"That's fuc—" he blushed. "Sorry. That's significant."

"Yes, it is. It's probably much bigger now. As a matter of fact, according to my research only two other petroleum companies have a larger market share than ENDICORP: PETROCOMP and World Energy; both publicly held."

Haydon was lost in thought for a moment; he snapped out of it when what was left of his compress began to steadily drip on his thigh. "What else did you find out on this Finley guy?" he asked while standing up to put the saturated handkerchief in the bucket Hildahl's assistant used to deliver the ice.

"Not a lot," she responded soberly. "Only that he's sole owner of ENDI-CORP—richer than Midas, of course. Inherited the company from his father. Unfortunately, I couldn't find anything else on the web that gave me any more information than that."

Haydon sat back down in his chair and gently rubbed his chin. He looked at the beautiful reporter pensively. "I don't know about you, Mary, but he sounds like a "made-to-order suspect" to me. If nothing else, he's a good place to start."

She nodded her agreement. "Alright. I'll line up an interview with this guy."

"How do you know he'll agree to it?"

The reporter, looking very confident, grinned. "Don't take this personally, Paul, but he'll agree to it because he's a man. All I need to do is stroke him a few times—express my admiration for him—and he'll roll over like a dog wanting his belly scratched. The tactic hasn't failed me yet. What's your next step, Paul?"

He stood up, rubbed his chin again and answered, "For what good it'll do me, I'll call the police again; see if they turned up anything on that license plate. Kidnappers, thieves and such that use get-away cars, usually switch vehicles quickly. I'll see if there've been any abandoned cars reported." When he reached the door he turned and added, "I wouldn't hold my breath if I were you, Mary."

Sadly she replied, "I won't."

A ship's whistle blew in the distance, its strident wail muffled by the aged brick wall facing the dirty harbor. To his right, through slit eyes he saw a large rat slowly sniffing various bits of debris strewn on the warped wooden floor beneath a shattered window; the rodent seemed to be oblivious to the three men he was sharing the room with. It was getting darker out and the fading light found it difficult to penetrate the two windows behind him encrusted with decades of grime.

Terrance McChaffee was sitting down with his hands tied behind the back of an old wooden chair. The rope was so tightly wrapped it was cutting into his flesh. But that was the least of his pain. His eyes were swollen, but not shut; with difficulty he could still see. His cheeks were raw from the numerous open hand slaps he'd received from Nick, who had yet to ask one question.

McChaffee sat tied to the chair for hours before Nick began to work him over. Having endured this tribulation for over two hours without being asked a single question, the engineer was convinced the man was beating him for his pure enjoyment. The young man suffered repeated blows to the face and stomach, had his fingers alternately broken and crushed, and was kicked savagely in the groin several times for good measure. He couldn't be sure, but he thought he had at least four broken fingers and maybe a couple of broken ribs. And there was that one terrifying moment when Nick placed a plastic bag over his head and kept it there until the searing pain of his burning lungs was about to drag him into an excruciating unconsciousness. Every blow now hurt more than the last, but McChaffee knew his tormentor was clearly holding back. He could've beaten him into unconsciousness by now if he'd wanted to, or just as easily killed him. What *was* he waiting for? McChaffee wondered as he braced himself for Nick's next strike. To be tortured this way required skill and experience, both of which this bastard clearly had.

After what seemed like an all-day drive, they arrived in an alley between two ancient warehouses. The bottom ten feet of the buildings were covered in gang graffiti and the alley full of trash. Across the rusty railroad tracks and wide pier was the harbor, beyond which McChaffee caught a quick glance of the distant New York skyline. For a brief moment he forgot about his predicament and forlornly thought how empty the city looked without the Twin Towers. A hand thrust into his back, pushing him toward one of the dilapidated buildings, instantly brought his mind back to his dire quandary. He quickly looked around and saw that except for them, the area was completely deserted. It was a god-forsaken place, so McChaffee figured they must be in New Jersey.

After entering the huge abandoned building they climbed three flights of creaky steel stairs to what at one time must have been an office; it overlooked the structure's cavernous interior. When they'd first entered he noticed how musty the place smelled; but the engineer couldn't even breathe anymore through this bleeding, swollen and disfigured nose.

While Nick was working on him, the guy who drove the van sat in a corner and read a newspaper. Now and then he'd glance at his watch, frown, then go back to reading. When Nick took a break from his labors and spoke to him, which wasn't often, his tormentor only referred to him as Mike, never using the man's last name. Occasionally Mike would peer from behind the newspaper to look at McChaffee. He never looked too long, and always went back to reading. He appeared unaffected, indifferent really, to the engineer's cries of pain and pitiful pleas for the beating to stop.

After a savage blow to McChaffee's mouth which loosened several of his teeth, Ragosta stepped back and lit a cigarette. Working up a sweat, he'd taken his coat off over an hour ago and laid it over the back of the chair Swenson was sitting in. While taking short puffs he studied the engineer, sneering as he contemplated where and how to strike next.

McChaffee was now continuously drooling blood from his mouth and when his tongue brushed up against his loose teeth, the stinging pain made him quiver. He spit out a mouthful of blood and slowly lifted his throbbing head. Looking at Ragosta through swollen eyes he asked, "Why…why are you doing this? What is it you want?"

The assassin spoke to him for the first time since the beating began. Yanking the cigarette out of his mouth he sneered, "Shut the fuck up, McChaffee. When the time comes, we'll be the ones asking questions."

Mike Swenson dropped his newspaper, looked at his watch and whined, "When the hell is he gonna get here? I'm gettin' hungry. I wanta wrap this up." The question caused McChaffee to tremble; "wrapping this up" surly meant his death.

Ragosta ignored his impatient colleague. He stepped up to the bruised and bloodied young man who dropped his head and braced himself for another blow. When one didn't come, he meekly lifted his head to see why. He saw his tormentor towering over him, contemptuously staring back at him and lighting another cigarette. "I'll tell ya this, McChaffee," he said with the cigarette bouncing between his lips, "If you don't cooperate like a good little boy, this *will* be the last day of your miserable life."

"You're going to kill me anyway," the young engineer retorted.

The assassin shrugged. "Maybe, maybe not."

They heard the slamming of a car door. Ragosta turned from McChaffee and walked over to one of the windows. He tried to see through the filthy pane but couldn't, so he walked over to another one where most of the glass was broken out of it. "He's here," the assassin declared.

"About time," Swenson mumbled.

McChaffee tensed as he heard the insipid echo of footsteps walking across the concrete floor; the sound became a dull sounding series of pings when the arrival began to come up the steel staircase. The reverberations of his footsteps were methodical and evil, coming ever closer; each step declaring that his imminent death was closer.

A tall, balding man Terrance McChaffee didn't recognize walked into the room. He was sharply dressed in a light blue shirt and dark suit, his loosened tie somehow gave him a look of unquestionable authority; the engineer could tell that the man was clearly agitated. He looked at Swenson. "It's getting dark in here. Go get the light," he ordered in a commanding voice. The private investigator nodded and quickly left the room.

He walked up to McChaffee and gazed down at the despondent young man; like Ragosta, his face was filled with disdain. He showed no reaction to McChaffee's severely bruised and battered face. Pensively he said, "So...this is the infamous Mister McChaffee." Haggerty studied him a moment longer then motioned for Ragosta to give him the chair Mike Swenson was sitting on. Haggerty took the chair, placed it in front of the engineer then twirled it around and sat down with crossed arms resting on the chair's back. He stared silently at McChaffee, his eyes darting from one abrasion to another, openly taking pleasure in the young man's misery. Turning to Ragosta he asked, "He tell you anything of interest?"

Ragosta shook his head, blew out a cloud of smoke from the side of his mouth then dropped his cigarette to the floor. While crushing it out with his foot he replied, "I didn't ask him anything. I saved that pleasure for you."

The owner of Noble Consultants produced a sad smile as he turned back to McChaffee. "Terrance, you've caused me a great deal of trouble. A great deal." He paused a moment to let the words sink in. "We're going to make this simple. I'm going to ask you a few questions. If I'm not satisfied with the answers, Nick here," he jerked his head toward Ragosta, who was standing behind him wearing a malicious smirk, "is going to persuade you to expound a little more, until I'm satisfied that you've truthfully told me everything you know. I assure you, Terrance, he can be *very* persuasive. I won't ask him to play around with you, like he did before I arrived. Now I'm going to insist he use all his professional talents on you. Do you understand?"

Looking down at him, Nick Ragosta considered Laurence Haggerty. How he'd changed over the last few years. From the benign father figure he was to Sandra Beach, to the cold, heartless person now ruthlessly interrogating a hapless young man. The assassin took no delight in the change; on the contrary, he thought it rather tragic.

McChaffee nodded. "Yes."

"Good," Haggerty sneered. "First question. When you spoke to Ms. Hildahl, what did you tell her Nick hired you for?"

McChaffee thought for a moment then answered, "Only that I'd been hired to rig Global Fuel Cell Technologies' demonstration vehicle to explode." He didn't see any purpose in brining Cynthia Klash into the picture. The woman was dead.

"Oh, I think you told her more than that," Haggerty said evenly. He eyed McChaffee suspiciously, dropped his arms from the back of the chair and crossed them over his chest. "What else did you tell her?" he demanded sternly.

The young man shook his head, tossing a rather significant amount of blood to the floor. "Just that. I swear!"

"*Nick!*" Haggerty called abruptly. He got up off the chair and took a step back. Ragosta came up to McChaffee, ripped open his pants and grabbed the engineer's testicials in his powerful hand.

The engineer looked at the hand in horror. "*WAI—*"

The assassin squeezed hard and McChaffee cried out in pain. Like most men, he'd been kicked in the balls a few times, but he'd never felt anything as excruciating as this. It was akin to someone slowly ripping out his intestines.

The assassin let go and took a step back. Haggerty again situated himself on the chair in front of the whimpering engineer. Mike Swenson appeared with a portable, battery-powered work light. He placed it on the floor a few feet from McChaffee, turned it on and pointed it directly at his face. It was very bright; reflexively he narrowed his inflamed eyes and averted them from the powerful beam.

"Look at me!" Haggerty demanded. Still squinting, the engineer turned his head to face the unknown man. "Next time I'll have Nick crush them. I don't have time to fuck around, McChaffee! Who was that man with you?"

The engineer didn't hesitate. "His name is Paul Haydon. He's a private investigator working with Mary Hildahl."

Ragosta rolled his eyes, "We know who *he* is, Laurence," he said impatiently. He pulled out another cigarette and lit it.

Annoyance flashed across Haggerty's face. He turned his head and gave the assassin an irate look, then continued grilling McChaffee. "What questions did Hildahl ask you?"

The engineer swallowed; it hurt terribly. Were it not for the blood he was swallowing, his throat would be completely parched; but it was also making him sick to his stomach. He licked some more blood from his lips and answered, "I…I don't remember everything she asked. Both she and Haydon asked me a bunch of questions."

"Do I have to call Nick again?"

"NO!" McChaffee shrieked in panic, snapping his legs together tightly. "I can't remember the specific questions they asked," he said hurriedly, "but I can tell you the gist of what they were getting at."

"Which *wasssss?*" Haggerty hissed.

"They believe…" he gagged and spit out more blood; he didn't want to swallow any more if he could help it. "They're convinced there's a conspiracy to destroy fuel cell technology." Haggerty and Ragosta immediately glanced at each other apprehensively. The assassin looked toward the ceiling, threw his hands in the air and mouthed the word *"fuck,"* while shaking his head.

McChaffee couldn't help notice their exchange but appeared to ignore it. He eagerly continued. "They asked questions like who hired me; what was I told by the guy who asked me to do this; did I contact the police…shit like that."

"Again, Mister McChaffee," Haggerty growled impatiently. "*What* did you tell them?"

"That I didn't know who hired me—which was the truth! Just that the guy's name was Nick, and that he wanted me to sabotage GFCT's vehicle…make it explode—in a big way." A tooth suddenly gave way and more blood began to cascade from the side of his mouth. The young engineer cringed, spit out the tooth and added, "That's…that's all I told them—all I knew."

Haggerty glared at him, resentment building in his unblinking eyes. Trying to avoid the hateful stare and that goddamned blinding light, McChaffee attempted to shift in his chair but couldn't—he was tied too tight. "Why'd you tell them anything at all?" Haggerty asked, anger building in his voice. "You were paid handsomely. Were you not?"

The engineer shook his head. "I…I…I just couldn't stand it any longer."

"Couldn't stand what?"

McChaffee threw his head back and let out a painful sigh. It hurt to breathe; it hurt to make any kind of movement. Blood trickled down his cheek and fell on his blood-soaked collar. Dropping his head back down he whispered softly, "The guilt."

Haggerty leaned in a little closer to him, looking perplexed. "*What?* I didn't hear you."

Ignoring the bright light shining in his eyes, McChaffee looked defiantly at Haggerty and spit out, "I couldn't stand the guilt—of killing someone. I have a conscious. I should've never agreed to cooperate with you...should've never taken the money."

The admission shook Laurence Haggerty. For a brief moment he too felt an undeniable pang of remorse; an emotion, he realized, that hadn't surface in him in a very long time. He pushed the unpleasant thought aside, grimaced and said evenly, "But you *did*, Mr. Chaffee. You did. You took the money then betrayed us."

His ordeal had been dragging on now for hours, and McChaffee was exhausted; any control he had over his emotions vanished. He started to tremble and cry. With tears streaming down his cheeks he begged, "*Pleaseeee* let me go! God, please! I...I have a little daughter. I won't say another word—I swear to God! I'll...I'll tell anybody anything you want!"

Almost remorsefully Haggerty replied, "I'm afraid that won't do any good, Mr. McChaffee. The damage is already done. The press now knows the explosion wasn't an accident."

"I was supposed to meet with Hildahl this morning—give her all the details," McChaffee offered in desperation. "I can still meet with her...change my story!"

Haggerty let out a defeated sigh and slowly stood up from the chair. He looked down at the frightened young man and for a moment searched his soul, but could find no pity. "No. You've caused me a tremendous amount of trouble," he said flatly, and without emotion. "And maybe millions of dollars too." He turned, nodded to Ragosta and walked out the door.

Mike Swenson took hold of the portable light but the assassin stopped him. "Leave it, Mike." Swenson released it and followed Haggerty out of the building.

Terrance McChaffee turned his terrified eyes to Nick Ragosta, who was reaching into his pocket. "*No! Oh no, please!*" he whimpered, tears flowing from his swollen eyes.

Ragosta produced the plastic bag he'd used earlier to torment the engineer. Looking at the bag he said, "The rats will eat well for the next couple of days." He walked up to the trembling young man who continued to plead for his life, and placed the bag over his head. He then pulled a large rubber band over the engineer's head and snapped the open end of the bag against his neck. As Terrance McChaffee began to spasm, Ragosta calmly walked out of the room, taking the portable lamp with him.

He joined the others waiting for him next to Haggerty's rental car. When he reached them Haggerty took Ragosta by the arm and began to lead him away. "Excuse us a minute, Mike." The private investigator nodded, relieved the assassin of the lamp and started to put it in the trunk of the car.

"Throw it in the harbor," Ragosta ordered over his shoulder as he walked away with Haggerty. Swenson nodded and headed toward the edge of the pier.

"What?" Ragosta asked when they were far enough away from Swenson.

"You made a mistake bringing Swenson here," Haggerty said quietly.

"I needed him," the assassin replied impassively.

"He knows too much. I don't trust him now. I'm afraid he'll try and blackmail me. And if he does that, both you and I can kiss the money goodbye."

Ragosta sighed and glanced sadly at the man standing at the edge of the pier. "Alright." With little enthusiasm he pulled out his pistol and began to walk toward Swenson, who had his back to him; he was now admiring the lighted New York skyline. "**Mike!**" the assassin shouted. Swenson turned around and saw the gun in Ragosta's hand. Bewildered, he looked from the pistol to Haggerty, who was standing solemnly in the distance. "Sorry partner, you know too much." Ragosta quickly raised the pistol and put a hole in the middle of Swenson's forehead.

The assassin threw the body into the van and with Haggerty's help, rolled it into the harbor. In silence they watched it sink, then got into Haggerty's car and drove off.

"Jesus Christ, Laurence…I'm getting tired of this!" Ragosta complained bitterly. He lit a cigarette, shook out the match and leaned back in his chair; his eyes remained locked on Haggerty. Still fuming he added, "I'm always one fuckin' step behind. I feel like I'm chasing my tail!"

"This should be the last one," Haggerty assured him confidently.

"*Yeah*? How do you figure?"

"Because she's wi—" Haggerty stopped talking when he saw the cocktail waitress approaching their table.

"Excuse me, sir," she said politely to Ragosta. "Smoking isn't allowed in this bar."

"Fuck off!" he snarled. Wide-eyed and absolutely stunned, the woman stepped back, hesitated a moment, then looking frightened quickly walked away.

"What I was about to say, Nick, is that she's with the press. *Convince* her to report only on the danger of fuel cells—dump the conspiracy theory, and this unpleasant situation will disappear. Fuel cells are to new to the market; nobody has them yet. I doubt there'll be any interest by other news agencies to pick up the story. And even if they do, they won't have the knowledge that Mary Hildahl has—you'll see to that. It's her story so I doubt she has any intentions of telling anybody else about it until it airs."

"What about this Paul Haydon guy?" Ragosta asked wearily.

Haggerty took a long sip of his Scotch then answered. "The fact that Haydon knows about it is of no consequence. Once Hildahl reports on the dangers of this technology the whole story will be sanitized—yesterday's news. At least in the mind of the public. This whole fucking mess will fade away."

Ragosta let out a tired sigh then said forcefully. "You'd better be right about this, Haggerty. After this one I'm walkin'—regardless of how P3 ends up. I'll want my money!"

The owner of Noble Consultants took another sip of his drink, keeping his eyes locked on the assassin and hoping like hell he was right, too.

CHAPTER 21

▼

Typically, just the mention of her name or her program, *Hour Report*, prompted either immediate cooperation or tenacious opposition. More often than not it was the latter. Normally it took several calls to gain access to those at the top rung of a corporation; in the case of ENDICORP it took a few more. However, once in contact with ENDICORP's executive secretary, the scheduling of Wendell Finley's on-camera interview only took a matter of minutes. As Mary Hildahl would soon learn, Wendell Finley was never one to miss an opportunity to talk about himself.

Initially it was a good sign; instead of promising a return call, she was placed on hold for the short time it took Finley's secretary to consult with him. While waiting, Hildahl began to dread the numerous questions she was always asked before a person of prominence would agree to an interview. *Why me? What will be discussed? Who else will be part of this story? Is there an escape clause if I don't approve of the interview? How long will it take? When will the show be aired?* And so on and so forth. By the time the questioning was over, it felt like most of the interview had already taken place. To her surprise, Wendell Finley only had one question before agreeing to talk. *Would his interview be the main feature of that week's program?* Pompous ass, she thought.

The CEO of the world's third largest oil company agreed to meet with her; and much sooner than she had anticipated. When his assistant informed Hildahl that Mr. Finley would grant her two hours of his precious time the day after tomorrow—ten o'clock in the morning, sharp—she was completely stunned. Caught off-guard, the reporter asked for one more day to properly prepare, but was curtly informed that this was the only time the busy executive would be available for the next three to four months.

Hildahl couldn't wait three months, not even three weeks. The tragedy in Las Vegas was still fresh news—a week from now some other cataclysm would occupy the public's fascination. The old adage, *strike while the iron is hot,* was distinctly true in this case. But with only one day to prepare, she was afraid she couldn't pull off the type of interview she had planned for Finley.

Close to panic, she called Paul Haydon and asked him to assist in the preparations. Her assistants could obtain the mundane facts and data; but he was better able to unearth any information that could possibly link Finley and his company to the fuel cell industry. She'd need all available time to bring everything together and formulate the questions that would hopefully cause the powerful oil executive to incriminate himself.

When Paul Haydon arrived at her office the reporter again thanked him for his help.

"Mary, you know I'll be happy to help," he said dismissively. "As a matter of fact, I've already put together scattered facts about several transactions I think will help in your line of questioning. Phrased properly, and with a little luck, they'll catch him off guard." He threw a folder on her desk.

Hildahl looked down at the folder and smiled. The fact that he was one step ahead of her didn't come as a surprise. "What would I do without you," she said with sincere warmth. Their eyes met and suddenly there was an awkwardness between them; a brief instance where they were drawn together by suppressed desire, an anguished yearning that turned into silent mourning for what could never be.

Reluctantly, she acted first; sheepishly averting her eyes from him she stepped over to her desk. As she passed by him, it took every ounce of self control Paul Haydon had not to reach out, grab her arm and pull her to him. Looking down at the top of her desk she pretended to straighten several stacks of papers.

Haydon took a small, tentative step toward her. "Ma—"

"Any luck finding McChaffee?" she quickly blurted out, turning to face him. Her eyes begging him not to say what they were both thinking...and feeling.

Haggerty stopped; a small, sad smile coming to his face. "I'm afraid not," he replied solemnly. "Several stolen cars have been reported, including the car they abducted McChaffee in. But no abandoned cars have been found that are similar to it." He sighed. "As much as I hate to say it, I think we have to write Mr. McChaffee off."

A distressing expression came over her face; she pursed her lips and shook her head. "The poor man," she said solemnly. She remained silent for a moment, as if reflecting, then looked at Haydon and said, "Paul, along with finding any links between ENDICORP and the fuel cell industry, if you have time I'd like you to dig up any dirt you can find on Finley himself."

"What purpose would that serve?"

"It's an insurance policy," she replied. "An old trick really—one we seldom use but like to have in our arsenal. We reporters insinuate…well, to be honest, threaten, to expose some nasty tidbit if we feel the interviewee is not being upfront. Usually works pretty good."

"Well…" Haydon grinned. "If it's dirty laundry you want, I've already found some."

The reporter's emerald eyes widened in anticipation. "*Really!* What?" she asked excitedly.

"In '71, shortly after graduating from Texas A&M, he raped two women. However, he was never convicted."

"Why not?" she asked in astonishment.

The private detective shrugged. "His father carried tremendous political clout. He apparently convinced the attorney general that it wasn't rape, but what we'd call date-rape today. In any case, his father paid a significant amount of hush-money to the girl's parents and they dropped the charges. Then, Finley senior quickly packed his son up and sent him into the Navy. I can only assume he wanted Wendell out of town and out of the public eye long enough to ensure the incident had blown over. Junior spent the next four years aboard the USS Cartwright as a signalman."

"How'd you find that out?" Hildahl asked in amazement.

"A simple records check; I have friends in the Oakland police department. I talked with one of the women. She's still upset with her parents for taking the money and keeping quiet, even though thanks to them she's never had to work a day in her life."

"What a pig!" she spit out in disgust. "Well, Paul, that will certainly be helpful, but please see what else you can find out on him. I'll need whatever else you can scrape up by tomorrow afternoon, five at the latest."

"When's the interview?"

"Friday morning; ten A.M. at his office. The network is flying me and my cameraman to Houston on the corporate jet."

Haydon gave her a quick nod. "If I find out anything else, Mary, you'll hear from me!"

Wendell Finley was thrilled that *Hour Report* called him and didn't think twice about agreeing to the interview when his secretary asked if he was interested. This was a wonderful opportunity for some free publicity. He'd always dreamed of running for governor and now with P3 behind him, he felt is was safe to do so. He was curious, though, how *Hour Report* got wind of his candidacy? He'd only made up his mind to run a few days ago and told just a handful of people about it at a cocktail party the other night. But telling one person who couldn't keep a secret was more than enough to start the rumor mill—especially in this town.

Now that the cat was out of the bag, he called up Theodore Kennelly, CEO of PETROCOMP. The "future governor," as Finley now liked to refer to himself, wanted to make sure both Kennelly and Kenneth Saxton, CEO of World Energy, were aware that he was running for public office. Finley knew both men held him in contempt, believing the only reason he was CEO of ENDICORP was because he inherited the company from his father. Though true, Finley was determined to show those arrogant sons-of-bitches from The Committee what he was capable of on his own. If he couldn't win the post on his own merit, he'd win it with his money. Either way, he was determined to be the next governor of Texas—those assholes could guess, but they'd never be completely sure how he pulled it off.

Not bothering with a salutation, the exasperated voice of Theodore Kennelly whispered, "Finley, we shouldn't be talking anymore. The agreement is over. We're back to being competitors."

"Come now, Ted. We went though a lot together," Finley said in a slightly condescending yet amiable voice.

"What is it you want?" Kennelly asked sharply.

"Want? Nothing really. I just called to tell you—and I'll be calling Saxton too—that I'm running for governor of Texas."

"Good for you," Kennelly replied indifferently, clearly not impressed.

Finley frowned. He didn't expect the CEO of PETROCOMP to be excited about the news, but he did expect Kennelly to be somewhat taken aback. Slighted by his apathetic response, the future governor decided to show him just how important he'd become. "I thought you might be interested in seeing me on TV. Tomorrow I'm being interviewed by *Hour Report.*"

"*WHAT?*" Kennelly blurted out apprehensively.

The CEO of ENDICORP mistook the tone of Kennelly's exclamation and proudly repeated, "I *said* I'm being interviewed by *Hour Report* tomorrow. "

"You *fuckin'* idiot!" Kennelly cried. "Cancel it!"

Finley gasped at the affront. Being chastised by those particular words turned him red with anger. "I will *not!*" he snapped. "Why the *hell* should I?"

Calmer, but still clearly agitated, Kennelly asked, "What do you think you're being interviewed for? Think, man!"

"Because I'm running for governor," Finley replied pugnaciously. "Why else would she want to talk to me?"

Kennelly sighed in exasperation. "Even *you* can't be that clueless! Finley, it hasn't been that long since…" he paused, hesitant to mention over the phone anything to do with the sabotage of Global Fuel Cell Technologies' exhibition vehicle. "Since the…incident that resolved our common problem. Follow me?"

The CEO of ENDICORP clearly knew what he was referring to, but because Finley considered P3 a success, he didn't believe a credible connection could be made between the incident in Las Vegas and the petroleum industry. Also, due to the denigration he was receiving at the hands of PETROCOMP's CEO, he didn't want to give Kennelly the satisfaction of caving into his demand.

"Yeah, I follow, Kennelly. But I don't think that topic will be brought up. And even if it is, so what? I'd just express my sympathies and move on to other issues."

The CEO of PETROCOMP attempted to reason with the arrogant son-of-a-bitch one more time. Trying his best to sound conciliatory he said, "Look, Wendell…why chance it? One slip of the tongue and you could arouse suspicion; could encourage them to reopen the investigation and dig deeper. They're tenacious bastards." He paused a moment then pleaded, "Wendell…for the love of God, cancel the interview."

Theodore Kennelly's appeal had no effect on Finley. "I'll let you know when the story airs," he said curtly, hanging up before Kennelly could get another word in. Wendell Finley then changed his mind; he wouldn't share the news with Kenneth Saxton.

An old, cantankerous security guard escorted Mary Hildahl and David Johnson, her cameraman, to Wendell Finley's executive secretary, an old, prune-faced woman who looked the reporter up and down and frowned in disapproval. She brought them to her boss's ornate and spacious office and asked them to wait for him there; he was in a conference that would end soon.

From the twenty-fifth floor of ENDICORP's corporate headquarters, his corner office had a marvelous view of the north and west sides of Houston. Experiencing the wonderful panorama was tarnished somewhat by the smell of stale cigar smoke, which seemed to emanate from the carpet and every piece of furniture in the room.

Hildahl followed her standard procedure when interviewing men; she wore a provocative, yet professional looking light blue dress. The outfit's hem was high enough to allow a generous view of her legs, made even more shapely by high heels, while also revealing a tantalizing amount of cleavage—something most men couldn't resist looking at.

She had recently heard a rumor that Katie Couric admired and tried to emulate her fashion sense—high praise indeed. Mary didn't particularly like dressing this way, but it gave her the upper hand when interviewing men. Consequently, she considered her wardrobe just another tool of her trade. She also took off her wedding ring; something she felt rather guilty doing and still intended to tell her husband about. However, she had yet to work up the courage to do so.

As David Johnson set up his equipment, Hildahl walked around the office and looked at the oil baron's paraphernalia. There was a considerable amount of it. She could usually get a good sense of what a person considered important by what they displayed in their office. From what she was seeing, Wendell Finley considered Wendell Finley important. There were pictures—lots of pictures. Of Finley with Jimmy Carter, of Finley with David Brinkley, of Finley with Ronald Reagan, of Finley with Peter Jennings, of Finley with George Bush—both junior and senior. Scattered about the room were numerous other pictures of Finley shaking hands with foreign dignitaries, famous actors and a few well-known authors she recognized. There were also pictures of Finley on oil rigs, Finley on snow skis, and Finley on horses. To her astonishment there wasn't a single picture of family—no wife, no children, not even a beloved pet for that matter. She hadn't even met the man yet, and already she didn't like him.

"I'm ready, Mary," her cameraman said, swinging camera two on its tripod and pointing it at one of the two chairs to be used for the interview. Hildahl wanted one camera on Finley at all times so she could later review his reactions to her questions. The other camera would be trained on her. If asked why two cameras, she'd tell the CEO of ENDICORP that the film from both cameras would be edited later to condense the interview for airing, and to ensure they use only the best shots of him.

Hildahl nodded and walked to the door. She signaled the executive secretary that they were ready, but the sour old woman gruffly told her to relax. Mr. Finley was still in conference. She was sure he'd be there as soon as he could.

Grimacing, the reporter stepped back in the office and began to make small-talk with her cameraman. She also took the time to review her questions, musing over whether or not they'd cause him to tip his hand. She was rarely nervous before an interview, but she was now.

Twenty minutes later Wendell Finley made his triumphant appearance. Hildahl thought he entered his office like a conquering hero strutting before a wild throng of cheering admirers. He was dressed impeccably; dark blue suit, silk tie and patent leather shoes. He even wore cufflinks—something she hadn't seen a man wear since her wedding. His cologne was powerful; it entered the room before he did. Like her husband, he used far too much. Blending with her perfume and the stench of stale cigars, the office was now a strange bouquet of smells.

"I'm sorry to have kept you waiting, Ms. Hildahl," he said sincerely, extending a pudgy hand. His big smile seemed forced, although Hildahl sensed that he was genuinely pleased to see her. It wasn't hard to tell when the person she was about to interview wasn't exactly thrilled to see her.

She took his hand and cringed internally; it was cold and clammy. "Thank you so much for agreeing to the interview, Mr. Finley."

"Please, call me Wendell."

The reporter smiled. "I'll be happy to off camera, but while we're taping it's more appropriate that I stick to the 'mister'." She turned and gestured to her cameraman. "This is David Johnson; he'll be working the cameras." The CEO looked at her colleague and gave him a curt nod, but didn't offer his hand. Johnson wasn't offended.

Hildahl walked over and took her seat; Finley followed. "Any questions before we get started, Wendell?" she asked while slowing crossing her legs. To protrude her breasts she slightly arched her back. Tight against her blouse, it was a sight no man could resist.

As intended, Finley's eyes instantly zeroed in on the cleavage that appeared to be struggling to erupt from the confines of the tight dress. The sight caused his talk with Theodore Kennelly to come to mind and arouse his suspicions. He was tempted to ask her what questions she would pose to him. But, so captivated was he by the beautiful reporter that he didn't want to appear nervous or unconfident. With difficulty, he tore his eyes away from her chest.

Mary Hildahl turned to her cameraman. "Dave, you ready?"

Johnson turned on the camera's bright lights. "Yep. We're rollin."

She shifted in her seat a little and turned back to face Finley. Dawning her warmest expression, she started the interview by saying, "Mr. Finley, thank you for being here today and agreeing to talk with us; it's quite an honor." With crossed legs and folded hands on his lap, looking every bit the successful corporate executive, Finley smiled and nodded affably. "Mr. Finley, ENDICORP has the unique distinction of not only being the third largest oil company in the world, but also privately held. Only PETROCOMP and World Energy have larger market shares." The mention of Kennelly's and Saxton's companies caused Finley to slightly wince. "To what do you attribute your company's success?"

Despite the mention of the other conspirators, the first question was encouraging. It left an opening to boast a little and perhaps steer the interview in the direction he wanted.

"That's an easy question for me to answer, Mary," Finley replied smugly. "Prudent management. Judicious management." He snapped the words out crisply while looking sternly at the camera. It was so practiced that Hildahl had to keep herself from rolling her eyes. Then, light-heartedly he continued. "I'd like to take full credit for my company's success, but I can't. As I'm sure you know, Mary, my company's assets pale in comparison to those of my two larger rivals. However, I'm able to compete because I'm surrounded by good people. That, of course, is crucial."

He leaned back in his chair and seemed to relax a little. Like a father lecturing to his son he added, "Anyone in a position of leadership, whether a chief executive officer, an army general, a president or even a governor for that matter, is only as good as the people advising him."

Hoping his answer would lead her to ask about his bid for governor, he was disappointed when she asked, "What do you see as the major obstacle to ENDI-CORP surpassing World Energy and PETROCOMP in annual revenue?"

He stared at her blankly for a moment, as if not comprehending the question, and then replied, "Environmental Regulations."

"How's that? Your competitors operate under the same set of rules you do, don't they?"

"Not necessarily, Mary," he said raising the palm of his hand to her. His reply was patient, even. "As you know, World Energy is a British conglomerate and operates under a different set of regulations—regulations that are much more business friendly. And PETROCOMP flourished during the years before any real environmental regulations were adopted. Or should I say, before those laws were actually enforced."

"But what difference would that make now, Mr. Finley, when so little of our oil is domestically produced?"

The executive's eyes darted down to catch a glimpse of her legs, then back up again. "It was really a matter of timing, Mary. ENDICORP was founded—just getting started—when those laws took effect. PETROCOMP had the good fortune of having been a mature, established company by that time. They acquired a tremendous amount of wealth during those years prior to the enforcement of environmental regulations, thus had plenty of capital to not only invest in new drilling technology, but…" he paused for a moment, trying to think how best to phrase his next statement. He wanted it to sting, yet sound partisan. "…also time to establish and develop beneficial relationships within what's now referred to as 'The Beltway'. That's the 495 loop around Washington, of course." After answering, he smiled demurely.

"You're referring to lobbyists, of course." Finley gave her a small nod. She smirked despite herself and asked with blatant skeptical sarcasm, "And…your company has no lobbyist in Washington D.C. Right?"

Finley pushed back against his chair and reversed his crossed legs; he was attempting to look at ease. "Well…I wouldn't go that far, Mary. Of course we do. But to this day, our relationships with influential lawmakers are, I regret to say, not as strong as those of our competitors—or those of many other industries…such as automotive or pharmaceutical.

"The point I'm making, Mary, is that moving forward, we can't rely on help from Washington—contrary to what most people like to believe."

"But your industry can," the reporter quickly shot back. "You just said your competitors have strong ties to influential lawmakers in Washington."

He gave her a wan smile. "Yes. *They* do. Pushing *their* agenda. We, ENDI-CORP, don't have that kind of influence. That's why leadership—strong, sound management is vital to the continued success, and growth of our company. It's the kind of leadership I hope to bring to the great state of Texas."

Again she didn't take the bait. Like a pit bull she hung on to what was becoming an annoying line of questioning. She glanced down at the yellow legal pad on her lap, wrote down a note and then asked, "Then you don't really consider your main competitors, PETROCOMP and World Energy, as an obstacle—a threat if you will—to your continued growth?"

"No. Not at all," he replied with a touch of irritation; his smile fading.

"What then *do* you consider a threat to the continued growth of ENDI-CORP?" Finley visibly stiffened; the question made him uncomfortable. She was heading in a direction that concerned him. Before he could answer she added, "Let me rephrase the question, Mr. Finley. Since the two largest oil companies don't concern you, what would you consider a threat to the petroleum industry as a whole?"

She noted with satisfaction the suspicious look he gave her; she had evidently struck a nerve. Finley cursed to himself. If she was dragging him into a discussion about fuel cells, that bastard Kennelly would be right. Having to admit he was wrong about the purpose of this interview, particularly to the arrogant CEO of PETROCOMP, was a humiliation Finley couldn't bear. He had to turn the conversation around.

He shifted uncomfortably in his seat and cleared his throat; it was becoming difficult for him to appear calm and composed. He breathed in deeply and replied, "Why, isn't it obvious, Mary? Political strife. Political instability and terrorism in Russia, the Middle East, the oil exporting countries of African, all threaten the supply of oil—particularly to the United States.

"South America, as a matter of fact, is *by far* the petroleum industry's biggest concern at the moment. There's talk of revolution in several exporting countries. And you're seeing these problems today—they're reflected in the price you're paying at the pump. You'd get the same answer from anyone in the industry." In a final push to turn the discussion back to his political ambitions he added, "That, Mary, is what keeps me up at night and why strong, competent leadership is so crucial. Particularly now. Not only in business, but also government. And I'm determined to provide that kind of leadership."

Hildahl struggled for a moment trying to understand the link between leadership and the supply of oil. But she quickly decided to let it go and not follow up—the last thing she wanted to talk about was his political aspirations. Besides, it was time to get to the real questions.

"That's not the kind of threat I was referring to, Mr. Finley. I'm sure you'd agree with me that there will always be political difficulties—particularly in third-world countries." Her resolute voice and expression made it clear to Finley that she had no intention of asking about his political future. She looked pointedly at him and he braced himself. "How does your industry plan on dealing with new energy producing technologies that threaten to replace fossil fuels such as oil and coal." She pretended to muse for a moment, tapping the end of her pencil against her pursed lips. She then pointed the pencil at him and added, "Let's take fuel cell technology as an example."

Wendell Finley stared at her blankly, as if completely at a loss for words. His mind began to race. Despite the persona he liked to project, he wasn't very good at thinking on his feet. Was she leading him into some kind of trap with regard to the Las Vegas incident? How could he avoid saying something that might be misinterpreted or sound incriminating? Damn the woman! He was betting that he could steer her away from the topic of fuel cells—and lost. He'd have to be extremely careful.

He had remained frozen in his vacant expression for so long that Hildahl was about to say something to prompt him. As she opened her mouth he squinted, shook his head and said, *"Fuel cells?"* as if the idea was preposterous; he mustn't have heard the question correctly.

She was somewhat caught off guard by his response; she was fully expecting him to just dismiss the idea out of hand. Instead, it appeared he was toying with her. "Why, yes…fuel cells," she replied with a touch of cynicism. "Surely you've heard of them?" she quipped, then regretted saying it. She could tell Finley wasn't amused by what she intended as a cute remark. She tried to recover by quickly saying, "Until recently, it appeared that fuel cells would be replacing gasoline-powered engines in just a matter of years. You can't possibly tell me that your industry ignored the potential of this technology to severely curtail the need for oil's main byproduct?"

Finley's expression turned incredulous. Dismissively he said, "I don't think the industry ever took fuel cells seriously."

"How could you not?" Hildahl retorted skeptically. "Global Fuel Cell Technologies was on the verge of mass producing a powertrain system that would eventually make gasoline obsolete. The majority of the oil ENDICORP produces or imports is refined into gasoline. If fuel cell powered cars were commercially successful, your company—all oil companies for that matter—would see a catastrophic drop in revenue."

Hildahl became concerned; ENDICORP's chief executive suddenly appeared relaxed. This wasn't good; it was imperative that she kept him on the defensive. Finley smiled warmly; all the tension in his body seemed to have evaporated. Gesturing with his hands he replied, "You hit the nail on the head, Mary. The key words are 'commercially successful', which fuel cells obviously aren't." He deliberated for a moment then added, "You can equate fuel cells to nuclear power. Because of its success in military applications—submarines, aircraft carriers and such—nuclear power was rushed to commercial use before it was ready. Consequently, to this day a majority of people consider nuclear power dangerous, even though it can be produced perfectly safe. Because of the high-profile accidents, Three Mile Island and in particular, Chernobyl, nuclear power got a bad rap that, in my opinion, it will never recover from. And that's a shame because nuclear power is a clean, safe and reliable source of energy.

"Now, look at what's happened to fuel cells—their potential cut short by a tragic accident that was no doubt caused by a zealous rush to market. Now, unfortunately, hydrogen's got a bad rap." Finley's steel gray eyes bored onto the reporter's. "Do you…see a pattern here, Mary?"

She couldn't reply—she was now the one at a loss for words. The pompous ass was now getting the better of her and she was starting to get angry.

On a roll, he continued. "Take solar power. Lots of hoopla in the '70's about its possibilities; and where is it today? Virtually non-existent. And it will remain that way until somebody figures out how to charge consumers for sunlight." He paused a brief moment to relish in Hildahl's body language. She was slouching a little in her chair with her arms tightly crossed over her chest. Her long, beautiful legs were still crossed but her foot was twirling about in a circular motion. She had a tight-lipped expression that clearly radiated resentment. Finley was pleased with himself; he was beating her at her own game.

"Oh!" he declared with sarcastic excitement. "And let's not forget about wind power! Practical, affordable, environmentally friendly, but it too has its drawbacks. A lot of generators are needed to produce a usable amount of electricity and worse, no matter how elegantly designed, the mills are an eyesore. I'm sure you've seen how they butcher a landscape. Nobody wants a wind farm in their backyard." He let out a long, pathetic sigh. "Just like those poor folks who've invested in these now debunked technologies, I'm afraid there're now a lot of disillusioned fuel cell investors out there."

Mary Hildahl swallowed hard. Finley made solid, factual points that couldn't easily be refuted. She remained silent for a long time, thinking how best to respond as the chief executive gazed upon her in an almost parental fashion, like a father waiting for his child to grasp a simple concept he'd just explained.

As she struggled with what to say, her frustration and anger with the direction of the interview grew; it was impeding her ability to think clearly. She had to push her hostile feelings aside, otherwise she wouldn't be able to turn the interview around—get Finley back against the ropes. And if she didn't do that, if she didn't get something from this man Paul Haydon could work with, she wouldn't be of any help to him. Worse yet, she thought, Terrance McChaffee—if indeed he was dead—will have died in vain.

Perhaps it was her aggravation that compelled her to rush ahead, but she decided to skip the rest of her questions and drive right to the heart of the matter. And given the direction this interview was going, she would clearly have to bait her next question. She straighten in her chair and composed herself. Looking Finley directly in the eye she said, "Mr. Finley, there have been…serious accusations from those within your industry. Accusations that some of the largest companies in your industry are conspiring to destroy fuel cell technology. To ensure it never makes it to market. Any truth to them?"

That question had the desired effect. A stunned expression came over the executive's face, followed a moment later by narrowed eyes that peered at the reporter with unbridled hostility. However, as quickly as the expressions came, they went and Finley appeared unperturbed. But there was no mistaking the anxiety the question caused him. His hands were again on his lap but she noticed that his right hand, covered by his left, was clenching into a fist.

His physical reaction to the question also jolted Mary Hildahl; it now appeared that McChaffee hadn't been lying. She never admitted it to Paul Haydon, but she not only questioned the information provided by the engineer, but also his motives. To her, the litmus test was getting a person in front of a camera. Right or wrong, she established a person's credibility and honesty by how they reacted during an interview with the camera rolling. She had been looking forward to interviewing McChaffee, but she'd never got the chance. She now had no choice but to believe that McChaffee had been on the up and up. Though, now she realized, the fact that he'd been abducted should've been proof enough for her.

The accusation caused Wendell Finley's stomach to spasm. Completely stunned, his mind raced to formulate an answer. He pulled himself together, relaxing his right hand and clasping them together on his lap. He forced himself to smile. "Well, that certainly is a loaded question," he replied with practiced jocularity. "Come on, Mary. I mean…who in their right mind wants more competition? However, I can't honestly say that I'm sorry fuel cells will never become a viable source of energy."

"That doesn't answer the question, Mr. Finley," the reporter said ingenuously. "To avoid the collapse of the petroleum industry as we know it today, isn't it true that certain people within the industry wanted to destroy any chance for fuel cells to become commercially successful? In particular, prevent them from replacing the internal combustion engine?"

Startled, Finley's head snapped back abruptly, as if he was punched square in the nose; he momentary glanced away to avoid eye contact with the reporter. He seemed to flush slightly, but Hildahl couldn't be sure. She noticed his left hand slowly grasping the chair's arm. He began to squeeze; so hard in fact that his knuckles turned white. He brought a fist to his mouth and coughed lightly, then turned back to her. She could clearly hear the agitation in his voice when he replied, "I sincerely doubt that fuel cell-powered vehicles would spell the end of the oil industry. Oil, as I'm sure you know, is used for many more products than just gasoline."

"Of course it is," Hildahl shot back instantly. "But the vast majority of crude oil," she glanced down at her notes, "eighty-four percent in fact, is refined into gasoline. No industry could survive that big of a drop in revenue. Not long after fuel cells enter the market—maybe ten, fifteen years, the estimated time needed for fuel cells to replace most of the gasoline engines on the road—there will undoubtedly be only a few oil companies left standing. And those that are will be nothing in comparison to their former glory."

Finley grimaced. With a wave of his hand he said, "Mary, it's all academic now anyway. It's a proven fact that fuel cells aren't safe."

Tenaciously, the reporter continued to push. "But you can't deny that fuel cells would devastate your industry?"

Finley frowned sourly. He rolled his eyes, sighed deeply and replied as calmly as he could, "They'd have a detrimental impact, yes."

With that admission she decided it was time to ask the question that she prayed would cause him to slip and give at least a tacit indication of the culpability of both himself and his industry. She fixed an icy stare on the executive and asked, "Mr. Finley, I have it on very good authority that it's not just accusation; that there *is* an actual plot within the petroleum industry to discredit fuel cell technology in the eyes of the public—to ensure it never gets a foothold in the market. Is ENDICORP in any way part of this…conspiracy?"

Completely shocked by the question as well as the impudence of this reporter, Wendell Finley's eyes instantly widened—Hildahl had never seen so much white in eyeballs before. Despite himself, he let out an audible gasp. He couldn't believe she, or anyone would address him in such an insolent manner. But her impertinence aside, it was really the question that completely unnerved him, and he knew it. His grip tightened; his fingernails raked the arms of the chair and he pushed himself back, as if trying to put as much distance as he could between himself and the reporter. *My God! I don't believe this,* he thought in horror. *Haggerty! That son-of-a-bitch! He lied! The bastard lied! Somehow word of the plot leaked.* There could be no other explanation for her allegation.

Suddenly the lights were terribly hot and tiny beads of perspiration began to appear on his forehead. Aware of his reaction he tried to appear unperturbed, even though it was too late for that. Planting both feet firmly on the floor he loosened his grip on the chair's arms and leaned forward slightly. He began to move his mouth but to his surprise, nothing came out.

His reaction and the astounded look on his face left no doubt in Hildahl's mind that she hit pay dirt. As far as she was concerned, this was all the proof she needed to confirm that she and Paul Haydon were on the right track. She now had the courage to deliver the final blow. Before he could get hold of himself and formulate a coherent response she added, "As a matter of fact, Mr. Finley, this same source mentioned you specifically—by name."

The CEO of ENDICORP began to burn red with anger. The sweat on his brow was prominent now and Hildahl noticed his hands begin to tremble. He flung his head from the reporter to the cameraman. Jumping to his feet he roared, *"Turn off the goddamn cameras! This interview is over!"*

Johnson lifted his head from the eyepiece. Casually he said, *"Mary?"*

Hildahl hesitated. Emotionless, she looked up at Finley, who was gazing at her with a murderous expression. A stare-down lasted several moments; the room was deathly silent. She then frowned, turned to her cameraman and let out a weary sigh. "Go ahead, Dave. Shut it down." He quickly complied and began to break down the equipment.

In a tremulous voice Finley snapped, "You've got your nerve young lady; waltzing in here and accusing me of some kind of scheme." In his anger he added, "I suppose you think *I* had something to do with the explosion in Las Vegas?" Any pretext of cordiality was gone from both his voice and manner.

Although she knew it was meant as a rhetorical question, she couldn't stop herself from coolly saying, "The thought had crossed my mind, yes."

Finley scowled. "Who fed you this line of shit?"

"I can't reveal my sources," she replied matter-of-factly, rising up out of her chair.

"Of course not," he sneered sarcastically. "It's a bunch of bullshit, Ms. Hildahl. I can assure you of that. And should you and *Hour Report* try and imply that I, that ENDICORP had anything to do with this so-called conspiracy or the tragedy in Las Vegas, I'll bring the entire might of not only my company, but of my entire industry down on you and your network. I'll sue your ass into the stone age!"

Hildahl remained composed, although his threat did unnerve her. She wasn't naïve enough to think for a minute that he wouldn't follow through on it. As David Johnson continued to break down the equipment, the two stood and stared defiantly at each other.

"You disappoint me, Ms. Hildahl," Finley finally said, breaking the silence between them. "I would've thought you were more intelligent than to fall for such a bogus story."

The insult didn't faze her. With fortitude she replied, "I'm convinced it's not spurious, Mr. Finley," then somberly added, "In fact, I'm quite certain a man is dead because of what he divulged to me."

Wendell Finley said nothing for a few moments; he just looked at her menacingly. Mary Hildahl was beginning to feel unsettled by the silence when he coarsely said, "I'm withdrawing my permission to air the interview, obviously. As far as I'm concerned, our little chat never took place. You can burn the tape for all I care."

"I still intend to air it, Mr. Finley," she replied defiantly. "You and your company will be central to my story."

"Like I said, Ms. Hildahl," Finley sneered, "should you slander me or my company, I'll file suit against both you and *Hour Report* the likes of which the media has never seen."

"I'll let our lawyers worry about that, Mr. Finley." Offering her hand she added, "Thank you for your time, Mr. Finley. This had been a very…informative interview. As soon as it's determined when this story will air, I'll have my assistant inform your office."

The CEO of ENDICORP looked repulsively at her extended hand for a moment. Then, breaking into a smirk—as if implying he knew damn well she wouldn't have the balls to follow through on her pledge to air the interview—shook it.

The moment she and her cameraman left his office he picked up the phone and began to dial furiously.

CHAPTER 22

▼

Paul Haydon watched the interview with Wendell Finley a second time. When it finished Mary Hildahl said, "I'm absolutely convinced he's one of the conspirators."

Still looking at the television screen the private investigator nodded. He then turned toward the reporter. "What we need now, Mary, is evidence. One solid piece is all it would take to convince the FBI to start crawling up Finley's ass."

"What about the P3 document itself?"

Haydon shook his head. "I thought about that, but they'd question its authenticity. In court, a good defense attorney would tear it to shreds. Besides, it doesn't mention Finley or his company, remember?"

Hildahl was leaning against the front of her desk with her arms crossed over her chest. She looked down at the floor and grimaced. "Then where do you suggest we look for it?"

Haydon sucked in his bottom lip, thought for a moment, and then replied, "That's a good question. I'll probably start with the phone logs of Finley's private number—if I can get my hands on them; see who he's been calling. If nothing else, that should lead us to whoever else is involved." He stood up and walked to the office door. Grabbing the doorknob he turned to her and asked, "When do you intend to air the interview?"

"The week after next. Thursday the 23rd."

"Your producer isn't worried that Finley will sue the network?"

"I haven't discussed the interview with Buddy yet," she said flatly. "The threat of a suit might spook him." She shrugged. "But in the end, I think he'll let it air. We get threatened with lawsuits all the time. It's nothing new."

"Well, if we've got until the 23rd, that will give us a little more time to find the evidence."

Two days later The Committee met in emergency session. Laurence Haggerty sat nervously at the end of the long table, three hostile faces glaring at him. He felt like he did years ago when he was in the Army Reserve. He was on the last day of his two weeks active duty and was caught borrowing his unit's truck to haul five kegs of beer to a friend's apartment for a party that night. He was grilled by his commanding officer, executive officer and the staff duty officer who needed the truck that day for legitimate business—business that never got done. Lieutenant Haggerty got off with a non-punitive letter of reprimand. He wished he'd be so lucky today.

"How the *hell* did this happen, Haggerty?" the CEO of World Energy demanded. Kenneth Saxton, normally composed and even-tempered, was beside himself. In an effort to calm their nerves, all three men had drinks in front of them; very unusual before a meeting—especially one that started at nine in the morning. It didn't escape Haggerty that nothing was offered to him, not even coffee. He looked longingly at the drinks—thinking what he wouldn't give for a straight Scotch right now.

The owner of Noble Consultants swallowed hard, grimaced and said, "There, uh…" he began to nervously rub his hands together, and then tucked them between his legs. "There was a small…slip."

"It doesn't appear very fucking small to us!" Theodore Kennelly growled.

"I'd demand my money back," Wendell Finley began to say brusquely, then shouted, *"except it won't do me any fuckin' good in prison!"*

"Why didn't you tell us about the breech?" Saxton asked, a little calmer now.

Haggerty shook his head, and then replied almost pleadingly, "It was such a *minor* slip that I didn't think it could, or would, amount to anything."

The three members of The Committee looked at each other acrimoniously, but said nothing. The CEO of PETROCORP stood and walked to the window, drink in hand. All eyes were on him, expecting him to say something. In the silence, Laurence Haggerty's mind wandered to his one-way ticket to Brazil.

Theodore Kennelly took a sip of his drink, his eyes staring out the window at the London skyline. He pursed his lips, turned to the others and evenly declared, "We're fucked."

Haggerty's mouth went dry and he sank a little in his chair. He began to debate with himself whether now was the time to tell his three clients what he'd ordered Nick Ragosta to do. But he decided not to—simply because of what he knew Kennelly was about to say.

"Now that the media has caught wind of this," Kennelly said dejectedly, walking back to his chair, "there's no suppressing it."

To hell with it, Haggerty thought. Composing himself, he folded his hands and placed them on top of the table before him. "The media *doesn't* have hold of it yet, Mr. Kennelly. Only *Hour Report*." He paused a moment to let his words sink in. "Mary Hildahl is not going to blow her exclusive by sharing it with her colleagues. This situation will only get out of hand if *Hour Report* actually airs the story—which I assure you, it will not."

Wendell Finley slammed his glass down on the table, Vodka and ice landed around his shaking hand. ***"I've had enough of your empty assurances, Haggerty!"***

As usual, the CEO of World Energy was the voice of reason. Given his earlier state of mind, Haggerty was both amazed and relieved. Placing a hand on Finley's arm, Kenneth Saxton soothingly said, "Wendell, we must give Mr. Haggerty the opportunity to correct his mistake." He slowly turned his head to look at Haggerty while ominously saying, "Which I truly hope will be his last." He took a sip of his straight Brandy then asked, "How do you plan on preventing the airing of this program and making this situation go away?"

Haggerty took in a deep breath, his eyes darting between the three men at the other end of the table. He quickly pursed his lips then said, "Extortion. We'll ensure she understands that she'll face dire personal consequences should she go through with the story."

A disgusted look came across Finley's face. "Why don't you just kill the bitch," he spit out.

"Because we *need* her," Haggerty immediately snapped. "We need her to make sure the story not only dies, but remains dead. The last thing we need is a high-profile murder investigation." He mused for a few seconds then added, "And keep in mind she has a cameraman. He needs to be handled also…though I'm not sure how much he actually knows."

"Christ!" Kennelly cried out in trepidation, running his hands over his face.

Haggerty glanced at him, ignoring the outcry. "Gentlemen," he said in a firm voice that again found its confidence, "you're forgetting that my ass is on the line here too. It's in *my* best interest to correct this situation immediately—and I will." The owner of Noble Consultants stared intensely at each of his clients in turn then concluded the meeting by saying, "By this time next week, I guarantee you this problem will be resolved and the book on P3 closed…forever."

She threw three twenty-dollar bills at the driver and was out the door before the taxi could come to a stop. Leaping from the car, she ran quickly through the doors of the emergency room; tears mixed with mascara were cascading down her cheeks, leaving long, dark streaks against her lightly freckled alabaster skin.

She still was feeling unjustified rage toward the cab driver; no matter how much she pushed the man to go faster, it wasn't fast enough—though in a small, detached portion of her mind she knew he was doing the best he possibly could. Regardless, the drive from the studio to the suburban hospital was the longest of her life.

Her panicked mind was racing in so many directions it was impossible for her to think coherently. She ran toward the reception desk with two men behind it. Disorientated, she briefly wondered why doctors would act as receptionists. The two male nurses turned to look at the approaching woman, their faces slowly registering recognition.

"My daughter, sons, hus, hus, husband!" she stammered, looking from man to man.

The young nurses recognized her frantic state of mind—they'd seen it a hundred times. "Hildahl, right?" the tall one with thick, flaxen hair asked.

"Yes," she replied breathlessly, rapidly nodding her head. Still staring apprehensively at the young men, she sniffled and used her sleeve to wipe her nose.

"I'll take her," the short, burly nurse said to his partner. It was an act of kindness the two extended to all worried family members when they worked the desk. Through experience they'd come to learn that half the time the hysterical people couldn't absorb the simple directions they'd give.

She followed the husky young man down a hall, around two corners and into a large, brightly lit room that smelled of disinfectant and was filled with all kinds of medical instruments. Standing at the other side of the room was an older woman dressed in a blue nurse's jumper; she was cradling a bundle in her arms. Mary Hildahl gasped and dashed up to the woman. Seeing Lauren's eyes closed and no movement from her tiny body, Mary froze in terror. She looked to the nurse with pleading eyes; the woman smiled reassuringly and said the little girl was fine, she was only sleeping. The words brought another rush of tears—tears of relief. She took her daughter in her arms and again gazed down at her, now noticing a large, ugly bruise on her forehead.

She turned to see Markie and Blake lying together on a bed. They too were asleep.

"We gave them a sedative," the nurse said softly. "Both boys were terrified when we tried to give them a local anesthetic and stitch their wounds. Normally, we try to avoid giving children sedatives. Even though we wrapped them up, they squirmed so much that sutures were impossible. The doctor decided they had to be calmed down." She turned from Mary to look at the sleeping boys and added, "They're going to be okay, though." Their mother solemnly nodded.

With Lauren still in her arms, Mary spun around to find her husband. She initially looked right past him—not recognizing the man in traction two beds down from where she was standing. "Your husband got the worse of it I'm afraid, Mrs. Hildahl," the nurse said. "A concussion, multiple fractures to his left leg and arm and some internal bleeding. The doctor will go over everything with you when he gets back."

Mary saw that her husband's left leg and arm was suspended by slings, he also had a thick bandage around his head. Were it not for the feel of Lauren in her arms, she would have thought she was in a bad dream. Everything seemed surreal.

Seeing his wife, Kevin Hildahl gave her a weak smile. She quickly walked over to him. "Oh…honey!" she said, fighting to hold back more tears. "Are you alright?"

Glancing at his limbs hung up in traction, he found the question hilarious and tried to laugh, but instead winced in pain. The nurse failed to mention that he also had three broken ribs. "I've been banged up worse than this," he replied. His wife knew that he wasn't making a cavalier comment to minimize his condition. He had been injured worse than this—several times.

They had been dating for about a month when he told her about his love for motor-cross racing. He was an avid racer and ranked one of the best in the sport. When he'd proposed to her about a year and a half later, she would only agree to marry him if he quit riding his motorcycle competitively. In their year-and-a-half courtship, he'd been hurt three times—once seriously. He loved racing and occasionally teased her that it was a tough decision to make.

She carefully sat down on the edge of his bed. The nurse came and took Lauren from Mary, who gave the woman a weak smile and nod of appreciation. She sniffled, wiped her eyes and then asked her husband, "What happened?"

Kevin Hildahl frowned bitterly and rocked his head back and forth several times on the pillow. "I…I don't know," he replied, sounding perplexed. "The truck, it…it came out of nowhere! Hit me broadside. And after he hit, he…he just kept going—actually speeded up!" He stared incredulously at his wife for a moment, as if asking her to confirm the implausibility of what he was telling her, then continued. "He pushed us to the side of the road. The wheels hit the curb and the van began to roll over from the momentum. But thankfully, a tree stopped us from rolling over completely." His wife said nothing; her red, puffy eyes just gazed at him despondently.

He turned his head away from her and stared at the ceiling. She could now hear a foreign emotion in her husband's voice—vulnerability. Emotionally, Kevin had always been strong and not one to expose his feelings. She was almost traumatized to hear him now. "I was pinned, Mary! The left side of the van was completely crushed—caved in. I was pinned and couldn't reach the kids. *Couldn't reach them!*" His inability to protect and aid his children during a time of danger filled him with fury and his eyes began to well up in rage. But he fought back the tears and calmed himself. "Hell...I didn't even know I'd broken anything until they cut me out of the van."

He paused a moment then continued; his voice now heated. "The van was crushed—fuckin' glass everywhere. The firemen had to cut us out. It took them over two hours to get all four of us out. In the meantime the boys were scared half to death." He looked at her angrily. "I still can't believe it, Mary; the son-of-a-bitch just kept going after he hit us!" He shook his head. "It had to be deliberate. Had to be! But...but *why?*"

"Who hit you? Who was the guy?" his wife asked.

"Wish I knew! I'd never seen the guy before. After the tree stopped our roll, he got out of the Hummer and—this is what really pisses me off—looked at me for a second. I...I could've sworn he smiled. Then the bastard got back in his Hummer and sped off!"

Mary Hildahl's mother offered to watch the children for the next couple of days; a Godsend that would allow Mary time to pull herself back together. During the drive home she just sat and silently looked out the window at the passing darkness; a blackness that paled in comparison to her mood. She was startled when the cab driver announced they'd reached her house.

She wanted to tell him so badly, but couldn't—not yet, anyway. The guilt of withholding from her husband what she suspected was tearing away at her conscience; made worse by the fact that she'd call and tell Paul Haydon as soon as she got home. She tried to ease her guilty conscience by telling herself she'd inform Kevin as soon as he got out of the hospital—there's no sense in getting him worked up, is there? It might only delay his recovery. But her promised intention to herself did little to help elevate her guilt.

The accident *was* intentional. From Kevin's account there was little doubt in her mind about that and it didn't take long for the name *Nick* to come to mind.

This was the man after Terrance McChaffee; the man who undoubtedly cold-cocked Paul Haydon and snatched the hapless engineer on his way to her studio that morning. And it would be naïve to think that this Nick didn't get whatever information he wanted out of McChaffee, including everything he told the investigative reporter from *Hour Report*. Desperate to suppress news of the conspiracy, it only made sense that Nick would be after her.

A cold chill ran down her spine and suddenly she became terrified. If she was correct, it was obvious that this man would stop at nothing to silence her. He must have thought she was in the van. If he was a professional—which he clearly was—he'd know she had small children; he'd know everything about her. The fact that her kids might be in the van with her clearly didn't deter him. *My God, what kind of monster was he?*

Hildahl thought hard about going to the police but decided against it. They were investigating the accident of course, for all the good it would do them. And what could she tell them anyway? All she had was her theory and the name Nick? Of course, there was always the possibility that it wasn't Nick—but rather just some nut in a Hummer that hit their van. She was sure Paul Haydon, who had learned the hard way how this Nick operated, could protect her until the story aired.

Perhaps the biggest reason she decided to leave the police out of it for now was the fact that if she went to them, she ran the risk of the story leaking; and a leaked story wouldn't have the desired impact she wanted. She knew it was terribly egotistical, but she still had to consider her career. She wanted both her audience and her network's executives to experience the full impact of her report on the fuel cell conspiracy.

The decision shamed her. She cursed her goddamn job and the devotion she had to it. She was protecting a story—possibly at the cost of her family's safety. What kind of person was her profession turning her into?

She paid the driver, and then started walking up the long stretch of sidewalk to the front door of her house. She stopped halfway to dig her keys out of her purse and noticed how dark and deathly quiet the neighborhood was—but that wasn't unusual for this time of night. The only sound she heard was a dog barking in the distance.

They lived in an exceptionally affluent neighborhood and her nearest neighbor was over a quarter mile away. They spent an extraordinary amount of money to live here, but it was more out of necessity than desire. Due to her notoriety, they needed a gated community if they were to enjoy any amount of privacy.

Finding her keys she picked out the one for the front door and inserted it into the lock. *Damn that Kevin,* she thought with no malice. *He forgot to lock the door again!* She stepped into the darkened house, closed the door and turned on the hallway light. She began walking down the hall; her footsteps seemed to echo thunderously through the large, deserted house. Suddenly she stopped. *"What the hell?"* she whispered to herself. She smelled cigarette smoke—neither she nor her husband smoked. Fear began to well up inside her and she tightened her grip on her purse. She nervously looked around the dark, cavernous dwelling; amazed at how something so familiar, like your own house, can seem so ominous when you're alone and full of anxiety. Suddenly she wished she had agreed to let her husband get that big, malicious looking dog he so desperately wanted.

Then, the tension in her body slackened as she remembered Constance, their housekeeper. She smoked. Mary had scolded her several times about smoking in the house, but occasionally, when alone, she'd sneak one. She laughed at her own paranoia and started walking again. She'd give Constance hell the next time she saw her. But she only took a few steps before stopping again. The smell was stronger now. It didn't seem like residual cigarette smoke she was smelling.

She looked to her left at the door to the study; the odor seemed to be coming from that room. She reached for the door knob, hesitated for a moment, then opened the door and stepped into the darkened room. She was about to reach for the light switch when she saw a ghostly amber glow move in the darkness at the other end of the room. The apparition shocked her and she gasped in fright, dropping her purse as her hands flew up to cover her gaping mouth. Instinctively, she took a step backwards. The high, narrow heel of her shoe caught on the thick carpeting and she stumbled, falling against the study's door and slamming it shut.

The lamps flicked on, illuminating the room in a soft, yellowish-white glow. Leaning against the study door, Mary Hildahl saw a man dropping his arm from the room's other light-switch. He was sitting in her husband's leather recliner with his legs crossed looking quite at home. He was casually smoking a cigarette and staring at her with a malevolent grin. She let out a piercing scream. The intruder didn't seem the least bit concerned by her outburst. He just took another drag of his cigarette and watched her cry out indifferently.

When the man didn't appear to be making a move toward her she stopped screaming. Still leaning against the study's door, she slowly pushed herself off it and stood. Her knees felt weak, and she had to struggle to keep from collapsing. Her eyes never left the intruder, her stare slowly intensifying in trepidation. Though frozen in horror, she surprised herself by feeling a twinge of curiosity that somehow wormed its way through the overwhelming sensation of terror engulfing her.

"That's much better," the man said in a tranquil, almost soothing voice. "I do so hate to hear women scream." Slowly, he brought the cigarette back to his mouth, his cold, dark eyes locked on hers. His head cocked back, he took a long, slow drag as his eyes continued to scrutinize her. He blew the smoke out of his mouth then said, "I hope you don't mind my dropping in, Mary. I was in the neighborhood, the door was unlocked so I thought (he shrugged)...what the hell! I'll invite myself in." He flashed a winning smile, nauseating Mary. "I also helped myself to a beer." He lifted up a bottle and tilted it toward her in way of salute. "I must say, your husband has excellent taste in beer. I love Sam Adams." He brought the bottle to his mouth and drained it.

Still looking quite at home in her husband's recliner the intruder twisted toward the end table beside the chair, put down the bottle and crushed out his cigarette, taking his eyes off Mary for the first time. "I apologize," he said, sounding almost sincere. "I looked all over for an ashtray but couldn't find one. I just took a saucer from your cupboard." He watched the cigarette crumble underneath his fingers.

The man confused Mary. He was so calm, so relaxed, it made her predicament almost surreal, as if she were caught in a bad dream from which she couldn't wake. She would've thought a person breaking into someone else's house would at least show a small amount of apprehension? His composure was uncanny.

Her hands were trembling slightly, so she hid them behind her, laying them flat against the door. She was still struggling to grasp what was happening to her, but the reality of the situation was becoming painfully clear. How could so many horrible things happen in just one day? Her world was turning upside down.

"I take it you folks don't smoke," he continued casually, as if he was their next door neighbor visiting over coffee. He turned back to Mary and crossed his legs in the other direction. "Good for you—it's a nasty habit." He paused for a brief second and stared callously at the terrified woman. Then, with a smirk he continued. "Constance here," he gestured with a tilt of his head to the corner of the room. Mary saw her housekeeper sitting in a dark corner, partially hidden by the sofa. She was tied and gagged and her wide eyes were wild with fear. "...suggested I use a saucer for an ashtray. But as you can see, it's a poor substitute. I'm afraid I got some ashes on your carpet. I hope you'll forgive me."

Mary Hildahl's mind was racing from one incoherent thought to another. Her eyes darted back and forth several times between her housekeeper and the intruder. The trembling in her hands was starting to move through her entire body. She tried to suppress it. "Wh…wh…who are you?" she finally managed to mumble feebly. But something told her she already knew who he was.

"Come now, Mary," the man replied patronizingly. "I think you know who I am. Surely your friend Terrance McChaffee must have mentioned me? After all, we were such good buddies."

"Nick!" she declared mellifluously in terrified conformation; the overtone of fear in her voice clearly amusing the assassin.

"See, you *do* know me!" Nick Ragosta exclaimed mockingly. "I'm touched. I'll confess, I've always wanted to meet you, Mary. You're one of my favorite T.V. personalities you know. Could I get your autograph?"

I've got to get out of here! Mary thought. *But how? Where?* She then decided that if she could get out of the house, she could outrun him. She was in great shape for a thirty-nine-year-old woman and if she kicked off her high-heels, she was sure she could lose him in the dark neighborhood. This is where all those years of jogging would pay off. Once she lost him, she could go to a neighbor's house and call the police.

Ragosta gestured congenially to the couch across from him. "Mary, won't you sit down? We need to have a little chat."

She looked from the assassin to the doorknob beside her. As quickly as she could, she pulled her arms out from behind her and reached for the doorknob—jumping back in astonishment as the knob exploded and disappeared inches from her hand. Mouth agape, she turned to Ragosta and saw he had a smoking gun in his hand. And in an instant, his expression turned from one of cordiality to furious rage; his black eyes burning with murderous intent. Incredibly, he had managed to shoot off the doorknob before she could reach it. She couldn't help but be impressed by his speed and accuracy.

Still appearing at ease in her husband's recliner, legs crossed, he kept his enraged eyes on her as he twisted the silencer off the pistol. He blew on it and put it back on the barrel of the weapon. "Hopefully, I won't need to use this again," he said evenly. He returned the pistol to the holster beneath his coat.

Mary again stared in awe at the shattered doorknob. It was only then that she felt the stinging in her left hand. Looking down at it she saw that it was bleeding—two punctures wounds in her palm and a large gash on her index finger. When the doorknob exploded, several small pieces of shattered metal lodged in her hand.

"Again…Mary, I invite you to join me." The overtone of impatience in his voice made clear she'd better not delay in complying. She slowly walked to the couch. As she sat down, she gave her housekeeper what she hoped was a comfort-

ing look. Constance was trembling and whimpering now; the gunshot eradicating the last traces of composure she still possessed. Her big brown eyes, filled with terror, glistened from the welling of tears that began to cascade down her cheeks.

Noticing her hand Ragosta asked, "Do you have a first aid kit?" He took her hand; while studying it he said, "I'm sorry about this. I'd hoped that I wouldn't be forced into harming you." It wasn't an empty statement. To her surprise, she noticed a trace of honesty and genuine compassion in his voice.

She stared at him in confusion. Realizing she was looking him in the eye, she quickly glanced down at her hand and said, "Ahhh…first aid kit. Yeah, we've got one in the kitchen."

The assassin stood up and walked over to the door, sticking his finger in the hole where the doorknob used to be. With little effort he yanked open the study's door and gestured for her to leave. He followed her to the kitchen. When she reached for the door of the cabinet Ragosta stopped her, seizing her wrist. He opened the door himself and took down the first aid kit. They returned to the study.

"Give me your hand," he demanded.

Hildahl shook her head. "No, I'll take—"

"Give me your fuckin' hand!" he said irritably, reaching over and roughly pulling her hand toward him. She offered no resistance. The antipathy she was feeling was like nothing she had ever experienced before. Watching him tend to her hand and feeling his fingers upon her flesh was repulsive, as if she was being forced to lie next to a rotting corpse. Her face hardened with disgust.

He was concentrating on her hand; dabbing away at the blood with his handkerchief. By the way he was examining her wounds it was clear he knew what he was doing. Still fixated on her hand he casually asked without looking up at her, "So…did you get my little message this afternoon?"

It took a moment for the question to sink in. When it did, her face filled with rage and she jerked her hand away. ***"YOU'RE RESPONSIBLE FOR THE ACCIDENT!"*** she roared.

The assassin looked at her with a calm callousness; he reached over and slowly took her hand back. She tried to draw her arm back but he was far too strong, and he continued to pull her hand toward him despite her resistance. Realizing the futility of her struggle she gave in.

"Yes. I was the one driving the car that hit your husband," he replied indifferently.

"My children were in the car, you bastard!" Again, she tried to escape his grip, but failed. She decided it was no use trying to resist and let her arm go limp.

Ragosta appeared unmoved by her heated retort. Still holding her hand in one of his, he dug through the first aid kit and produced a tweezers. He began to probe one of the puncture wounds in her palm. She winced in pain. Pulling out a small piece of metal and examining it he said, "I assure you, Mary, your children were in no danger." Intensely looking at her hand again, he began to probe the second wound. "I trust you understand why I did it?"

"I think I have a pretty good idea," Mary replied tersely.

"Humor me. Why would that be?"

"You want me to drop the fuel cell story."

"Very…" he pulled out the second piece of metal; Mary let out a sharp gasp. "Good. But…" he dropped the small piece of shrapnel on his lap, then looked up at her. "I don't necessarily want you to drop the entire story. Are you up to date on your Tetneous shots?" He began to look at her finger. "I think you'll need stitches for this."

Ignoring his medical opinion she gave him a questioning look. "*What?* I don't understand."

Dabbing the blood away from her finger he replied, "I *want* you to do the story on fuel cells, Mary. But I only want you to report on how dangerous they are. How—because of their fuel source—they will *never* be a viable source of energy or means for powering cars. The incident in Las Vegas clearly proved that—don't you think?"

Carefully, almost tenderly, Nick Ragosta began to bandage her hand. The kindness he'd shown in caring for her wound stunned and confused her even more. For a moment she couldn't think of how to respond.

Since first learning of the conspiracy, Mary Hildahl had been researching fuel cells with a vigor she hadn't felt since college. She spent a considerable amount of time learning the basics of the technology not only because she needed the knowledge to accurately report on the subject, but also because she began to take a genuine interest in them.

Everything she'd read about fuel cells she found extremely encouraging; particularly the potential benefits of the devices. Affordable, "green" energy generated from a fuel source of unlimited supply. No more dependency on oil from the Middle East, or anywhere else for that matter; no constantly rising gas prices; a massive reduction of green-house gases; and most importantly, no more soldiers dying to keep the supply of oil flowing—it was almost to good to be true. From the viewpoint of a consumer, if there was a downside to this technology, she couldn't find it.

It was her intention to make her report on fuel cells extremely positive—which wouldn't be hard to do. And even if she and Paul Haydon couldn't prove a conspiracy existed by the time she had to air, she would leave no doubt in the mind of the audience that one exists, and is responsible for the tragedy in Las Vegas. Considering the enormous benefits of moving to a hydrogen economy, the thought of her condemning fuel cells on *Hour Report* was completely unpalatable. But watching Nick wrap the bandage around her hand she came to grips with not only what kind of man he was, but what kind of people he was working for, and knew she'd have little choice.

"You want me to report on the dangers of fuel cells," she replied flatly.

Finished with her hand, Nick Ragosta leaned back in the chair, lit another cigarette, and then looked her square in the eye. "Exactly. I want your story to be so damning, so negative, that no one in their right mind would ever consider fuel cells as a replacement for the internal combustion engine."

"Since the explosion in Vegas, there have been countless stories damning fuel cells," Mary scoffed.

Ragosta shrugged. Indifferently he replied, "I could say that yours will be just one more then—that it could be considered positive reinforcement. But those I work for believe—and I tend to agree with them—that a negative report from you will carry more legitimacy than all the others because you were there, in Las Vegas. Your initial report was used by most of the news networks."

Mary scowled. "That's what this is all about: oil. Isn't it?" she snapped peevishly.

The assassin took a long drag on his cigarette, blew out the smoke and watched it rise to the ceiling. He looked back down at Mary stridently. "If you must know, yes. There are certain individuals who have a vested interest in maintaining the status quo. They've hired me to ensure that happens."

She looked at him in disgust. "What about our future—the future of our children? Surely you must know that in probably less than fifty years we'll have used up most, if not all, of the world's oil reserves." She gave him a piercing look, her voice rising a couple of octaves. "What will we...*Christ*, what will the *world* do then? If we don't start developing alternative energy now, the world is headed for complete chaos!" Then, turning away from him she murmured dolefully, "Hell, if we're not too late already."

Nick Ragosta studied her for a moment, smirked and replied sarcastically, "I don't have children, and in fifty years I'll be dead." He had hoped to get a rise out of the woman but instead Mary just gave him a quick side-glance that clearly illustrated her contempt; she then crossed her arms defiantly over her chest and fumed. Ragosta looked at her for a moment, then dropped the smirk. His face turned serious and in a subdued tone of voice he said, "Believe it or not, Mary, but I'm aware of the consequences of continuing to depend on oil." Slowly, she turned toward him; her face registering a trace of astonishment. "But don't be so naïve as to think that the people who run the oil companies, and their stockholders for that matter, give a damn." He slowly shook his head, his face stone. "They don't. In my opinion they're the most selfish, self-centered, greedy bastards you'll ever meet." He began to crush out his cigarette. "They don't give a shit about anybody but themselves—their own self-interest."

"And you differ...how?" she asked scornfully.

He let loose a short chuckle and a smile crossed his face. "I guess I don't," he replied jovially. "The bottom line here as far as I'm concerned is that I'm being handsomely compensated for my services—I'll do my job."

"What if I refuse to report the story the way you want?" Mary asked defiantly.

The assassin stared gravely at her for a moment, then in one fluid motion he pulled the pistol from his coat, pointed the gun at Constance and put a bullet in the middle of her forehead. The woman's head flew back against the wall. Then she slowly tipped over; her mouth agape and her wide eyes fixed and glazed. As she slid down, the back of her head left a trail of blood and brains streaked against the wall.

It happened so quickly that Mary didn't comprehend what had happened. Then she screamed; a loud, high-pitched shriek that actually caused Ragosta to wince. *"CONSTANCE!"* she wailed. *"OH MY GOD! CONSTANCE."* She began to shake uncontrollably. Trembling hands covered her mouth; she turned and gaped at the assassin with wild, terror filled eyes.

"That's what will happen if you don't do the story exactly as I say," Ragosta said with horrendous maliciousness while his black eyes bored into her very soul. "To your husband, your children, and you—in that order." He stood up and returned the pistol to the inside of his coat. He looked down murderously at the woman seated before him on the couch. He was infuriated with her for what she just forced him to do. He hated killing women, but felt he had to kill the housekeeper to make his point crystal clear. He was done fucking around.

"Goddamn it Hildahl! I would've thought my earlier message made my intentions reasonably fucking clear." He paused for a moment to collect himself. Still staring down at her he added, "Are you listening, Hildahl? I want to make one thing perfectly clear." Mary didn't look up at him. Weeping, she only nodded her head and continued to stare in disbelief at her dead housekeeper through tear-filled eyes. "Good. Should you have a change of heart and not condemn fuel cells on your show, you'll force me to call on your family again. And I assure you, *Ms. Hildahl*, there will be a horrible finality to my message."

Mary dropped her head and stared blankly at the floor; she couldn't bear to look at Constance any longer. She felt numb; as if every ounce of life and energy had been brutally sucked out of her. Neither one of them uttered a word for several minutes and the room remained deathly quiet. Only Mary's intermittent sniffles broke the silence.

Ragosta was growing impatient. He was about to speak when Mary slowly turned her head and sheepishly looked up at him. "I'll...I'll do it," she stuttered meekly.

"I know you will," Ragosta replied coldly. He then flashed her a satirical smile. "I hate to eat and run as they say, but I really must be going. I can't tell you how much I'm looking forward to seeing your show." He walked over to the study's door, stopped, and glanced at the short, jagged pieces of metal that was once a doorknob and said lightheartedly, "You really should get that fixed."

He turned to leave but then stopped. He brought his hand to his chin and seemed to contemplate for a moment. He then turned back to the beautiful woman still softly crying on the study's couch. Shaking his index finger like a college professor stressing a point during a lecture he said, "Oh, one more thing, Mary. I'm sure I don't have to tell you this, but don't try anything cute like asking Paul Haydon to help you out of this." At the mention of the detective's name, Mary's head shot up and she stared at him in surprise. "Yes, Mary. I know about him." Of course he did, she thought. He was the one who laid Paul out in front of her building. "I know *everything*. Don't forget that!"

She turned to look at her dead housekeeper, and then back at Ragosta. "The police will get involved," she protested. "What am I suppose to tell them about Constance?"

The assassin shrugged. Indifferently he replied, "Tell them anything you want. Tell them the truth. They'll never find me. You see, I don't exist."

"I wish you didn't!" Mary snapped back with unbridled hatred.

Nick Ragosta smiled affably at her and left. Mary heard the kitchen door to the garage shut. A moment later she heard the grind of the garage door opener. *That son-of-a-bitch had the nerve to park in my garage!* she thought bitterly. She fell back on the sofa and began to wonder what she was going to do. She then threw her hands to her face and burst into tears.

CHAPTER 23

▼

"As it turned out, Buddy, there was no conspiracy after all," Mary Hildahl said to her producer, Buddy Worther. Despite her best effort, she knew she didn't make the statement with the necessary conviction to convince her boss.

The producer eyed her suspiciously. She wasn't herself. She seemed uncharacteristically somber, almost restrained. He leaned back in his chair; genuine concern written over his face. "Mary...are you alright?" he inquired with narrowed eyes.

She gave him a weary smile. "Yes, I'm alright. I'm just a little tired. I spent most of the night at the hospital."

"Yeah, I was sorry to hear about the accident. Please, sit down;" he gestured to the chairs in front of his desk. "Or would you rather go home?"

"No, no, no," she answered with a flippant wave of her hand. She took a seat. She didn't cross her legs, which Worther found both odd and somewhat disappointing. She always crossed her legs. It was a clear sign to him that she really wasn't alright; but he decided not to push the issue. "I'm fine—just a little disappointed." She paused a moment to look down at her folded hands, sighed, and then continued. "It's just that my interview with Wendell Finely produced nothing incriminating and Paul Haydon hasn't come up with any hard evidence. I'm...I'm afraid that part of the story is dead, Buddy."

Worther raised an eyebrow in surprise. "That part? I thought you wanted the entire story to center around the conspiracy?"

The veteran reporter was ready for that question. "The more I dug into fuel cells the more I learned how *really* dangerous they are. As far as I'm concerned,

Global Fuel Cell Technologies was about to sell a virtual time bomb to the public."

Buddy Worther studied her intensely for a moment; he was troubled by the lack of conviction in her voice. Tired or not, normally she was incredibly convincing. That wasn't the case now. "Really? Any evidence of that?"

"Isn't the disaster in Vega enough?"

Worther mused for a moment. He wanted to question her further; see if he could find out why she's had such a sudden and unpersuasive change of heart. But he knew he didn't have the time. He glanced at his watch, sighed and said, "Could you build a story around that? I'm not comfortable with it, but it's too late to fill that slot with another story."

"Consider it done, Buddy," she quickly responded.

"Alright then, go with it."

Another obstacle out of the way, she thought as she walked out of the producer's office. Earlier that day she had convinced her cameraman with the same story she just gave Worther. But Dave was easy; he wasn't privy to any of the information she had about P3 other than the questions she'd posed to Finley. Besides, he didn't give a shit about anything.

But now she had to confront her most difficult obstacle—Paul Haydon.

"Tell me this is some kind of joke, Mary!" the private investigator pleaded incredulously. As she thought, Paul wasn't taking this well. But how could he? He'd put an inordinate amount of time and effort into this investigation. Now, she was asking him to throw it all away; to pretend it never happened. He had every right to be angry.

Mary sat at her desk in complete desolation. She found it difficult to look at the man she had grown so fond of. Staring off into nowhere she said, "*God*, how I wish it *were* a joke, Paul. But it's not. It's a nightmare! That man is terrifying and absolutely ruthless…pure evil." Just the mention of Nick caused a chill to run through her. She now turned to Haydon with a dazed expression. "He killed my housekeeper right in front of me—in cold blood!" She paused a moment, shook her head and added, "There's no doubt in my mind he'll make good on his threat. None whatsoever. I've got no choice; I have to do what he says."

"Mary, give me time to track him down. I'll—"

"PAUL," she shrieked, "*my family* is at stake here! Can't you see that?" Then, turning away from him she quietly added, "There's nothing you can do."

Haydon's face and spirits came crashing down. He was loathed to let the conspiracy succeed after all the time and effort he'd put into it. The worst of it was that he'll have let down his friend, Rick Miller. But then his daughter and grandson came to mind. If he were in her position, would he do any different? He sighed heavily, bowed his head dejectedly and said, "I understand, Mary."

As he reached for the doorknob he looked at his watch. It was nine-thirty in the morning. He didn't particularly care for morning meetings but this was one he'd been looking forward to for a long time. He'd actually wished the meeting was first thing this morning so he could be done and on his way by now. To his surprise he was a little excited—an emotion he rarely felt. This would be the last official meeting of his career.

Stepping into the office Nick Ragosta grinned and shook his head. Laurence Haggerty was already drinking. The assassin walked over to the pot of coffee Haggerty's secretary always brewed in the morning—apparently in vain. He poured himself a cup and then sat down on the couch and crossed his legs. After blowing on the coffee and taking a sip he asked flatly, "Got the money, Laurence?"

The owner of Noble Consultants gave him a quick nod, then turned around in his chair, got up and one at a time picked up four large suitcases. Each one thudded loudly as he placed them on top of his desk. "As they say down south, 'ya done good,' Nick. All in cash—fifties and hundreds, as you requested. I'll help you carry them down to your car."

Ragosta took another sip of coffee, put the cup down and approached the desk. He opened one of the suitcases to find hundreds of bundles of bills. Gazing solemnly at the money he said, "No need to count it I trust."

Haggerty took a sip of his scotch and shook his head. "Go ahead. Count it if you like. There's fifty million, as agreed."

The assassin closed the first suit case then peeked into the other three. As he snapped the last one closed he asked with spurious concern, "Are Kennelly, Saxton and Finley happy now?"

The consultant leaned back in his chair and took another sip of his drink; an air of smugness came over him. "The answer to that, my dear friend, is in those suitcases," he replied, gesturing to the luggage on his desk. However, if they're the least bit dissatisfied, they won't be after tonight. *Hour Report* airs." He paused a moment, studied the glass in his hand then looked sharply at Ragosta. With a trace of apprehension he asked, "There's...no chance of Mary Hildahl fuckin' us over, is there?"

Ragosta shook his head. "None whatsoever. I made it perfectly clear to her what would happen if she didn't do exactly as I said. I got the impression that she's a mother first, reporter second. She won't gamble with her family's life."

Haggerty nodded. "Good."

The consultant helped Nick Ragosta bring his money to his car. After closing the trunk, Ragosta turned to Haggerty and said, "I'm off, Laurence. Northern Minnesota is calling me. It's my fervent hope to never see, or hear from you again."

The owner of Noble Consultants chuckled. "You won't, Mr. Ragosta." They shook hands and Haggerty watched him drive off.

Back in his office, Haggerty poured himself another generous glass of scotch, opened the top drawer of his desk, pulled out his ticket to Rio and tore it up. He sat down, looked out the window and in the distance noticed a car pulling into a gas station. He sipped his drink, and with a smile watched the woman fill her tank.

It was the kind of news that had to be delivered in person—like informing the family of a soldier their son or daughter had died. He wanted to make sure Rick understood the whole story; why it turned out the way it did—he deserved that much. He also didn't want Rick to think he threw in the towel for financial or other reasons. Paul Haydon wouldn't admit it to himself, but he needed absolution from his friend. He owed Rick his life. He'd done everything he possibly could to bring the conspiracy to light, but in the end the stakes were too high. He didn't want blood on his hands—least of all the blood of Mary Hildahl and her family. He was sure Rick would understand that.

After arriving at Milwaukee's General Mitchell International airport, the private investigator rented a car for the forty minute drive to Minnawaka. Along the way he again thought about how best to break the news; but once again he failed to find the right combination of words. As he took the exit that would bring him to the small town he gave up in frustration—there was no easy way to say it.

Rick Miller was surprised and delighted by the unexpected visit of his friend. While Paul was greeting Terri, Rick ran to the kitchen and came back with three cans of beers. He handed one to his wife and one to his guest, then ushered them into the living room.

Rick's high spirits made Haydon feel even more distraught over what he'd come to tell them. He couldn't have felt more morose and he wanted something to stiffen his resolve. He looked at the beverage in his hand and silently wished it was a strong glass of bourbon. As he walked to the living room he cracked his can of beer and took a long swallow—it was better than nothing.

After they all sat down Rick opened his beer, took a sip and said, "It's been a long time since I heard from you, Paul. So, what's the latest on the conspiracy? Are ya close to nailin' the sons-of-bitches yet?"

Haydon's sudden long face extinguished Rick's enthusiastic disposition like water on fire. He knew something was wrong. Terri gave her husband a concerned look. "I'm sorry, Rick, but...but it's over." His despondent articulation had a finality to it that left no room for interpretation.

Taken aback, Rick stared at him in silent disbelief for a moment, then dropped his head and frowned. The room became uncomfortably silent. With a vacant expression, Rick looked at his wife, then back at his friend. Slowly shaking his head he said, "You...you must be kidding, right? I mean, you worked so hard on the case, Paul. Hell...*I* worked so hard to be part of this promising new industry. What the hell happened?"

Rick Miller was totally disheartened by the news. Earlier on in the investigation, he would have understood if Paul dropped the case; if for no other reason than to stop his financial bleeding. Rick even suggested he do so. But when his friend insisted on continuing, Rick's hopes that the conspirators would be flushed out began to build. Because he hadn't heard from Paul in such a long time, Rick just assumed he was making substantial progress.

Paul Haydon began to tell Rick and his wife everything that had happened since the tragedy in Las Vegas—in detail. The two sat silently, asking few questions as their friend outlined the saga as best he could. Rick was shocked and saddened to hear about Terrance McChaffee, and felt some amount of responsibility for his disappearance. The engineer's body had not yet been found.

Eight beers and two hours later Haydon came to the conclusion. "So the bottom line, Rick, Terri, is that the oil barons will get away with it—all of it! Destroying the fuel cell industry, murder and the continued pollution of the planet. Not to mention keeping the world dependant on a limited natural resource." He looked incredulously at Terri. "Can you imagine how the nations of the world will respond when we do start running out of oil—with no alternative developed? *God*, I hope I don't live to see it!"

Haydon stood, shoved his hands in his pockets and shook his head. "I can't prevent it," he murmured despondently. Turning to Rick he pleaded, "I hope you understand. I just can't risk the lives of Mary Hildahl's family." Terri reached up and gently touched his arm in a gesture of sympathetic understanding. He looked at her hand and grimaced sadly, then sat back down.

Rick was blankly looking off into space, thinking of all the time and energy he'd wasted working with Unlimited Energy Systems and Global Fuel Cell Technologies. He then scolded himself for his selfish lack of concern; the welfare of future generations was far more important then his loss of sales. He was drawn out of his thoughts when he heard Paul proclaim, "The power these guys wield—the power they have over our lives is…well, unbelievable. Almost inconceivable really."

Haydon let out a weary sigh; he decided he'd done enough talking. He looked apprehensively at Rick and asked, "What's going on now at Unlimited Energy Systems and Global Fuel Cell Technologies?"

The salesman frowned; evenly he replied, "Nothing. Absolutely nothing. I've talked several times with the few remaining engineering and purchasing contacts I have left. It wasn't long after the explosion in Las Vegas that both companies began lying off people. All new programs have been shelved. It appears the companies—as they are—are just going to tinker with what they have for now." He paused for a moment and downed his remaining beer. Looking disgusted at the empty can in his hand he said, "You hear the same goddamn thing you heard about fuel cells ten years ago: 'It's going to be another ten years.' And in ten years it will be another fucking ten years. *Christ!*"

The three remained silent for a minute or so, lost in their own thoughts. Then, Rick looked at his watch. "It's time," he said sullenly. As his wife reached for the remote and turned on the television, Rick said, "A golden opportunity was lost here, Paul. A real chance to make a change for the better—one that would benefit every person on earth. Now it's lost. Gone. All on account of the greed of a few people."

The living room, darkening with the setting sun reflected their mood. The three sat in silence and watched *Hour Report.*

Mark James Regan
October 1, 2005

ACKNOWLEDGEMENTS

I could not have accomplished the writing of *The First Element* without the help and knowledge of many people. In particular I'd like to thank Jeff Jerdee, one of the finest engineers to grace the profession and a friend who never laughed at my mechanical ineptitude. Also Paul Andraschko; undoubtedly one of the brightest executives in the corporate world, he was never to busy too take my countless calls and educate me in the ways of big business. Dale Tiemeyer, without whose friendship and encouragement I could never have continued writing. Last but not least, my wife Barb. Her editing skills are surpassed only by her understanding and patience with a flawed husband. Any mistakes or inaccuracies in this novel are mine and mine alone.

978-0-595-36975-1
0-595-36975-8

Printed in the United States
38952LVS00004B/28-57

9 780595 369751